D0388902

Spider Dance

Sketch by Wilhelm von Kaulbach

By Carole Nelson Douglas from Tom Doherty Associates

MYSTERY

IRENE ADLER ADVENTURES
Good Night, Mr. Holmes
The Adventuress* (Good Morning, Irene)
A Soul of Steel* (Irene at Large)
Another Scandal in Bohemia* (Irene's Last Waltz)
Chapel Noir
Castle Rouge
Femme Fatale
Spider Dance

MIDNIGHT LOUIE MYSTERIES

Catnap	*Cat on a Hyacinth Hunt*
Pussyfoot	*Cat in an Indigo Mood*
Cat on a Blue Monday	*Cat in a Jeweled Jumpsuit*
Cat in a Crimson Haze	*Cat in a Kiwi Con*
Cat in a Diamond Dazzle	*Cat in a Leopard Spot*
Cat with an Emerald Eye	*Cat in a Midnight Choir*
Cat in a Flamingo Fedora	*Cat in a Neon Nightmare*
Cat in a Golden Garland	*Cat in an Orange Twist*

Cat in a Hot Pink Pursuit
Midnight Louie's Pet Detectives (editor of anthology)

Marilyn: Shades of Blonde (editor of anthology)

HISTORICAL ROMANCE

Amberleigh**   *Lady Rogue***
Fair Wind, Fiery Star

SCIENCE FICTION
Probe**
Counterprobe**

FANTASY

TALISWOMAN
Cup of Clay
Seed upon the Wind

SWORD AND CIRCLET

Six of Swords   *Keepers of Edanvant*
Exiles of the Rynth   *Heir of Rengarth*
Seven of Swords

*These are revised editions   **also mystery

Spider Dance

A Novel of Suspense featuring
Irene Adler and Sherlock Holmes

Carole Nelson Douglas

FORGE

A Tom Doherty Associates Book
New York

SPIDER DANCE

This book is printed on acid-free paper.

Edited by Claire Eddy

Maps by Darla Tagrin

Portrait sketch of Lola Montez by Wilhelm von Kaulbach, courtesy of California History Room, California State Library, Sacramento, California

A Forge Book
Published by Tom Doherty Associates, LLC
175 Fifth Avenue
New York, NY 10010

www.tor.com

Forge® is a registered trademark of Tom Doherty Associates, LLC.

Library of Congress Cataloging-in-Publication Data

Douglas, Carole Nelson.
    Spider dance: a novel of suspense featuring Irene Adler and Sherlock Holmes.—1st ed.
        p.   cm.
    "A Tom Doherty Associates book."
    ISBN 0-765-30683-2
    EAN 978-0765-30683-8
    1. Adler, Irene (Fictitious character)—Fiction.   2. Holmes, Sherlock (Fictitious
character)—Fiction.   3. Women private investigators—California—Fiction.
4. Birthparents—Identification—Fiction.   5. Bly, Nellie, 1864–1922—Fiction.
6. California—Fiction.   I. Title.

PS3554.O8237S65 2004
813'.54—dc22

                                                                                           2004053282

First Edition: December 2004

Printed in the United States of America

0   9   8   7   6   5   4   3   2   1

For the many loyal readers
who've asked for, supported, and enjoyed the further adventures of
Irene Adler and company

C*ontents*

To all the men and women
of every land
who are not afraid of *themselves,*
who trust so much in their own souls that
they dare to stand up in the might of their
own individuality
to meet the tidal currents of the world.

—DEDICATION TO *THE ARTS OF BEAUTY*

I would give a great deal to know what inevitable stages of incident produced the likes of Irene Adler. Show me a method of forming more women so, and I would show more interest in women.

—SHERLOCK HOLMES, *GOOD NIGHT, MR. HOLMES,*
CAROLE NELSON DOUGLAS

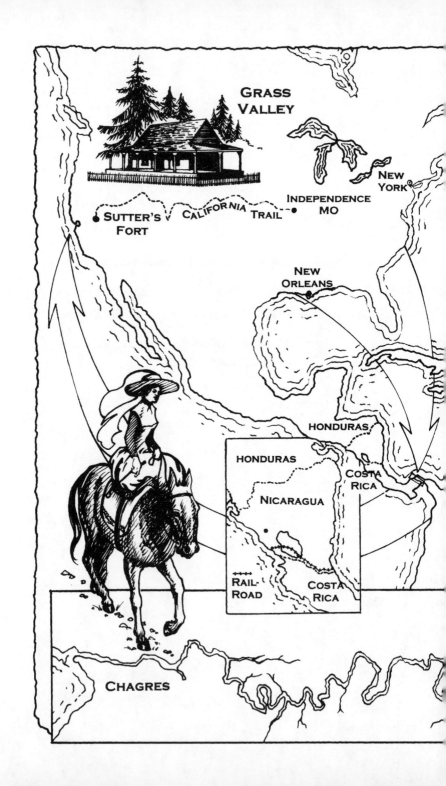

GRASS VALLEY

NEW YORK

INDEPENDENCE MO

SUTTER'S FORT

CALIFORNIA TRAIL

NEW ORLEANS

HONDURAS

HONDURAS

COSTA RICA

NICARAGUA

RAIL-ROAD

COSTA RICA

CHAGRES

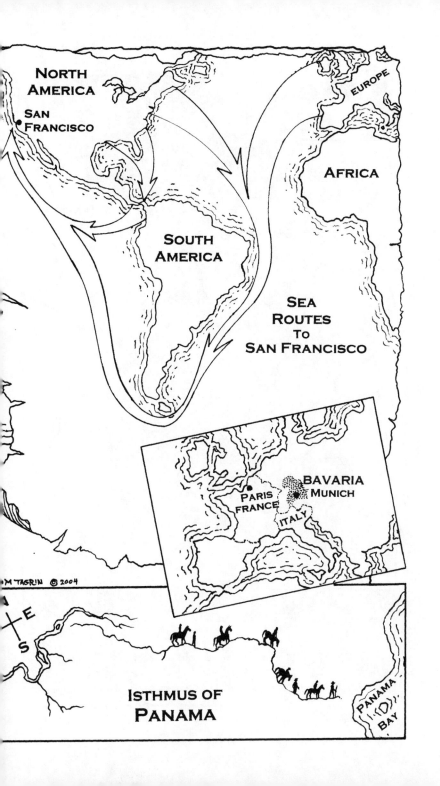

NORTH
AMERICA

SAN
FRANCISCO

EUROPE

AFRICA

SOUTH
AMERICA

SEA
ROUTES
TO
SAN FRANCISCO

BAVARIA
MUNICH

PARIS
FRANCE

ITALY

M TAGRIN © 2004

E

S

ISTHMUS OF
PANAMA

PANAMA
BAY

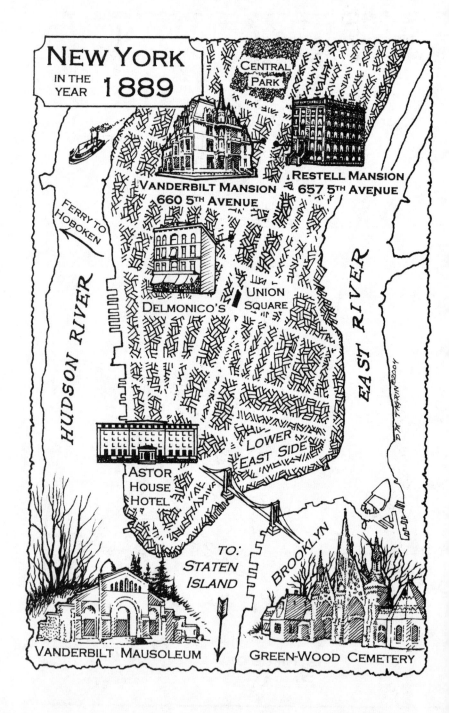

NEW YORK
IN THE YEAR 1889

CENTRAL PARK

RESTELL MANSION
657 5TH AVENUE

VANDERBILT MANSION
660 5TH AVENUE

FERRY TO HOBOKEN

HUDSON RIVER

EAST RIVER

DELMONICO'S

UNION SQUARE

LOWER EAST SIDE

ASTOR HOUSE HOTEL

TO: STATEN ISLAND

BROOKLYN

VANDERBILT MAUSOLEUM

GREEN-WOOD CEMETERY

Cast of Continuing Characters

Irene Adler Norton: an American abroad who outwitted the King of Bohemia and Sherlock Holmes in the Conan Doyle story, "A Scandal in Bohemia," reintroduced as the diva-turned-detective protagonist of her own adventures in the novel, *Good Night, Mr. Holmes*

Sherlock Holmes: the London consulting detective building a global reputation for feats of deduction

John H. Watson, M.D.: British medical man and Sherlock Holmes's sometime roommate and frequent companion in crime solving

Godfrey Norton: the British barrister who married Irene just before they escaped to Paris to elude Holmes and the King

Penelope "Nell" Huxleigh: the orphaned British parson's daughter Irene rescued from poverty in London in 1881; a former governess and "typewriter girl" who lived with Irene and worked for Godfrey before the two met and married, and who now resides with them in Paris

Quentin Stanhope: the uncle of Nell's former charges when she was a London governess; now a British agent in Eastern Europe and the Mideast

Nellie Bly, aka *Pink:* the journalistic pseudonym and family nickname of Elizabeth Jane Cochrane, involved in the Continental pursuit of Jack the Ripper in *Chapel Noir* and *Castle Rouge;* a young American woman with a nose for the sensational and possessed of her own agenda

Baron Alphonse de Rothschild: head of the international banking family's most powerful French branch and of the finest intelligence network in Europe, frequent employer of Irene, Godfrey, and Nell in various capacities, especially in *Another Scandal in Bohemia*

Portrait of an Adventuress

[She] came . . . one day, in the full zenith of her evil fame, bound for California. A good-looking, bold woman with fine, bad eyes, and a determined bearing, dressing ostentatiously in perfect male attire with shirt-collar turned down over a velvet-lapeled coat, rich worked shirt-front, black hat, French unmentionables, and natty polished boots with spurs. She carried in her hand a handsome riding crop, which she could use as well in the streets of Cruces as in the towns of Europe; for an impertinent American, presuming, perhaps not unnaturally, upon her reputation, laid hold jestingly of the tails of her long coat, and, as a lesson, received a cut across his face that must have marked him for some days. I did not wait to see the row that followed, and was glad when the wretched woman rode off the following morning.

—FROM THE MEMOIRS OF MRS. SEACOLE, AN ENGLISH LADY, 1851

I was never in Cruces and had gone by way of Nicaragua.

—THE NOTORIOUS ADVENTURESS IN QUESTION

Prelude: Memoirs of a Dangerous Woman

Exile 1847

*Recognize the abyss that you are digging beneath your feet,
an abyss that will swallow you up together with the monarchy
if you persist in the direction you have taken.*

—BARON DE LOS VALLES OF SPAIN

 They drag me in from the balcony, kicking and screaming and brandishing my pistol. They prattle of danger from the mob outside, but I will face them off, one by one or by the tens and hundreds and thousands. I've always been more of a danger to myself than anyone else could ever be to me.

I have said that only twice is the life of a woman not intolerably dangerous: before she is old enough to bear a child and after she is too old to bear a child.

My life has been intolerably dangerous, I still reside in that danger zone, and I have given back what opposition I have gotten in full measure.

Of course, dangers depend. They are not always murderous mobs. They may be runaway horses, or runaway men . . . evil tongues or tongues that don't wag about a woman at all. (In fine, I would rather be the victim of calumny than of indifference.)

Dangers can be unwanted children, or, as equally, wanted children. And equally dangerous are faithless lovers and faithful husbands.

A woman is thought to have no will of her own. I have spent my life disputing that assumption. I have been famous, and once a woman dares to become so, she is then labeled infamous. I have struggled to have something, and came to want for nothing. Then lost it, found it, lost it again.

The one thing I have not done is give in. I give no quarter, nor do I take it.

This may be why I have been a wanderer, often persecuted and reviled. Still, I can't regret anything, even now as I lay dying, virtually alone, and not quite penniless, but come down a great deal in the world.

Once I could have been a queen and an impossibly rich woman. Certainly I flouted convention and conventional religion. I had ideals of governance for the common people, and for my ideals I was hounded by an ancient conspiracy that wishes to keep all power in the hands of a few old and hidden men. Pharisees in the temple! Pretending to be noble even as they scheme to amass and cheaply spend everyone else's lives and money and faith.

Now I am a supplicant at the foot of Our Lord's cross, a Magdalene despite myself. I truly regret a great deal in my life, so perhaps that sincere contrition will open the gates of paradise to me. I am weary beyond my years, and have lived to see my fabled beauty fade to a ghost in the mirror, my arms that once wielded whip and pistol like an Amazon withered with inaction. My spirit that once dared anything fades into the wispy smoke that used to wreath my head almost constantly.

On the other hand, some things I will never regret, because they were honest and true, though I know they will never be written down that way. So I sit in this barren room, writing, as I have so often done in years past, only now my words must be formed slowly and deliberately when before they came as swift and forceful as the fire and fury of a dragon's breath.

She was as wild as the wind, my younger self, and even before I reach forty or die—and that will be a race to the end—she has already been lied about on three continents. In this new land of America I will write my own ending to the tempestuous and misunderstood history the world associates with my name.

Which, of course, is not really my name.

1

Unsuitable People

~∽∾~

I only caught a glimpse of her at the moment, but she was a lovely woman, with a face that a man might die for.
—SHERLOCK HOLMES ON IRENE ADLER, "A SCANDAL IN BOHEMIA"

New York City, August 1889

Perhaps I have presumed. I, Penelope Huxleigh, have always considered myself the sole recorder of the life and times of my friend Irene, née Adler, now Norton. (Irene, having performed grand opera under her maiden name for some years, now uses both surnames in private life. Propriety was never a sufficiently strong argument with this American-born diva with whom I have spent almost ten—can it be?—years of my life.)

So I was taken aback to witness Irene entering the sitting room of our New York hotel, her arms bearing a bundle of writing paper as if it were an infant of her recent and fond delivery. Her distinctive penmanship, exercised in eccentric green ink, galloped over the visible top page like a runaway horse.

"Is this the 'something' you said you had for the post?" I asked, setting aside my own handiwork, a petit point bellpull. There was no use for such a thing in a hotel, but I hoped that we would not forever dwell in a hotel, although it seemed as though we had already.

She regarded her foolscap progeny's bulky form as if seeing it clearly for the first time.

"I suppose this is more in the way of a parcel than a letter, but I had so much to tell, and even as many cables as I send Godfrey about our American adventures can barely scratch the surface."

She sat to straighten the unmannerly sheets on her lap. "Godfrey must be half-mad by now, languishing in the dully bucolic Bavarian countryside. I'm sure he'll welcome this more thorough report on our recent investigations in America."

"Godfrey would welcome reading the London city charter from your hand, but you can't possibly have told him about all of the unsuitable people we have met here in New York."

"Er, which unsuitable people? I'm sure, Nell, you could name a good many, but how am I to acquaint Godfrey with the outcome of our quest if I do not mention Salamandra, or Professor Marvel, or the Pig Lady?"

"Although those are unsuitable people, which I am thankful that you recognize, I did not have *them* in mind."

"Oh." Irene sat back in the small tapestried chair, sinking into her combing gown of puffed white silk and sky blue ribbons as into an exceedingly comfortable and flattering cloud. "You meant to say 'Unsuitable Person.' Singular."

"Sherlock Holmes is very singular, as well as very unsuitable."

"Then you will be relieved to know that I did not mention him to Godfrey."

"Not once, in all those pages and pages of exclamation points? Don't bother to deny it, Irene. You write as if you were singing grand opera. Every paragraph is an aria, every sentence a dramatic revelation, and every word an impossibly high note."

"Do I take it that you find my writing persuasive?"

"Excessively so. And yet you have used the most uncharacteristic restraint in omitting Sherlock Holmes from the cast list! I find that even more troubling than including him."

"How so?"

Irene played the innocent as well as she portrayed the femme fatale. It struck me then that she would best serve her absent spouse by having her photograph made and sent to him, just as she appeared now.

I have never seen a woman who looked so unnervingly well in the morning, her color warm even without the light enhancement of paint, her chestnut hair flashing gold and red glints like cherry amber, her face serene as a Madonna's. Unfortunately, not many Madonnas were to be found in grand opera.

Needless to say that Irene and I were, like most longtime companions, night and day in temperament. We were also opposite in looks, although Irene insisted, in her usual optimistic moments, that I was attractive.

She was now frowning prettily and paging through her opus. "I suppose I could slip mention of Sherlock Holmes into one of these pages, if it would satisfy you, Nell."

"Me? It has nothing to do with me. And why trouble Godfrey when he is too far away to do anything about it?"

"What would Godfrey do if he were here?"

"Escort you everywhere, so you had no opportunity to consort improperly with that miserable man."

Irene smiled. "We really had very little to do with Mr. Holmes during our New York inquiries."

"No, he only appeared at the end when you had solved the unspeakable death, to drop portentous hints about your lost mother's identity . . . in a graveyard, no less, and then marched off without even a word of farewell."

"Perhaps he expects to see us again," she murmured to the infant serial novel on her lap. Just loud enough so that I could hear it.

"And will he?"

She looked up through her dark eyelashes, as contrite as Miss Allegra Turnpenny at age fourteen, and I was cast suddenly again in my role of stern governess.

"I hope not," Irene finally said with deep feeling, an emotion I could heartily endorse.

I allowed myself to take a breath of relief.

"When I follow someone, especially Mr. Sherlock Holmes, I would hope to be quite invisible."

I should have known that Irene would be determined to pick up the gauntlet he had tossed at our feet at Green-Wood Cemetery in Brooklyn two days earlier.

How Sherlock Holmes had been lured from London, and Irene and I from the pleasant village of Neuilly-sur-Seine near Paris, to arrive at this place of gravestones near Manhattan Island, would require a book to detail in all its convolutions.

Nellie Bly, the crusading American newspaper reporter had been the catalyst, by tempting Irene with the notion that she had a long-lost mother whose life was being threatened. Irene, abandoned soon after birth, had always stoutly denied any sentimental need to find a delinquent mother, but add the melodrama of possible murder, and she would go anywhere. We'd discovered more than I wanted to know about Irene's childhood years, and a truly appalling candidate for the role of Irene's mother.

So Irene and I culminated our investigations with a visit to the burial site of "the wickedest woman in New York," or so the long-dead creature had been called more than a decade earlier, in 1877 on the occasion of her shocking demise. This pseudonymously named Madame Restell (she was an Englishwoman born, can you imagine!) had ministered to "women's problems," for decades, even to the point of forestalling births. Some considered this an abomination, others a boon. It was not precisely illegal in Madame Restell's day, and the woman had become conspicuously wealthy, even building a grand mansion on Fifth Avenue where her clients would come to a side door in the dark of night. That some of them came from the surrounding mansions protected the Restell enterprise for decades. She also offered the same services to poor women at far less costly rates. Her clients regarded her as a savior. Her detractors considered her a devil. Charged by a morals crusader named Comstock, she had supposedly cut her own throat with a butcher knife on the eve of her sentencing, adding the sin of suicide to any roster of wrongdoing she would have to answer for before the Final Bar.

Some question remained whether this lost soul had been the "Woman in Black," who had apparently abandoned Irene at an early age to the care of the most freakish assemblage of theatrical folk I had ever seen, onstage or off.

We had contemplated that very fact as we gazed at the monument for what might be Irene's mother. I sincerely hoped not.

Then who should appear but Sherlock Holmes in top hat and city garb, quite appropriate for the cemetery, actually, and the sober act of visiting the dead. He led us to another hill in the vast and picturesque park and to a small headstone that bore the very common name of Eliza Gilbert. *Mrs.* Eliza Gilbert, I noted to my great ease of mind.

And there he had left us with the unspoken implication that this unknown woman was more likely to be Irene's mother than "the wickedest woman in New York." I was foolishly relieved. At the time.

"How would he know?" I demanded as I unpinned my hat when we had returned to the Astor House Hotel on Broadway.

"Apparently he does know, and knows more than I do. Than we do. I do not for a moment believe that Sherlock Holmes is in New York City in answer to Nellie Bly's summons. He has business of his own here. The fact that I had come here on the thin trail of a mother who disowned me, and who might be in danger of death, according to our daredevil reporter friend, meant nothing but a moment's mental diversion for Sherlock Holmes. Yet he insists on dogging my movements."

"Perhaps because you pursue these inquiries."

"How would he know, or suspect, who the Woman in Black was? He must have found clues here, for neither of us had the least interest in her until Nellie Bly's cables drew us both across the Atlantic."

"And we shall have to cross that horrible, heaving body of water to return home to Paris again! I do not believe I can stomach that."

"Poor girl." Irene patted my hand. "You didn't stomach it at all on the voyage over."

"A week of terror and distress. I would almost volunteer to remain in this savage land rather than return by sea."

"You cannot fly, Nell. And walking on water is a prerogative of the Lord you would not wish to usurp. But fear not. We will stay on until we solve the riddle of Eliza Gilbert, and by then you may have somewhat forgotten the inconveniences of the voyage."

"You have today put me between the devil and the deep blue sea, Irene, and I don't know which is the worst to contemplate."

"Then don't think about either." She bent her eyes to her pages and turned several periods into exclamation marks.

Poor Godfrey. A benighted barrister toiling away on dull legal matters in Bavaria for the Rothschild banking interests, bereft of wife and unaware that she was bent on trying to out-Sherlock Sherlock Holmes himself.

Brilliantly blind Irene! She was quite unaware that the cold-minded man of logic had developed an unreasonable addiction to her brains and beauty as well as cocaine and who knew what other vices?

What a bother! I would have to make sure that Irene did not dance too near the flame when she sought to turn the tables on Sherlock Holmes.

That might be just what the irritating fellow was hoping for.

2

Busybodies

‷‴

A fair reader who confesses to an honorable admiration for the intrepid and energetic Nellie Bly of The World, writes to inquire if this is the real name of that enterprising young woman. The World's Nellie Bly is, I believe, in private life, a Miss Pink Jane Elizabeth Cochrane.

—*TOWN TOPICS* GOSSIP SHEET, AUGUST 1888

‷FROM NELLIE BLY'S JOURNAL‴

Though they would deny it to a man, and to the death, there is no gossiping old biddy worse than a gentleman of the press.

So it was that their sly looks, and slyer chuckles, greeted me as I entered the *New York World*'s offices that summer afternoon.

Immediately several men in my vicinity stopped hawking tobacco juice into their rank spittoons and began whistling "Nellie Bly."

Oh, I am so sick of the song that gave me my byline! Yet it does stick in the mind of the public, and that is a boon you can't buy.

I ignored their merriment and went to the desk I am given the use of. I come and go a great deal, and when I am off on one of my stunt impersonations, I am not to be found at the office for days or even weeks.

"Don't get too settled, Nellie," Walters the sports columnist finally advised me for the room at large. "You'll be in Pulitzer's office soon enough."

Now, that was meant to strike fear into me. I confess the brave crimson feather on my hat might have quivered a bit. Our new owner was a most demanding editor. But ambition is a close friend of mine also, and I had determined to drive Bessie Bramble and Nell Nelson and all my rival sisters of the press from the front pages of this teeming city and the entire eastern seaboard.

I was even now working on a most scandalous, shocking, and sad story, an outgrowth of my recent frustrating sojourn with my expatriate countrywoman, Irene Adler Norton. In trying to extract the secret of her American past, I had ended up finding mysterious deaths among a forgotten group of variety performers. Hardly front page material. If only I were free to reveal the indomitable Irene's discoveries about the identity of Jack the Ripper . . . but I was bound and gagged on that account, by some of the crowned heads of Europe, no less.

Ah, well. There is always another sensation somewhere.

My current investigation, for one, should shake New York society to its roots.

So I sat at the desk, writing on lined paper until the threatened summons from Mr. Pulitzer should arrive, if it did.

I regarded my colleagues from under what I knew to be a particularly winsome hat, sapphire blue velvet with one large crimson ostrich plume rampant among the flock of smaller dove gray feathers.

Most of my jocular persecutors were almost twice my age of twenty-four. "I'd relish talking to Mr. Pulitzer," I said to no one in particular. "I've got a very keen story in the works."

Their unkempt brows knit below their balding heads as some twiddled their thumbs over swelling waistcoats dotted with lunches past. They tolerated my presence as an unnatural wonder, and were sometimes quite kind, and sometimes quite cutting. I weathered whatever way their winds blew. Elizabeth Jane Cochrane had learned to speak up for herself against a brutal and drunken stepfather at an early age. Speaking up for myself had made me into a daredevil reporter.

I heard an office door crack open as the murmur of masculine voices oozed from the editor's offices.

Broadhurst, the drama critic who came into the office as seldom as I did, took pity on me. "It's not Pulitzer'll be wanting to talk to you, Nellie. It's some Brit toff."

Well! There were, of course, no mirrors in the totally masculine *New York*

World offices, but I did reach up to make sure my hat was properly anchored by the foot-long pin festooned with a glass-bead butterfly.

I believe a woman should be attractively dressed, whatever her role in life.

And . . . Quentin Stanhope looked a man who could appreciate that fact, despite poor stumbling Nell's blissful ignorance of such things, and despite being my least favored nationality, English. No doubt it was because Mr. Stanhope was a renegade Englishman who had gone native in the world's most exotic corners. My. How our reticent Miss Nell Huxleigh would fret to know that Quentin had called upon me at the *New York World*.

I heard the usual small talk of farewell, then firm footsteps approaching me across the wooden floors layered in newsprint, a concession to my long skirts, so they should not sweep up trails of tobacco juice that had missed the spittoons. Newsmen were no different from the grubby newsboys hawking on the street corners: they reveled in the mischief of always looking and speaking too rudely for church.

I turned, for I prefer to confront rather than to be confronted.

Gracious! My visitor was *not* the dashing Quentin Stanhope. He was another sort of Englishman entirely, one most unworthy of my new hat, and one hardly in my good graces.

"Good day . . . Miss Bly?" Sherlock Holmes towered over me like some character from Dickens, quirking his angular head to the side in a habitual inquisitive gesture.

"That will do nicely," I said, for few people knew my real name was Elizabeth Cochrane, even less that I had been called "Pink" from childhood.

"Mr. Pulitzer agreed that you might be helpful to me."

So it was a conspiracy. "Pull up a chair. Most of us come and go, so any open desk or seat is fair game. Nothing 'drawing room' about a newspaper office."

He immediately turned to claim a golden oak armchair, not upholstered but still one of the more substantial, and heavy, chairs about the place.

So he seated himself, cutaway coat, pinstriped trousers and all. His top hat and cane he laid across the newsprint-strewn desk.

I smiled at the notion of Sherlock Holmes being taken for a city slicker by my compatriots. They hadn't seen London and all the men running about the streets dressed up like undertakers at a robber baron's funeral.

"I suppose," I said, "this place is a bit crude for your taste."

"Not in the slightest, Miss Bly." He turned to survey the room as alertly as a hawk on a telephone wire. "Fascinating. And it even offers the charming fogs of my home city."

I sighed at his reference to the clouds of cigar smoke polluting the air. A newsroom was something of men's club, after all. And, at bottom, I was not as welcome in it as even an unknown Englishman like Sherlock Holmes. But he didn't need to know that.

"How did Mr. Pulitzer think I could help you?"

"With the lay of the land, specifically regarding the first families of New York. I am quite the new student in that regard."

"And why do they deserve your study?"

"Call it an English eccentricity." His eyes were hooded, his expression bland. "We put much stock in family and title."

"There are no titles here, except what the newspaper cartoonists come up with, and they are invariably rude."

"Exactly so. I need not tiptoe around the information I seek, but ask it openly of an expert source like yourself."

If I didn't know better, I would think we were fencing. Or flirting. "I'm no expert. My stories are about the girl in the street, and how she's abused by all and sundry. The Four Hundred are as above me as the Queen must be above you."

"Oh, I fear you underestimate us both." Before I could decipher his reference to the Queen of England—Had he really met her? Had he in fact been of service to her? It was possible—he spoke on. "The fact is that rich Americans do not shirk publicity. I must say that as a consulting detective I applaud such refreshing frankness. Much about them is common knowledge that would never be publicly discussed about the London nobility. However, it is not common knowledge to a newcomer to your shores. I wish to be as knowledgeable as the man on the street, that's all."

"Which families interested you?"

"I have heard some names. Belmont, Vanderbilt, Astor."

"You've heard right. That's the Holy Trinity of New York society, all right, though some of them are less holy than others."

"Exactly what I needed to know."

I leaned back in my own wooden chair, thinking madly. What did Sherlock Holmes *really* want to know, and, more important, why? How had he gotten entrée to and aid from my boss, Mr. Joseph Pulitzer? Not that we didn't get on. Mr. Pulitzer liked my "pluck." That didn't save me from getting stuck with some stupid flower show story now and again. I always had to fight for my big stories, had to go out and do things like checking myself into a madhouse to get good placement in the paper. Trouble was, I'd done all the usual street stories. My latest project did in fact touch on the same high levels of society that Mr. Holmes was inquiring about.

"So you're not leaving New York immediately?"

"I'm not eager to waste a week of ocean travel by turning right around again. I understand that crime runs as rife here as anywhere."

"Even among the Four Hundred?"

"I would assume especially so. Where there is great wealth and display there's always some magpie eye on it. And some hunting hawk watching the magpie."

"You are the hawk, no doubt."

"I am a mere seeker of what's common knowledge to most New Yorkers. What is unholy about these three families?"

"Ambition, Mr. Holmes."

"That is not unknown among even costermongers."

When I frowned, he quickly added, "Street peddlers."

"Yes, but among the rich it's two-pronged." I had interested him. "The men are rabid to outdo each other at business, buying entire railroads just to foil a rival. The women, however, cross swords socially. Mrs. John Jacob Astor was the undisputed queen of New York society."

"Was."

"The famous Four Hundred was the exact number of first citizens who could fit into her ballroom. And mere money did not qualify for an invitation from Mrs. Astor."

"So who *with* money did not fit in her ballroom?"

"Commodore Vanderbilt and all his many progeny. Didn't bother the old man, who died a few years ago, one bit. But his eldest grandson's wife, Alva, was a different story. She besieged Fifth Avenue, put up a gleaming white Parisian chateau amidst all the glowering, four-square brownstones of the Astors and their ilk, the ones rather like Madame Restell's unhappy former residence across the avenue from 660 Fifth. Of course Mrs. Astor would not recognize her new neighbor, Mrs. William K. Vanderbilt, until Alva held a ball so extravagant that Mrs. Astor's own daughters were mad to attend. You can imagine the outcome."

"Mrs. Astor surrendered to placate her daughters and Mrs. Vanderbilt now is the hostess of the moment."

"You show an alarming accuracy about the rivalries of New York society ladies, Mr. Holmes."

His laugh of acknowledgment was as short as a bulldog's bark. "I doubt they differ much from the rivalries of the Corsican brotherhood, only it is blood feuds over ballrooms."

"Well, Alva's ball was six years ago and the Astor and Vanderbilt men are still outbuilding each other with larger and more extravagant seagoing yachts."

"And the women?"

"Are still enriching the milliners and dressmakers and jewelers of the city and the Continent. It is a War of Millionaires."

"I see." He swept his cane and hat off the desk.

"That is all you wish to know?"

"It is. For now."

"And what about matters that I might wish to know of?"

He paused before standing to take his leave. "I suppose I owe you pence for pound."

Despite his warning that he would be a stingy source, I pressed on. "Have you seen Mrs. Norton of late?"

"Not of late."

Was there the merest hesitation?

I went on. "The matter of Madame Restell was tragic and settled mysteries almost older than I am, but it resulted in no modern revelation suitable for the public print."

"Such sordid matters do not belong in the newspapers."

"I disagree there." He had not quite denied the case's relevancy to current events. "I'm investigating an offshoot of that unhappy history. It should cause quite a stir."

"I believe that 'stirs' are what your profession seeks. I count myself successful when matters are resolved privately, or why else would a consulting detective like myself be called in?"

"Then you *have* been called in on some matter in New York beyond the crimes that surrounded the quest for Irene Adler Norton's origins?"

He stood and smiled with that superior British aplomb I so loathe, looking down that arrogantly beaked nose at me.

"I am no more at liberty to discuss my possible cases than you are eager to reveal your possible 'stories,' Miss Bly. The only difference is that the results of your inquiries will eventually see the light of public amazement in the papers."

"Not always," I interrupted, standing. "Sometimes I am gagged."

"Then you understand my position. I don't seek revelation but solution, and my clients seek discretion. Good day."

It was not. I watched him leave with a swift step that was also annoyingly confident.

The whistled chorus of Stephen Foster's "Nellie Bly" grew as deafening as a chorale of crickets. A nearing cloud of smoke almost asphyxiated me.

"Brit gent come a-calling," Walters said loud enough for several men to hear. "You going to run off with some titled English bloke and leave us flat, Nellie?"

Speculation on my private life fired many a bull session at the *World* and I knew it. I was young, not unlovely, and somewhat famous. It was assumed I would wed the first good prospect that came my way. That is exactly why I would not.

"I'd never leave my handsome knights errant of the press."

They guffawed at my coy rejoinder. They knew I was not coy and they also knew themselves for an uncouth, opinionated, whiskey-and-cigar-loving lot no lady of gentle rearing would embrace.

I was no lady of gentle rearing, but neither was I eager to surrender my hard-won independence for any man. And that attitude would astonish them more than any wild stunt I might ever perform, even were I to ride Jumbo the elephant in the late P. T. Barnum's circus.

"We'll never understand you, Nellie," old Broadhurst swore melodramatically, with a hand to his heart.

And didn't I prefer it that way.

3

A Pocket Full of Death

New York City is cursed with its universal chocolate coating of the most hideous stone ever quarried.

—EDITH WHARTON IN 1882, THE YEAR THE VANDERBILTS'
SHINING WHITE CHÂTEAU WENT UP

My house was the death of the brownstone front.

—ALVA VANDERBILT, UNPUBLISHED MEMOIRS, 1917

⊰FROM THE CASE NOTES OF SHERLOCK HOLMES⊱

I had expected an urgent summons from a master of commerce on Fifth Avenue. Trifling as the game with the Renaissance chess set had been, I saw some hidden horror behind it.

Anyone, or any force, that would toy with millionaires and a priceless ancient artifact is capable of far greater games on a far more relevant board, such as our very lives and times.

The summons was even more urgent than I had anticipated, and from the wrong party.

"Mr. Holmes! Mr. Holmes!"

I heard the voice as soon as it exited the lift, playing counterpoint to the thump of pounding footsteps on the thick hall carpet. This may have been

New York, not Mayfair, but even here such frantic gallops through hotel halls are unheard of.

Further, the fellow weighed at least twenty stone and had a limp, probably from birth, that he was pushing to its limit.

I greeted him at my open suite door.

Breathless, he hugged the doorframe, one leg tellingly cocked, the booted toe barely touching the Oriental runner.

On seeing me, he had lost his voice and stood panting.

"I'd ask you in, my good man, but we have no time to spare, I see. Have you a hack waiting?"

He nodded twice in answer to each of my comments. Although heavy-set, his bland, round face and meticulously trimmed mustache bespoke a man of little action but great acuity for all that is detailed in life.

"I'll just fetch my hat and stick—"

"Hurry, please, sir."

Quick as can be, I had taken his arm and was playing walking stick as I took the weight of his game leg so he could hop back down the hall as fast as a jackrabbit.

At the elevator he leaped up and down on his good leg in impatience until the creaking car finally returned to our level. His breath appeared to be on permanent leave, and I didn't question him.

My friend Dr. Watson, were he present, would have wondered why, but the answer was obvious: I had learned all I need know from his appearance and clothing.

His gasps had turned to huffs as I sped him through the lobby and to the waiting conveyance. No city hack but a private carriage pulled by a very pretty pair of matched chestnuts.

He seemed surprised by my strength in assisting him up the one high step into the carriage, but my practice of the martial art of baritsu has made me far more powerful than I appear to be. I smiled to think that not a week before I had contemplated performing my old trick of bending a fireplace poker for my friends in the theatrical boardinghouse. But that had been in another guise, and that case was closed, along with my fledgling American stage career as well, alas.

"Mr. Holmes," he sputtered valiantly as the carriage jerked into motion, then proceeded on silken springs. We entered the clopping and grinding traffic of New York City, which was no greater or different than that of Mother London.

"Save your breath, man. I am aware of most of the particulars already."

"Someone else . . . reached you . . . first. Im . . . possible."

"You told me yourself."

"Are you mad? I can . . . only . . . speak now."

"But your person has told the story far more eloquently. Although I am not surprised that an event of horrific import has occurred on Fifth Avenue, I am rather amazed that Mr. William K. Vanderbilt's private secretary should be dispatched to fetch me rather than some more suitable body servant from the staff. The need for secrecy must be dire."

His pupils, small as dried berries behind his thick spectacles, grew smaller still as his irises widened against a sea of white.

"You know all that? Who has betrayed us?"

"Yourself, as I said before."

"I spoke only your name since leaving the house. How is it you know which house I came from, and my station with my employer? He said you could be a wonder worker. Are you a spiritualist, sir?"

I could not restrain my laughter. "Quite the opposite. I depend solely upon solid physical evidence. Before I even laid eyes upon you I was aware that you were in your early forties, occupied in sedentary pursuits, so sedentary that only the gravest crisis would call you away from your post as Mr. Vanderbilt's secretary. I fear this footrace he has set you upon today will tax your crooked ankle for some time."

He glanced down at his high laced boots. "It seldom troubles me at all. But you are right, sir; I do not move much for a living. And I am employed by Mr. Vanderbilt, how did you know that?"

"In your haste you brushed against the stone railing as you left the house. None other on Fifth Avenue is a white-stone monument to French architecture. Your right pocket looks as if it has been floured."

"True enough, true enough." His wide eyes narrowed and his worried face frowned. "Now that you explain it your assumptions are not such a wonder as I thought."

Watsons, God bless them, are everywhere. So I did not add that he also had a sister who played the harp, a brother who played the ponies, and a small addiction to pastilles.

"And the reason for my summons?" he asked after some time in silence.

"Life and death, of course."

He shuddered slightly. "Fearful death."

I did not say more. I wished to see the scene first, and hear from whoever had been first to discover it.

Shortly we passed the dark square house that had once belonged to the ill-fated Madame Restell. Most of the "mansions" along Fifth Avenue were of that somber ilk.

When I spied a flash of sepulcher white from the coach window, I picked up my cane.

"My name is Wilson," my carriage partner said suddenly.

"Mr. Charles Wilson," I retorted. He blanched again.

"The initials CAW are on the handkerchief that peeks from your breast pocket. I doubt that parents with the surname of Wilson would stray far from Mrs. Grundy's baby-naming recommendations. Pray do not tell me your name is actually Cuthbert. I shall be shattered."

"Cuthbert? I should hope not. Charlie it's been since I could first gimp about on my bad ankle."

"Well done, Mr. Wilson. We are here in record time, I am sure."

I stepped out without waiting for the servant's assistance and handed the now evenly breathing secretary onto the white limestone sidewalk. Beyond the shining peaked château at 660 Fifth Avenue loomed the dark Gothic spires of a mighty church. The other mansions along the street seemed as somber and forbidding as a Lower East Side tenement compared to the fanciful Vanderbilt edifice.

It was odd to contemplate "mansions" so contained, more like dark, Italianate crypts than the much-added-onto sprawl of London's great houses. Of course London mansions had been imposing since the sixteenth century, and poor Fifth Avenue was a mere upstart of forty years at best, for I understood that commercial buildings were ever being driven farther north by these millionaires' exercises in instant opulence.

We dashed up the paltry six steps leading to the entry. A waiting butler held the door open so as not to impede our progress. From first glance the house showed itself not to be what it seemed, which I find an interesting comment on the persons who inhabited it. The pale stone walls had been carved into the likeness of well-fringed fabrics.

Dark carpets floated on snowy stone floors in the wide hall beyond that extended perhaps sixty feet to an elaborate pair of doors.

"We must hurry," Mr. Wilson urged.

"First I must know which is the room."

"There! Ahead. To the right."

"The first or second door?"

Mr. Wilson cast an anxious look at the impassive butler who had taken our hats and my walking stick.

"The second."

Nodding, I led the way down the hall, along the stone and sparing the carpet any more impressions than it bore already.

"And this first room to the left?" I asked.

"The Grinling Gibbons room, for small receptions or daytime callers."

Pale stone, carved within an inch of its life with geometrical and floral patterns paneled the walls. "Grinling Gibbons?" I asked. "Was he not the author of a treatise on ancient Rome?"

Mr. Wilson eyed me with some of Watson's amazement. "He was the noted seventeenth-century carver and sculptor, nothing to do with Romans."

"Ah." All this decorative busywork was a rather trivial pursuit in my opinion. "And the room we hasten to?"

Mr. Wilson stopped and seemed to gather himself. "The billiard room, sir."

"Hmmm." I was not optimistic about encountering anything truly fearful in a chamber as frivolous as a billiard room. So far the floors had been disappointingly blank, not a spec of dust allowed to sully their surfaces. The carpeting looked as if it had been cleaned by one of those devilish electrified machines that Americans favored, which sucked up and swallowed anything in the nature of a clue.

Even as I noted the stunning size and scale of the place, a well-upholstered woman descended the grand staircase to the right. She was as handsome and adamant as Lady Liberty in the New York Harbor, although attired in the expensive fripperies that pass for the latest Paris fashions, which somehow did not flatter her overshot lower jaw that spoke of bulldog resolve.

My guide stiffened as he spied her, so I watched her imperious advance much as a courtier might await a royal personage coming abreast.

When she arrived even with us, her gaze was only for my conductor. He bowed his head at her passage. Her sharp footsteps never faltered, and I was accorded only the slightest glance and that at my clothing.

The door behind us opened to admit the clatter of Fifth Avenue. I heard the butler murmur that madam's carriage was awaiting at the curb. Then the door closed again and we were left to the lonely silence of a mausoleum.

Mr. Wilson swallowed audibly.

"Mrs. Vanderbilt, I take it?"

He only nodded. I surmised that he would not be displeased if some unearthly force took Mrs. Vanderbilt from us all. America prided itself for its egalitarianism, but it struck me that its queens of society were as imperious as any Empress of All the Russias.

I was also struck by the difference between these two American women, Mrs. Vanderbilt and *the* woman, Madam Irene. Mrs. Norton was infinitely more comely if not less expensively attired, but Mrs. Vanderbilt moved as if she commanded every creature within her purview, man or mouse. And as if man would soon be reduced to mouse. Madam Irene was in admirable command of herself, but did not seek to erase the presence of others, witness how she had tended the poor injured churchman I had played to gain entry to her house in St. John's Wood when we first met two years earlier.

Had I played the same disabled role with Mrs. Vanderbilt as she entered her carriage, she would no doubt have used me as stepping-stone.

American women, I was beginning to suspect, were like their sisters everywhere, not to be trusted, but in addition as willful as wolverines.

"This way, sir." My guide was polishing his ruddy perspiration-dewed cheeks with his handkerchief.

And so we proceeded down that wide hallway, our bootheels the only sound in that palatial expanse.

As we passed the grand curving stairway from which Mrs. Vanderbilt had descended, I spied a dark-haired elfin sprite crouched at the top of the stairs, gazing down on us wistfully.

My work occasionally had brought me into grand halls and palaces, but none so oppressive as this, despite the light-colored stone of its construction.

At a pair of ornate wooden doors, Mr. Wilson stopped, tapping upon his game leg with impatience.

I stood back to let Mr. Wilson open the doors, but he then beckoned me inside and whirled to shut the doors behind us as if sealing out Satan himself.

He had moved so fast I could not object that he had disarranged the threshold before I could examine it.

A familiar stench filled the room, undignified death in its most disagreeable form. I catalogued the immediately obvious contents of the large chamber. Its centerpiece was a billiard table set upon ornate wooden legs so stout and swollen they seemed to suffer from gout. Enough gilt fringe to circle several lampshades dangled from the corner pockets. Gilt metal inlay, probably gold, glinted from every curve in the carving.

The thing more resembled some bloated pagan altar than a gaming table. Over it hung an immense branched electric lamp of brass and opaque stained glass.

And on its green felt surface, the only ordinary thing about the table, lay a form that was the source of odor, arms stretched out and . . .

A soberly dressed fellow stood near a massive sofa several feet from the billiard table.

I spoke. "I must examine the entire room thoroughly, from the bottom up. Starting with the threshold. Mr. Wilson, if you will open the doors again."

"No one in the house must know." The man by the sofa's voice creaked with recent disuse, but it held a modicum of command.

"Mr. William K. Vanderbilt, I presume." I faced a man of no great height, but of regular, even bland, barefaced features, most notable for the waves of dark hair parted in the middle.

"Who is this dead man?" I asked.

"I don't know."

"You have no idea why he's in your house? Are any servants or workmen missing?"

"I'm not about to upset the house with such inquiries, but everything has been perfectly normal this morning. One would never know—" His glance slid toward the table, then avoided it. "No one in the house must suspect any problem. Your investigation must be completely discreet."

"Then I require your patience. It is crucial that the floor and furnishings of the room be as untrampled as possible. The sooner I make my examination, the sooner those doors can be bolted again."

He finally nodded, and Wilson opened first one, then the other door, gazing anxiously down the hall.

But no one approached and I was soon on hands and knees, magnifying glass a monocle before my right eye, surveying the hallway stone for any mite of evidence.

"How often are the floors swept?" I asked.

From the silence I knew that both men regarded my posture with amazement.

"I may look as if I'm playing a schoolroom game, gentlemen, but you have no idea how many conclusions may be gathered from the testimony of the trail a pair of shoes or boots may leave on stone and carpeting. I see, for instance, that Mr. Wilson was the first to discover this tragedy when he entered the room before breakfast this morning."

"How, sir, would you know that?" he said.

"Beyond the inequity of the depth in this set of impressions on the carpet, here they are made by shoes with an arch, so only sole and heel show. You, sir," I noted to the master of the house, "are dressed, but still shod in leather house slippers. These flat, potato-shaped impressions reveal almost the entire foot. Obviously you were urgently summoned here by Mr. Wilson from the breakfast table, where, I also perceive, you enjoyed a finnan haddie in asparagus sauce."

"Are you a chef, man, or a detective?" the businessman huffed.

"That is a very fine-figured smoking jacket, Mr. Vanderbilt, but the paisley can't conceal the dropped fragments of your final forkful at Mr. Wilson's obviously urgent summons.

"Scared the living kidney pie out of me," Mr. Vanderbilt admitted. "And . . . this." He glanced at the top of the billiards table with a shudder. "I am a man of industry and a yachtsman, but no hunter or meat dresser. I am lucky that more of my breakfast doesn't adorn my jacket front."

"Indeed. If you gentlemen will remain standing where you are, I'll complete my examination of the floor. Then you may leave."

Mr. Vanderbilt raised an eyebrow at my instructions, but said nothing. I had quickly realized that he was used to heeding domestic directions. I had only to seize the reins and he would go where I led.

"What disposition do you plan to make of the body when my examination is done?" I asked.

"No one must know, most particularly my wife. She would wish never to set foot in this house again. It cost three millions six years ago and would cost a million more today."

"The body must be removed and an autopsy performed," I said. "I am not a medical man. And then buried."

"Wilson will see to that. I have influence with the authorities, so they will remove the remains discreetly. Fortunately the house is large, with a maze of service areas at the rear. This truly unfortunate fellow will pass out of this house as discreetly as a drunkard from my wife's dinner party last night."

Answered if not satisfied, I bent back to my task, crawling my way around the room's perimeter in narrowing circles until I came up short on one of the billiard table's gargantuan legs. One would think I was kowtowing before one of the ancient world's wonders, the Colossus of Rhodes.

My labors had given me little more than a pocketful of rye: a few tiny and sere blades of grass tracked in from the nearby park, no doubt.

I nodded at the master of the house, and a great many more things, as I stood. "I will do the rest alone."

Vanderbilt skated on his flat-soled slippers to the door, erasing my tracks as well as his own and Wilson's, the sizes of which I had paused to record in a pocket notebook.

"Wilson will wait outside the door until you are done, Mr. Holmes, then escort you to my library, where we will talk. In the meantime I will call those discreet enough to remove the er . . . cadaver."

I nodded, or bowed, depending on how the observer wished to take it. Both men left the room and closed the door.

For a moment I mulled my astounding conclusion: other than the foot marks of Mssrs. Vanderbilt and Wilson, and now my own, there were no other foot tracks in the room. None.

I glanced at the savaged body on the green felt.

The feet were bare.

Ah, now what would Watson title a story on this grisly corpse in the millionaire's billiard room? An American Conundrum, perhaps, though I feared it would be nothing so tasteful. Perhaps "The Adventure of the Barefoot Corpse?"

I bent to the second, more repellent stage of my work, wishing my physician friend were here to put the purest mayhem I had ever witnessed—save for the depredations beneath Paris this past spring—into the distancing drone of a medical opinion.

4
Clothes that Make the Woman

~⚬ᵥᵤ⚬~

When he tried in vain
To raise her to his embrace...
She bounded off... as she knew
He could not touch her, so was tolerant
He had cared to try....

—ELIZABETH BARRETT BROWNING, "AURORA LEIGH"

A knock at the hotel suite door surprised me.

Irene would have used her key. I confess to feeling a bit uneasy about being left alone in a hotel room in New York City, but Irene had insisted that I stay here and "rest," from what exertion I cannot imagine.

So I had occupied myself with brushing our travel-weary clothing. The contents of each of our small trunks had been intended to last for ten days. Now it seemed our exile in America was to extend far beyond that.

The knock sounded again. No doubt it was some emissary from the hotel desk, seeking boots to polish or to perform some other petty service that required being rewarded with the extravagance of an American fifty-cent piece.

I swung the wide door open, a no of refusal already formed on my lips. It swiftly transformed into an oh of pleasure followed fast by panic.

Quentin Stanhope stood on the threshold, his hazel eyes merry with the knowledge of what a surprise his presence was.

"Nell, you look radiant," he informed me. I could hardly say that this desirable feminine condition was due to a hard hour of sponging and pressing like a ladies' maid.

"Come in." I stepped back, even as I weighed the propriety of inviting a bachelor gentleman into hotel rooms occupied by a spinster lady.

But then, this was America, and propriety seemed to have been subdued and permanently confined to the cellar as far as Stateside customs went.

"Irene is out," I informed him as he set his hat, a soft-crowned affair, on the nearby table.

"I know. I saw her uptown."

"Uptown?"

"Farther north on Fifth Avenue."

"What did she have to say for herself?"

"Nothing." He arched an eyebrow toward the sofa.

"Do sit." I was less interested in playing hostess than solving why Irene had snubbed Quentin. She had been mightily put out with him a few days earlier for consorting with Nellie Bly at Delmonico's, but Irene was the last person to hold a grudge. "She said nothing to you?"

"She didn't see me."

"Were you trying not to be seen?"

"Oh, no. This is a spy's holiday for me. I am not known in this country, and have hardly any duties at all. Except, perhaps, accompanying intrepid ladies to Coney Island."

"Oh, Quentin, I was not at all intrepid at Coney Island!" I paused, appalled and confused to the point of momentary speechlessness. He immediately sensed my distress.

"What is it? An unhappy memory of the Ferris wheel?"

"Ah, no. I was just wondering, that is, I can't exactly remember, if we had formally agreed to being on informal terms."

The twinkle in his eyes was growing wicked. "How so on informal terms?" Distinctly not unhappy memories of our jaunt to Coney Island swept over me.

"Meeting unchaperoned in hotels, I mean. Of course."

"Of course. You are right, Nell. It does seem a . . . significant step."

"Apparently we have taken it," I pointed out with a bit of annoyance.

He grinned at me, and I suddenly wished for distraction.

The only thing that occurred to me would involve my being even more intrepid than going on a ferris wheel ride. I would have to use the black beast crouching on a circular end table.

"May I offer you some refreshment?"

He immediately glanced at the decanter by the desk.

"Tea, I meant."

"Of course. Tea."

I picked up the ignoble instrument and waited for a human voice to acknowledge my bold move. In very little time one did, barking "Yes?"

I ordered a tea service for two and gladly relinquished hold on the telephone, for only Irene had used it since our arrival ten days before.

"Tea." Quentin leaned back in the sofa and smiled, closing his eyes. "It will feel just like home."

"But you call the odd corners of the entire world home these days. Quentin."

His eyes opened, rebuking my reminder. "That is where I work. Home is where tea is hot and sweet instead of salty, and the servers are charming English ladies instead of squatting Bedouins."

"I thought you liked the nomadic life."

"I do, when I want adventure. But when I want comfort . . . there is nothing like a good English tea."

"I can't guarantee the Astor House will come anywhere near that standard, although . . . the cooking here is actually quite agreeable."

He laughed and shook his head. "Nell, you are learning the first lesson of the Englishman or woman abroad."

"And that is?"

"The English can't cook."

"I don't agree. And I certainly find the reputation of the French in that regard overrated."

He just shook his head.

"So," I asked, "what was Irene doing when you saw her and she did not see you? It is so unlike her to be oblivious."

"She was leaving the B. Altman's Department Store."

"Ah. No wonder she was distracted. Now that we have resolved to stay on in America, I imagine she has decided to supplement her meager wardrobe. You know how naked Irene feels without a full repertoire of clothing to suit every occasion from walking out in gentleman's guise to playing the belle of the ball."

I only then realized that I had used the word "naked" in a gentleman's presence. I felt the "radiance" acquired from working escalate into a blush that suffused my whole face.

Quentin, however, was looking down, studying the highly polished boot-toe on his casually crossed leg. "Forced to leave the stage that was her natural arena, she brings it with her, costumes, props, and all. And sometimes supernumeraries like ourselves, Nell."

"Oh, we are not mere supernumeraries," I said hastily as he looked up at my face again. Surely my crimson tide of embarrassment was ebbing by now. "Rather I would think of us as supporting players."

"Well," he said briskly, "she is playing some part today, for she was wearing an extremely plain gown of modest black."

"Not when she left here!"

He shrugged. "I know, Nell, that her quest in this country was to find her mother, who had apparently abandoned her at a young age. Is she . . . in mourning?"

"Well, I can't say. We did visit Green-Wood Cemetery and saw the grave of a woman who could have been Irene's mother. There is also some question that another dead woman may possibly . . . er, have the honor. But I never thought this quest had affected Irene so deeply that she would resort to wearing mourning!"

"You and I take knowing our parents for granted." He rose to answer a knock that had given me another start. "How can we understand what it must be like to grow up having no one to call mother or father? Ah."

He admitted a waiter bearing a huge silver tray as if it were made of lace instead of metal. This was deposited on the cloth covering the low table set before the sofa Quentin had taken.

Quentin saw the waiter to the door and skillfully slipped him a coin for his trouble, something I would never have thought of, and never have managed without attracting great attention to what should have been a subtle gesture. Would I never become a woman of the world? That is what comes of being born a country parson's daughter. Yet, as Quentin had just pointed out, there was comfort in knowing that, a comfort Irene had never felt.

He took my hand—another "informality" I was not certain we had agreed to—and led me around the table to sit beside him on the sofa.

"Mourning," I repeated, pouring tea and making sure Quentin's had two lumps of sugar. As I poured a few drops of milk into my cup, I couldn't help thinking of bitter tears flowing. "I had no idea Irene was so affected by this quest. We really can't believe she is the daughter of 'the wickedest woman in New York,' especially now another candidate has reared her, er, headstone, so to speak."

"What do you mean, Nell?" Quentin rose and went to the brandy decanter to pour a bit into his tea.

Before I could lower my eyebrows, he'd brought the decanter to me. "A bit for flavor?"

"Will it sweeten the tea?"

"No, but it may ease your anxiety." He poured some in without further ado. "I must tell you that Irene looked very unlike a woman in mourning when I saw her. She looked most pleased with herself. In fact, she was rushing along the avenue as if trying to catch a streetcar."

"How puzzling. She said nothing to me before she left, only that she had some errands and I must expect surprises." My first sip made me rear back. "This is far more heady than beer, Quentin."

"Brandy is for heroes, the saying goes. And heroines."

"Then certainly not for me." I frowned. "So that is why you came here. You had seen that Irene was out and wanted to know why she was wearing mourning attire."

"No. I saw that she was out and, clever agent that I am, surmised that you would be here alone."

There came another knock, only this was my heartbeat rapping at the cage of my chest.

Perversely, I longed for the intrusion of an actual knock on the door. A worldlier woman would have asked why Quentin wanted to visit me privately.

All I could do was rattle the tea things and exert all my will to keep from clearing my throat.

"Have I upset you?" he asked.

"No, but you have pointed out that our being . . . closeted here is somewhat improper." Suddenly my throat was clear and I found my voice, which seemed to be telling me a thing or two, more than him. "Although that is a bit ridiculous, as Irene would point out were she here. I am hardly a young, marriageable female that must be safeguarded at all times, and never was."

"I'm shocked. You mean to say that you are married?"

"No! Of course not! Never."

"You seem quite adamant against the state." He frowned slightly enough to indicate that he was railing me. "Then you must be about to confess that you are not female. I must confess in turn that I won't believe you, even were you to don Irene's walking-out clothes."

"Of course I would claim no such thing. One cannot deny one's gender, lowly as it is."

"Then you must have meant that you are not young. If so, I am in desperate straits, for I am older than you."

"How do you know?"

"Because I was already in the army when I first saw you and you were a governess so young you seemed on the same footing with your charges."

"That was years ago, Quentin. And you were startlingly youthful then too. I only meant that it's absurd for a spinster of a certain age to feel she must answer to some nameless critic for every step she takes."

"You did not take many steps here today, Nell. I called upon you. You merely answered the door. But I'm glad you have concluded that you . . . we . . . no longer need a chaperon."

Strange how one can find oneself coming to a brand-new conclusion, a revelation, in fact, by the act of speaking to someone else, and hearing yourself as if for the first time.

In fact, there was no one left in my life to scandalize . . . my parson father, the ladies of the town, people who passed me in the street and knew me not at all, and never would.

And Irene was impossible to scandalize.

I took a deep breath. "I quite agree, Quentin, that we do not require a chaperon. Then why do I feel that one is in order, despite everything?"

He leaned near, so I saw the lines of his smile etched in white against his sun-darkened complexion.

"Do you know, Nell, that I take that remark as a compliment?"

Was I woman, or was I mouse? I begrudged Pink the association with Quentin that events had demanded, but when he appeared here, of his own will, I hardly knew what to do with him.

"I'm sure you deserve many compliments," I said, "and from persons far more important than I."

"I can think of no such person."

Gracious. He had contrived that we sit very close together on the sofa, or somehow our positions had merged.

My heart was pounding as if a Spanish dancer had suddenly become resident. My face felt hot, my hands cold, my feet numb.

Quentin's wonderful hazel eyes were looking deeply into mine, and I was feeling such turbulence of emotions, knowing I had to choose whether to trust him or not, for he could as surely destroy me as delight me.

As if reading my thoughts, he took my hand.

"Nell, I ask only one question of you."

"That's odd. I have about a thousand for you."

"I ask only if you feel anything for me. Anything at all."

"Of course I do. My goodness, you are my onetime charge Allegra's uncle. I saw you as a very young man off to war, and now, here you are a seasoned agent for the Foreign Office, sent all around the world. I am very proud of you, Quentin, and especially of how you have lived such an adventurous life in frightening times and places, and done such good service for queen and country."

"That is the former governess speaking. I had something else in mind."

"What could there be but my sincere admiration, and gratitude?"

"Nell," he rebuked me.

"And . . . I do indeed feel a certain . . . camaraderie from dangers we have shared."

"Nell."

"And certain other . . . oh, a certain deep regard."

I gave up, for he was staring into my eyes in such a way that I could hardly think, much less speak.

The spell was breathtaking, and I felt such panic that it seemed imperative to break it.

"Why must I list my feelings, when I know nothing of yours? It is most unequal."

We stared at each other for what seemed like infinity.

"We are unequal," he said finally. "I find myself drawn to you, Nell. You know that I did from the moment we met in my niece's schoolroom, back at Berkeley Square in London. I still see the breathless girl in you, forced into service by circumstance. I want her back. I want to make her come back, to me."

I may have been somewhat obtuse by nature and education about what transpires between men and women, but there was no mistaking how Quentin thought he could recall that phantom of myself I had interred years ago.

"That moment is past. I am not the same."

"But you could be. I could make you be the same."

He lifted my hand to his lips. I felt warm breath, then flesh along them, and a thumb stroking the palm of my hand.

"Quentin, there are many other women more suitable—" Except for Nellie Bly, of course.

His lips and breath had moved to the inside of my wrist.

How I wished there were someone I could ask what this meant, and what I should do, or not do! Irene was out, of course, but I knew instantly that I could not refer this matter even to her. I wanted no other soul to know of it.

And yet . . . what did it mean? What would he do? I do? What would come of it?

How could I be again that green girl I had been for those few moments, and still protect myself from the harm another can do one for all the best reasons in the world. These moments were not new for Quentin, but they were for me. Once they were created, would the mystery and magic fade? Would I be left, like Elaine, the lily maid of Astelot, with only an abandoned image of myself in a cracked mirror?

Yet the feelings I felt, that Quentin had asked me about, were so strange and rare I couldn't bear to let them escape.

He brought my hand to his mouth, his lips on my unfolded palm, and I knew that I was lost.

5

A Bloody Game

As the playing conditions improved, so did the proficiency of the top players with the spot-stroke.
—PETER AINSWORTH, *A BRIEF HISTORY OF BILLIARDS AND THE TOOLS OF THE TRADE*

⊰FROM THE CASE NOTES OF SHERLOCK HOLMES⊱

I will say one thing for my Continent-wide pursuit of Madam Irene and her cohorts during my mission to put Jack the Ripper to rest last spring: It had prepared me for the most gruesome killings on the planet.

Here again was one such before me.

First I examined each carved curlicue of wood in the four massive pillars that upheld the table. My magnifying glass was hard put to spy a spec of dust, much less evidence. Then I studied the bank where green felt met ruddy wood.

At last I stepped back to view the body on its felt-lined bier of solid mahogany.

The stained-glass lighting fixture above it was nigh as long and wide as the table, illuminating each ornate leather pocket as if they were gopher holes to oblivion. Now it cast the half-clothed body of the man below it into harsh relief, like a cameo of death.

His skin was indeed that pale. Though the face, neck, and hands may have been ruddy once, they were now the gray of clay, of lifeless human clay.

The man lay centered precisely on the felt, arms stretched out to each side at shoulder height. Curled knuckles just brushed the billiard table's banked sides.

He was clothed only in trousers so rent and stained that it was difficult to determine their original manufacture. A far from young man, this fact made the violent nature of his death all the more shocking. One likes to think that the old have declined into a state of terminal innocence, although the second most vicious blackmailer I ever knew had been almost ninety.

Death's rigor had stiffened his form into temporary stone, but an examination of the felt beneath him revealed bloodstains. He had been limp, and possibly still living when placed upon the surface.

My usual methods would not suffice in this case. His hands had been so mutilated—fingertips missing, or nails wrenched from their roots—that the abuses obscured whatever calluses and lines his life's work and habits had scribed into his skin.

The bare feet were equally abused. Torture was the only answer, and merciless torture the civilized world had not known in centuries. Why had no one in the house heard his screams? It was huge, of course, and the long, stone-lined hall kept sounds confined to the rooms along it.

I examined the features, which were crusted with rivulets of dried blood. Were the corners of the mouth damaged by a gag?

Never had I so wished for Watson's seasoned medical presence. Usually I can sink myself so deeply into my scrutinies that I barely contemplate the larger ironies of violent death. I leave that sort of thing to Watson.

Now I had no partner in the bloody work and felt an alien unease. Something about this murder was more Watson's sphere than my usual orbit. Cruelty, vicious anger, murderous rage . . . I see the results of these stormy emotions and weigh and measure them and feel only curiosity and a determination to undo the doer. Watson, on the other hand, worries, fears, expresses all the emotions I find too distracting to note, much less feel.

I stood back. There was more to this picture . . . it was indeed a "picture," almost a painting. Something from an earlier age.

My brown study was interrupted by a voice from the adjacent room, half-muffled.

"All the staff is supposed to be upstairs cleaning this morning. Master's orders. What are you doing here?"

I was slightly surprised to note the British accent in that admonition, and even more surprised when the voice of Erin answered with a soprano lilt.

"Master wanted his billiard balls dusted up, now didn't he tell me, just? This mornin'. And dustin' all the other folderol around the place. I was just gettin'—"

"So you loiter in the back stairwell, my girl?"

"I don't do any of that there 'loiterin'' you mention. I was just adjustin' me collar and cuffs, 'case I was seen by the gentry."

"Then be about it. Mr. Vanderbilt is extremely particular about the billiard room."

That very Mr. Vanderbilt's wish to keep the contents of this room secret held me silent.

I heard two sets of footsteps, light ones scurrying this way and heavier ones ascending an unseen staircase.

I began to step around the billiard table to block the view of the body, but the admonished maid darted into the room like a scalded black-and-white hen, a flurry of dark skirts and a flourish of feather duster.

"Oh! Sorry, Sir." She kept her voice low, at least. "I didn't know a gennelman was about the place."

Her skin, as white as her cuffs and collar, was strewn with pale freckles. Her hair was the burning-bush scarlet of Ireland, abundantly escaping her white cap.

In attempting to back out of the room, she sidled away from me . . . and into full view of the thing on the billiard table.

Her eyes widened to cue-ball rounds. "Holy Mother o' God! 'Tis a dead man, for sure." Her fingers moved to forehead, breast, and shoulders in a sign of the cross. Then her voice took on a deeper, awestruck tone. "Crucified, begorrah, like the holy martyrs of old."

Crucified! Of course. Would even Watson have realized this? Perhaps only a Roman Catholic, an ignorant, superstitiously devout underhousemaid.

"Listen, my girl." I stepped toward her with finger on lips. "I am from the police. The master doesn't wish anyone to know of this. You mustn't scream."

She paused her frantic Latin muttering and breast-beating to eye me. "I'm not one to scream, Sir, I—"

At that her eyes rolled up in her head and she began to swoon.

I caught her before she made a confounded thump on the floor that would bring the butler back, and deposited her on a long velvet-upholstered bench from which the losers must have watched the winners finish up the table.

Her eyelashes batted open again before I could turn away to finish inspecting the scene, now from the vantage of a new and profane manner of death.

Her white little hands clamped onto my sleeve like the teeth of a deep sea conger.

"Oh, please, Sir. Don't tell anyone I came in here. 'Twas only to escape that awful Masher footman. Was he killed here, that poor man?" She crossed herself yet again.

"It's none of your affair. And your dereliction of duty will soon be at least Mr. Vanderbilt's knowledge. I can't say that I think it will go well for you with him. Now, no more swoons. Stay still and keep silent."

Sometimes it is necessary to be firm, and I am no more mindful of hushing a housemaid than shushing a Royal when it comes to ensuring that I am free to go about my work undistracted.

Crucified, though. I approached the billiard table again. The Vanderbilt family was not Roman Catholic, that I knew. Why would a corpse defaced in such a manner be deposited in their great city house? This was fast becoming a far more fascinating case than that of the missing Astor chess set that had originally entangled me with the first families of New York City.

I examined the corpse's hands and feet once more, bending very close with the glass. The central wounds were not gross enough to have been made by thick, ancient nails, but indeed his hands had been pierced by something sharp and long, perhaps a very narrow dagger. I glimpsed minuscule flakes of metal in the wounds, betokening great force.

Mr. Vanderbilt would not welcome this diagnosis of the murder on his premises, but it would be interesting to observe his reaction.

I turned as the door from the hall opened, my eyes passing over the recumbent maid.

She was gone.

6

Together Again

I cannot conceive how men who are husbands, brothers, or fathers can give utterance to an idea so intrinsically bad and infamous, that their wives, their sisters, or their daughters, want but the opportunities and 'facilities' to be vicious, and if they are not so, it is not from an innate principle of virtue, but from fear.

—MADAME RESTELL

 A key scrabbled at the lock and then Irene was in the room, hat and hat-pin already in hand, hair windblown, her cape opening on a skirt of black sateen, just as Quentin had described.

I had leaped up at her entry.

She was as surprised as I. "Nell! What are you doing?"

"Having tea. What are you doing, or rather, what *were* you doing? And where?"

It was a stalemate. We had both managed something we rarely did after all our years of living together. We had surprised each other at one and the same time.

"Quentin." Irene advanced on our . . . no, my . . . guest, gloved hand extended. "Please don't get up. It looks as if you and Nell have consumed far too many tea cakes to permit unneeded leaps."

"I'm sorry there's nothing left." I turned toward the telephone. "I can order more."

"Don't bother." Irene had sat on the occasional chair and unfastened her summer cape hook. It fell away from her black gown as she began easing her fingers out of tight, pale kid gloves. "My appetite is not quite right anyway," she muttered.

"Where have you been?" I was not to be drawn away.

"Out. Investigating."

"What have you to investigate now that the matter of 'the wickedest woman in New York' is resolved?"

"Nothing's ever quite resolved, is it? You remember that we have that most fascinating and annoying book in code?"

I had forgotten the infernal book, a coded Who's Who to illegitimate births in New York City at midcentury.

Quentin was looking politely bemused as only an Englishman born can. Neither Irene nor I chose to enlighten him. I almost suggested he have a look at the code, for he was a seasoned spy, but felt the book was Irene's private matter and didn't want to speak for her.

So Irene sat smiling vaguely at us, stroking the empty kid gloves in her lap. "I have had quite a walk. Much of it inside B. Altman's and Macy's. Mercy! What massive emporiums. But I've ordered a few more articles useful for our prolonged stay here, Nell. They should arrive tomorrow."

"Excellent," Quentin said. "Word of a 'prolonged stay' is most welcome."

"To you," Irene noted. "Others would not be so happy to know of our remaining here."

Quentin exchanged a glance with me. It was odd to know more of what he was thinking than what Irene was. And not entirely comfortable.

Irene sat, lost in thought. She didn't even twit me indirectly about my recent seclusion with Quentin. This was most unlike her. Also, as a former diva, she was used to sweeping onto each new scene and mastering it at once. Now it was as if she had bumbled onstage into a play starring Quentin and myself, quite without having a role in it.

Quentin finally disobeyed her and rose. "This has been a delightful repast," he said with a bow to me, "but I must be about some trying business with the banks. Extended visits abroad are costly."

Irene nodded, leaving me to see Quentin to the door, through which he swiftly drew me into the hall.

"Irene is not herself," he whispered. To whisper just outside the not-quite-closed door required him to lean his face very close to mine. "What do you suppose is going on?"

"I haven't the slightest idea," I whispered back.

"Then perhaps you had better find out."

His breath warmed my cheek as his lips brushed the hair at my temple.

It was a farewell gesture that one could consider brotherly. And, then again, that one could not.

"I've slipped the address and telephone number of my hotel into your pocket, in case you should need me."

"My pocket?" My hand went to the folds of my skirt. "When? How?" I was beginning to blush.

"Espionage begets many skills. Irene is not quite herself, and after the personal strains she has been under, I can understand why. You should have someone else to call upon."

"It's this maddening quest for her mother. She cared nothing about it until Nellie Bly started making such a false fuss about it, and now . . . I'm afraid a hornet's nest has been unearthed. And that miserable Sherlock Holmes has only fed the flames. I wish we had never seen either of them."

Quentin wisely did not comment on my two bête noirs, nor my abominably mixed metaphors, but donned his hat and gloves and nodded good-bye.

I slipped back into the room to find Irene still seated on the chair and frowning into the distance.

"What's the matter?"

She visibly shook herself out of her pondering mood. Her palms lifted and struck the arms of her chair with fresh resolve. "I must concentrate on attending to the unfinished business started by Nellie Bly, that's all there is to it."

"I've been afraid of that very thing." I sank onto the sofa so recently vacated by Quentin. "You are never one to let well enough alone."

"And what is well enough?" Irene responded indignantly.

"You know what I mean," I answered, drawing some fancy work from the bag beside the sofa and proceeding to untangle threads. That I would not watch her aggravated Irene even more. Persuasion depended on the full impact of her person.

She stood, the better to pace back and forth and wear out the Astor House's fine Turkey carpets. It was a pity there was no operatic score for *The Merchant of Venice,* for Irene was very fond of lapsing into what I called the Portia role.

It was also a pity women today were still not allowed to be barristers, for at such times Irene quite rivaled or even surpassed Godfrey for fire and eloquence in court. The greatest pity was that it was wasted on an unswayable audience as myself.

"The fact is, Nell, that we have been issued a challenge on two fronts."

"We?"

"You are here, aren't you? With me? What shall you do if you disapprove of my actions? Take a steamer—a great, huge, wave-wallowing, endlessly rocking, seasick-making ocean steamer—back to France? Swim?"

"I merely suggested that I am not an indispensable element. Besides, I saw only one challenge issued, and that was more of a taunt, if you ask me," I said.

"You refer to Sherlock Holmes's behavior by the old grave in Green-Wood Cemetery."

"I refer to him *following* us to Green-Wood Cemetery."

"And *I* refer to him then telling us the grave site we visited *first* could not possibly contain my lost mother. Is that not extraordinary behavior?"

"For an ordinary person, yes, I grant you. It is the kind of rude meddling *I* expect of the man. To then lead us on an unconscionably long trek through the graveyard to another headstone was even more of an imposition."

"He implied that this Eliza Gilbert was more likely to be my mother. What am I to do? Let the implication lie there like forty pounds of memorial marble? Is Sherlock Holmes to know more of my antecedents than I do?"

"Really, Irene. You are being most immature. When Nellie Bly's cable to Neuilly a few weeks ago first raised the ghost of your mother, you insisted you had never known a mother and had no wish to do so now. Yet you ended by uprooting me and condemning us both to a week's sentence on the heaving Atlantic."

"Nellie Bly also cried bloody murder."

"And there was indeed murder afoot, both past and present. But at the end of it you learned that your childhood was exactly as you'd thought: you'd been reared as an orphan by theatrical folk. For a while it looked as though 'the wickedest woman in New York' at midcentury might be your mother. I almost think that you're disappointed now that she may *not* be. And you are thus convinced by what? On the word, nay hint, of whom? Mr. Sherlock Holmes? Hardly a trusted boon companion."

"Not like yourself," Irene murmured. Slyly.

If she knew, as I did, of *the* man's secret admiration for her she would realize how little he was to be trusted. They had first crossed swords in London two years ago over the King of Bohemia's claim upon one of Irene's possessions, if no longer on her heart. It was later that I glimpsed some fatuous unpublished scribblings by his physician friend, John H. Watson, purporting to tell the tale of "A Scandal in Bohemia." Never would I wish Irene to know how much her wit and beauty had touched this heartless detecting machine, an unrepentant drug and tobacco fiend as well as one with no natural liking for women, to read the doctor's story.

Now we were marooned on this wild continent of America, she and I, her stalwart husband, Godfrey, in Bavaria on urgent business for the international Rothschild banking interests. Marooned here with Sherlock Holmes. Never had my self-assigned role of chaperon been more needed, even though Irene was a married woman and I was still a spinster. My unwedded state did not mean that I was unable to harbor strong suspicions.

"We have Madame Restell's coded book about who had abortions and who had children given up for adoption,' Irene said, switching subjects. "Nellie Bly would give her reporter's eyeteeth to lay her hands on a listing of all the unwed births or aborted pregnancies of New York society dating from the '20s to the '50s of this century."

"That is old news, Irene, at this late date of 1889."

"Not when some of the children of society misses were placed secretly in new foster families. Think of the heirs and heiresses today . . . Astors, Belmonts, Vanderbilts . . . who would tremble in their dancing shoes to know an unacknowledged sibling lurked somewhere to share the booty."

"I know the volume is dangerous. That's why I believe we should leave it untranslated. And your interest is not really in shaking the foundations of New York society, about which you never did give a fig. You want to see if you yourself are listed there. You, who loudly insisted you neither had nor needed a mother, are now intent on finding her out: the unnamed 'woman in black' who came to the theaters to play with you as a child. Besides, if you are to believe Sherlock Holmes, she is already dead and you know her name. Eliza Gilbert. *Mrs.* Eliza Gilbert. Is that not enough?"

Whenever I waxed as eloquent or lengthy as Irene (who was used to delivering whole arias and thus had breath to speak three times as long), she invariably resorted to the cigarettes or small cigars she favored.

By now her soufflé of a chestnut-colored pompadour was wreathed in veils of blue smoke. The scent of sulphur lingered on the air even though the lucifer with which she'd lit her cigarette was ashes in the crystal tray. I wouldn't doubt that some shadow of Beelzebub lingered in the room, scenting a new Pandora about to open another forbidden box.

"Everything you say is true, Nell. As always. Yet I find that, as little as I cared to know my family past, I as much dislike other people knowing more about it than I do. ' 'Tis a poor thing, but mine own.' "

"Shakespeare was referring to repute, not a past. A reputation is a woman's only past. And yours will be not be enhanced if your mother proves to be exactly the sort of woman who abandons a child."

"You forget the 'Mrs.' you immediately rhapsodized over on Eliza Gilbert's headstone when Mr. Holmes led us there."

"What sort of married woman deserts a child?"

"One driven to it."

"And leaves a small girl to the keeping of a gypsy assortment of variety performers and freaks?"

"One who may know that people are seldom what they seem to be. From the admittedly haphazard care of those 'gypsies' and 'freaks' I went on to become the first American diva to establish a performing career in the Old World, on its terms, not as a touring star performer from the States."

"Oh, they are inoffensive, I suppose, and very careless as to family ties, but well-meaning. If the Woman in Black was able to visit backstage all those many times, why could she not acknowledge you as her daughter?"

Irene paced again. "I don't know, Nell. That is what I must find out."

"And how will you do it?"

"It would be fastest to ask Nellie Bly for help. She knows the city like Sherlock Holmes knows London, and would have access to such information."

"No!" I dropped my lapful of satin threads and immediately snatched them up in a new tangle, only then remembering that our fat Persian cat, Lucifer, was far from interfering with my handiwork. The old black devil was back in Neuilly smacking his whiskers at Casanova in his parrot cage.

Irene paused, inhaled on the hateful cigarette impaled in an elegant holder like dead leaves rolled in a Baccarat crystal vase, and spat out a stream of wispy smoke.

"Well, then. Since the only two people in New York who might know more than we do on this subject are rivals rather than allies, we'd better investigate this ourselves. As usual. It is, after all, my business."

I felt both dismayed and pleased. Much as I disapproved of Irene's headstrong determination to solve all riddles, no matter how perilous, I did like her to rely upon me rather than others in pursuit of such foolishness.

Irene finally snuffed out the cigarette. "What, by the way, did Quentin want here?"

"It should be obvious. Tea and talk." I returned to sorting my slippery little eel's nest of threads all over again.

"Oh, it is obvious, Nell. All too obvious."

I ignored Irene's smile as I vigorously pursued my work.

7

Millionaire or Mouse?

*Find a poor patrician woman who knows everybody
and loves to spend money.*

—RULE FOUR ON HOW TO BREAK INTO SOCIETY, THE REV. CHARLES WILBUR DE LYON

NICHOLS, *THE ULTRA-EXCLUSIVE PEERAGE OF AMERICA,* 1904

⊰FROM THE CASE NOTES OF SHERLOCK HOLMES⊱

"Brandy?" Mr. William Kissam Vanderbilt asked when Wilson escorted me into the library at the front of the house.

I'd been led directly there, so swiftly that I knew he hoped his wife would never glimpse hide nor hat of me. For one who has not been unwelcome at Windsor, this sense of being hustled in and out like an unwanted tradesman was irritating.

What an odd notion—not brandy in the morning after a severe shock—but situating a library overlooking a busy metropolitan street. However, the rows of gilded book spines marching across the shelves in perfect formation told me that effect, rather than function, was the major purpose of this room.

That and the amber brandy decanter sitting amid a flash of silver and crystal.

Vanderbilt was swift enough to read my glance. "Yes, there was a brandy service in the billiards room, but . . . that's no place for partaking at the moment. I have cigars as well."

"I am an almost exclusive pipe smoker, Mr. Vanderbilt, and I bring my kit with me."

I produced the old briarwood I had packed for foreign travel and accepted the light my host offered.

He poured for himself, a generous amount. Then he gestured to an armchair while he settled behind the long rococo library table. Obviously the air of an office soothed a man of business.

These American empire builders are quite an intriguing breed. I confess that my interest has always perked up when one has found his way to Baker Street. What a pity Watson is not here to capture this one with his pen. Vanderbilt appears surprisingly youthful for the richest man in America, the richest of continents.

Had I not known his particulars I still would have known him for what, if not who, he was. An American nabob, certainly. He radiates the hallmarks of a man of business. Under the library table I could see that his high-polished shoes were scuffed on the left side over the small toe and on the right over the large toe. The habitual desk sitter often crosses his feet behind the closed-in skirt of his office desk; not even rigorous polish can obscure the scuffs of daily habit.

To the contrary, the right jacket sleeve and cuff edge of his shirt bore the polish of frequent sweeps across papers and bare mahogany. Even a man of millionaire's means can't replace suits and shirts fast enough to prevent the wear of daily work from showing.

As for his character, I judged it extraordinarily amiable for a man of such power. No doubt he needed to be to tolerate his wife's extravagant social ambitions.

"You come highly recommended, Mr. Holmes," he said after two long swallows of brandy, "but I hadn't planned to confront you with slaughter in my billiard room."

"What first convinced you that you needed a consulting detective at all?"

"Not just a consulting detective. There are Pinkertons aplenty in New York City, for all their home office is in Chicago. No, this matter is . . . delicate, and even more so now, after this atrocity."

I waited. I wanted him to speak unhalted, tumbling out his thoughts in one unconsidered rush.

He picked up a fountain pen and twirled it between his forefinger and thumb. Yes, truly right-handed. "We Vanderbilts are the third generation of

New York wealth, yet only recently vital to New York society, Mr. Holmes," he explained. "Mrs. Astor queened it over Fifth Avenue for years, with her balls and 'Four Hundred' guests deemed worthy of inviting to them. No Vanderbilt was on the list."

"We in England have been familiar with that sort of quandary since the time of the Conqueror."

"This is our time of the conqueror. The great fortunes are being made here and now in this century, and this city is the crown jewel of our industrial kingdoms. Here we establish fiefdoms, we Vanderbilts, Astors, Morgans, Belmonts, Goulds, and Fisks. This section of upper Fifth Avenue between Fifty-first and Fifty-eighth is known as Vanderbilt Row since we began building our latest town houses in the past decade, were you aware of that?"

"I am now, but I am more aware of the dead man in your billiard room, and in fact, know more about him than I do of American millionaires."

He waved a vapid hand. "I merely bring you up to date on these matters because a scandal of this sort . . . a man slaughtered in the billiard room of six-sixty Fifth Avenue would destroy what my wife has worked for, and spent lavishly on, for years. This house is an architectural wonder of New York City, yet she would not abide in it a moment longer if she knew what lay in the billiard room."

"So you require discretion in order to not upset your wife."

"Women can be very odd about such things, you know."

"That is not an area in which I am expert."

"What man is? At any rate, Alva was planning to be out most of today, thankfully. Wilson will collect us when the . . . er, undertakers arrive so we can supervise them. Or you can. I understand you are most particular about observing every action before and after a crime has been committed. Or so Astor has told me."

"The forgery of the ancient chess set Astor bought was hardly this sort of crime. It was committed in Cremona three centuries ago. I merely detected the minuscule but unmistakable marks the forgers left in turning an ancient curiosity into a thing of false provenance and outrageous profit. A million dollars indeed! You men of Fifth Avenue are multimillionaires in extravagance as well as worth, though I suppose that is what the game is all about."

"A million? Astor paid a million for a worthless forgery?"

"Not quite worthless." I smiled, and left him to wonder why. "Perhaps he will next be envying your interesting corpse."

"Heaven forbid! Much as the thought of an Astor envying a Vanderbilt is enjoyable. No one must know of this."

"There is more to this conviction of yours than worries about your wife's repudiating this house."

Vanderbilt laid his cigar in a huge cut-crystal tray and watched the smoke idle upwards from its end. I puffed contentedly on my pipe. I could have been camping out in Central Park at this moment and have been just as content there with my humble shag. Great wealth brings great worries.

"Why did you wish to engage my services?"

"I'm sorry, Mr. Holmes, that the problem I'm facing became so evident before our appointment later today, and in a way I'd never dreamed. The matter seemed to involve only absurd but disquieting threats. Now this, which must be part of the puzzle! When I wrote to engage your services after Astor mentioned you were in New York, I had no idea that a stranger would be murdered so brutally in my house."

I waved away his apology. I wanted to hear what he thought was the matter. Only then could I begin to determine what was actually wrong. And, indeed, he might well be part of it.

"I've been getting threatening communications, Mr. Holmes. I know, all of us millionaires do. But these are beyond the offerings of the ordinary crackpot. They warn me that if I don't go along with what the men, or man, wants, there will be dire consequences."

"The state of your billiard room is indeed dire. I must see these 'communications.'"

He went to a tall cabinet, unlocked it, and brought out a green leather letter box. After lifting the cover, he placed the box on the table beside me.

I reached into my pocket for a pair of tweezers. The dark Vanderbilt eyebrows rose as I used the implement to turn over what soon proved itself to be seven pieces of paper.

"Hmmm." I flipped my way through the collection. "Ha! And ha again!"

"What have you found? Something incriminating?"

"Something nonsensical. These threats are vague and their form is laughable."

"I fail to see the hilarity."

I held up a sheet of cheap yellow paper in the tweezers I always carry. Childish as the collection was, the papers still merited close study. "A cablegram. Really, Mr. Vanderbilt, one of the simplest things in the world to trace.

The time, date, and place of origin are represented by the numbers above the message. And this . . . this note on plain paper with the words formed from letters cut out from the daily newspaper . . . the *New York Herald* if I recall the typeface rightly. And then, this! It is beyond the amateur to the point that I truly sense something sinister behind it. Such well-calculated buffoonery can only be serious. The typeface is delicate, even arty. It is from some weekly or monthly journal that I am sure no menacing party would subscribe to or even know about. All these were addressed to you, not to your wife?"

"Alva knows nothing about it, and matters must remain that way."

"I shall take these for study."

A knock at the door made us look up.

"Enter," Vanderbilt said uncertainly, then told the butler to return later.

It was plain he was not truly master in his own house, but then a man whose bedroom slippers stuck slightly to the carpet would not be.

"Have you a gymnasium in the house?" I asked him. The traces of rosin I had noticed on the slippers he wore earlier was obvious.

He blinked at the apparent inanity of my question. "Why, yes. On the third floor. The children, you know. But how did *you* know?"

"And your bedchamber is located nearby?"

"Next to it."

I nodded. Mrs. Vanderbilt, no doubt, had a palatial suite to herself on the second floor (which we should call first in England.) Why a wealthy man might marry to be relegated to a Cinderella's lot, I cannot say.

"Why is secrecy so vital in your own house?" I asked Vanderbilt. Beyond the heavy draperies, I heard the ceaseless sounds of passing horses and equipages, again struck by the folly of situating a library facing the street.

Obviously, the room was for show rather than retreat, yet my host appeared more at ease in this room than anywhere else in the house, including the masculine sanctuary of the billiard room.

"Vital? Of course it is, Mr. Holmes. The markets are volatile. We are the richest family in America. Any whisper of upset in our well-being, and fortunes would fall. Not just ours but those of the hundreds and even thousands who have caught on to our coattails. It is a crushing responsibility."

"And these extortion notes have been coming for how long?"

"Two, perhaps three months."

I considered the contents of the letter box again.

"Who has handled these?"

"Myself alone. At first I took them for a joke. Some of the social maneuvers among the first families of New York are so intense that such distractions would not be unexpected. One would think kingdoms depended on which grand dame's grand ball is deemed the most successful."

I carefully arranged the collection of notes, letters, and cablegrams into chronological order. The first was a cablegram that stated only "Pay what thou owest."

"This first cable seems more a platitude than a threat," I noted.

"So I thought. The phrase is merely a foundation of good business."

"The second cable embroiders on that theme, but only slightly: 'Pay what you know you owe.' It's dated two weeks after the first. Did you grow uneasy then?"

He shrugged and opened a brazilwood humidor on his desk. The scent of tobacco as well aged as a fine brandy pervaded the room. By now he knew better than to offer me a cigar, and lit his own ceremoniously before answering.

After an inaugural puff, he replied. "I must have been feeling ever so slightly uneasy already, because I'd put the first cablegram in this box. I can't say I was surprised to receive a third communication in the same vein."

I lifted the envelope postmarked three weeks earlier. From Paris.

"This paper is of German manufacture. It's called Dresden deckle and has been manufactured for perhaps forty years." I opened the single sheet within. Hand printed thereon was another phrase: "Do what thou wilt, but pay what thou owest." "This correspondent favors the mode of biblical exhortation, I see. The authors of most threatening communications prefer that tone."

"I am amazed." Vanderbilt had sat forward, still puffing on his cigar. "You're sure the paper originated in Germany?"

"Of course. That doesn't mean to say it was used in Germany, although it is suggestive. This is the first personal correspondence and may be either a clue or a deliberate attempt to force wrong conclusions."

I plucked up the fourth communication. Another letter, this time on the thin paper intended for trans-Atlantic passage. This one was postmarked London, two weeks earlier.

"Victoria Station posting," I observed. "From the very heart of London, where millions pass by each week. Your correspondent both advertises his movements and despises the usual means of tracking his movements. He is not to be underestimated."

"You assume a personal enemy?"

"I assume only someone who wishes to be paid what he believes is owed. Have you any 'debts' of that sort?"

"Of course not. In an unstable business climate, any breath of insolvency is suicide."

"Are you operating in an unstable business climate?"

"Anyone of my wealth is, Mr. Holmes, but the United States government is particularly vulnerable at the moment, with the argument for the silver standard versus the gold standard at white-hot fever. That is why the subsequent messages become more sinister."

By now our correspondent had arrived at local New York City postmarks and the use of innocuous small envelopes, the sort that might include invitations to the lady of the house. Yet the contents were hardly invitations.

I read one message: "Pay what you owe or the consequences will be dire."

"Do you have any notion what payment is demanded?" I asked Vanderbilt.

He shook his dapper head. With his center part and dark waves to either side, I could not help but think of some of the slipperier variety artistes I had briefly encountered during my excursion into Madam Irene Adler Norton's rather lurid American past. I almost smiled, but of course Vanderbilt would misinterpret mirth at this juncture.

"This next billet-doux, for it is on quite frivolous paper, finally becomes specific and demands 'the gold and the jewels.' Have you any idea what gold and which jewels are meant?"

"Mine, I suppose. My gold and my wife's jewels, which are formidable."

"Are they also in safekeeping?"

"Some in banks and others in our own safes."

"How much actual gold do you have?"

Here he shifted uneasily so the huge leather chair squeaked most disagreeably, like a lapdog with its tail stepped upon.

"Now there, Mr. Holmes, you tread upon what you might call a state secret. There are three or four of us . . . millionaires, that is . . . who have enormous gold reserves. Not Vanderbilts. The others won't say how much, because that could set the markets soaring or plummeting. And then, too, the government is mighty interested, and it's to the financiers' advantage to keep them guessing as well."

"You are saying that the monetary state of the United States is best kept a mystery?"

"From my point of view, and the government's, yes."

"*Hmmm.* Even your unnamed correspondent seems willing to keep this all a mystery. And this is the last message, until the presumed object lesson left upon your billiard table?"

"Yes."

"Obviously, he, or they, had intended to kill that poor old fellow all along, for his presence here only announces that these are not people to be crossed."

"You assume more than one."

"One man would be sorely tried to import a body into a household as large as yours. There are at least two, and the entire sequence smacks of some sort of cadre. These written notes are in different hands. What is most disturbing is not the wretched soul left on your billiard table but the vagueness of the demands. It is almost as if the blackmailer expects you to know exactly what is wanted: how much gold and which jewels. Can you explain this?"

"Mr. Holmes, I cannot. I am a millionaire. I am known for amassing money, and the finest form of money is in hard gold bars. It does not rot. My wife is the leader of New York society and as such has always impressed upon me that it is my duty to swath her in jewels."

"As far as you know, none of your gold or jewels is missing?"

"Not one gold bar, not one diamond brooch. It would appear that these thugs are so vague because they want it all. Of course that can't happen. Before I call out the entire New York City Police Department, such as it is, I would rather work through you and the Pinkertons or my own discreet staff members."

"Indeed. These are rather interesting criminals. They threaten before they make their demands known. I suspect a determined band of brigands. I also suspect further warnings, probably even more appalling than the man you will shortly remove from your house. They tortured him for some reason, and are letting you know that they are on the trail of the goods you have that they claim."

"But all I have is the means I inherited from my grandfather, the Commodore, and that my own father multiplied many times over in the eight years he lived after my grandfather died, and left to me and my brothers and sisters. Who would claim the whole of the Vanderbilt fortune?"

"Who indeed, but a criminal, or criminals, as paramount in the world of misdeeds as the Vanderbilts are in the world of finance? I predict that we confront a truly fiendish scheme concocted by men who are prepared to use any atrocity to accomplish their ends. Were we in London, I know whom I would suspect. Here in America, the possibilities are endless."

"Then it is hopeless. I must convert my house into a fortress and forbid my family all egress."

"This house was not designed to be defended, Mr. Vanderbilt, even though some call it a castle. The only solution is to discover who these people are and what specifically they want, and perhaps why they want it from the Vanderbilts. Are there any your family exploited to rise in the world?"

"Many, probably."

" 'Many' alone will not do. A few ruthless men driven by desires too dark to divine readily must be behind this mystery, and it must have to do with your family history."

"How can you say that? Being a captain of industry makes for ruthless competition, and may produce violent unrest among the working force, but none of this rude jostling among the lower classes touches the ruling families."

"Yes, that is quite obviously the case, Mr. Vanderbilt." My scathing tone was lost on the American millionaire, as it had been on the King of Bohemia earlier. Absolute power not only corrupts absolutely but it apparently renders the possessors deaf and blind.

"Good heavens, Mr. Holmes! I would have to say our most vicious enemies are the newspaper cartoonists. Though they are indeed merciless with pen and ink, I hardly think they would torment old men with knives."

"I saw nothing artistic in the indignities done to him, although there is a certain element of ritual to the method, if not the means."

"This is a brutal and senseless puzzle."

"The first, yes, but I beg to differ on the second. It is a commonplace to call what is brutal senseless, but I have found the opposite to be the case. It is simply that the motive is not evident and makes no sense to us yet."

8

Family Mystery

❧

In any appreciation of the American Renaissance, as the period from the 1870s to the first world war is sometimes called, the era that saw the United States emerge from its earlier republican simplicity and isolation to ingest the glories of European art and culture, some account has to be taken of the Vanderbilts.

—LOUIS AUCHINCLOSS

❧ FROM THE CASE NOTES OF SHERLOCK HOLMES ❧

I'd gotten my old briarwood going and rose to stretch my legs while I marshaled my thoughts into a form that would penetrate a millionaire's brain, addled as it must be with buying and selling men and machines.

I was, in a sense, taking the stage in order to keep the attention of this surprisingly dense man. He made Watson glitter like the veriest Aristotle by comparison.

"Mr. Vanderbilt, I have had cases laid before me by everyone from humble clerks to the crowned heads of Europe. In each instance, they reported a puzzle or a dilemma that often had them fearing for their fortunes, their lives, their very sanity. At all times the circumstances that brought them to me were strange, frightening, and contradictory. In all cases, every one, I was the mere epilogue to a string of events that were rooted firmly in my clients' pasts.

"I am not much a reader of fiction or drama, but I can say that if there is a motto that guides my detection work, it was uttered by England's Will Shakespeare four hundred years ago. 'The past is prologue.' I know not the play or the speaker, and I don't care. To help you, I must know your past and that of your forebears."

"My father has been dead these five years, and my grandfather, the Commodore, has been gone for twelve."

"Again to quote the Bard, and I assure you I don't have a large store of such: 'Age cannot wither nor custom stale' the interest to be found in a saga of worldly success built from a pittance. I presume that was the Commodore's story, or was he truly a well-born and placed soul?"

And so I invited upon myself the usual rags-to-riches fairy story, save that it was set against the rude American background of a frontier becoming a world force.

Invited to tell the family tale, the affable William Kissam Vanderbilt, a handsome man only a few years my senior, selected another Havana cigar and gestured me back into the comfortable armchair.

"The Commodore was not an official title, as you divined," be began. "It came as a result of his extensive shipping interests, and, I suppose, a certain commanding manner."

He nodded at a black-and-white sketch on the wall framed by a broad border of gilt that would have overpowered the subject had he not been a lean old man of martial bearing. His hat and cane occupied each hand, and he wore a high-buttoned frock coat with the soft collar and tie favored at midcentury, or earlier.

"A large man, I see, muscular and athletic. Something of a frontiersman in his youth, like your president, Andrew Jackson."

My dapper host blinked in amazement. Ah, it is good to encounter a portable Watson now and then. "How on earth did you know that, Mr. Holmes? There can't be much knowledge of our family's roots in England."

I nodded at the sketch. "All the knowledge I need is there. His size I determined from the length of his arms and size of the hat in relation to the figure we see from head to knees. His firm grasp upon the walking stick implies a man who has had more concrete rudders in his hands than metaphorical ones. The knuckles are also enlarged, either the sign of a pugilist or a laborer."

"My grandfather was born in a Staten Island farmhouse."

"Modest, I presume."

"Quite. He had no education, but a journalist once said that 'he would have become rich on a desert island.' "

I nodded at the Commodore's strong old face. With the fashion in which he wore his hair, one need only add a goatee and a hat clothed in Old Glory and he would make an excellent "Uncle Sam." I said so.

"Unfortunately, your observation is correct, Mr. Holmes, including the cruder aspect of life earlier in the century. The Commodore was never ashamed of himself, but the fact is he was not socially acceptable."

"How so?"

"He cussed like a pirate's parrot, loudly, pinched the servant girls black and blue, used chewing tobacco, and believed in the occult. But he never was a true robber baron, like Fisk and Gould. He never preyed on other people's investments. He simply built huge transportation concerns for a burgeoning country . . . shipping lines all over the world, railroads that crossed the continent as far afield as Nicaragua, where he made a million a year for saving prospectors six hundred miles on the Central American overland route to the gold fields of California. When he died January fourth in 1877, his fortune exceeded the cash reserves of the entire United States government."

"And how did he leave his wealth?"

Vanderbilt laid his cigar in the crystal tray. Its scent perfumed the air, quite overwhelming my modest pipe.

"There's the rub. He had ten surviving children. My father, William Henry, the eldest son, was virtually the sole heir of a hundred million dollars."

"Did this occasion some rancor between the survivors, then?"

"Rancor, Mr. Holmes? It unleashed a firestorm. True, none of the boys were cut entirely off; they were given from two to five million each. Our scapegrace uncle Jerry, Cornelius Jeremy, got nothing, nor did any of my father's many sisters. They did challenge the will in court."

"On what grounds, sir?"

Vanderbilt squirmed in his chair, ill at ease for the first time. "It was quite ugly, Mr. Holmes. My father was a gentle soul whom my grandfather dismissed as a 'blatherskite' when he was alive."

The son gazed at the smoking cigar in its tray and some emotion passed over his features.

"There's a family story, Mr. Holmes. The Commodore took the entire clan to Europe on the *North Star,* the largest private yacht in the world, in '53. My father was a married man of thirty then, but when the Commodore caught him smoking a cigar on the deck, he denounced tobacco as 'a dirty habit' and offered my father ten thousand dollars if he never touched it again. My father immediately tossed his prime Havana overboard. He didn't need the money, he told the Commodore. He would do it to please him.

"At that the old man took out his own Havana, grinned, and lit up."

Vanderbilt shook his head. "My father was a greatly underestimated man. He'd overworked himself into a nervous breakdown on Wall Street trying to please the Commodore in vain, but when relegated out of sight to a Staten Island farm, he made such a profitable go of it the old man finally took him seriously. It was my father who expanded the railroad holdings, even beyond the U.S. borders, and he did it paying decent wages. When the Commodore's will was challenged, he was charged in court with heinous things that did little to make our family acceptable to the Four Hundred. Perhaps that's why my father died only eight years later, but he had managed to double the inheritance by then."

" 'The past is prologue,' " I quoted again. I fancied I could be quite as commanding as the Commodore when I chose to be so.

The younger Vanderbilts struck me more as pot metal than of the Commodore's steel, no matter how crudely smelted.

"Uncle Jerry and the aunts accused my father of manipulating an old man by . . . 'procuring' was the term . . . parlormaids. They said my father had arranged with phoney spiritualists to manipulate my grandfather into giving him all the money. He was even accused of bribing the Commodore's young second wife into assisting with the charade. My father was a man who had married a modest minister's daughter. It quite leveled my mother. The newspapers and the cartoonists ran riot."

"Hmm. And this was when?"

"The trial ran from late '78 to early '79. At the end, my father had to settle with the dissidents. He actually drove in his carriage to each of their homes and handed over a million in bonds to Uncle Jerry, and half a million each to the aunts."

"I assume the eldest son is still the heir, in your case."

"Yes, only now it is the two eldest. My brother Cornelius and I share the wealth, and the onus of managing it. When my poor father died, he was the wealthiest man in the world."

"And what killed him?"

"Wear and tear, Mr. Holmes, wear and tear. He'd made an unfortunate misstep in front of the press seven years ago. It was during a railroad junket with some of his fellow moguls. The Chicago press wanted an interview and my father explained that he maintained the crack passenger service between Chicago and New York less from profit than to keep the rival Pennsylvania Railroad out of the market. Didn't he feel that good passenger service was a duty to the rail-riding public? he was asked. My father, relaxed and thinking only of his rivalry, answered 'The public be damned,' and was vilified for that ever after, which for him turned out only to be three years, no doubt due to the onslaught of vicious cartoons portraying him as a heartless robber baron. He retired soon after, and began work on the Staten Island mausoleum he had promised the Commodore he would build. Ironically, he was all too soon serving himself. He died almost four years ago, while lunching at home, just down the avenue. The president of the B & O Railroad had a bone to pick and went over Neily and myself to call on my father, who collapsed of a stroke the moment he rose to receive him."

"A pity. It does indeed seem that your father had a fine head for business, but no heart for it. How did he leave his millions? Was another scandalous court case necessary?"

"He would have died to prevent it." Vanderbilt frowned, realizing what he had said. "He often announced that the Vanderbilt fortune had become 'too great a load for any brain or back to bear.' He said he had no son on whom he would wish such a burden. We elder sons were the major heirs, but he created two forty-million-dollar trusts that all eight of us shared equally, one was untouchable except for interest, the other not."

I nodded, amused by the unthinkably enormous sums Vanderbilt bandied about.

"And the Vanderbilts are still social outcasts?"

"Indeed, no! My own wife, Alva, produced a ball so lavish a few years ago to inaugurate this very house that even Mrs. Astor's daughters were begging their mother for invitations."

"And the result?" I asked, although I already knew it, thanks to Miss Bly.

He laughed. "Total truce. Mrs. Astor capitulated completely and accepted Alva into the bosom of New York society." He nodded at another wall where a framed photograph was hung.

I recognized the imperious lady of the morning, although her aspect was much altered. She was arrayed in an elaborate gown with a train long enough for a coronation curled around her feet. Stuffed doves perched upon her wrists and fluttered like courtiers on the carpet before her. Pearls and diamonds draped her neck, wrists, and bosom. She wore some haloing headdress. I was reminded of representations of the Roman goddess Juno, she of the signature bird, the peacock, and of the upheld hand of Lady Liberty in her spiked crown of copper.

I rose to further inspect this apparition, reminded of another, simpler cabinet photo that sat on my mantel in Baker Street. The face set in all this glory was as adamant as a dyspeptic bulldog's.

"Alva's shining moment," he said.

"These jewels—"

"The pearls were my latest gift at the time. They'd belonged to Catherine the Great of Russia, and later the Empress Eugénie of France."

"Jewels worth a queen's ransom indeed. Are they stored securely?"

"Of course, in our own vault—Oh, I take your meaning, Mr. Holmes. Given the recent . . . incident, it might be best to remove them to a bank vault."

"Jewels were mentioned in the threats. The difficulty, though, is whether it's safer to move them or to leave them be, even perhaps to leave them as bait."

"Which do you recommend?"

I turned, more than ready to leave this oppressive pile, but I had one more task to finish this day.

"I will smoke some pipes of shag over that question, Mr. Vanderbilt, over the complete problem, in fact. This is a pretty, if particularly grisly, conundrum. I assume the Commodore would have been pleased to have presented me with such a challenge. Like many self-made men, he must have thrived on goading others to their utmost. A side mystery here is why these ruffians play so coy as to their demands, but first I must request sequestered time in your billiard room until I'm satisfied that I've wrung every clue from the premises."

"Mr. Holmes, you've gone over the place with more energy and thoroughness than my army of cleaning staff. Given Alva's habit of going through every room in a long white kid glove and immediately firing any maid who allows one visible particle of dust to linger, that's saying something."

"As with your wife, it takes a great deal to satisfy me. I must have the chamber completely to myself until I leave."

"I'll notify Wilson to await your departure, whether it is three this afternoon, or three in the morning. And I look forward to hearing your suggestions, sir, but more to hearing your solution."

By then Wilson had entered and shut the door behind him. "They are here to remove the, uh, atrocity, sir."

We doused our respective smokes. Vanderbilt stood and took one last swallow of brandy. "We shall go along to supervise. Fetch Mr. Holmes an envelope first."

Wilson, surprised, opened the top drawer of a smaller desk and produced a large envelope. He watched while I deposited the papers within via my tweezers. It must have looked as if I were handling dead insects instead of a lively batch of threatening communications.

Vanderbilt and I shook hands, and then I left the library to return to the mysteries of the billiard room.

I had a great deal to think about, and no one waiting at my hotel room to pester me for the estimated time of my return, or for premature conclusions.

This case was beginning to show some intriguing features.

Chief among them was the poor soul about to be bundled away to a secret autopsy and then a pauper's grave, no doubt.

I quite deplored this shabby and secretive course of action. Only in America would a wealthy man like Vanderbilt have the power or nerve to attempt such a violation of police routines. Yet his willingness to do so, and his need to call on a visiting foreign investigator, told me that he was not a total innocent in some business practices.

Or perhaps he was merely terrified of his wife, should she learn of the irregularities in her fabled household. From what I had glimpsed of the lady, she was a far more immediate threat to him than any unknown villain. As I have often warned Watson, women are not to be trusted, not even the best of them. And when it comes to the worst of them . . . I shudder, Watson. I shudder.

9

Clearing the Table

❧❦❧

As a rule, the more bizarre a thing is, the less mysterious it proves to be. It is your commonplace, featureless crimes which are really puzzling, just as a commonplace face is the most difficult to identify.
—SHERLOCK HOLMES, "THE RED-HEADED LEAGUE"

⊰FROM THE CASE NOTES OF SHERLOCK HOLMES⊱

Once the body had been spirited away, I returned to the room that had so far defeated me. Vanderbilt was correct; he had watched me scour the premises inch by inch and fiber by fiber.

Wilson had shut the doors behind me and secured the entry from the serving halls beyond by stationing a footman there. I stood just inside the doors and studied everything in the room as I would a stage set.

It was not only that a man had been murdered. I doubted that had occurred here. It was that the murderer, and more likely murderers, had stage-managed the discovery of his death for some still-hidden purpose of their own.

The billiard table had been kept pristine of all mortal signs. I recalled the superstitious maid's emotion, her curled fingers beating at her forehead and breast over and over in the sign of the cross.

By now I was circling the room, drawing closer to the imposing table on every circuit, my mind mimicking the relentless spiral of my memories and thoughts.

I would never have thought of a crucifixion, though the flung-out arms of the corpse caught my attention at once. As Watson often takes me to task, I am not a religious man in any standard sense. One will not find me before an altar when a chemist's table calls me.

This is perhaps a failing; certainly it was so in this instance, for I'm convinced the girl in her ignorant instincts was right.

Yet what religion sacrifices the old and frail and the time-burdened instead of the young and the whole and the innocent? (One reason I don't hold much with religious sects, which seem to eat their young.)

And what sort of criminal needs to confound as well as confront?

The surface of the table lies before me, a great lawn of felt soiled by a patch of dried blood.

If the carpeting that surrounds the table bore no marks of passage . . .

I spring up, a hand on the elaborate wooden border and perch there like a monkey.

Such feats convince the conventional onlooker that I'm half-mad, but there is no witness here, not even Watson.

I stand on Mr. Vanderbilt's billiard table's rim and picture again the dead man stretched before me.

If no mark on the carpet testifies to his murderers' passage . . .

I bend to peer up into the truly massive fixture that lights the entire tabletop, now so close to my head.

Its stained-glassed canopy has an eighteen-inch rim, and inside it's a maze of electrified brass lights, a modern candelabra big and bright enough to illuminate a cathedral, were it set on high instead of low over a billiard table.

Even these hidden arms have been dusted, but not as recently as the room below.

My magnifying glass spies places of bright brass amid lengths of metal lightly fogged by the merest breath of dust.

It is enough, O my foes, it is enough.

Vanderbilt and Wilson would truly wonder now, for I leap from table lip to table lip, until I have discovered four disturbed points. Then I bound back to the carpet and hie along the paneled walls. I am forced at length to wrestle one of the uselessly heavy Gothic chairs along the wall to a position by the far door where the inquisitive maid had entered.

With it for a ladder I can at last inspect the paneling and discover a small hole, into which a stout hook was screwed recently, onto which a strong rope was wound.

I glanced back at the lighting fixture over the billiard table. Within its decorative boundaries, I see a fatal web of metal and glass, and one poor victim trussed and waiting, not for Death, who has already bitten him to dust but for revelation.

The villains! They waited for the room to be cleaned before they revealed their perfidy, as a stage manager directs the opening of a curtain on a play. Once traces of their presence were wiped away, they loosed the rope that held the body suspended in the arms of the lighting fixture. Who would look up from a billiard table that everyone looks down on?

Had the table been used the night before? Had bowed heads concentrated on the intricate clicks of ivory ball against ivory ball and never suspected the atrocity looming over them?

Suspended by ropes at wrists and ankles, wrapped over the trouser legs and arms, I think, but how were they retrieved? For the ropes would have to be retrieved, from above, to produce the puzzle of an undisturbed surface below.

I pictured the scene again. A trained monkey, perhaps, or an acrobatic child. Someone primitive. I seemed to be dealing here with conjurors and circus tricks.

And blasphemers.

A truly interesting consortium.

I must inspect the body and clothing again. The scent of conspiracy and revenge overlies the reek of greed.

The past is prologue.

10

Speaking Volumes

꙳ᑍꙮᑈ꙳

. . . an amiable and simple-minded nonconformist clergyman.
—SIR ARTHUR CONAN DOYLE, "A SCANDAL IN BOHEMIA"

Irene was pensive the rest of that day and into the next. I couldn't determine if it had to do with Quentin's unexpected call (about which she was most annoyingly incurious), or with some matter involving the details we had recently learned of her bizarre childhood.

After lunch in the hotel dining room, we returned to our rooms. She brought out the forbidding volume she had literally unearthed following a ghastly night of death and danger at a house only a mile or so up Fifth Avenue.

We had left a purported "suicide" behind in that house, and were very lucky to leave it at all, at least upright under our own power.

Irene had also borne away with her a book that Nellie Bly, authoress of the sensational *Ten Days in a Mad-House*, would have spent *twenty* days in a mad-house to get her hands upon.

The paper was lined, as in a ledger or an account book. Faded ink in an old-fashioned hand had strung numbers and letters together into page after page of gibberish.

Irene now brought me the book. "Madame Restell's real surname was Lohman, née Trow. She was English-born, Nell."

"Don't remind me! It's so galling to think that a person with such a positive start in life could immigrate to America and shortly after become known as 'the wickedest woman in New York.'"

"Perhaps you will be better able to crack this cipher."

"I have nothing in common with the woman, except country of origin."

"But you are so clever at puzzles."

"—and she's more than ten years dead. I am? Clever at puzzles?"

"Much more so than I am. Perhaps it's because you have such a keen eye and hand for fancywork, which is all patterns, after all."

"But—"

"An eye that can follow a cross-stitch schematic can surely untangle a few pages of letters and numbers."

True, my humble sketches had been of some use in our previous investigation . . . no! Now I was thinking of this cursed, coded book as part of an investigation.

"Don't worry, Nell. This is but one end of our investigation. I only meant you to have this book so that you could apply yourself to studying it in the odd free hour."

"And when do I have an 'odd free hour,' pray?"

"I don't know. Perhaps not if Mr. Stanhope is to make himself a fixture around here."

"One visit does not make a fixture."

"I see signs, Nell. I see signs." Irene rose airily to collect her summer gloves and the single straw hat she had allowed herself for our supposedly brief visit to American shores.

"You are going somewhere?"

"Indeed. And you may go with me, if you like."

Although my remaining alone at the hotel yesterday had produced the pleasant surprise of a tête-à-tea with Quentin, I can't say that I liked sitting at "home" and getting reports of Irene's whereabouts and doings secondhand.

"Indeed I will and do," I said, standing to prove my intentions. Was it possible that Irene *wanted* me to let her roam the streets of New York unescorted? If so, that happy liberty would not occur.

I joined Irene at the mirror in pinning my own hat into the stubborn "rats" that underlay my hairdressing. (I had quickly learned Irene's stage tricks, and indeed, these new wide-brimmed hats, besides functioning as "sails" in a windstorm, required a fuller hairstyle as a foundation.)

Irene showed no dismay at my resolve to accompany her. Instead, her tor-toiseshell eyes, half-brown, half-golden, shone as if polished.

"You had no appetite at breakfast," I noted suspiciously.

"I have regained my girlish zest since we lunched quickly in the hotel din-ing room."

"These Americans eat so fast," I complained, taking up my parasol, for my complexion was fairer than Irene's and tended to the occasional freckle. For some reason the occasional freckle now seemed a fate worse than death.

"They have places to go and people to see there. And so do we." Irene swept open the door.

"And we are going—where?"

"Where indeed," said a shadowy figure in the hall.

I gasped. Even Irene drew back as if confronted with . . . well, that truly bestial fellow from our last heedless adventure.

It was, however, only Sherlock Holmes, I realized with some relief (given the alternative, i.e., Jack the Ripper). Irene, however, looked as displeased to see him as I usually did.

"Why are you lingering in our hall, sir?" she asked.

"Precisely the question I came to ask you in regard to another location. I see you are going out. May I come in first?"

It was not a question, of course, and Irene visibly teetered on the brink of a rude reply.

It was odd to see her so testy with London's only consulting detective. Usually that was my role. So . . . I took up her usual stance.

"Yes, do come in, Mr. Holmes. It's so frightfully common to stand gab-bling in public hotel passages."

He favored me with a slight smile. "And no one present is in the least bit common, Miss Huxleigh."

Irene shot daggers of resentment my way. How nice it was to be the one to take the lead, for a change. I could afford to be magnanimous to "*the* man" af-ter spending a blissful private hour yesterday with Quentin, which was quite improper but most . . . emboldening.

We returned to our parlor, which Mr. Holmes inspected with one sweep-ing glance.

"Well, now, Mr. Holmes." Irene wheeled on him the moment the hall door was safely shut. "You can see we were about to leave. You do see that?"

"And a great deal more."

She ignored his comment. "I can't imagine why you'd need to detain us."

He said nothing.

"Will we be needing to actually sit down to discuss this? Shall we have to remove our hats?"

When she wanted to, Irene could be as imperious as a czarina, but I stared at her. Beneath the bravado of her performance, a longtime and intimate audience like myself scented an unlikely odor of . . . unease.

Why would this tall, aloof observing machine make Irene Adler Norton, prima donna and veteran of myriad opening nights on the world's most intimidating operatic stages, nervous in her own hotel room?

"I came to warn you, madam," he said. "On the first occasion we met, I admit I was attired in mind and body to deceive you to your disadvantage."

I was transported two years back to the charming St. John's Wood villa Irene and I had occupied then in London, from which she and her new husband, Godfrey, had fled to Europe to evade the King of Bohemia and his paid agent, Sherlock Holmes.

I had stayed behind, disguised by Irene as an elderly servant. In that case I had been the observant one, for I saw how the King regretted the escape of the woman he loved but would not marry. I also saw that Sherlock Holmes held King Willie in as little respect as I did. It was the one thing about the man I could commend.

So his confession now was very gratifying. What a sneak and liar! He had disguised himself as a feeble old clergyman, not unlike my own deceased Church of England father. In this falsely benign guise Holmes had feigned a fainting episode on the street before our door. Irene, with the empathetic heart of an actress, had succored the poor old fellow and seen him brought into our front parlor and laid upon a couch . . . from which vantage point he was ready when his henchman, the physician named Watson, heaved smoke bomb into our innocent parlor.

This entire charade had been enacted to stir Irene into revealing the secret wall niche where lay the photo of the King of Bohemia in her company . . . and with Irene wearing the crown jewels at his behest. Grounds for an international scandal if such an indiscreet photograph should show the world the King had pretended to offer queenship to a mere American commoner like Irene, while betrothed from birth to a princess royal.

I remembered these events with a revived resentment as I pictured the elderly innocent Irene had invited into our parlor: fine, snowy hair, a stooped, hesitating posture, spectacles perched precariously on a long, hooked nose.

I eyed the upright, hale man of thirty-five years before me. Had he no shame? Aping a defenseless old man in order to deceive two much-tried women, themselves fleeing for their reputations and even their lives?

Now *his* face grew accusing, and Irene was looking decidedly nervous even holding her own ground.

Why was Sherlock Holmes recalling this incident so far distant in all our pasts?

Irene had twined her fingers in her pale kid gloves, reminding me of Miss Bo-Peep fretting over her lost sheep.

"You have overstepped yourself," he said.

Irene's hands became stone-still.

"Not in St. John's Wood," he added, "later that night in London. 'Good night, Mr. Sherlock Holmes' indeed. Passing my very doorstep in men's dress, playing the baritone, verifying my identity and risking all for a gesture of pure cheek."

Irene lowered her hands and lifted her head. "What of it? You were too late to catch me the next morning, in any event, and that is all that mattered."

He shrugged. "I was never enamored of the chase, or the case. I am under a certain noblesse oblige to honor royal requests, since my own queen has called upon me from time to time. Given the delicate political brink that Europe ever teeters upon, it's never amiss to extend my reach beyond Mother England."

"Hence you are here in America. Why?"

"Nothing to do with you, madam."

"Are you sure? You have had a great deal to do with me since our encounter in St. John's Wood. Perhaps it has become a habit."

"Even," I added sternly, dipping into my secret well of knowledge about the man's many personal weaknesses, "an addiction."

At this his sharp eyes finally pricked me directly. I suppose they were gray. I found them so cold and speculative that they might have been the color of water. Iced water, the way Americans like it.

"A subject," he said as icily as he glanced at me, "on which you are no doubt well and personally versed, Miss Huxleigh."

"I? I have no habits of that nature."

But he had already turned back to Irene. "Suffice it to say I have just today realized that our positions from two years ago have reversed. You were pursuing *me*, madam, in humble guise, and managed to intrude yourself into a house I occupied and feign a swoon sufficient to acquaint you with what you wished to know. What was that, and why?"

"Nonsense!" I said. "You flatter yourself, sir, even beyond your own usual extremes, if you delude yourself that Irene would deign to follow you in any guise."

Irene cleared her throat, but I wasn't done. "Furthermore, you are correct in at least one assumption; there is no readily apparent reason Irene would do any such thing."

"Ha!" His eagle eye darted from myself to her. "I agree, Miss Huxleigh, which is why I have taken the time to come here and ask the lady herself. In St. John's Wood, she eluded me. Here she cannot."

I was about to order him to "begone" like a melodrama villain when Irene shrugged, spread her forearms and hands in a graceful gesture of utter capitulation, and sat, very prettily, I might mention, on the sofa.

"Nell, if you would kindly order some tea, I believe that Mr. Holmes will be staying to partake."

"I don't have time for tea," said he, still standing.

"Oh, do sit down," Irene suggested with leading lady aplomb, removing her hat. "You were cheated of your inquisition with me in St. John's Wood, so you might as well make an afternoon of it now. I am trapped, am I not? In my own hotel rooms. What alternative do I have but to answer your every question?"

This charming capitulation held even *the* man temporarily speechless. Indeed, Irene gazed up at him with such an air of wry innocence that I found myself standing by the awful telephone (thank goodness we had seen some at the American area of Paris Exposition last spring or I should never have been able to contend with it now) to order a round of tea and crumpets. Although Americans only offered tea and something common they called cookies.

Mr. Holmes removed his hat at last, then pinched off his gloves and laid them in the upside-down crown. Once hat and stick were reposing upon the desk near the door, he pulled the occasional chair to face the sofa and sat.

Tea, I saw, was a mere civil excuse to dress up an interrogation. Or perhaps a duel of words, for Irene was looking far too self-possessed to play the meek penitent.

I watched them in the mirror as I unfastened my own hat. Hatless, Mr. Holmes looked older. His hairline bared a high prominent forehead and framed his angular face like a hood of black mail. Perhaps it was only my dislike of the man that made his every feature seem so severe. Perhaps it was my association with Godfrey that had made me prize a temperament formed of good nature and ease of presence.

Still, Mr. Holmes was very good for my posture, for I went to sit as upright as a headstone on the remaining occasional chair, considering myself an odd blend of tea server and referee.

So we sat making inane comments on the weather in England and France as compared with New York City in high summer. Finally a knock at the door signified the arrival of a welcome distraction. I directed the serving man to lay the heavy tea service and assorted serving trays on the high table before the sofa.

"I will pour," Irene said, sitting forward in a posture to mimic my own.

I raised an eyebrow.

"Oscar Wilde has always said that a tea table is as often the scene of slaughter as a battlefield," she noted.

"So, I imagine, is a billiard room," Mr. Holmes commented.

This made Irene hesitate in pouring a cup, but only slightly. "Milk? Sugar?" she inquired of our guest.

"Neither."

She poured my cup, liberally laced with milk, and selected a sunny slice of clove-implanted lemon for her own sugared serving.

"A billiard room," Irene mused after a careful sip. "I shall have to mention that idea to Oscar Wilde when we return to Paris. He is always looking for unlikely settings in which to showcase his wit."

"Speaking of unlikely settings," Mr. Holmes noted, "why were you at the Willie Vanderbilt house on Fifth Avenue at eleven o'clock this morning?"

"Why were you?" she shot back. "And you must be mistaken. I was rummaging at B. Altman's at the time, buying assorted fripperies for Nell and myself. The city has filled with thriving new emporiums since I left."

"You plan to remain in New York for a while, then?"

"Possibly. It has been suggested to us that I might have relatives here to dig up."

"And that is why you were following me."

Irene sipped and said nothing, leaving me to defend her honor, or at least her veracity.

"Why would Irene follow you?" I asked.

"She might have thought that my movements here have something to do with her lost family origins."

Irene interrupted us. "We have not ascertained that I was where Mr. Holmes claims I was."

He set down his untouched cup on the tea table. "Come now. There is no point in denying it. Once the idea had struck me, I saw the whole sequence of events. Had I not been concentrating on the . . . unfortunate surface of the Vanderbilt billiard table, I would have seen through your imposture then and there."

"Well, had I not been distracted by the poor unfortunate fallen clergyman outside my door in St. John's Wood, I would have seen through your ploy to use fire to force me to reveal the location of my hidden safe that very moment, instead of half an hour later."

I looked from one to the other. "Is Mr. Holmes implying that you were . . . lurking outside the Vanderbilt house after following him there, that you actually entered? The Vanderbilts are the wealthiest family in the country, Irene. Breaking into their home is like . . . sneaking into Windsor Palace. How could you?"

" 'How' was not difficult for a clever woman." Mr. Holmes seemed to be enjoying my astonishment and relished enlightening me. He turned back to Irene, in his element. "After you so conveniently swooned and then vanished, I made inquiries belowstairs. The laundry facilities there make a supply of fresh white cuffs, collars, and caps always available, to anyone. You wore black that morning, not in tribute to the Woman in Black who haunted the variety theaters when you were a mere infant but because it's the easiest way to blend into the landscape of a great house on any continent. The ungoverned mop of curly red hair you had already adopted, knowing the hordes of Irish in service in this city—two-thirds of all domestic servants, isn't it? The only thing you had not taken into account was that I had been called in to examine a body on the billiard table, a body with such violence done to it that it rivals the depredations of Jack the Ripper in Whitechapel, and beyond.

"I am curious, madam. Did the sight of that brutalized body indeed cause you a siege of faintness? Or was that another ruse to escape my attention for a moment so you could retreat before I was called out of the room?"

"Those are not *my* questions," I put in. "Why, Irene, would you follow Mr. Holmes at all?"

He started to answer but Irene's strong stage voice overrode his. "It's obvious. He dropped that maddening hint about my mother's identity at the grave site in Green-Wood Cemetery. Obviously someone he has been talking to in this country has given Mr. Holmes information on the subject that we don't have yet. I followed him to find out who."

"But . . . Irene. You have yourself walked me along upper Fifth Avenue and pointed out Vanderbilt Row, all those high, imposing mansions the family's many members have built. Am I to understand you masqueraded as a maid at Willie Vanderbilt's house—only the most palatial of them all? Why on earth would you go inside when you saw that was Mr. Holmes's destination? His errand could have nothing at all to do with you."

At that Mr. Holmes gave one of his rare bursts of laughter. "Your logic is impeccable, Miss Huxleigh, but your quarry was not acting on logic, was she? She followed me inside because she thought my business might be *her* business, of course."

I stared again at Irene, who was momentarily silent and looking studiously away from us both, as Lucifer the cat will do when he's been caught overturning the cream pitcher to lap up the contents.

"Irene!" I was shocked. "You thought . . . you thought *you* might be . . . *related* to the Vanderbilts?"

"There are an awful lot of them, Nell. The founder, the Commodore, who never went to sea except in his own yachts, had—what?—nine or ten or a dozen offspring. It's possible a child might have gotten lost in that lot, particularly if it was a by-blow."

"Irene, that you would even think such a thing, much less consider acting on it! It makes you look like a fortune-hunter."

"Ha!" Holmes was observing us like an audience at an entertaining play. "Madam Irene is not unfamiliar with the term 'adventuress,' " he told me, "but I believe that she would claim only legitimate interest in the estate, although she could no doubt convince what I have seen of Mr. Vanderbilt that she was his long-lost first cousin. Mrs. Vanderbilt, however, would be a different matter."

"It's true," I said, "that Irene is a consummate actress and mimic."

Irene snapped her cup onto its saucer to regain our attention. "The question is not what I *could* do, but what I would. And I would never stoop to bilking even the Vanderbilts. Which is why I left as soon as I determined that your business with them was merely another morbid crime."

"Hmmm." Mr. Holmes savored this assertion, then stood. "I trust then, that I shall not have to be on the look-out for any amateur competition as I conduct my business here in future. I can swear to you upon your mother's grave, if it is indeed so, that this has nothing, in any respect, to do with you personally."

"Of course not." Irene sounded indignant as she stood to see him to the door. "I can assure you that I will not bother myself with your movements now that I know you are merely pursuing another insane murderer. Though it is interesting that the victim so devilishly abused was a man, and an aged one—"

"Not interesting but appalling," I put in, following them to the door.

"Yes, Nell. Of course." Irene smiled at me. "We have had enough of the appalling. We remain here in the United States merely for matters of genealogical research. I don't suppose, Mr. Holmes, that you so earnestly wish me to find other occupations than following you . . . that you'd now drop a more concrete hint than a name I've never heard of written on a headstone?"

He donned gloves and then hat, saying nothing until this parting dictum: "I have your word that you will meddle no more with Vanderbilts?"

Irene nodded. "From what I saw, they're a rather vulgar family anyway. Nouveau riche. I should not wish to claim a relation even if I could."

"Then I will suggest to you, and to Miss Huxleigh, that when you sought news of the mysterious 'Woman in Black' you primarily, and quite naturally, interrogated the distaff side of your old acquaintances. Perhaps the gentlemen would have taken more, and a different kind of, note of her."

Irene's eyes glittered like fool's gold on hearing this. "How generous of you to share such insight. You could have saved me an unpleasant journey up Fifth Avenue had you told me this at Green-Wood Cemetery."

"At Green-Wood Cemetery I was not quick enough to anticipate to what lengths you'd go."

"As you were not in St. John's Wood. Perhaps there is a lesson here, my dear Mr. Holmes?"

"Oh, there is, but I much doubt that you will learn it, my dear madam. Good day. Miss."

As soon as Irene shut the door she leaned her back against it and rolled her eyes. Then she clamped a hand over her mouth.

I couldn't tell if she was furious or amused.

"Well?" I demanded.

She put a quick finger to her lips, then turned her ear against the wood to listen.

Finally, she took my wrist and led me to the window overlooking Fifth

Avenue. While we gazed down, we finally spied the top of Mr. Holmes's hat turning left up the avenue.

"He's gone," I said.

"Oh, that could be a dupe in hat and coat, carrying his cane."

"Would he really go so far to spy on you?"

She shrugged. "Perhaps not, but I do believe that he has a gruesome and puzzling case on his hands and will be far too busy to meddle in minor melodramas regarding the family origins of a retired opera singer."

"Was he right? Were you following him yesterday? Did you pass yourself off as a maid at the Vanderbilt house? That huge white one next to the church? One hardly knows which spire denotes the place of worship from the place of commerce rewarded."

"Yes," she answered simply, to all my questions.

"I can't believe it! You thought you might have been born a Vanderbilt? This is worse than thinking you could be the Queen of Bohemia."

"No, it's far more likely, Nell. At least I was born here in America. I had a mother we know of, this Eliza Gilbert buried in Green-Wood Cemetery. At least Mr. Holmes would like me to think she is my possible mother. And Green-Wood is a fashionable cemetery, Nell. Not just anyone is buried there. She must have been someone."

"Everyone is someone." I sounded prissy even to myself.

"Of course, but I am speaking of how the larger world regards things, and people. Poor Ann Lohman helped many women from New York's first families when they found themselves in the family way without having first wed."

"It troubles me that you assume you were of . . . unsanctioned birth. That headstone read '*Mrs.* Eliza Gilbert.' "

"Nell, children are seldom left for strangers to rear when their births are . . . regular. I've always assumed I was illegitimate, and I refuse to be cowed by the notion. From my views of most mothers and fathers, they are not such a lot as one would care to spend much time around them."

"My father was—"

"He was a saint, I know. You were lucky, Nell, but you must consider that neither Godfrey nor myself have an ordinary upbringing to look back upon. Our fathers apparently had no use for us, leaving us to mothers forced to foist us off on others. We shouldn't suffer for it now, as we had to then."

"Oh, goodness! I didn't mean—No, of course they don't mean anything.

Origins, that is. Mr. Holmes may spring from a perfectly conventional family, and look how he turned out!"

"And how is that, Nell?"

"High-handed, annoying, impossibly arrogant."

"So did half of England, then." Irene returned to the tea table and poured what must have been an utterly cold cup. She sat and proceeded to sip at it like the veriest savage imported to Windsor Castle and knowing no better.

"Sherlock Holmes," she said, "is typical of his gender and class. At least this humiliating interview has given me a clue to follow regarding my sole concern in New York City: finding the mother I never had, the woman who left me behind, whether she lies under a headstone in Green-Wood Cemetery or still lurks somewhere out in the streets of New York."

"So that dead body on the billiard table doesn't interest you?"

"Of course it interests me! No human being could see another slain in such an odious manner and not care. But we have risked life and limb in the pursuit of one such demented killer. Let Mr. Holmes have a crack at another with the benefit of all he has learned in our wake. Here and now we will pursue nothing but my dead past, and then we will go home."

"Is that a promise?"

"It is a solemn vow."

Irene spoke most convincingly, but then she had always mastered her lines perfectly.

11

Raiding the Morgue, Act I

⚜

It is a capital mistake to theorize before you have all the evidence.
—SHERLOCK HOLMES, "A STUDY IN SCARLET"

Mr. Vanderbilt's carriage called for me at midnight.

I was waiting outside my hotel to assist in the subterfuge.

"Mr. Holmes?" the driver inquired from his perch.

I nodded and sprang inside, noting that the side lamps were half-shuttered.

There are some kings of small countries in Europe who could not arrange such secrecy to save their thrones.

The ride was not far. As soon as I saw the distant lights tracing a cluster of buildings, I knew where we were going: Bellevue, New York's grande dame of city hospitals, as St. Bartholomew's is London's.

Vanderbilt's civic power impressed me even more. He'd had the inconvenient body removed from his house directly to the city morgue attached to Bellevue, yet expected secrecy to be maintained. That meant that officialdom in every version was at his service.

Those who were harrying him had perhaps taken on a foe who might not be made of their same violent metal, but outmatched them in sweep and power.

I had strolled by Bellevue in daylight. Walking is the only way to truly take the measure of a city, and naturally such a large institution should catch my interest. It was at St. Bart's where I had first heard of some affordable rooms on Baker Street and met the medical man who needed another single young fellow to share them. Alas, Watson had not remained single for long, and so I became the solitary occupant of 221 B.

Bellevue sat on several acres at Twenty-sixth and First Avenue, on the lip of the East River, as the Paris Morgue sits upon the banks of the Seine. Like many institutions, it had grown over the decades into a cluster of two- and four-story buildings, a bit haphazard as to architectural style, which only testi-fied to its vigorous roots in the community.

In fact, I was aware of one paramount fact about Bellevue. It was the first hospital in the world to use hypodermic syringes. Thus a colonial outpost managed to lead a British institution to much that is useful, and, in my case, pleasurable. The business I was on would not be in the least pleasurable.

I was not sure where on the grounds the carriage stopped, but no sooner had I alighted then another man met me.

"Mr. Holmes?" he inquired.

I was beginning to feel like an oddly welcome guest at a country house party where I knew no one.

"Yes."

"This way, sir."

The way was lit by his lantern, though once we were inside a few electric lights stared from the wall fixtures. Those used to the flickering glamour of flame or the gas jet find electric illumination rather relentless, but I welcome these steady beams that permit no misinterpretation.

I was taken down a passage so plain it obviously led to those unable to note its austerity: the dead. Entering a room, I felt the artificially cold air of a mor-tuary keeping room.

My guide lifted his lantern to touch a switch. Cold electric light flooded the concrete-and-steel table before me.

There, nude, lay the old man once cushioned on green felt in a million-aire's residence.

"We have fifteen minutes before the night watchman returns to where your carriage waits."

"Ten will be sufficient. Hold up your lantern, please."

"The electric lights—"

"Are splendid, but I need as much and more."

My guide, a youngish Irishman whose wife and four children must be gnawing upon his unaccustomed absence from home this night, reluctantly stepped near the makeshift bier. He held up the lantern until I felt its slight warmth on my face.

Nothing would warm the face below me, bloodless now and gray as granite.

I had examined the mutilated hands and feet before, but now bent again to each extremity. The wounds were as sere as ancient papyrus, all blood washed away, the skin puckering along the gashes like parchment.

Now I could truly see. Now I knew what to look for.

I moved, and my able assistant moved the lantern with me.

Yes! Rope burns at the wrists and ankles. Very faint, for the man had been dying, or freshly dead when trussed up in the Vanderbilt lighting fixture.

What hath Edison wrought? Without such cold sources of light, such huge fixtures would not be possible. Without such an opportunity, this man would not have been used as a deus ex machina in some ancient play, lowered like the god in the machine to strike awe and fear into his audience. His audience of one man only: William Kissam Vanderbilt.

What could this mild-mannered millionaire have done to invoke such bloodthirsty enemies? And why?

The answer was bound to be both confounding and intriguing.

12

Raiding the Morgue, Act II

❧

Of incalculable value to any large newspaper is its 'morgue' or library. Hardly an hour passes that some situation does not arise which requires reference to previous items . . . a treasure of necessary information.

—STANLEY WALKER, CITY EDITOR, *NEW YORK HERALD TRIBUNE*, 1934

Herald Square clearly took its name from the *New York Herald* office building that faced Thirty-fifth Street. This was a pleasantly low-profile two-story building faced with graceful Italianate arches. Not far away the Sixth Avenue Elevated roared past, and the area thronged with the marquees of theaters, dance halls, and even an opera house, as well as restaurants.

"Pink works for the *New York World*," I repeated for the third time as we stood on the bustling sidewalk and gazed at the unassuming building.

"Yes, Nell. But I have no intention of allowing Miss Elizabeth Jane Cochrane, familiarly known as Pink and publicly known as Nellie Bly, another opportunity to use my past as the key to a sensational newspaper story."

I wore my new town gown that Irene had purchased for me at B. Altman during her shopping spree before broaching the Vanderbilt mansion in the guise of an Irish maid. For a ready-made costume it was fairly respectable. It was of cream-and-green plaid sateen, with the new three-quarter sleeves that were met by longer gloves, and the new slightly puffed sleeve at the shoulder.

Irene was also attired for city business, but her ensemble mimicked an eighteenth-century riding costume with its dashing copper-colored satin jacket with large revers and cuffs over a skirt striped in peacock green and copper. She carried a large black leather handbag rather than the more formal reticule that she preferred. And inside the handbag was a letter in a long envelope of heavy linen paper that I had seen for the first time that morning at our hotel rooms.

"What is that?" I'd asked when she'd paused to place it in her newly acquired handbag.

"It is a precaution, Nell."

"Usually precautions are actions, not physical items."

"This is both." Her gloved fingers waved it once before she latched the bag shut. "Before we left Paris, I asked Baron Alphonse for a letter of introduction from the Rothschild agent in New York. This awaited us at our hotel."

"You never mentioned it to me."

"Things were rather hectic, as you recall. Besides, I had no use for it until now."

"And what will you use it for today?"

"To introduce ourselves to Mr. James Gordon Bennett Jr. and to induce him to allow us to see the newspaper files for 1861."

"The year Mrs. Eliza Gilbert died and was buried."

"Exactly, Nell. I am weary of other people waving hints of my family origins at me. I will know the truth, and the entire truth."

"Then you meant what you told Mr. Holmes."

"Which was?"

"That you hadn't the slightest intention of intruding on his assignment involving the Vanderbilts."

"Oh, that. Of course I did. I will settle the identity of this Gilbert woman, discover whether there is any possibility she might have been my mother, and then we will unfurl our sails and breeze back to Paris and Godfrey as fast as Mother Ocean will let us."

"Godfrey is not in Paris."

"He ought to be." Irene shook her head as if trying to dislodge the veil furled on the keel of her sweeping hat brim. "What can be so fascinating in Bavaria that it should occupy an English barrister more than a week or two? I intend to wire the baron to that effect if Godfrey is not soon released."

I could see that Irene meant every word she said. For me the news was both happy and, oddly, sad. We would track down the history of the dead Eliza Gilbert. We would confront our new theatrical acquaintances (actually Irene's childhood caretakers) with whatever facts we found and either confirm or eliminate the woman as a possibility for Irene's mother. We would then speed home again, a consummation devoutly to be wished . . . save that I might be leaving Quentin Stanhope behind. Along, or even alone, with Elizabeth Pink Nellie! Not a thing to be wished in any event.

So I regarded the dour office building now before us with a glum mood. Quentin had made it clear that his sojourn in New York City was Foreign Office business. He could not leave until it was accomplished. And I could not banish the conviction that, no matter how charmingly he partnered me at tea, his assignment had much to do with that inescapable and annoyingly forward and attractive young person named Pink!

"She is only a few years our junior, Nell," Irene pointed out beside me.

"What?" Irene's new habit of commenting on my unspoken thoughts was becoming as annoying as Pink herself!

"Our friend Nellie. She lied in Paris. She is in her midtwenties, and we have only edged past thirty."

"How did you—?"

"You have been throttling the neck of the rose silk reticule I bought you at Macy's ever since the child in the large pink straw hat brimmed with pink roses passed by."

"Really? I didn't notice her, Irene."

"In any case," Irene went on, "I agree that we are better off leaving Pink to her own devices and attending to ours. I hope this letter will be an 'open sesame.'"

With that she mounted the short flight of stairs to the building, I in her wake.

For some reason newspaper editorial offices sit on the topmost floor. Irene and I labored upward, the building having no elevator, feeling the risers tremble beneath our feet as the great hidden presses kept their noisy pace.

We exited at a floor as filled with smoke as a variety theater. Ladies were not often expected here, for the floors were dusted with ashes and dark disgusting islands where that awful American habit of "chewing tobacco" has missed arriving at the awfully but aptly named spittoons.

Even the Rothschild letter, one would think, would not deign to be delivered here, were any such action up to a mere letter.

Irene sailed through the muck in an evasive path that missed the worst of the filth and I followed in her footsteps.

Our unusual presence finally inspired a man in rolled-up shirtsleeves and a homburg (indoors!) to lower his booted feet from a desktop and inquire, "Lookin' for something special, ladies?"

"Mr. Bennett," Irene said, smiling.

The man removed a thick cigar stub from his mouth and pointed with it to a closed door. "You're lucky. He seldom visits the U. S. but he's just back from Paris for a short time. There."

There we went. Irene knocked. "Come in, dammit," a voice commanded.

Within was an office as civilized as the outer areas were not, though the smoke and clatter drifted in.

Mr. Bennett was standing at a large mahogany desk, frowning at sheets of newsprint and chewing on the stump of an expired cigar like a mastiff on a bone.

"Mr. Bennett," Irene said for the second time.

"Not me," the cigar chewer said. "Him."

We turned to regard a well-tailored man sitting in a leather club chair before the desk. His hair was edged in middle-aged silver, but his large, pointed mustache was still jet black.

He rose at once. "I am Bennett. How may I help you, madam?"

"You may indeed help, but it is Baron de Rothschild and his agent, Mr. Belmont, you will oblige the most by helping me."

Irene extended the letter even as the man's eyes moved from Irene to myself, and then back to Irene. "And you are—?"

"Mrs. Godfrey Norton, and this is my companion, Miss Huxleigh."

By then he had opened and skimmed the letter sufficiently to return it to the envelope and hand it back.

"How may I assist you?"

"I need to consult the back issues of your newspaper for a certain date, or a few dates."

"What are they?"

"Quite old, I fear. January of 1861."

"Ah, the Civil War years."

"That will cause a difficulty?"

"On the contrary. This newspaper dates back to early in the century, but news chases the future, not the past, and copies were not always kept well. However, the war years would be more likely to be preserved. Davis." He turned his eyes and voice to the man fretting over the desk full of newsprint. "Write these ladies a chit so the dragon who guards the back copies below will let them browse amongst our wares." He turned back to us. "You may only consult the papers, not take them."

"Information is all we seek," Irene said.

"And what would two such genteel ladies need with ink-stained editions from nearly thirty years ago?"

"I seek to trace relations."

"Ah. Lost in the war, eh? Not likely to be found at this late date. Dispense with your gloves, is my advice. Ah. Thank you, Davis. You can return to worrying the front page."

Irene held the note between her white-gloved fingertips. "Thank you so much for your assistance, and your sanitary advice."

"The morgue—what we call our library—is on the basement level. My regards to Mr. Belmont. I hope to see him in Paris again one of these weeks. I live abroad now that I've founded the *International Herald* English edition. Good day."

"Perhaps I can return your hospitality in Paris one day," Irene said. "We live there as well."

His eyebrows peaked with surprise, giving him a slightly satanic look, as we murmured the appropriate farewells and returned to the loud, reeking room outside.

"Basement," I commented, shuddering. "I had enough of cellars and catacombs and other dread underground places last spring."

" 'Dragon.' " Irene quoted our former host. "That should be fascinating."

The basement was indeed belowstairs, and as dark and dank a near neighbor of Gehenna itself as one would fear.

Similar ropes of electrical wires that swagged ten feet high across every New York City thoroughfare like giant musical staffs also had done their duty for this "morgue." Bare electric lightbulbs dangled over the aisles between rows upon rows of filing boxes on shelves. The watery light they gave created as much shadow as illumination, and the rectilineal vastness and order was indeed reminiscent of a graveyard.

"Note from Mr. Davis, eh?" demanded a bent, wizened old man whose spectacles pinched his nose so hard it had turned scarlet. Or else the drink had done it.

"Ladies," he further observed, looking us up and down and left and right in a most ungentlemanly manner. "Don't get much ladies down here. I suppose it's some picture of yourselves at Mrs. Astor's latest ball you forgot to save and now must ransack my files to get. No issue leaves this place, not one, for no one."

He plucked a huge cigar from its resting place in a white porcelain soap dish and puffed until we were wreathed in smoke.

"Our quest is not so lighthearted as you had hoped," Irene said soberly, as if breaking bad news to our guide and gatekeeper. "We are in search of an obituary."

He peered through his own fog. "You're not wearing black."

"The deceased passed on in 1861. I believe the traditional time for wearing black is long past."

He harumphed in admission of his wrong inference and puffed more smoke. If he had been the big bad wolf and we had been pigs' houses, we would have been blown down by now.

But smoke was not a deterrent to Irene, and I had grown used to being so assaulted, although I coughed delicately, by way of a hint. A hint not taken, or even noticed.

"Sixty-one." His eyes narrowed above the spectacles, though that may have been more from his own smoke than a pretense at deep thought.

Irene gave him the date.

"I can show you the section, but you ladies will have to get your dainty white gloves dirty, for you'll have to page through the papers yourselves."

"We can remove our gloves, Mr.—?"

"Wheems. And here I thought you ladies were born with them on."

He turned and led us down a maze of aisles: straight ahead, left, right, ahead again.

In the eerie silence our skirts rustled behind him like the dragging tails of herded rats in a dungeon . . . and I do have reason to know that loathsome sound.

"In luck, ladies." He had paused to peer at a shoulder-height shelf. "This here's the very box you want."

He assailed the box in question with several puffs of smoke, then looked at us.

Obviously such a bent wizened creature couldn't get the box off the shelf, especially with the cigar in his careful custody.

So Irene reached up to slide a corner free, and we both caught it.

"A table?" I asked.

"This here's not the public library on Fifth Avenue," he reminded us unnecessarily. "No lions outside *our* door. There's a table around the end of the aisle. Put the box back when you leave."

This last instruction was called back over his shoulder in a haze of departing smoke.

"Irene . . ."

"I know, Nell. It is a filthy habit. I do plan to renounce it."

"When?"

"Not when I am a stranger on another shore, digging through newsprint almost thirty years old."

We huffed and puffed our own way to the opposite end of the aisle and found the promised table, a slatternly thing of peeling paint and split boards and protruding nails and . . . spiderwebs bracketing its legs.

"*Ooooh!*" Irene let her half of the box thump to the tabletop with a creak of old wood. "Old newsprint smells fusty and mildewy."

"Our gloves are already a loss," I said, sliding my half of the box onto the uncertain surface and raising my dust-smudged palms.

"Gloves will wash, Nell. The past only rarely opens its gates to us. Eliza Gilbert must at least be mentioned in the contents of this box for the date of her interment, if she did not merit a separate death notice."

We took off our gloves, and removed the first papers.

"Ah!" Irene read the first page. "The funeral was the nineteenth of January and these papers are stacked from last to first of the month. We shall have a slightly shorter dig than the other way around."

"Not by much." I coughed as she set down the first edition and a billow of yellow dust wafted up with a noxious ink and mold odor. "Who would have thought anything on earth would have competed with Mr. Wheems's choice of cheap tobacco?"

Irene was too intent disinterring edition after edition to agree.

I made sure they stacked neatly, observing the narrow, old-fashioned columns and the paragraph-long headlines above the stories.

"Here it is. The nineteenth!"

The paper shook slightly in Irene's hands as she laid it open on the pile of previous editions and began studying the double pages.

"The obituaries," I suggested, "are always toward the back."

"Who knows where they were then, and Mrs. Eliza Gilbert may have merited more prominent mention."

"Irene, you always weave fairy tales around the simplest facts. This may be some mischief devised by Sherlock Holmes to keep you out of his way, which you have a habit of getting into."

She stopped to regard me. "You believe that Sherlock Holmes can be mischievous?"

"Ah, no. Alas not. But he might be mischievous in a devious, obstructive sort of way. He must have been just that kind of boy."

"And you have a habit, dear Nell, or imagining us all as recalcitrant children who have escaped your tender supervision." She frowned and started paging backward. "The obituaries are on the last page of the first section, but no Eliza Gilbert is listed there. If only we could take this edition with us to study in decent light."

"We can't."

"Actually, we can." Irene lifted her hem while eyeing me significantly. "It could be gently rolled and put into a petticoat pocket."

"That would be stealing, Irene."

"It would be borrowing."

"You plan to broach the Dragon Wheems again, coax him into taking down this same box, and surreptitiously returning the missing paper during a second visit?"

"That is a possibility. I could say I needed to check additional facts."

"Adding lying to thievery."

"I need this paper, Nell."

"Not in *my* petticoat pocket."

"Very well. It will go in mine. All I require is your silence."

I looked at the ceiling, which unfortunately forced me to stare at one of those confounded electric lightbulbs of Mr. Edison. Progress was very wearing.

"Silence," she repeated.

It was only one miserable newspaper, but it might be the only one from that date. "I will not return to this obnoxious place," I said. "You will have to replace it on your own."

"I will, Nell. In fact, I wish I *had* come here on my own."

At that we both rustled back down the myriad aisles, reinstalling the looted box in its place, and then finally finding Mr. Wheems's small station.

He stared at our hands, which could have been shoveling coal.

Irene smiled as if he were President Harrison. "We will tell Mr. Davis of your cheerful cooperation. I may have to look up one more thing at a later date, if I may."

"You may, but if Mr. Davis don't say it's right, you mayn't."

Irene didn't bother telling him that Mr. Davis had offered her carte blanche once he had seen Mr. Belmont's letter. She would manage the return, I was sure, if she had to don her walking-out clothes and break into the place by night to do so.

Once we had regained the ground floor and then the street, she eyed the avenue up and down until she spied a tearoom.

"There! We can get a seat by the window and study this terrible smudged old print in daylight."

And so we did. But rake the obituary listing up and down as many times as we liked, we never came across the names Eliza or Gilbert.

Memoirs of a Dangerous Woman:

Countess of Landsfeld

~❧~

I speak of Jesuitical lies . . . It was said, also, that I tamed wild horses, horsewhipped gendarmes, knocked flies with a pistol ball of the bald heads of aldermen, fought duels . . . and a multitude of other similar feats. Now, sir, do you see the sly Jesuitical, infamous design of all this? It was simply to unsex me—to deprive me of that high, noble, chivalrous protection, which is so universally accorded woman in this country.

—LETTER FROM LOLA MONTEZ TO THE *BOSTON DAILY EVENING TRANSCRIPT*, 1852

 I've been called many names, some of them quite rude: strumpet, whore, Republican. At the time I evoke here, I was known as Marie, countess of Landsfeld. Ludwig's advisors wore out his ears trying to stop him from bestowing a Bavarian title on me, but I won out. I had been winning out so roundly over the Jesuits and Ultramontanes that they resorted to every subterfuge to turn the people against me: slander and lies were their sword and pistol. I determined that nothing should drive me out of Bavaria, not names, not death itself.

The mob of six thousand assaulting my palace windows that night in Munich used most of the rude names granted me, and then some. I appreciate invention in an opponent, even it if has six thousand throats.

My loyal Alemannia—young, brave, handsome fellows, my small army of student-soldiers and my self-appointed honor guard—stood inside with me, ready to defend me against all attackers. How many, I wonder, still live today?

For although the events that are burned into my brain occurred on another continent and more than a decade ago, they visit my dreams even now. Especially poor old Würtz, who was murdered so vilely.

I saw him dead before I quit that place I had once loved as nowhere else. To this day it is as if a photographer's flash powder lit that scene. Only that convinced me to abandon my palace. Did I say that I saw him dead? More than that. I saw him after having been tortured to death by the damned, conniving Ultramontanes, his brutalized body left in my own elegant rooms! Who knows why, perhaps merely to freeze my notoriously temperamental Latin blood.

Now I am myself not dead but nearly so. I live in no palace now, but rented quarters in a humble area of a bustling city, on the sufferance of others. Once I ordered. Now I ask. I will not write "beg." There is not much that I want now, after all.

I was once famous for the variety, fame, and number of my reputed lovers—Liszt, Dumas, princes petty and pettier. My most intimate companion now is the Cough, which visits often, but without warning. The Cough racks me so violently that my pen grows palsied on the paper, so I must stop. And my left side is crippled by a stroke. Yet I can lift a pen in my right hand and write between the Cough's ceaseless spasms. I can't hold a cigarette anymore.

I am told that I was the first woman to be photographed holding a cigarette. Why not? I was painted and photographed my whole life through. Until now I had hoped for a more distinguished record of achievement. I am also the first white woman to have been photographed with an Indian. I smile as I view that portrait from 1852. I was still handsome then, my face framed by dark curls above a sweet round white collar. So demure, so dangerous. My left hand, still useful, was linked through Chief Light in the Clouds's arm, although he stared ahead like a statue, his dark face framed by long black braids.

Always the opportunist, I first escaped what others determined should be my life by jumping the traces and running while barely in my teens: a fourteen-year-old girl pledged to a disgusting old man. I'd rather have been mistress to an unrespectable young man, and achieved that ambition several times in my life.

Chief Light in the Clouds knew nothing of my history or reputation, nor I of his. We met at a Philadelphia photography studio, he fresh from visiting the "Great White Father in Washington," I fresh from adventures and disappointments in Europe.

We were both hopeful in that photograph, and both born to be betrayed long after it was taken.

Do people in their last days always digress? I feel as old as Lilith, but am not yet forty.

The room is cold. This winter season in a northern clime befits my decline: it is the autumn of 1860. Even as the sounds of rocks crashing through windows and chipping at stones echo in my memory, someone comes in and knocks the cot leg with the chamber pot. Consider it a triangle sounding in a funeral march.

Is that always the outcome of history? Once I made it. I broke hearts and made newspaper headlines and even toppled a kingdom, now . . . now I don't have the strength to finish filling the space on this small page . . . to wield a pen, much less a whip or a pistol.

Lord God, I do fervently wish I could have a cigarette! One last cigarette before the firing squad. But the Cough, my constant companion now, says no.

13

Tea and Treachery

Jealousy, the jaundice of the soul.
—DRYDEN

Irene withdrew to a retiring room to install her ill-gotten gain in her petticoat pocket, which was easier to extract from than return to.

I sipped my tepid Earl Gray. Americans seemed afraid to make really good scalding hot tea. I gazed idly at the street. Sitting in a tearoom is one of the few places where a lady is free to stare at passersby. I found myself smiling to recall that a tearoom was where Irene and I first met, and she had resorted to thievery on that occasion also . . . slipping the remaining cakes and sandwiches on our tray into her capacious muff for later consumption.

Of course we had both been half-starving young spinsters then, Irene an aspiring opera singer, myself an unemployed governess, and then an unemployed drapery clerk.

The paper was a minor matter, and I was glad to see Irene pursuing her own past rather than the lurid murder she had stumbled onto just as Sherlock Holmes was consulting on the event.

I should be grateful that Irene was committing only petty theft now, instead of traipsing after Sherlock Holmes on a gruesome case as awful as the Ripper hunt.

I sipped more tea and blinked my eyes open as I recognized a hat passing on the opposite side of the avenue. Pink Cochrane! How that girl flaunted her lavish-brimmed hats and her eighteen-inch waist!

The *New York World* was erecting an impossibly high building next to the *Herald* and the *Times* . . . twenty-six stories, I had read in the *Times*. The new owner, a Polish immigrant named Pulitzer, sought to bring the less regarded *World* into direct competition with the larger newspapers.

Apparently "Miss Bly" was inspecting the new quarters, which would be crowned with a gilded dome like St. Peter's in Rome, only smaller, one would hope. Nothing like Roman Catholics and newspapers for sensational display!

While I was exercising my Anglican distaste for show, I suddenly spilled what was left of my tea into the saucer. Pink had an escort for her promenade up Fifth Avenue . . . Quentin Stanhope. Even now he was lifting his walking stick to indicate some point high on the *Sun* and *Times* buildings.

I half stood to better view the pair, and in so doing, tilted my tea-filled saucer into my lap, where it drenched my new green plaid skirt.

Thus Irene found me, flailing with a napkin at my skirt and craning my neck nearly around the window frame to catch the last, unwelcome glimpse of the passing couple.

"Nell! You've had an upset."

An upset indeed! "Yes, I turned to look out the window and my cuff must have caught on the teacup."

"Gracious. It will dry, of course, and we can have the hotel staff clean and press the skirt when we return."

"We must return right away. I am not about to stroll Fifth Avenue looking like something a pet Pekingese has had its way with."

"But my next destination is on the way downtown, and I am anxious to put this matter of Eliza Gilbert to rest."

"Eliza Gilbert has already been put to rest by those more entitled to do it than you."

"Nell!" she rebuked me for my temper.

"Oh, I'm sorry, Irene. I'm even sorrier that everything is ruined."

"It's only a department-store skirt, Nell. We can get another tomorrow if the mishap ruins the outfit for you."

"You're right, Irene. Spilled tea is hardly spoiled expectations or ruined hopes. But our gloves are unwearable, and—"

"August in New York is quite warm enough to do without gloves. We shan't be the first women to dispense with them."

I sniffed, but had no heart to argue proper attire with her. What did it matter where I went, wearing what?

14

Taking the Fifth

※

It is admitted by everybody that the newspaper woman does better work than her male competitors on the society and fashion pages of the great dailies. Nellie Bly has shown that a woman can make her mark as a traveling correspondent and as a special writer. Still, there is the general impression that the newspaper woman is confined to a narrow field. Perhaps this is a mistake.

—THE *ATLANTA CONSTITUTION*

⸢FROM NELLIE BLY'S JOURNAL⸣

I gazed at the bare ground across from Park Row, then back at the towering facades of the *New York Tribune* and the *Times* building to its right. It was all I could do not to whoop a hurrah at the impressive sight of what was known as Newspaper Row.

Then I turned my attention to my escort. He did quite nicely, for all that he was of that abominable, self-satisfied breed, an Englishman.

I was often recognized on the street nowadays, not only because we girl stunt reporters were the talk of the newspapers themselves but because my novel, *The Mystery of Central Park,* had appeared last year with my likeness, wearing a large and most becoming hat, on the cover.

I must admit that I was one of the first to dispense with the fashion of the modest little bonnet and embrace the newly popular hats with their swashbuckling wide brims and plumed panache. As rare as girl reporters still were, it didn't hurt to have an instantly recognizable trademark (unless I was undercover), and a hat can't be missed.

And, of course, I stirred a great deal of curiosity about my gentleman friends. How odd that when a woman becomes known for the work she does, the first thing people want is to marry her off.

I made sure no scandal attached to my attachments, and they were nearly nonexistent. All the better to have people talking about one. And the more they talked about me, the better stories I would be allowed to pursue and the more I would cement my position.

I summed up the Englishman beside me as I knew the people who nodded to me in passing were doing.

Of course there is nothing like an Englishman for tailoring, and in this Quentin Stanhope was in the running with the best of his breed. No sacklike lounge suits for him! He wore summerweight wool in a gray-and-ivory check, although he had conceded to the heat with a straw boater hat. Despite the soft summer tones, he seemed as hard as a steel etching, perhaps because his light eyes narrowed at all he examined, as if he took instant measure of every person and thing around him. His sun-darkened skin was oddly attractive against the light clothes, and he flourished his walking stick with an ease that reminded one it could also be used as a club. He was, in fact, a walking contradiction, a thoroughly civilized Englishman, as few Americans can emulate, and a thoroughly dangerous man.

At the moment he was being charming, but I was well aware his fount of that was about to run out.

"You said," he reminded me in his clipped accent, "that this stroll would be enlightening."

My, was that fabled British patience wearing porcelain thin? I was irritated to consider that while he chafed to serve as my escort, he would willingly consort with that ninny Nell Huxleigh.

"This hole in the ground is very enlightening," I told him. "You see how the *Tribune* and *Times* buildings face the park along here?"

"Quite impressive," he said, sounding not at all impressed. "They must tower fifteen stories or so, and the single spire atop the *Tribune* must reach twenty. I don't doubt that Wonders of the World will soon be springing up in New York City."

"And I intend to be one of them."

His lazy gaze sharpened on me in that intimidating manner. "Aren't you getting a trifle above yourself?"

"I aim high and am not ashamed to say it. The new *World* building goes right here. It'll be twenty-six stories and have a gilt dome atop it."

"Rather like St. Peter's in Rome."

"Like nothing in New York, except City Hall next door, and the *World* dome will be much, much bigger and higher. It will be the tallest building in the world when finished next year. There's a story about Mr. Pulitzer. This site where the *World* will soon reign supreme housed the elegant French's Hotel at Park Row until Mr. Pulitzer bought and razed it to make way for the new *World* building."

"Amazing waste." Quentin shook his head. "We're not so hasty to tear down the old and erect the new in London. We wait a few hundred years at least."

"Ah, but here's the rest of the story. A bit more than twenty years ago, when Mr. Pulitzer was a fresh Hungarian immigrant and volunteer Union Army cavalryman during the Civil War, he was ejected from French's Hotel because his battle-frayed uniform annoyed the fashionable guests. You see what this says about America?"

"That snobs are everywhere?"

"Don't tease, Quentin! This is a land of limitless opportunity. In just a few years, Mr. Pulitzer has managed to bring the *World* to dwarfing the circulation of James Gordon Bennett's *Herald.* Now his new *World* building will literally dwarf the neighboring presence of Charles Henry Dana's *Sun.*

"Mr. Pulitzer plans to excel the *Tribune* and the *Times* as New York's most important newspaper, and I intend to be part of that."

"What are you telling me, Pink?"

I must say that the sound of my nickname in that accent, on those hard-cut lips, was far more inciting than the many sweet nothings American gentlemen had whispered in my impervious ear.

I would not be deflected by them, and I would not be deflected by him.

"Only that my silence on the capture of Jack the Ripper last spring is an extraordinary requirement. To obey it, I must have extraordinary support."

"I can't remain in America as your nursemaid for much longer," he warned.

"I never had, nor needed, a nursemaid. I'm telling you that I want a story. A story the entire world will marvel over. I don't care in what odd corner of the globe it may be found, and I know you are very familiar with the world's oddest corners. I want a sensation, and soon, or I will give Mr. Pulitzer the only such story I have: Jack the Ripper."

All pleasantries were over. Quentin Stanhope looked exasperated enough to consider beating me with his walking stick. Of course he did no such thing.

"Doing that would seriously antagonize the governments of several European nations, and the queen and prime minister of England."

"Not to mention Mr. Sherlock Holmes." I couldn't help laughing. "I'm not afraid of any of you. So perhaps you'd better think of another story I can pursue that will earn me the unbridled support of the governments of several European nations."

"I, and those I represent, do not deal with blackmailers."

"We have a free press in this country, Quentin. So free it's sometimes a free-for-all. All I'm asking for is one little global sensation. Surely in your bag of espionage tricks you can come up with a maharajah who beheads his wives . . . a modern Bluebeard. That would be a start."

"You Americans are a bloodthirsty lot."

"We just don't pretend to be 'civilized' when we're not. So. Will you find me another Jack the Ripper sensation?"

"My dear Pink," he said softly.

I imagine that Nell Huxleigh would have swooned if Quentin Stanhope had whispered her name with such exact articulation in her ear. I met his challenging glance with my own. He took my elbow a bit more firmly than needed and steered me along the street, away from the fascinating hole in the ground that would soon become my new professional home, the only home that truly mattered to me.

"My dear Pink," he repeated, "I will do my humble best to find you something to outdo catching Jack the Ripper. Only give me a little time."

"Of course. The new building will not be ready for some months. I want to be on the front page when it becomes a reality. Meanwhile, you can hobnob with your friends Irene and Nell. I imagine they won't much object to that."

His hand tightened on my elbow warningly.

"What I do has been called The Great Game in the eastern corner of the world, but I assure you, Pink, it is not a game and it is not safe to toy with me, merely because my hands are tied. They won't always be."

"This is not a game with me, either. I've never backed down from anybody, including my drunken brute of a stepfather, which is why the name of

Nellie Bly is a force in this city. I wish her to become a force in the whole wide world, that is all. Is that so bad?"

"No worse than what Attila the Hun wanted," he said, amusement masking the iron in his voice. "Let me think about it. Meanwhile, you may excuse me from future strolls down the avenue. I shall be far too busy hunting up a sensation extravagant enough for Nellie Bly."

I pulled away from his male custody and dusted the palms of my gloves together.

"Go, then. I'm sure others would cherish your presence more than I."

He bit back a reply, tipped his boater, and called a hansom over to the curb.

He paid the driver in advance, handed me in like Prince Charming, and bowed as I drove off.

His eyes were as narrow as stilettos, and I knew he wished me in the lowest circle of hell.

I didn't mind, not as long as he found me the story I needed.

15

The Purloined Paper

~•~

*Beautiful she was, with those wonderful eyes, blazing forth now and
then from under heavy, long drooping lashes, the masked batteries
of passion; her dark soft abundant hair, gathered back from her
low forehead in lovely shining ripples, and lit by some gorgeous tropical
flower. Yet to me there was something sad in her passionate, defiant,
utterly unpeaceful face.*

—GRACE GREENWOOD, 1853

So we left the tearoom and hailed a cab to take us downtown, Irene eyeing my docile accommodation to her wishes like a cat expecting a pug
to bite at any moment.

I paid no attention to where we were going, although I peered at
the passing street and pedestrians. No dashing dark blue hat surmounted by crimson roses was in view, and certainly no dashing Englishman
of my acquaintance.

Slowly the passersby changed in age and appearance. People were either
older or younger than the fine figures strolling the avenue farther north. Gangs
of shabby children threaded the crowds. Peddlers carts jammed the verge
between street and walkway. Old women not unlike the head-scarved
"babushkas" of Prague moved slowly among the busy throngs. And most of
the men were either old and feeble or young, sullen, and ill-kempt.

All the able-bodied, or law-abiding, women and men in these districts were either toiling in the tenement shops and in the shipyards and slaughterhouses or ill in the cheap boardinghouses that extended for blocks in every direction, some becoming tenements farther afield.

The growing unsavory look of the street life roused me from my fit of pique. I did not like to feel so divided in myself, but longed for former days, when I was serenely indifferent to what people of my acquaintance might choose to do . . . unless it was quite wrong. And there was nothing wrong in Quentin Stanhope escorting Miss Nellie Bly down Fifth Avenue, was there?

"Where are we?" I asked Irene.

"South of your favorite neighborhood," she told me brightly. "The theatrical district." That phrase she endowed with melodramatic emphasis.

She was not to get a rise out of me this time. I had resolved to remain calm and let nothing nor anyone else disturb me.

"Why?" was all I asked.

"When stymied in an investigation, and being forbidden on grounds of pride from simply asking Sherlock Holmes about it, I've decided to take his 'hint.' We call on Professor Marvel."

"Oh." I warmed. I liked the old fellow, despite his strange profession. He reminded me of the harmless village elders in Shropshire, more ready to indulge in a pint and a gossip than the mischief those of a younger generation might get up to. "Why do you think he can help us?"

"He knows everything, doesn't he? His performing placard advertises the fact."

"That encyclopedic knowledge owes itself to the thousands of cards and memorabilia in that enormous frock coat of his, not to real, daily life."

"Ah, but we are not investigating 'real, daily life.' We are exploring the past."

Irene paid the driver his fifty cents and caught my elbow to steer me into the grim brownstone before us.

She was in fine spirits that day (having seen nothing to disquiet her) and eager to be on the hunt.

I oft wondered if the tension and excitement of stage performance was not a sort of drug, a drug quite the opposite of the dream-inducing cocaine in which Mr. Holmes repeatedly indulged. How odd that the man of intellect chose dreams as an escape, and the woman of emotion and theatrical fantasies sought the unpredictable dangers of crime-solving for challenge.

Here, though, the only crime was one abandoned orphan child. Herself. And, gazing at Irene's face as she studied the brownstone's facade, anticipating what might be discovered within, I thought that she, born a beauty and thus indifferent to that fairy gift, had never looked lovelier, and livelier.

She had not missed my downcast state, for her hand tightened on my elbow and she leaned close to whisper, "Courage, Nell. We will find out at least what Mr. Holmes suspected, and perhaps solve the mystery of the Woman in Black. Then I can pen a companion novel to Mr. Wilkie Collins's *The Woman in White,* and become a famous lady novelist. What do you think?"

"I think you're always writing your own plays to appear in, anyway. And I doubt that Professor Marvel can point us to the proper streetcar stop, much less your family origins. But if the children are playing quietly in the nursery, one might as well let them have their fun."

"Thank you, Madam Governess."

We went up the stairs together, rather faster than I would have liked, and soon were knocking on the self-styled "professor's" door.

"He's not likely to be in since we have called without notice," I pointed out.

"Nonsense. It is just noon. Theatrical performers never leave their nests before noon."

"You still retain the habit, and let poor Godfrey leave for Paris in the morning quite uncatered to, except by our cook, Sophie."

"Ah, but I am in splendid fettle to greet him effusively in the evening when he returns, and if you were to ask him, he would much prefer that state and consider himself far more catered to, as you put it, Nell."

Of course I would ask Godfrey no such thing. But I took heart. A *morning* stroll on Fifth Avenue, then, was not the pathway to a man's heart.

"Perhaps we should ask Quentin to dine with us," I said.

Irene turned to me, startled. "That is not a bad idea, Nell, but why do you speak of it now?"

"It just came to me. He is a stranger in this city, as are we. It would be only polite. Thoughtful."

"Very politic, I think. I'll write to his hotel as soon as we return to ours this afternoon. You can debut the new Battenberg lace jacket I bought you at B. Altman's on Ladies' Mile. It elevates everything and is so appropriate to the summer heat."

"It's only a ready-made piece, Irene."

"But sure to be charming on you. You really must let me dress you. It salves my disconsolate loss of my theatrical ways."

"Oh." I did know how deeply Irene missed the life of the theater, which

alternated dull routine with feverishly frantic moments and a constant emphasis on costume. Since I did not have Pink's flair for millinery, I would have to
rely on Irene's frustrated urges as a dresser. I resolved to accept whatever frip-
pery she launched at me. That blue-and-crimson hat on Fifth Avenue was a
declaration of war, as far as I was concerned. And soldiers did require handsome and awe-inspiring uniforms to impress the enemy.

"I can't wait to see what you have brought me," I commented with more
fervor than ususal.

Irene eyed me again with that confused but suspicious glance.

At that moment, the well-worn door opened and Professor Marvel stood
there in all his portly glory.

"Irene, my child! Always a joy to see the blooming woman you have become. And the delightful Miss Huxleigh. Do come in. I have just arisen and
performed my ablutions, so am ready for company, as it happens."

Irene threw a knowing look at me over her fashionably puffed shoulder as she
preceded me into the professor's humble but fascinatingly cluttered front room.

We had barely seated ourselves on his threadbare sofa when a soft knock
came at the door.

He opened it to Edith, the Pig Lady's pansy of a daughter, just six.

How hard to believe this neatly attired child was the waif we had found
at the top of a tenement only a week before! Her mother had survived doing
sewing piecework from dawn to sunset beside a filthy window after time had
made her services as a "pig-faced woman" on the variety circuit unwanted. I had
never seen far into the deep shadow cast by the poke bonnet the Pig Lady
invariably wore, but now, thanks to Irene's ability to draw on the Rothschild
credit while abroad, she and Edith had moved to the professor's boardinghouse.

"Come in, my dear," the professor caroled in the voice useful for shy children. "Look who's come to visit us. Miss Irene Adler, the internationally famed
diva, and Miss Nell Huxleigh, one of the world's first type-writer girls, I am
given to understand."

Edith stood hanging off the doorjamb in the shy manner of her age. This
shabby yet genteel rooming house was a far cry from the cramped garret in
which we had first met her.

"Edith!" I welcomed her, holding out my hand. "How wonderful to see you
again. That frock is most becoming. Did your mother sew it for you? Come
over and let me see it."

My combination of cajoling and order brought her to me in shy steps.

Edith today indeed eclipsed the drawn, timorous child we had met, and her shiny dark curls were caught up in a charming gingham bow.

"Anna Scofield is sewing for all us board-treaders now," the professor said, smiling benignly on the child. "No more shirts by the dozen for pennies a day. She has airy quarters a floor up, which allows me daily visits from the pretty Miss Edith, but soon she will be going to school and I shall see that she gets there and back each day. It's good for a man of my years to provide escort duties for a charming young lady."

Edith blushed at this courtly patter, but I sensed the idea of "school" frightened her.

"School will be most instructive," I said, taking her hand. "I used to teach school, as a matter of fact." Of course I had been a governess, and my "school" had been a room and two or three pupils until the tutors arrived for the boys, and the lady elocutionist, sketch artist, and comportment coach for the girls.

"Is that true, Miss Huxleigh? Will they speak and look like you?"

Irene intervened. "They will not have an English accent, but they will teach you. And that is a very grand thing."

Edith nodded, then offered to "get the tea things" for the professor.

"She loves her 'teas,' " he confided as the girl disappeared behind the curtain that hid a tiny pantry, no doubt. "We have berry jams and marmalade. And only cold tea, I'm afraid, Miss Huxleigh, but not cold enough to qualify as iced. I can't let the child handle the stove."

"Of course not. Cold tea is very . . . bracing."

"I'm glad you found her mother's rooms upstairs," Irene said in an undertone. "Thank God you moved her out of that garret."

"Thank God you found her after all these years. We had no idea she lived in such straits, or about Edith."

"Yes, there are many overlooked children in any great city," Irene said, "and I am the older self of one."

"I imagine being reared by a moth-eaten collection of Vaudeville has-beens was no romp at the Rialto."

Irene took the old man's hands. "On the contrary! It was the making of me," she insisted. "I dance, I act, I sing. I've been a professional mermaid and an amateur hypnotist. And I shoot almost as straight as Annie Oakley."

"And you did most of that at an age younger than Edith," he agreed. "I'm glad you've found your bag of parlor tricks useful in later life, but singing was always your greatest gift."

We all fell silent, for singing was the one thing Irene had been forced to give up by circumstances. Once forced into hiding by the King of Bohemia more than two years ago, the arc of her career had vanished like one-half of a rainbow into a cloud.

"But there is more to the past than performance," she said with the air of moving firmly beyond any melancholy. "There is still the Woman in Black who visited me backstage during my youngest years before vanishing forever. It seems I am doomed to investigate my own mystery for a change. And I'm hoping you can point me in a direction that will identify my lost mother."

"I? What makes you think that?"

"You know everything," I said.

His genial face, mostly nose, ears, and multiple chins, shone with self-deprecation.

"So my advertising placards boast, Miss Huxleigh, but you know that theater is nine-tenths fraud and one-tenth luck."

"And six-tenths talent," Irene said. "Your area of expertise may be abstruse, Professor, but I believe it can't be underestimated."

He shrugged, pleased despite himself. "How can I help you?" he asked Irene.

"You have an encyclopedic memory. I suspect that a woman named Eliza Gilbert, who was buried at Green-Wood Cemetery in mid-January of 1861 may have something to do with my birth. Yet her obituary is not in the *Herald* for that date."

"I hate to point this out, but New York City is rife with newspapers. Perhaps you should consult them all."

I couldn't help groaning aloud. "No more 'dragons' and no more 'dungeons,'" I entreated Irene.

The professor frowned his understandable confusion at my comment, but Irene grasped it entirely.

"A person buried in Green-Wood would be prominent enough to merit attention in every paper," she said, "and the *Herald* is no fly-by-night journal, but has been established since the early years of this century."

Professor Marvel reached flying fingers into the innumerable pockets of an invisible coat, miming his own stage act, producing facts from the air.

"Eliza. The desperate mother fleeing over the ice floes in a river from an evil slave-owner in a novel by Harriet Beecher Stowe. W. S. Gilbert, a British composer of light opera. Humphrey Gilbert, discovered Newfoundland for Queen Elizabeth the First.

"But no Eliza Gilbert, Irene. I'm sorry. I'd love to produce a magic card, some tangible map that would reunite you with your mother, but the name means nothing to me."

Irene produced the purloined copy of the *Herald*. "Her tombstone exists. Nell and I and . . . someone else saw it. It reads January seventeenth. I checked the papers on either side of this most likely date. Eliza Gilbert is nowhere to be found."

He took the paper and scanned the page to which it was turned, moving his spectacles over the actual type like a magnifying glass. "You are as observant as ever, my dear Irene. I'm sorry, but I can't help you. I only pretend to know everything."

"You come close," she said with a smile, disappointment still peering through it.

Irene had made a career of a world of make-believe, and there was still in her that childlike sense that something wonderful could possibly happen at any moment.

For young Edith, rescued from an isolated, obscure penury, that had been true, partly through Irene and my efforts, which made me very proud. For Irene, though, my great grown-up charge and dear friend, the magic was thinner and more infrequent, and my heart ached for her doomed quest.

Perhaps it was best this kind old man, who had known her as child, should be the end of the obsession. She had at least reclaimed the people from her past, even if they were not blood relations.

"My, look at this headline." He chuckled at a story on a page opposite the obituary listings. "I remember that, but had forgotten it, if that makes sense. How things have changed, and not changed. Look at this story of the arrest of Kid Glove Rosey, the shoplifter. Saints and sinners have always been with us, and they often make the newspapers, the sinners more often than the saints."

"I wonder if there is any mention of a theatrical sort? Those were the days. I was doing a mind-reading act then."

Irene's rueful eyes met mine. Our "clue," obtained by ridiculous lengths, had become a path down memory lane for our aged friend.

Edith came in bearing a plate of raspberry tarts . . . goodness, so we each took one while the professor rambled through the faded ink of yesterday, and waited politely for him to recollect our presence. The old are like that. I saw that Edith knew that too. She smiled at us and bided her time until he should notice that she had a sweet to offer him.

"That rascal! Biggest thief in office until the present lot." He rattled the pages to find new sources of indignation or nostalgia.

And then he stood. "I have indeed heard the name Eliza Gilbert, by God," he thundered. "But only once, so long ago that I'd forgotten it.

"I and the world knew her by another name for years, you see. A few of our performing lot went to the interment, quite a crowd for one so fast fallen from fame. Later, when the headstone had been placed, I returned to visit her grave. I had to check the site with the office, which finally directed me to 'Eliza Gilbert,' and I soon forgot that forgettable name. Why she was buried under that mystifying name I don't know, but it ensured the obscurity of her grave."

Irene had stood up, the tart dropping to the floor.

Her face was drained of everything but astonishment, as empty of expression as a milliner's mannequin. She was suspended on the professor's next words.

He looked over the edge of the yellowed pages just then, equally astonished. "Irene, the paper is full of this woman. Here, on the front page."

"The front page!" I looked at it. "There was nothing but type about politicians and a series of their sketches."

"A sketch, yes, though nothing like the others I have seen, but a full story as well." He turned the front page to face us. The few illustrations were as small as a large man's thumbprint, and all of men, except for one woman.

16

Imposter Mother

~ฒุ๛~

*The woman is so hard
Upon the woman.*
—TENNYSON, "THE PRINCESS"

Irene shook the paper she had snatched from his hand in the professor's face.

"The headline mentions no name, only 'Foreign Dancer Dies in New York City.' This is not Eliza Gilbert."

"This is, however," he said mildly, "a lady I can tell you much about, for a finer likeness of her than this postage-stamp sketch hangs on that wall and she did die on the date you mention. Also," he added, "a cartoon of her from the papers at midcentury inhabits one of the myriad pockets in my Coat of Many Memories."

Irene glanced at the wall he indicated, which was papered with theatrical posters and photographs. She then stalked over, the folded paper in her hand.

I leaped up to follow, for I had not yet studied the newspaper page and was mad to see what woman we had overlooked.

Practically bouncing up and down behind Irene's shoulder to see the paper folded in her hand, I watched her examine every female image on the wall.

There were a good many, and a good many of them wore the scandalous pale tights, colored pink in actuality, of a variety performer. The costume was reminiscent of medieval gentlemen in tights and puffed pantaloons and quite shocking to see on a modern, corseted woman instead of a skirt.

At last Irene stopped searching the wall high and low and left to right. She paused before one likeness. Which was a very good thing, because I had grown quite dizzy without having yet had a clear look at the sketch in the newspaper.

"This must be the woman." Irene nodded at a photograph set dead center of the entire display, a dignified portrait, I was relieved to see, with indeed only the woman's hands and face exposed. No tights. No long lower limbs utterly revealed.

The photographed woman sat by the base of a large classical pillar, clothed in a great dark swath of velvet sleeves and cloak, almost like a tent. Little could be seen of her hair, for a soft velvet hat edged with a large feather concealed it. Only the narrow white border of a collar and cuffs contrasted with the dark dignity of her figure. Her face was as blandly pretty as her drooping white fingers, and in her right hand she held a most out-of-place object, a slender riding crop.

This photograph had so snared Irene's interest that I recalled her American singing master. He had mesmerized her to erase a particularly gruesome shock that had, for a time, stolen her singing voice. The trances had also erased many good memories of her girlhood.

Yet now a quite different force held Irene entranced. This was fascination, perhaps with an alternate image of herself. This woman was dressed as Irene might have been for an operatic role. Knowing the way Irene's fevered theatrical mind would erect serial novels from the slightest hint of a story, I suppose she envisioned her possible mother as a great stage performer, a Shakespearian actress perhaps.

Certainly a woman as circumspect as I, a modest parson's daughter, would happily claim the serene woman in the portrait as a mother, even if she had been so unsuitably employed upon the stage.

The professor had come up behind us. "That is my favorite likeness, even though it's perhaps the most unlike her, oddly enough. She had a face that could launch a thousand ships, but in other ways she had a thousand faces. The most fascinating woman of my era."

"Your era—?" Irene had turned to interrogate him. Despite the gentle, familial nature of her quest, she was as focused as a hunting dog on a scent.

He shrugged, disarranging his loosely tailored coat. "I mean a time when I was young, or still could be considered young, the forties and fifties."

"She died young?" Irene glanced back at the classical figure in the photograph.

"According to her." His smile was cryptic as well as fond.

"According to you and the *Herald,* in January of 1861. I would have been two or three then."

"If you had truly been born in 1858, as you were told," I pointed out.

Irene frowned over her shoulder at me. She wanted to hear of no more uncertainties in this tenuous quest.

"And there," said the professor, lifting an age-spotted hand to another framed picture on the wall, "is a newspaper sketch done when she first crossed the Atlantic to our shores."

Irene and I gasped in tandem, like overworked horses in the same traces. We stared at a drawing of a leaping woman in a ballerina skirt that barely covered her knees. She was poised in a small boat with a swan figurehead and Cupid, the bow pointing his arrow at a shore crowded with the crowned heads of Europe. The caption was "Europe, farewell! America, I come!"

Irene immediately dropped her eyes to the tiny faded print on the yellowed page of the *Herald.*

She read aloud the first sentence: " 'Some of the City's first citizens commented today on the passing of a woman whose name was known to so many'—all right, then, so what is it?—'but who was personally known to so few.' "

Irene declaimed salient phrases: " 'many warm friends . . . generous to a fault . . . excitable to pity and kindly sympathies.' "

I nodded approval.

" 'Many acts of generosity, especially to poor people . . .' "

Even as Irene's voice grew more and more disbelieving, I rejoiced the more.

" 'Generous . . . forgiving and affectionate . . .' What was she, a performer or a saint? And what the devil was her name? Ah, here. At last. A whole string of them . . . 'Maria Dolores Eliza Rosana *Gilbert*!' "

"She was Spanish?" My enthusiasm rapidly waned.

"Yes. Then she must have married a Gilbert."

The professor chuckled behind us.

"Ah, some mention of her position in life." Irene read approvingly, " 'Her natural talents were of the highest order . . . her accomplishments manifold—' " here she fixed me with an I-told-you-so look—" 'and in some respects, marvelous.' "

The professor's chuckles had become an elderly giggle.

Irene frowned and stopped reading aloud, although her pace of silent reading quickened.

A new and confusing burst of quotes issued forth next: "From Ireland . . . 'neither creditable to her native land nor useful to society . . .' England: 'We do not think it desirable to narrate the adventures of unfortunates of her class, however prominent.'"

"'Unfortunates,'" I burst out. "Irene, in London that means—"

"I well know what that means." Irene regarded Professor Marvel with eyes of cut steel. "Who *is* this Maria Dolores Eliza Rosana Gilbert who I have never heard of, but apparently the whole world knows, or knew, and you personally as well."

He shrugged again. "She was best known by a diminutive which became her stage name. I think you have heard it. Lola. Lola Montez."

Irene stepped back from the wall. Her arm fell to her side like a duelist who has fired her one and only shot and now must await the fate of another's action. I was able to slip the newspaper from her nerveless fingers and finally read it for myself.

"Lola Montez," Irene repeated in tones of deep contempt.

She might have just been told she was suspected of having a black widow spider for a mother. Indeed, the mysterious woman of her earliest childhood had reportedly worn black.

"That name is vaguely familiar," said I, hardly realizing I spoke aloud.

Both ignored me. Irene had turned to face the professor as if they were opponents in a court of law.

"You realize," she said, "that I am seeking the identity of the mother who bore me. You realize that person cannot possibly be *Lola Montez*."

"Certainly not, Irene," I put in. "If she was indeed an 'unfortunate,' no one of that immoral class could possibly be your mother."

"Of course she could, Nell!" Irene turned on me, with something resembling fury. "All the more reason for bearing an inconvenient child and abandoning it. But I would claim *any* unfortunate save her. Do you know who, and what, she was?"

"Immoral?"

"Worse!"

"Worse?"

"Say if I exaggerate, Professor! She was considered . . . haughty, vain, selfish, and worst of all, an abominably untalented dancer and an even more execrable actress. She was booed and hissed off the major stages of Europe for her sheer ineptitude. She can't possibly have been my mother; I would have been born without a scintilla of talent. I would have booed her myself from the womb. How, Professor, can you have admired such a woman, even in your benighted youth?"

His expression retained the warmth of benign memory. "She was a great beauty, Irene. You should have seen her. No painting or photograph captures her. She exploded with vitality. Black, shining hair, eyes of brilliant dark blue, flashing bolts from the gods on Mount Olympus. The daintiest little foot to touch hardwood stage floor and enough fiery spirit to instill the wildest stallion. It didn't matter how well she did anything, Irene. Everything she did was with her whole heart and spirit and that was always . . . electric."

" '*Mrs*. Eliza Gilbert' was on her headstone," I said softly.

"And a bigamist, if I recall!" Irene charged suddenly. "The more I remember, the more I am appalled."

"She had an irregular childhood," the professor said.

Irene would hear nothing of the old man's defense. "So did I. But I can sing on key. And act outside of an opera. And dance better in my sleep, no doubt."

"Can you dance?" I asked, thinking that might settle the matter.

"Yes. And fence. And I have never been booed off a stage."

"A pity," said the professor. "One can never learn true humility until one has faced that cruel situation." He clearly had.

"I do not need to learn true humility," Irene retorted.

"Spoken like the late Lola Montez." The professor smiled.

Meanwhile, I had been rapidly looking farther than the article's first page, which quoted both damning and admiring summations of Lola Montez's life.

"She was involved with King Ludwig of Bavaria?" I asked the professor in some amazement.

"Her most famous, or infamous association. She, and he, claimed their friendship was purely platonic. He had a queen, after all, but he made her Countess of Landsfeld and a citizen of Bavaria, under her duress, it was said. She was forced to flee the country during the late '40s revolution that cost Ludwig his throne. Many blamed his association with Lola for that."

I glanced at my friend. "How interesting. Irene was . . . acquainted with the King of Bohemia."

The professor beamed. "Like mother, like daughter."

"You sly rascal," Irene challenged him. "You are enjoying comparing me to this wretched woman. I do not have blue eyes, electric or otherwise, in case you hadn't noticed."

"I believe a father is involved in this process," he said.

"And," I said slowly, "she did perform upon the stage."

"Nell," Irene warned me, beginning to pace. She also began to dig in her reticule for her cigarette case and lucifers while continuing her interrogation.

"It says in this newspaper, Professor," I went on, "that she first had a stroke, then died of pneumonia contracted during a walk in wet weather. And she was not yet forty!'

"Some say, scurrilously, that she died of diseases associated with her immoral life, but in fact she had always had weak lungs."

"Weak lungs? Well, she certainly could not have sung."

"But she smoked."

Irene stopped pacing, a telltale cigarette sending a flurry of smoke signals thick enough for a Red Indian to read into the air above her hat. "Smoked?"

"Incessantly," the professor said as Irene hurriedly stabbed her cigarette to death on her teacup saucer. "She was high-tempered," he went on, nodding to the photograph again. "That riding crop was a frequent accessory, and she used it, whether on an impudent man who accosted her in public or a mob screaming for her blood in Bavaria. She was as fearless as a cavalry officer."

"Irene," I told him informatively, "once took a riding crop to a set of gossiping women at the salon of Maison Worth in Paris."

"Really?"

The professor joined me in studying Irene as she continued to pace before us.

"Lola would wear men's clothes on occasion," he said. "To escape Bavaria, for instance, or during the harsh overland Panama crossing to the California gold fields."

"Irene has done that very thing," I told him, with the sense of discovering I was chatting with someone with whom I had much in common, "and more than rarely. She fought a duel with swords in male disguise once, and Sherlock Holmes himself could testify personally how effective she was in such guise, much to his chagrin and professional embarrassment—"

"Don't be ridiculous!" she told us. "A man like Sherlock Holmes does not embarrass, and neither do I. You are both enjoying tweaking my self-respect, but these are the merest coincidences. Any independent woman in this age of milksop females might be expected to be as inventive and forceful in her habits and actions. I shall have to see a great deal more evidence before I believe that there is any possibility that woman could be my mother."

"You are in luck," the professor said. "I believe that more has been written about her than any woman who lived in the middle of this century with the possible exception of your queen, Miss Huxleigh. In fact, she has written one of these books herself. She retired from the dancing stage here in New York after her return from California. Following a few final trips to Europe, she became a noted lecturer. I never saw her stage work, but in the lecture hall she was spellbinding. Alas, her decline in health soon followed. I believe she became quite religious in her last year."

"Professor," I asked, "do you preface your last sentence with 'Alas' because her health declined or because she became religious?"

His watery eyes regarded me for a long moment. "I must have meant only the former, Miss Huxleigh, for I believe it only right that a person leaves this earth in good order with her God."

At that Irene threw her hands into the air and returned to her chair before the tea table.

"This is arrant nonsense," she said in calmer tones. "This is some foolish lark dreamed up by you and Sherlock Holmes to distract me from a search for my genuine mother."

"I do not know this Mr. Holmes," he objected.

"I'm surprised he didn't contact you since he arrived in America. He is a possessive man, and our paths have crossed during his investigation of his various cases, as well during mine."

"Ah, yes. Your youthful work as an Pinkerton agent here in New York. You have continued with this in Europe?"

"I do private inquiry work at times, yes. So simply because Sherlock Holmes leads me to a headstone in Green-Wood Cemetery does not mean the inhabitant of that grave leads back to me."

She picked up her cigarette case again, lighting one with deliberate, lingering grace, as if to blow smoke in the face of this theory. Then she spoke again, to the wall of memorabilia.

"I do fancy the idea of carrying a riding crop, though. It does make so much more sense for the modern woman than a parasol."

She regarded the professor. "Since this woman had snared your youthful imagination, I will investigate her further, if only to utterly disabuse you of this fancy. Can you suggest where we should begin?"

"Irene, I—"

The professor spread wide his hands. "All of New York City is filled with the ephemera of Lola Montez. You should begin as one of those fevered collectors do, and find the books and posters of thirty and more years ago."

Irene frowned. "New York City has no Left Bank like that in Paris, full of book vendors' stalls and old and quaint memoirs of the past."

"No," the professor conceded, "but here we have do have the Rialto area of bookshops and especially Brentano's Literary Emporium, and that should be a fine place to start."

Memoirs of a Dangerous Woman:

Panama Passage

Came Lola Montez one day, in the full zenith of her evil fame, bound for California. A good-looking, bold woman, with fine, bad eyes, and a determined bearing, dressing ostentatiously in perfect male attire . . . She carried in her hand a handsome riding crop, which she could use as well in the streets of Cruces as in the towns of Europe.

—FROM THE MEMOIRS OF MRS. SEACOLE, AN ENGLISH LADY, 1851

I was never in Cruces and had gone by way of Nicaragua.

—THE NOTORIOUS ADVENTURESS IN QUESTION

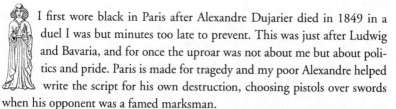 I first wore black in Paris after Alexandre Dujarier died in 1849 in a duel I was but minutes too late to prevent. This was just after Ludwig and Bavaria, and for once the uproar was not about me but about politics and pride. Paris is made for tragedy and my poor Alexandre helped write the script for his own destruction, choosing pistols over swords when his opponent was a famed marksman.

I did not wear only black, however. I put a red flower in my hair to remind me of the one true love in my life. He had left me some theater stock and shares in his newspaper but soon I was caught up in the "gold fever" searing all of Paris, and invested several thousands in a California gold mine called the Eureka.

In 1849 all the world echoed with the Gold Rush. California! Eureka! The very words rang with adventure and optimism. Shortly after, all Paris was buzzing that the companies selling mine stock were fraudulent. I was forced to find less costly quarters.

Still, I was not yet forced to find less eminent escorts. I renewed an acquaintance with Prince Jung Bahadoor, an Oxford graduate who was the ambassador for Nepal. Parisians called him "the educated barbarian" but he was a man of the highest caste in his land. We amused ourselves by startling the sneering Parisians when we would chat together at length in a Hindu dialect. How odd that a notably accomplished man of foreign lineage and a slandered woman of suspect talents were both gossiped about . . . and invited everywhere.

The prince and I attended Meyerbeer's *L'Africaine* at the opera house, which had been refitted to resemble a San Francisco theater . . . red velvet on the seats, red silk upon the walls.

I sat there as the music surged around me, my mind adazzle with Africa! California!

Watching eyes showered disdain on the prince and myself but whenever could outward disapproval quench the inner fire?

During the intermission, the audience murmured its disapproval of an actress in the piece who smoked a cigar. I mutely applauded her, though I had stopped the smoking habit I had learned from George Sand. For a while.

The prince returned to Nepal and all Paris talked. He had abandoned me, I was penniless and broken. The prince sent me a box dripping with precious stones and a shawl worked in diamonds and gold as a "mark of his esteem."

Still Paris gabbled. I was weak and penitent and would soon retire to the Carmelites at Madrid.

Their gossip made me angry. My Nepalese prince was not the only royalty I could appeal to. I wrote Ludwig, and he restored my pension. I shopped the boulevards for carpets and paintings and furnishings for a new house on the rue Blanche.

They called me Lola Noir and said I was in my decline. It was only a matter of time.

It was only a matter of time before the countess of Landsfeld sent out invitations for a grande soiree. Every distinguished personage in Paris attended.

I set aside my mourning black to don the color that named the street I now dwelled upon: a white watered silk gown slashed across by the grand cordon from King Ludwig, with a white camellia in my black, black hair.

Paris declared me a great lady and clamored for another soiree. I was, it seems, fashionable.

Then influenza laid all Paris flat, including myself. I kept to my house for three months, as into my fever dreams came Dujarier. He clasped my hands, whispered to me. When I awoke after many weeks, he was gone. Fate has torn many lovers from me, but only one love.

Paris shook off the influenza like a bad dream. Its gay, heedless life resumed. I arose from my sickbed and found myself still a phenomenon though I felt like a phantom. A horse named after me won the grand prize in the races at Chantilly. I barely had the strength to walk to the corner.

Sick to my soul and facing new debts, I sought out the dance master Mabille. Now I was truly weak, if not penitent. Every day for three months he drilled me like a soldier at Jardin Mabille. I emerged with six new dances, fine notices from a circle of friends, and returned to the stage. I suppose it was a triumph but the ghost of Dujarier danced with me.

I was, of course, rumored to have taken a host of new lovers. If I had bothered to collect all these falsehoods about myself they would form a mountain higher than Chimborazo in Ecuador.

"Lola Montez bathes in lavender water and dries herself with rose leaves," wrote a San Francisco reporter in the *Pacific News*.

All these fairy tales found their way to me via my agent, M. Roux, who passed them on in hopes of getting his 25 percent for every page.

I was past thirty, though I could pass myself off as twenty-five, and did. The influenza had taken my hair by handfuls, and I was forced to wear a wig. When the actress who had smoked at the opera burst in upon me without notice backstage and found me wigless, she cried, "Imagine you wearing another woman's hair!"

Vicious civet! I eyed her cashmere shawl, and retorted, "Imagine you wearing another sheep's clothing!"

I did not tell her that I myself smoked again, incessantly, for my nerves were as ragged as my hair.

I went to other cities in Europe that would welcome me until I had danced away my old fever dreams of entrancing a king and liberating a country and . . . of Dujarier. Then I went to America, and, finally, California.

New Orleans is the most European and thus the Queen of Cities in America. It was both the scene of my finest stage triumphs during my American tours and of my most volatile fracases, in court and out.

So it was that, forfeiting $500 bail but not the goodwill of the New Orleans citizenry for my travails, I set sail from Jackson Square April 22, 1853, on the U.S. mail ship *Philadelphia,* bound for Aspinwall on the coast of Panama, and from there for the gold fields of California.

In those days only three routes offered passage to California: Overland for months. Or by sea around Cape Horn at the notoriously stormy tip of South America, often used for freight, for months. (Being notoriously stormy myself, this route appealed to me, although I did not like the notion of being confused with baggage. . . .) Or across Central America via Panama or Nicaragua by rail, riverboat, and pack mule, more often used for people and their luggage, for weeks.

As I had told the court in Louisiana about a gentleman who had accosted me in a theatrical fracas: I would rather be kicked by a horse than an ass. The Central American route, and its mules, appealed to me despite tales of steamy jungles and resident insects and fevers.

After all, I had survived many jungles before, most of the them man-made. Or woman-made in one case. My reasons for going to California were many. First, performers followed the gold, and my brother and sister acts were already tackling the gold fields. For another, I was weary of these court battles, not just the latest in New Orleans but that atrocity in 1849 that ruined my marriage to George Heald, a charming young man who offered me the protection of his name after I'd fled Bavaria to Switzerland and then returned to London. His zealous aunt did not even allow us a month of marriage before she sent an inspector to arrest me for bigamy! We fled to London, then Spain, where he abandoned me. That is what one gets for marrying a boy of twenty-one, no matter how charming and devoted. Although I assured my dear "Luis" by letter that the marriage was merely one of convenience, he was most grumpy about it and cut my pension in half. Alas, Ludwig had been a king and couldn't understand that a woman on her own must make accommodations, even if her heart is breaking, and especially if her bank account is.

As my funds ran low, I was forced back to the footlights of Paris, where I was always welcome. A foray into Prussia ended when the police director banned my appearance, saying the Countess of Landsfeld's presence might incite public demonstrations by liberals, socialists, and communists. Of course it was the cursed Jesuits again.

Luckily, I'd met a most charming man in Paris, a brother of James Gordon Bennett, publisher of the *New York Herald*. He was much taken with me and suggested I follow Fanny Eissler and Jenny Lind in conquering American audiences.

I considered the matter. Meanwhile Mr. Bennett and his brother raised so much speculation about my possible arrival in New York that the *Times* commented, "We shall be sadly disappointed if this creature has any degree of success in the United States. She has no special reputation as a dancer. She is known to the world only as a shameless and abandoned woman."

I'd been abandoned by my husband, Heald, all right, and "this creature" was indeed shameless about flying into the teeth of her enemies. I resolved to go, for the *Times* couldn't have given me better advance publicity had I paid for it!

My New York performances were well attended and lucrative, but after a year or so of touring most of the major northeastern cities and the middle of America, I longed for fresh challenges. That niggling suit by a variety hall manager in New Orleans forced me to take over my own defense on an assault and battery charge. The spectators in court applauded me as if I were dancing. Indeed I danced out the courtroom door and straight onto a steamer to far California.

The *Philadelphia* plied the Caribbean Sea's aquamarine waters for a full week before landing at Aspinwall. The first two days featured would-be gold miners hanging over the rails. When they recovered, they hung over the rails to discharge their new-bought Colt revolvers at the dolphins capering beside the steamer. These huge, smiling fish seemed protected by the water, but I didn't hesitate to draw my own pistol, far better used than theirs, for I had been a crack shot for years, to dissuade them from troubling the sea life.

These men had read and heard the same siren call to the gold fields and thus resembled a scruffy band of brothers: all wore red flannel shirts and slouch hats, and had hung themselves with a least one revolver and a Bowie knife, and most were beginning to grow beards.

One could not even take a walk around the deck, it was so occupied with idiotic contraptions for the quicker mining of gold these gullible fellows had bought with their last cash.

Naturally, prices at every step of the journey were exorbitant, and I had a larger party than most: myself, my manager, my new maid, Hyacinth, whom I renamed Periwinkle after her blue-gray eyes, and my lapdog, Flora.

Naturally, I did not ascribe to the extortion that was common.

Ladies, I may point out, rarely made this brutal journey. Especially not ladies with entourages. Or ladies with daggers in their boots, pistols in their pockets, and whips in their hands.

Aspinwall proved to be a shantytown built on stilts over a swamp. The hotel could sit two hundred for a meal, but accommodations were so cramped that most men slept on cots on balconies in the humid night air buzzing with insects.

I was fascinated by the towering coco palm trees and the airy vines which intertwined like lace above the matted jungle growths.

Even the lowliest cot in Aspinwall was a prize. I required a private bedroom, and a cot for poor little Flora. The hotel manager claimed that men were sleeping on the floor, and he couldn't spare a cot for a dog.

"Sir," I said delicately around the cigarette that much more pleasantly occupied my mouth than arguments with craven and greedy innkeepers. "I don't know where or how your guests sleep, but I'd have you know my dog has slept in palaces. Get the cot, and say no more."

Of course in the morning the miserable worm presented a bill of five dollars for Flora's bed. I was forced to draw my pistol to negotiate a reasonable compromise.

Indeed, I saw many men treated worse than coatless dogs on that journey, all these hopeful fools, mortgaging everything they could lay their hands on to head for the fabled gold fields.

Pistols were prominent in their belts, along with sun-shading hats and bravado. None had the nerve of Lola to use them.

Not all those California-bound were luckless gold-seekers. Senators and journalists also thronged west, some from the Gold Coast, others traveling there to make their mark on the thriving communities springing up everywhere.

Here is where for a time I donned mannish garb à la Amelia Bloomer. When the railroad stopped at Gabon, we and our goods were loaded into fragile native canoes and paddled up the murky Charges River to Gorgona, where we faced a twenty-mile trek by mule to Panama City on the Pacific side. I wanted no insects stinging me to death through delicate women's dresses, which I had brought with me in many trunks.

In Gorgona it was every man for himself to find and engage a reliable guide and mules for the rough journey.

Weary travelers to the gold fields gained new resolve from the sight of long mule trains coming the other way, from east to west. Each animal was burdened with large saddlebags holding pure gold nuggets and dust. Only two armed men would accompany each train of fifteen or so mules.

When I marveled at the slim number of guardian riders for such rich mule trains, I was told that each box of gold weighed so much that only a foolhardy man would attempt to take one. And even then such a fool would be shot dead before he could stagger fifteen feet away. And certainly no mule, especially so laden, is fast enough to be herded away by a highwayman.

Many men there, though, would steal if they could, what they could.

I kept my whip constantly in hand. Soon my many wardrobe trunks lay atop the backs of my own train of many mules. This way I could see them at all times and no one could steal the contents. I also ensured that our noble beasts of burden didn't carry more than they could, and berated with tongue and whip any greedy fool who attempted to abuse them within my sight.

And so it was that the humble mule carried fortunes on his back across the Isthmus of Panama . . . and Lola's magnificent wardrobe. This array would soon dazzle all of San Francisco, the storied city at the end and the beginning (depending on which way one was going) of the fabulous Gold Coast.

At last the mules' narrow footpath opened onto the view of a bustling settlement. Panama City. Here civilization had set up her tents on the outskirts of another mighty ocean.

Here we would wait, and jostle, to command passage on a ship to San Francisco.

Here Lola Montez would begin to stamp her presence upon the minds and hearts and the history of the region. Not since I had come to Bavaria had I felt such a sense of destiny. O brave New World! You are mine!

The Cocoa Grove Hotel was the only reputable hostelry in town. I took rooms there and found myself among political appointees from the new Franklin Pierce administration just arrived from New York City, as well as the editor-owners of three prominent San Francisco newspapers. Oh, my. When I was not castigating the newspapers for spreading slander about my art and life, I was getting along quite well with their owners, such as Mr. Bennett of the *Herald* in New York.

While we waited our places on the next steamer to San Francisco, it was simple to set up a salon at the hotel. The hard-bitten newspaper men who expected to meet a hulking Amazon wielding a whip went away praising my "delicate frame, regular and handsome features, pair of brilliant and expressive eyes, and an exceedingly winning address."

Hah! They soon saw the mettle of Lola.

While Mr. Middleton of the *Panama Star* and other such men sat talking with me by the hotel's entrance, a man of their number rose to stroll the premises and wandered into the utter darkness beyond the gate. Then we heard two rapid revolver clicks, yet no discharge. The stroller cried that a man was trying to shoot him. Again came a few more revolver clicks, but apparently the endless tropical damp had disarmed the gun.

I rose from my chair, told the men to fetch a light, and dashed into the darkness. The other men were at my heels, along with the one who found a light. We glimpsed the back of an escaping villain. One of my followers fired a pistol, but again the tropical humidity made a mockery of gunpowder. (There is a reason I consider a whip an ideal weapon. It never fails, unlike a pistol, and lets me keep my distance, unlike a knife.)

Mr. Milne stood shaking when we reached him. I led him back to the hotel veranda, asking all the way who might wish him ill. Since he could produce no enemies (a sign of a milksop personality, in my view) I concluded that the hotel keepers were patroling the fringes, forcing people to shelter in their establishments.

"How," I asked the poor-spirited Milne, "could you stand there like a rooted target? When you heard the pistol clicks, you should have dashed into the darkness, taken the offender by the hair and shouted for help whilst you admonished him. So I would have done, and he would have run off sooner."

Mr. Milne could not answer, other than to beg that I remain in Panama City, and perform at their theater.

I had performed enough at the scene of the foiled "shooting."

My newspaper gentlemen sang my praises in rotation. Two days later I boarded the Pacific Mail Steamship Company's sidewheeler, the *Northerner,* bound—where else?—north for San Francisco, a heroine in search of another territory to conquer. From the Atlantic might of New York City, I had come to the Pacific power of San Francisco a full continent away, and teeming with enterprise and the raw gleam of gold.

I breathed in a fresh cigarillo on deck. I was smoking perhaps five hundred a day now, but only taking a few puffs on each one. Men followed and gathered around me to hand me the pungent lighted brands, a trademark of my "wild and willful, but never wicked" ways. And who was I to scorn any one of my charming courtiers?

17

House Alert

❦

The land is full of bloody crimes, and the city is full of violence.
—EZEKIEL 7:23

❧ FROM THE CASE NOTES OF SHERLOCK HOLMES ❦

While I smoked a considering pipe, I examined my position and its advantages: the intersection of Fifth Avenue and Fifty-second Street, directly across from the notorious Madame Restell's house. That dark brownstone block of a house had been the scene of a horrifically dangerous denouement involving myself and Irene Adler Norton and her loyal friend, Miss Huxleigh, only days before. What melodrama Watson would make of such events neither I nor the panting public will ever know, to the peace of mind of both. I turned away from the recent past with a grim smile to regard my present, the huge white stone carcass that was the Willie K. Vanderbilt's triumphal city mansion. Even the princeliest city mansion must sit parapet by paperboy on the city streets, and Fifth Avenue hosted as many peddlers and hucksters as any New York neighborhood.

Homeless urchins are, unfortunately for them, to be found in every major metropolis. Fortunately for me, New York was enough of a great metropolis to sprout a particularly large and enterprising population of these threadbare entrepreneurs. A good many of them hawk newspapers, so they are well informed of the day's most lurid events and in addition have become quick studies of the ways and means of passing humanity.

Arriving early on the corner of Fifth Avenue with my rented cart, I established my place of business and identity in one fell swoop. Jimmy Crackcorn, dealer in tools and tinware. A peddler had rented me cart and contents for a ten-dollar gold piece and immediately hied himself to the nearest saloon.

I spent the morning engaging the small merchants of the city street in palaver and dispensing American dimes to them. By noon the Vanderbilt house was under the eagle eyes of a company of utterly ignored rapscallions whose loyalty was ensured by promises of quarters and even a dollar to the lad who described the most interesting visitor to the Vanderbilt château, fore and aft and from port to starboard.

Of course I had no time to create a company as loyal and well instructed as the Baker Street Irregulars, but I used the same quasi-military cant that enchants boys everywhere, and coin of the realm, or the republic, speaks the same language everywhere.

I am not well-known in New York, yet my guise as an old peddler came easily. I exchanged my English accent for the brogue of Ireland and immediately was as worth overlooking as any of my barefooted boys.

There is a far greater tolerance in America of people of different classes mingling in the streets. I soon made the acquaintance of other confreres, and sisters, loitering about with the intention of perpetrating no good on the honest citizens bustling to and fro.

These alone recognized me as a new face, and came toddling round to eye me and warn me to beware of treading on their turf.

First came a stout, matronly lady of sixty and middling height, all in widow's black from her now old-fashioned bonnet to her long black cape. Gray eyes, gray hair, almost-gray complexion, and an Irish lilt to give mine the test of truth.

"Good day, Sir. I see yer new to commerce on this corner."

"Aye, mum, jest off the ship, with me feet fresh on American soil."

"You've got a lot of nose for a son of the auld sod, m'boy."

"Ah, there was likely a German in the peat bog, back when every man jack was invadin' the isle, don't you know?"

"German's all right, long as it's no Englishman."

"Heaven forbid," I said piously.

"And what game you got goin', lad?"

I nodded at the grandiose Vanderbilt mansion, inspired, as I often am when creating a fictitious persona. "I'm not sayin' there's not a game or three I got playin', but all I do here and now is not for gamin' but for subjects closer to a man's heart. There's a maid in yon mansion, a very fair maid, and 'tis hard for a man to find a way to her inside one of these blasted castles."

"Like a fairy tale." The old lady cackled. "Well, good luck to you, lad. They call me Old Mother Hubbard, but me given name's Margaret, with a few last names to go wi' it."

"Aye. I'm Liam, but whether 'tis Kelly or Casey depends on the day and time and the person."

"And what is this fair lass like?"

"Hair as red as any burnin' bush under her white cap, and a quick bright eye, and sings like the thrush in springtime."

"I can see yer enamored, lad, best watch yer step. Those who work for the great houses get turned-up noses quick."

Now that Mother Hubbard had stayed to chat, we were joined by two of her kindred: street pickpockets and satchel robbers, and banco artists and swindlers.

"Why, 'tis Lord Courtenay," Mother Hubbard hailed one. The appellation didn't surprise me. He stood over six feet, like myself, an exception on the metropolitan street, but he was bronzed of skin, slim, with dark hair and a light mustache. I am sorry to say that his chin, unlike mine, was weak, and that immediately conveyed an air that underlined his masquerade: an English Lord.

"M'lord," said I, with a facile bow.

"One of the brethren," Mother Hubbard said quickly.

"A pretty good bow, for a street fellow," the false lord said in upper-crust tones.

"Who are ye this time?" Mother Hubbard inquired.

"Sir Harry Vane of Her Majesty's Lights. The ladies rip the gold buttons off my British Royal Navy uniform when I present myself at balls. American ladies are bold and easily bowled over."

"Indeed," said I. "I hope that applies to an Irish maid in America."

"Ye seem presentable enough, my boy," Mother Hubbard said. "Why won't yer little maid walk out wi' ye?"

"Alas, I have but seen her from afar. And I fear that some ither fellow with better access to the Great House is beatin' me to the punch."

"Ah." The old lady nodded. "That's why ye've stationed these gutter rats all about the place. D'ye know his name or his trade?"

"That's jest it, I do not. I've asked the lads to report anyone who seems to linger or not have real business there."

"That's the newest Vanderbilt mansion, my poor man," Sir Harry explained. "I could waltz in the front, of course, but I'm no good for telling you about tradesmen who come and go." He eyed the place like a connoisseur studying a Burmese ruby. "Ah, what marks abound within there. But strike a pose as English nobleman and you will pick them clean. I am known under many titles, from Montreal to the Indies, sir, but as Sir Hugh Leslie Courtenay of the British Royal Navy I lived on credit in Baltimore for almost a year and had any man's money and many a woman's at my beck and call."

"You aim too high," said the second man who had joined our group, heretofore silent. He was youthful and well presented, and introduced himself to me by his street name, Hungry Joe.

"Now, when I run a banco," he said, "I don't pretend to be other than I am, which is a damn good talker."

He too was near forty, and well dressed, and he began to demonstrate his skills with a will.

"I have run my game in every major city in the U.S. of A.," he said, speaking rapidly and with a sort of singsong cant that shortly held us spellbound.

"There isn't an opening that I can't squeeze into, whether it be in conversation or a bank vault.

"I study the passenger list of arrivals on the great lines. That is how I picked up Oscar Wilde when he toured the States, and followed him to his hotel. Why, we were best friends at the Hotel Brunswick, and closed down the café with our palaver. I had five thousand American out of him, but the codger put it in a check and tumbled before I could cash it. I do better with old coots like this Manchester merchant I managed to 'run into' while he was strolling down Broadway. I called his name and bowed. He was much surprised and I explained I was the steamship captain's nephew and had heard a good deal of him from my uncle at dinner the night before. Flattery is the key to turning folks loose of their money. So we linked up and soon I had him at a confederate's office, where I engaged in a three-card monte, but ran out of cash and the old fool got so excited he staked me. Well, I got so excited I took the five hundred dollars and ran."

He patted his pocket. "What will you do when your charms with the ladies pale, 'Sir Harry'?"

The faux lord looked at me. "I shall be this fellow, then, I suppose, standing outside looking in. For now I can get inside and look out, and will do so as long as I can. I have studied all the pedigrees of England as well as its complicated legal system. There are a great many descendants of Old Blighty in the U.S. hoping to hear of an English inheritance, and I am Johnny-on-the-spot with that confidence game."

I recalled one American who had recently been hoping to hear of an American inheritance, and had to cough to conceal my chuckle.

"Do ye smoke, Liam," Mother Hubbard asked in a maternal tone.

"I do, ma'am."

"It'll be the death of ye," she said, shaking her head. "Oh, look. One of your lads is come running."

Indeed he was, to report the arrival and departure of the ice man.

"And was he a young fellow?" I asked in view of my new acquaintances, to demonstrate that I was the love-struck swain indeed.

"No, sir. He was fat and som'at past sixty."

"Very good, my lad. Here's a dime. Now watch further."

Sir Harry shook his head. "Such effort for a parlormaid. You will never go far in America."

"The prince climbed the glass mountain and slipped back three times before he won fair lady," Mother Hubbard said, pinching my cheek. "Now you lads be about your business and let poor Liam be about his."

We parted, but I was to see this trio cruising Fifth Avenue as long as I held to my humble stall.

By nightfall I had reports of all the servicemen who visited the premises in a day, a staggering number of butchers and greengrocers, bakers and laundrymen.

It was young Archie who won the dollar of the day, though, when he told me of the man who watched with him at the rear of the building.

By now the gaslights and electric lights were brightening on whatever streets they served, and the passing coaches were driven by a pedigreed breed of horse as New York society dressed up and drove out.

All the peddlers carts were gone save mine, and the newsboys had been replaced by match and flower girls.

"He's been standing there all day, in the shadow of the house opposite," Archie said. "I noticed him about noon, for he never left to eat."

"Did he look a respectable gentleman?"

My young informant frowned. "Not respectable, not unso, if you know what I mean?"

"Nondescript?"

His dingy face stared at me as I realized I was not speaking the same language.

"Rich, poor?"

"Not either. Very quiet. I didn't notice him for ages. No one you'd look at twice."

"And when did he leave?"

"He's still there—"

I pressed a dollar into his hand, ignored his startled look and blathered thanks. "Tomorrow," I said. "Early. Same time, same place. Another dollar if you stow my cart someplace safe around here."

"I'll have to stay with it the night."

"Another dollar."

By now his eye whites glimmered as large as dollar coins.

"Yes, sir!"

I'd have the Irregulars up to snuff in no time.

But first I needed to find the nondescript man on watch.

Dark had descended like a black theater curtain. I pulled my shabby pea-coat collar over my ears and my dark cap down over my eyes.

In two minutes I was at the rear of the Vanderbilt property, watching the man who watched the house. This action reminded me of my hours alone in Whitechapel, but here there was no fog, and no murders in the street. I'd have to be clever and quiet to follow anyone and I certainly intended to follow this man when he left.

He didn't leave until past three in the morning.

By then the Vanderbilt coach with its bright side lamps had paused in the front to release its passengers and clattered to the back area to stable the horses.

I wished for a London fog, but New York was a city of light, not murk. That made it harder on criminals, and detectives.

My prey was as the boy had described him: bland, undistinguished. He wore a long dark coat and a soft hat pulled over his eyes.

He never lit up and smoked while I watched, though my own fingers itched for the comfortable companionship of my pipe. In Whitechapel, my pipe was a stage prop that suited the atmosphere. Here it would be a distraction, a betraying blot of light in an emptying night.

The sound of traffic on Fifth Avenue had almost died away until the early morning dray wagons began arriving with goods for the waking city.

My man moved. A blot of darkness pulled away from the surrounding inkiness and began walking away from Fifth Avenue.

So did I, on my gummed soles. My pulse quickened. Whoever had delivered threatening notes and the dead body to Vanderbilt had to have been watching him then. That anyone was watching his house now indicated the game was far from over, and possibly the dead bodies.

I slipped past streetlight after streetlight, ducking into doorways, a shadow that was more a figment of the flitting moonlight than of anyone's notice.

I saw other shadows on my way, huddled black and shapeless in niches. The homeless, some of them my newsboys, no doubt.

These did not stir, lost in the exhausted sleep of those too worn to care for their own safety.

My man's footsteps were as soft as fog. He had been at this game for a long time.

His path was erratic, and he paused often to stop and listen.

He heard nothing but the distant creak of wheels, the bay of a stray dog.

Finally we reached a street as somnolent as any in New York City.

He vanished into a five-story brownstone building. I subsided into a doorway, out of sight down the street, and finally relit my pipe.

In two or three hours, when the poor folk who keep the great city running began arriving by foot and by horse cart, I asked them until I found one who knew what that building was.

It was not one of the innumerable brownstone boardinghouses that make up most of New York residences.

It was, my grizzled informant stated in a broad American drawl, "The Episcopal Club of New York, sir, full of high churchmen and bishops and all."

Bishops and all. Kings and queens. And perhaps knights, and pawns, and rooks.

18
Spiderwebs

～◦⋉◦～

The spiders accumulate and the danseuse stamps. They appear in myriads—hairy monsters with five clawed feelers and nimble shakes—they 'crawl and sprattle' about the stage, invading the fringe of Milady's pettycoats . . . It is Lola versus the spiders.

—SAN FRANCISCO *WHIG*, 1853

At first I slept that night. Then I woke even before the streetlights had dimmed for the night. Fragments of my dreams still floated at the edges of the darkened room like ghosts at a séance. I saw the Woman in Black at the center of a huge sticky web, but her face was veiled. . . .

I saw, as if from the window of my room, masses of spiders scurrying through the streets of New York below. In the corner of my room, I glimpsed Quentin caught in silvery strands like pearls, or dew-jeweled webs. The spider-woman from the fringes was edging nearer in her black gown and showing the face of Nellie Bly! . . .

After such a parade of half-seen horrors, I could not sleep again to save my soul.

I quietly lit the paraffin lamp, then listened to judge if Irene had heard my stirrings in the next room. Apparently not. My clumsy attempt at stealth had been successful.

I was not so selfish that I wished another's sleep to be disturbed because I had lost the knack. And . . . I wanted to consider what kept me awake and what I could best do about it. I had long ago learned that the finest cure for any malady is useful occupation.

Unfortunately, most of my cords and crochet hooks were back in the cottage at Neuilly that we had all abandoned for a time to our caretaking French couple.

So I sat up against my pillows, twiddled my thumbs instead, and thought.

First, I could do nothing about Quentin's insistence on associating with our acquaintance Pink. He had told Irene and myself that his work for the British Foreign Office required him to come to this country and keep an eye on her. I had to agree that her promise to keep quiet on the recent Jack the Ripper matter, made to the governments of three nations, was a touchy thing. Still, as a foreign agent, Quentin's forte had been going "native" in the exotic eastern climes of India and Afghanistan. Playing nanny to a rash American daredevil reporter in a semicivilized modern city like New York must be quite a comedown for the poor man. As time passed, Pink's instinct to pursue a sensational story would overcome any sensible course to let the matter rest. Only one thing would distract her from the recent hunt through Europe: a new sensation on her own shores, something that fell into her own lap.

If I could provide such a *divertissement,* as the French say so prettily, Quentin would no longer be obliged to escort her about New York City.

Whether he would then choose to squire me about, I couldn't predict, but my greatest wish, and worry, was that he be free to leave Pink to her own devices.

It was, however, highly unlikely that I could produce a sensation sufficiently distracting for a girl who had committed herself to an insane asylum and a bordello before she was five-and-twenty, merely for the sake of a "story." True, shocking conditions needed exposing, but these modern "New Women" delighted in making themselves the centerpiece of their "crusades," and their social consciences came topped with a healthy serving of self-aggrandizement.

I know my limitations, and the sensational is the last thing I would have any skill at invoking, or provoking.

As I twisted in the fine bed linens, twiddling and plotting like a dreaded web-weaver myself, a truly ignoble thought sprang to mind like a pouncing spider.

It was so terribly ignoble that I cried a sharp "Oh!" aloud to myself, then clapped my hands over my traitorous mouth, hoping Irene hadn't heard. For Irene could never, never hear of this.

I slithered out of bed and tiptoed over to the bureau. From a drawer that I opened by careful quarter inches, I withdrew the small coded book Irene and I had unearthed at the very thoroughly late Madame Restell's house.

This prize Irene had not wanted Sherlock Holmes to have, but I much doubt he cared about illegitimate births among New York City society families more than thirty years ago.

I, on the other hand, had skimmed some of Miss Pink's "Nellie Bly" newspaper stories in the *World* since we had arrived here. She did not always write the "shocker" stories she was famed for, such as getting herself arrested and then reporting the unspeakable indignities suffered by women inmates.

She had recently also discussed her adventures riding a newfangled bicycle, and had visited the pugilist John L. Sullivan at his training camp to pester him with such impertinent (and trivial) questions as Do you take cold showers and How much money do you make?

(I must admit that I find pugilists fascinating for no reason I can name, although I have never confessed this to anyone and would be loath to think that I shared any interests in common with our Miss Pink. Other than Quentin, I suppose.)

At any rate, in following the journalistic adventures of our former associate, I'd noticed that she had recently been dispatched to the fashionable resorts of Newport and Narragansett as well as Bar Harbor and Saratoga Springs to report "the gay goings-on" of people whose money is their sole claim to fame.

Such place names meant little to me, save that they were patronized by the rich, apparently serving as the American equivalent of Bath. Surely Miss Pink would pursue a scandal among them . . . could I but find one, a nice juicy one involving persons long dead so no real harm could be done in the present. That would be the very thing to divert her from our affairs.

But first I must decipher this blasted book . . . or at least appear to. The paraffin lamp flickered in the darkness, barely lighting the pages of tangled letters and numbers squirming like worms on the cramped pages before me.

Irene had said I was clever with patterns. Could I be as clever at unweaving patterns?

I set to work with a will.

19

A Bookish Sortie

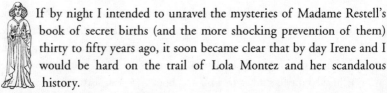

*Agosto Brentano, a Sicilian immigrant, had for years run
a newspaper stand in front of the New York Hotel.... After
amassing capital selling foreign and domestic papers, he branched into
books and play scripts, opening Brentano's Literary Emporium in
1876. It became a popular rendezvous for the theatrical elite.*
—GOTHAM: A HISTORY OF NEW YORK CITY TO 1898

If by night I intended to unravel the mysteries of Madame Restell's book of secret births (and the more shocking prevention of them) thirty to fifty years ago, it soon became clear that by day Irene and I would be hard on the trail of Lola Montez and her scandalous history.

I had at first supposed it spoke to Irene's moral sense that she was not so much searching for a forebear as being determined to prove this particular woman could not possibly be any relation to her. But, no, Irene was driven by other concerns.

This became clear when we hied the next day to the newsstands and bookshops at the "Rialto," the theatrical district clustered around Union and Madison Squares.

Mrs. Eliza Gilbert was completely unknown there, but Lola Montez was everywhere. At Brentano's Literary Emporium, a shop that stocked the London and Paris papers among many other foreign journals, we found the clerk ecstatic to guide us to the full complement of written material relating to Miss Montez. Or perhaps I should say, La Montez.

This young man, possessed of a snowy celluloid collar, shirtsleeves, and rather loud suspenders, radiated the incessant energy native to this large and exhausting city.

"Lola Montez? You have found a gold mine, ladies, speaking of which we also have many volumes about the Gold Rush of '49 in which she figures as a minor but always colorful character. And Brentano's Literary Emporium, with our situation in the heart of the theatrical district, has many actual play scripts for sale, including several relating to the acting career of the lady you mention."

"Really." Irene sounded as icy as a dowager duchess. "I didn't think she acted."

"Oh, in many plays, ma'am, including the one of her own life, which was most popular in the olden days." He stopped his patter long enough to regard Irene's expressionless face. "Oh, I see. You have been reading the critics! I fear we don't have newspapers old enough to contain reviews of Lola Montez on the stage, but the books quote lavishly from the journals of the day, and you will find all you need here at Brentano's, I promise you.

"Are you ladies planning to pen a volume on this most interesting lady?"

He looked expectantly from one to the other of us, and I suspect he found the same appalled, even revolted, expression on both of our faces.

Indefatigable, the young man shrugged. "Someone does a new one every five years or so, so there's lots to choose from. And we stock her own books, as well."

"She wrote books?" Irene sounded as incredulous as I felt.

"And volumes of letters to the newspapers, usually defending herself from what she called 'calumny.' My, they used forty-dollar words in the olden days. She was as fast on the draw with her pen as she was her riding crop."

"Why is America so enamored of this Lola Montez?" I asked.

"She did raise Cain everywhere she went, and we weren't so cosmopolitan back then," he explained. "Visiting celebrities from Europe always turned our heads. Why, when that poet fellow Oscar Wilde came through, I was just a boy, but I remember the whole country was in a stir about him from East to West."

"He was not from 'Europe.'" I adopted Irene's chilly tone. "He was from England. England is an island. It is *not* part of Europe."

"It's right close, ma'am, and Europe is a pretty big continent. What would England be otherwise, a barrier island?"

"One could only hope," I answered, "but unfortunately that was not enough to keep the French away in 1066."

He frowned prodigiously. "Are you speaking of an hour or a year, ma'am? Anyway, it's only ten years or so since Oscar burned a trail down Broadway, and I 'spect we'll be talking about him and his velvet knickers as long as we have gossiped about Lola and her riding whip."

I sighed. Heavily.

"We will take everything you have available on her," Irene said in a new tone that I can only describe as martyred.

He was off without a second glance. That is one thing that I both like and loathe about America: as long as you carry a reticule or a handbag you can enter any establishment and be taken quite seriously. Money tops birth and station.

A half hour later we left with our pocketbooks considerably lighter of paper bills and coins, but both arms burdened with common paper-wrapped parcels.

Irene's expression was grim. "We have our work cut out for us, the size of sailcloth, it appears."

"Don't worry, Irene." I balanced so many packages I needed my chin as a third hand to hold them together. "A woman this notorious could hardly have sneaked into variety theaters as the Woman in Black."

"One would hope. But there are veils. We must hail a cab."

"I have no hand, much less an arm free, and besides, they never pay attention to me."

"I have part of my right hand free," Irene said, waggling the gloved fingers in question over the top of a stack of wrapped books she also anchored with her chin.

One would think a gentleman would observe our quandary and offer assistance, but they all brushed by, as busy as newsboys with fresh editions to hawk.

Irene put two fingers in her mouth and used her operatic lungs to blow a whistle so loud and shrill that every cab within a hundred yards came to a halt.

One driver nosed closest to us first, and we leaned in to dump our parcels on the seat first, before stuffing ourselves in after.

The ride was spent rearranging the booty into portable piles. There was barely room for us to perch on the edge of the seat, but then there was barely time for us to rearrange ourselves before we were on Broadway again and at the Astor House Hotel entrance.

Irene probed her reticule. "I have nothing left to pay the driver."

At that moment our hack door swept open and brown packages tumbled out toward the doorman's feet. While I instructed him to fetch a boy to tote the things inside, Irene slipped into the lobby and withdrew some more cash from the hotel safe.

By the time the cab was emptied, she was back to press a generous dollar into the driver's grubby glove.

Our course was set: we would spend the next day or two sequestered with the literary legacy of Lola Montez, apparently the most notorious woman of the century.

For Irene, it was sure to be a lurid journey into the life and times of the woman who may have birthed her.

For me, it was a distasteful yet welcome opportunity to make sure that Irene remained as far as possible from Sherlock Holmes, the pretentious Vanderbilt "castle" on Fifth Avenue, and the body in a disgusting state of disrepair that she had spied on the billiard table within.

Ever since Irene had been consulted by Bram Stoker years ago about the drowned sailor on his dining room table, she had shown an unnatural curiosity about these ghoulish matters.

I had hoped the extremely gruesome trail of the Ripper she had followed last spring might possibly have sated this unbecoming curiosity, but I fear that Irene was not one to let convention stop her.

Already she had one characteristic in common with the despised Lola, not to mention smoking and a stage career. I could only pray that Irene's real mother had died on her birth-bed, or had been a consumptive and home-bound wife whose bereaved husband had been forced to give up his only daughter to those better equipped to handle an infant. Why those should turn out to be itinerant variety hall performers I have no idea, but stranger things have happened. In fact, had the Vanderbilt family not already figured in a matter involving the odious Sherlock Holmes, I would have been happy to applaud Irene's operatic hope that she was a lost heir to an American fortune. Being illegitimately born to a Captain of Industry had far more future than being illegitimately born to a Woman with a Past.

20
Spider Dancer

Our first feelings always remain our last memories.
—LOLA MONTEZ

How could I have dreamed that the hunt for Lola Montez among this landslide of paper would prove to be the most enjoyable time Irene and I spent in New York? Perhaps it only seems so in retrospect because of the cataclysmic events that came later.

But for this period—the lull before the storm—the intimidating telephone became our newest ally as we ordered first dinner, then breakfast and lunch, picnicking among a sea of books strewing the carpeting, the chair seats, the tabletop.

There was no help for it but to lounge on the rugs in our dressing gowns like schoolroom girls, each consuming cakes and fruit and wine and sarsparilla (a nonliquorous soda I was becoming quite fond of) along with great dollops of the impossible life of an impossible woman.

Irene, I'm happy to say, was always the first to quote aloud some unflattering bit, to the extent that despite myself I found it necessary to soften the damning picture that was assuming almost sentient life in our midst.

I was the readiest, however, to cast the first and most damning stone.

"Look here! She was *Irish,* Irene, not Spanish at all."

"Irish? Then she need not apply for the position of my mother." Irene made a face disavowing her previous words. "I'm sorry, Nell, but I find the

Irish a delightful and gritty people. That is no mark against her in my book. You'll have to search further."

"Aha! I have the source of the tombstone name; She was born Elizabeth Rosana Gilbert, but her mother always called her Eliza."

"That's odd. Why should she put that diminutive on her tombstone? This book says she hated her mother for planning to marry her off at age fourteen to a sixty-four-year-old major general who just happened to be her mother's husband's commanding officer. I'm afraid I'm solidly on young Eliza's side here. Her own mama was 'selling' her into marriage with her stepfather's superior officer."

"Such a marriage would have had assured Eliza status and security."

"Nell! Fourteen and sixty-four? Have you any notion what an unthinkable age difference that is? A child of fourteen—granted, a pretty, precocious child—to a man . . ." figures had never been Irene's strong point, so she counted on her fingers ". . . ten, twenty, thirty, forty . . . goodness, *fifty* years her senior? She would remain in her teens while he crept toward seventy! Most unnatural!"

"I suppose so," I said, but I was really as shocked as Irene by the notion of a girl so young wedding a man so old. "That is why she ran away with the young soldier."

"Even he was almost thirty, twice her age."

"She could not have married a fourteen-year-old!"

"Not unless she'd lived in the Middle Ages when noble children were betrothed from birth. You may not see the peril in such great age differences, but trust me, Nell, superior experience conveys power, and it is never good when a man has that much more knowledge and power than a woman."

"But don't they all?" I asked, thinking of Quentin, who was ever so much more worldly than myself, if not that much older, surely. Just how old *was* Quentin? I would have to find out.

"Amen," Irene said, "or at least that's the way too many of them would like to keep it."

"You sound like a suffragist."

"Not I. I have not half the courage."

"You? You are the bravest woman I have ever seen."

Her head shook. "I might contemplate a hunger strike in the right cause, but I could never face the force-feeding: that awful metal apparatus jammed down one's throat, the delicate tissues ripped and abraded raw, the vocal cords stretched . . . no, no, I could never do it."

"That is because safeguarding your throat has been a professional necessity since before you were twenty, although smoking those foul cigars and cigarettes certainly can't be good for it. In other matters, I am sure you would match a suffragist for nerve. Even Sherlock Holmes thinks you a wonder of audacity."

"He thinks I'm . . . audacious?" She sounded much too flattered for her own good. "How do you know, Nell?"

Oh, dear. I knew because I had peered into one of Dr. Watson's unpublished stories about his friend. This I could not admit, so I merely said, "Oh, he may have expressed some such sentiment when we were searching the dungeons for Godfrey and Bram Stoker."

"You found time *then* to pause to discuss my character?"

"Well, no, matters were rather . . . grave. Oh, I don't know, Irene. I probably just dreamed it. Look! I have found reference to Lola's marital quandary in her autobiography: 'So in flying from that marriage with ghastly and gouty old age, the child lost her mother, and gained what proved to be only the outside shell of a husband, who had neither a brain which she could respect, nor a heart which it was possible for her to love. Runaway matches, like runaway horses, are almost sure to end in a smash-up.' "

"She obviously wrote that passage from the other end of the telescope," Irene noted, "when that youthful act was seen small and wee from the vantage of middle age."

Irene was less interested in Lola's youthful escapades and more in her theatrical reputation. She was reading raptly again. "This is more like it. This is the creature I recall hearing about. Listen to this review of her appearance on the Paris Opéra stage, the foremost theater in France:

" 'Mlle. Lola Montez is a very beautiful person, who is endowed with a lovely figure and the most beautiful eyes in the world. . . . Unfortunately . . . Mlle. Lola Montez doesn't know how to dance; she doesn't know the first elements of choreography. Her figure and her eyes which she paraded before the auditorium with martial assurance did not disarm the spectators, who welcomed her with indulgence at her first dance, but who at her second hissed her with such vehemence that it determined the withdrawal of her name from the bills.' "

"How humiliating!" said I, who could no more imagine appearing on a stage than flying. "I could never have set toe to board again after such a publicly reported failure. Of course, the French are notoriously particular. What was this dance that they found so scandalous?"

"Something Lola made up, like much of her life history," Irene replied, paging through our collection of books with eager fingers. "Unbelievable gall. What a glorious fraud! What verve. What nerve! Listen to this, Nell: Before her debut as a dancer, she encountered no less a personage than the earl of Malmesbury on the train from Southampton to London. She represented herself as the widow of a Spanish Republican who had attempted to overthrow Queen Isabella the Second and had been promptly shot."

"Why should she want to pose as a traitor's wife?"

"Because all London was swooning over the young rebel who'd refused to flee to save his life. Lola claimed to be his penniless widow and ended up selling Spanish veils and fans at a benefit concert arranged for her at the earl's home. It was the earl who introduced Lola to the impresario of Her Majesty's Theater in London, where she would debut her Spider Dance, and the impresario, Lumley, who then introduced Lola to the London journalist who would serve as her herald."

"You're saying that because of the mere chance of sharing a train ride with an earl, Lola became the toast of London?"

" 'Mere chance' is but Act One in the game of life, Nell. It's what the enterprising spirit does with 'mere chance' that makes all the difference. It was 'mere chance' that we met on a London street, after all, and look what has come of that."

Luckily, Irene rushed on without giving me opportunity to answer.

"Do you realize that Lola was doing all this forty years ago! That she was indeed a political force? She didn't have to aspire to any intellectual life at all, but she was highly informed for a woman of her time. As for her dancing, it's clear she was judged against the tradition of ballet, when flamenco is a dance of the people. No wonder the critics didn't know what to make of her, so they tried to make a joke of her.

"Listen to this article describing how Lola was to 'introduce for the first time the Spanish dance to the English public.' "

" *This* member of the 'the English public' sees no need to be introduced to the Spanish dance at all."

Irene, however, had become so caught up in the report of Lola's debut that she leaped up and began to act out the words as she read them.

" 'The French *danseuse*,' " she declared, taking on the ripe voice of Sarah Bernhardt, " 'executes her *pas* with ze feet, ze legs, and ze hips alone.' "

"That already strikes me as a great deal more than is decent."

Irene was undeterred by my Greek chorus of objections, as ever.

" 'The Spaniard dances with the body, the lips, the eyes, the head, the neck, and with . . . the heart. Her dance is the history of a passion . . . "Lolah Montes" is a purely Spanish dancer. In person she is truly the Spanish woman— in style, she is emphatically the Spanish dancer. . . . The variety of passion which the Spider Dance embodies—the languor, the abandon, the love, the pride, the scorn—one of the steps which is called *death to the tarantula* and is a favorite *pas* of the country, is the very poetry of avenging contempt—it cannot be surpassed. The head lifted and thrown back, the flashing eye, the fierce and protruded foot which crushes the insect, make a subject for the painter which would scarcely be easy to forget.' "

Irene, having evoked all these motions and emotions, awaited my reaction. Or possibly my applause, although she should have known better.

"A person making those same movements in Shropshire would be judged as having fits and sent to a madhouse for life."

"Exactly why Shropshire doesn't have Her Majesty's Theater in its environs. But you miss the point, Nell. Lola was as Spanish as your left foot! It was all . . . a glorious fraud. Here's the prestigious London *Times*: 'grateful at last to have seen a Spanish dance by a Spaniard, executed after the Spanish fashion.' "

"I don't see that England had or has any need for either French *danseuses* or Spanish dancers."

"Or Irish frauds?" Irene asked impishly. "I may be an Irish fraud myself."

This quieted me. Irene was coming to relish rather than deplore the adventures of Lola Montez. I tried to compare the audacious young woman who had passed herself off as a Spanish heroine to the penniless young woman on her own who created scandal everywhere she went, yet had always spent freely for the good of others less fortunate, and had ended her days in the bosom of the Church (even if it was Episcopal; at least it was not Catholic!).

"And . . . Lola had always claimed that the Jesuits had slandered and persecuted her. I'm sure the Jesuits would have slandered and persecuted me, had they been aware of my existence, or I of theirs."

So. What was I to make of Lola, really? She had begun to matter to Irene. From the accounts of Lola's final illness, a certain Father Hawks had been deeply moved by her conversion in her last years.

What was I to make of her that she hadn't made of herself? I didn't know. I was used to knowing exactly what I thought about everything, but

Lola Montez had defeated me. She had crushed my inborn certainty under the drumming of her flashing feet, and, through the veil of the decades, had fixed her stunning blue eyes on my heart and head, daring me to dismiss her at my own peril.

Memoirs of a Dangerous Woman

California Dreaming

 San Francisco, a city of fifty thousand souls, was but four years old when I arrived. Anything was possible here for anyone. Buildings of brick and stone had sprouted like mushrooms. San Francisco's new American Theater held three thousand and they all had heard of the Countess of Landsfeld.

Despite not having a contract and having had to fire my manager (again) on arrival, I opened five days after as Lady Teazle in *The School for Scandal*. I knew the part and the resident company knew the play.

Seats went for the scandalous sum of five dollars apiece, five times the rate in the finest New York theatrical house. The box office collected almost five thousand dollars on my opening night alone. Truly California was a fairyland of instant riches, and the price to play in it was very high indeed.

While the company of the American Theater was learning my signature play, *Lola Montez in Bavaria,* I entertained audiences with *Yelva,* in which I played a mute Russian orphan, and with performances of my Spider Dance.

The California critics found my skirts lower and my art higher than had been anticipated, and my Bavarian play soon opened, an utter triumph. One critic went so far to say . . . now, where is that newspaper squib? . . . to say, "The play represents Lola as a coquettish, wayward, reckless woman, intent on good . . . but not the wily diplomatist, the able leader which she is represented in history. She counsels the King with all the enthusiasm of a Red Republican sophomore. . . . History pays her a higher compliment than her own play."

Ah, and isn't that how everyone wanted to see me? Flirting with revolution, dancing my way into dangerous diplomatic waters? Good history doesn't make good theater. Or good profits. *Lola Montez in Bavaria* made me $16,000 my first week at the American. And I made almost as many friends.

Viva California!

I tried to enlist my dear Miska, a charming violinist sponsored by P. T. Barnum at one time, into forming a company of solo acts to take to the smaller cities and mining camps where a full play couldn't be mounted. And to him I confided that I would marry the Patrick Hull, whom I'd met on the *Northern* en route here. (Some ungentle observers would comment that I tended to find new lovers or husbands on every voyage. Perhaps that's because I was never still enough on land to linger long with one man.)

"Why marry?" Miska asked. "You seem to have found the fountain of youth, stalling in high summer under the two glorious day-stars of your incomparable eyes. I would think no one man would match you."

"He is a fascinating fellow, dear Miska," I told him. "A big, roaring lion of an Irishman. He's handsome and he makes me laugh. In truth, I enjoy the company of men even if they are not material for love. Hull has made a Benjamin Franklin of me! He took me to the offices of the *San Francisco Whig and Commercial Advertiser* and taught me to set type. (I was later to amaze associates in New York by this skill.) I weary of constant travel. This sunset land of the West is more than holes of gold in the earth. I might settle here, have children. Don't laugh, Miska! The touring theatrical life won't always be for me."

I had arrived in San Francisco in early May. By July the marriage was made, a Catholic ceremony which began with me offering two vases of white silk roses to the Virgin. And so Maria Dolores Eliza Rosana Landsfeld Heald (as I had been styling myself after my second husband, George Heald, a handsome but weak young man under his spinster aunt's thumb) took a third husband and became Mrs. Hull. We celebrated at the reception with cake, wine, and cigars and cigarettes! We moved to the foothills of the Sierras in Grass Valley, which reminded me of the Himalayas as seen from Simla when I was a child in India and the lovely Alps of my beloved Bavaria. I could offer a child no better birthplace.

A pity it only lasted two months, but it soon became bitterly apparent, after he sold his newspaper, that Hull wished only to live on my money, and I was forced to throw him out. Divorce? I don't believe in it, and reverted to using the surname of my second husband, Heald, when I traveled incognito.

Of course I'd told Father Fontaine, the officiating priest at our marriage, that I was twenty-seven. (Although I didn't mention my undissolved youthful alliance with Lieutenant James. The laws of England might want to put me in legal limbo for eternity, but that marriage was long null and void in my head and heart, such ancient history!)

It would have never done to admit to thirty-two and exceed my bridegroom in age! Husbands may come and go, but these facts are put on record, after all. The newspapers do have an annoying habit of going back to look them up and keep track. Always so inquisitive about one's age, the newspapers. . . .

21

Pottering About

*I look forward with great pleasure to my return to N.Y., for it is the
only city in America where I prefer living....*

If someone had told me that I would one day journey to New York City
in search of my friend Irene Adler Norton's mother . . .

If that same someone had said that in the course of this inquiry I
would be obliged to call upon the Episcopal bishop of the city to ask
him about the most notorious woman in the world . . .

If that very individual had also asserted that the need to call upon the
bishop arose from information found in the "morgue" of a New York City
newspaper . . . well, I would have said I knew a liar three times over.

Alas, no one had warned me of these eventualities, so I had no one to
blame for this turn of events but myself, or perhaps my shameless companion
who would plot herself into any preposterous situation and carry it through on
sheer bravado.

We owed this one respectable call of our stay in New York to another expedition to visit the ogre of the *New York Herald*. He greeted our return to his
dingy subterranean domain with a sort of evil glee.

When Irene told him we sought news of a Bishop Potter of the Episcopal
Church in 1861, he led us down another confusion of aisles, cackling all the
way.

"A bishop you want now? That would be on the churchly aisle, all the denominations together, as they so seldom are in life. In the same pew, so to speak."

When we finally stopped, his mottled hand waved at a row that looked longer than the nave of a major cathedral. My heart sank, and then I sneezed.

"Bless you, ma'am. It's the paper dust. And all the weevils and spiders and that sort down here. Shouldn't wonder if you'd inhaled some dead spider legs. Paper is nasty stuff. The ink smudges and powders. The pages rot and crumble, you know, and attract vermin."

By now I was ready to retch as well as sneeze.

"Not a place for ladies, newspapers, not even in the offices upstairs. And especially not down here."

His voice had risen into the strident tone of an itinerant preacher admonishing a flock.

"The sooner we find what we need the sooner we will be gone," Irene said, and if a soft voice could turn away wrath, hers was warm honey.

"Suppose so. Watch yer hems, they'll be sweeping up mouse and rat droppings."

Thus warned, we were led to the middle of the aisle. "Lucky for you Potter has been a hallowed name hereabouts for thirty-five years; still is."

Our glances met as our hearts leaped up.

"So Bishop Potter is still the prelate here in New York," Irene said.

"Must be," our guide grumbled. "They is always writing about him in the paper."

He's alive, thank the Lord. That is the phrase that came unbidden into my mind. If we had to investigate the life, and death, of this troublesome woman, it would be luck indeed that an honored churchman could add a personal recollection to the lurid stories the newspapers had recorded.

Of course Bishop Potter may not have visited her deathbed personally, but from the accounts of her passing, an Episcopal priest, the reverend Francis Lister Hawks, had been beside her reading from the Good Book at the end. His account of her death brought tears to my eyes.

Irene had sniffed and said that deathbed conversions played well enough on the stage, but that she always mistrusted them in real life.

I do believe that, as much as Irene was mortified by a possible mother who was inept onstage, she was even more embarrassed by a penitent one.

"Here it is." Mr. Wheems pulled an actual file from the shelf. "You ladies know where the table is."

We didn't, not in this maze of glaring electric lights beaming down on us, creating shadows larger than ourselves.

Irene told him so, and he led us back to the rickety table we had used on our first visit. The dust we had left undisturbed still lay there.

This time we had clippings of articles to scan, all in a huge envelope marked "Potter, Bishop."

As soon as Mr. Wheems's departing shuffles had died to a whisper, Irene began drawing out leaves of yellowed paper from the large envelope. I showed my agreement with our guide about the lamentable condition of old newsprint by sneezing several more times.

Irene snatched the papers from my vicinity like a mother saving a child from a fire. "Here's my handkerchief. We don't want the ink to blur."

She sifted through the collection. "These are filed from the most recent dates to years back. Let's see . . . 'Bishop Potter Addresses Episcopalian Club. This spring. Henry Codman Potter Succeeds to Bishopric of New York City. . . .'"

"But that announcement is dated only two years ago!" She frowned and eyed me with astonishment.

"How could he be 'Bishop Potter' in the 1861 news report and be made 'Bishop Potter' in 1887? Instead of a cart before the horse that puts a bishop before a priest."

Irene was riffling back through more of the musty clippings. "Ah, here! 'Henry Codman Potter Consecrated Assistant to His Uncle Horatio Potter, Ailing Bishop of New York.'"

I couldn't believe the coincidence. "Irene, there are *two* Bishop Potters! Horatio must have been the bishop referred to in 1861. So now he's dead, and only two years ago. How unfortunate!"

Irene's toe tapped the rough brick floor, unmindful of any passing vermin she might be sending to their maker.

"Yes, *he's* dead. But the nephew might be aware of his uncle's . . . what do they call it in churchy circles, Nell? . . . his uncle's reign?"

"Your mind turns too much upon kings and worldly monarchs," I said. "Bishops are elected or appointed, so it would be called a term of office."

"Apparently his nephew was a shoo-in to replace him. Sounds mighty like a dynasty to me. Anyway, according to the newspaper stories, our man . . . the living Bishop Potter, that is . . . is something of a social reformer, a supporter of working men's clubs, missions, kindergartens, improved saloons."

I frowned at that last mention. "I don't see how saloons can be improved."

"Neither do I. They have served well as is for centuries."

"I meant that they were too debased to be improved."

"Well, apparently Lola Montez was not, to read the exceedingly treacly narrative of her last hours on earth." Her forefinger stabbed Bishop Potter's name in a current headline. "We shall have to call upon the good bishop."

"How? You can't just ring up and ask for an appointment for no reason."

"I shall have the best of reasons."

"Which is?"

"A donation to one of the bishop's pet projects. I wonder if the Magdalen Asylum is still operative. That would lead nicely into the subject of the late, lamented Lola, for she left a bequest to it."

"Irene, not only is this scheme dishonest and shabby but you would be required to make an actual donation."

She shrugged. "One must sacrifice for the greater good at times, and what else use is that lovely letter to the Rothschild agent in New York? I am sure the charming Mr. Belmont can arrange for my bank in Paris to cable authorization for a few hundred dollars here to New York."

"A few hundred dollars! Irene, that is an immense sum to pay for a chance of speaking to someone who perhaps remembers or more likely knows nothing of importance about Lola Montez."

She whisked the clippings back into their envelope. "It's for a good cause, Nell, in any event. And a paltry donation would not get us an audience with the bishop."

"Us! I will not be present while you hoodwink a prelate of the Church."

"Oh, don't be stuffy, Nell. He isn't even Anglican."

"He isn't?"

"No, they started out that way but now they've become completely Americanized, which is why they're called Episcopalians. It's not like they're Church of England."

"Oh."

"So you wouldn't be mocking the faith of your father, et cetera. Besides, our cause is good."

"What is it?"

Irene did not think long. "We wish to found a New Magdalen Society, inspired by the touching conversion of Lola Montez and . . . and the eloquent detective investigations of Miss Nellie Bly into the sore-tried lot of the working girls and the poor."

Her skirts swished back down the aisle as she returned the compendium of Bishops Potter I and II, to their shelf.

I remained nailed to the spot, contemplating how Irene had managed to transform herself into the fictional emissary for two such divergent persons as Lola Montez and Nellie Bly. It was utterly audacious. On this and this alone, Sherlock Holmes and I were in concord.

Only Irene, and only in New York.

22

An American Atrocity

A good while ago we gave you a tip to investigate Insane Asylum——you remember——and we suppose that 'Nellie Bly' is the result.
—NOTE TO JOSEPH PULITZER AFTER BLY WROTE AN EXPOSÉ OF
TEN DAYS SPENT IN A MADHOUSE

⊰FROM NELLIE BLY'S JOURNAL⊱

The Affair at Noll Cottage burst upon the New York scene on August 26 of the summer of 1889 like the Johnstown Flood. Unlike the flood of the preceding spring that leveled thousands, this was an intimate atrocity, but no less devastating.

I will never forget that date. By a stroke of good luck, the shocking event all the city talked about combined the boring society coverage I had been relegated to lately with the elements of the most thundering melodrama on view in the Rialto theatrical district.

A bloodstained dagger!

A wailing infant!

Two hysterical women!

A mistress, a wife, a betraying nursemaid, a socially eminent husband.

Of course the *World* reported every breathless detail.

Imagine a late summer luncheon at fashionable Noll Cottage in Atlantic

City. (Noll Cottage, of course, was as much a true "cottage" as the Vanderbilt, Du Pont, and Astor "cottages" in Newport, Rhode Island.)

The guests, men and women attired in the pale shades of late summer, are seating themselves at tables laid out in pastel summer linens, flowers everywhere.

Into this tranquil setting come, from above, a woman's hysterical screams and the crash of fine furnishings smashing to smithereens.

Below, the men in their beige summer suits, the women in their white silks and dimities, are pushing back their chairs, deserting the melon balls and cold cuts and ices to stand, looking upward.

A waiter is the only one to act.

He runs upstairs to the find the nursery is the source of the commotion, to find his employers struggling and bloody.

The husband: Robert Roy Hamilton, yes, those Hamiltons. Grandson of Alexander Hamilton, who himself died in a duel.

The wife: Eva, beautiful as all society wives are beautiful, blond hair disheveled, stabbing at everything within reach with a bloody dagger.

The infant: only six months, wailing and flailing on the bed.

And on the floor, the child's nursemaid: bloodied and unconscious.

Of course I was not allowed to cover a crime story, a front-page news story. I read of this event in the newspapers like everybody else. I was, however, perfectly free to find my own angle on it, and luckily, I'd already been investigating the general subject. I forgot all about Quentin Stanhope's quest to keep me quiet about the Ripper.

I was now on the trail of a true and native American sensation.

The facts baldly stated were scandalous enough. The lies and deceit that underlay them might take weeks to reveal and must be even more sensational.

The *World* laid every one of those facts bare in the following days, but by then I was following one strand in the web of lies: the infant on the bed was not Hamilton's own child, was not the supposed reason for his marrying Eva, his mistress of some time, and making an honest woman of one who previously had entertained in brothels for years.

The infant on the bed was, in fact it was later found, the *fourth* false offspring that Eva and her cohorts had palmed off on the befuddled Hamilton. The first infant had died, as had a replacement. A third didn't resemble the first enough to fool even Hamilton, who was apparently easy to dupe, so this last child had been installed in the Hamilton cradle.

Only the nurse had detected the several switches and had revealed the truth to Hamilton that serene August luncheon day. She had testified in front of his traitorous wife, who drew a dagger and attacked. (One does wonder how poor little Eva ended up accessorized by a dagger like some hot-tempered Spanish dancer. I would think such foresight would only occur to the redoubtable Irene Adler Norton.)

Yet Eva, I sensed, was not the mastermind of the trickery. I read it all in the *World,* far more fascinated by Eva's unsavory man "friend," Joshua Mann, and his so-called "mother," Mrs. T. Anna Swinton, who had produced the train of false infants.

This situation reminded me of one I had encountered before, involving a so-called Madame Restell, a midcentury New York abortionist who dabbled in such scandalous practices as contraception and placing society women's unwanted children in unrelated homes.

Madame Restell's doings and death was old news, twelve years old. Despite the sensational new information about her I'd learned through the New York investigations of Irene Adler Norton, I could make nothing newsworthy of it for today's readers.

The Hamilton case was another story. My story, did I but pursue it in my own special way. Undercover, of course.

I had a homemade sensation to track down before I conquered the rest of the world.

In print in the *World.*

Quentin Stanhope, who was as attractive as he was obstructive, would have to wait.

Or would he?

Perhaps I had found a way to make him pay for balking my best journalistic instincts, along with all his cohorts.

23

A Changed Woman

The greatest of all seems to be Lola Montez, who alone is able to keep up the applause and excitement which she created when she first appeared behind the reading desk of Hope Chapel. In fact, Lola seems to have beaten all her illustrious rivals clear out of the field.

—THE *NEW YORK HERALD* ON THE DAY'S LEADING LECTURERS,

INCLUDING HORACE GREELEY, 1859

Even Irene Adler could not conquer time and space.

It took a full two days before sufficient funds were cabled to the New York bank and we were granted an appointment with Bishop Potter, also thanks to the offices of Mr. Belmont.

"A good banker," Irene pronounced after initiating the procedures, "is worth his weight in watch chains."

"Especially when he is Baron de Rothschild himself," I commented tartly.

In fact, we had all of us been employed by the baron to investigate delicate matters across Europe. Godfrey was even now tending to the Rothschild interests in Bavaria.

Which reminded me . . . "Irene, there is another King Ludwig in Bavaria now. Is it like the Bishops Potter here?"

"A succession, yes. But I believe Ludwig the Second is a grandson of the notorious Ludwig the First of Lola Montez fame."

"Do you suppose Godfrey could find anything out about her on his end?"

"I'm sure he could, but I think that period of her life has been copiously documented in those many books in our possession. Also, I don't wish to interfere with Godfrey's business matters. That is a wife's worst mistake."

"If you *didn't* interfere, Godfrey would find it more disturbing than if you did."

"Tut, Nell. I trust I know how to keep our lives interesting by not insisting on overmuch collaboration. 'Absence makes the heart grow fonder' is not an adage for nothing. Of course I miss Godfrey dreadfully, and don't doubt his similar sentiments, but I also anticipate a most . . . refreshing reunion. Especially when I can share what I've learned about my origins, which will remake me to an extent in his eyes. It's important in life, as in acting on the stage, to be someone of whom others can eternally learn more. What Godfrey *doesn't* know about me and what I am doing at any given moment is infinitely more intriguing than what he does. That is always the way of it between men and women."

"Really?" I turned my speculations to another couple entirely.

"Now," Irene said, "we must go shopping."

"Why must we?"

"We have nothing suitable to wear when calling upon a bishop."

"But . . . all our money has gone into your 'donation.'"

"Not all," said Irene, donning her gloves and a mischievous smile. "I made sure that enough money was sent to last us a good long time here in the New World, as well as provide for any fresh emergencies on the scale of visiting a bishop."

I barely had time to stick a pin through my hat and catch up my gloves before she had swept out the door.

The Episcopal Club had been founded, Irene told me, for high churchmen. Women were seldom present, unless they were on the cleaning staff.

"Then why are we not dressed as maids?" I asked as our hired carriage jolted down Fifth Avenue.

"You saw the limitations of the role of maid for yourself just a few days ago: one may always be ordered out of the way. It is an ungrateful role on the stage and even more so in real life. I merely point out that this is an exclusively male compound we broach."

"That is nothing new to you, nor was it to Lola Montez, come to think of it. Her 'salons' often had only male guests, so she smoked cigars and drank wine with the best, and the worst, of them."

"That woman had a nerve, especially when you think her day was in the '40s and '50s. We will be among far more refined, and older, men. I merely warn you, Nell, that they may not know quite what to make of us."

"I must say that you have attired us like a pair of extremely rich temperance ladies."

Irene beamed at my praise, since I rarely gave it on matters of dress. I treated her like the prettiest child at a garden party: it would not do to comment on the charm of her face and gown, for then one would have a spoiled child.

"It was most difficult to come up with something suitably 'serious' during this frothy summer season." Irene brushed her dark puffed sleeves to attention. "A pity to spend so much money on such dull goods."

Dull goods! True, the colors were not as riotous as petunias, but in honor of this charitable outing, I had allowed Irene to attire me with the latest fashion. I was also perhaps thinking of the stylish Miss Bly with her exotic hats and eighteen-inch waist.

Irene had chosen a steel gray silk gown with full sleeves from shoulder to elbow. A black lace high collar and neckline was underlined by a thick, glittering rainfall of solid jet beads over the bosom. A diamond pattern of jet beads crisscrossed the skirt as if it were quilted, and she wore a broad-brimmed summer black straw hat surmounted with gray ostrich plumes.

I also wore summer black straw, but my plumes were green, as was my tailored riding-habit-styled gown. I was the more experimental of us two, for once; my gown had an upstanding white collar like a gentleman's, and a slim black satin tie. It struck me as a most businesslike ensemble, and I couldn't complain, or, rather, chose not to.

We descended from the hired carriage at a sober-fronted brownstone building that bore only a gilt number on the glass window above the door. Soon we were admitted by a butler as dignified as any MP. When the heavy door shut behind us, we were enveloped by an eerie hush. The constant street sounds faded as if sent to bed early.

"How may I assist you ladies?" the butler asked softly.

"We have," Irene said with equal discretion, "an appointment with Bishop Potter. I am Mrs. Norton and my companion is Miss Huxleigh."

He nodded and showed us into a front parlor.

As in the hall, the carpet here was maroon colored and heavy. Thick velvet curtains shut out both the light and noise of the avenue. Several small bronze lamps set around the room (no glaring electric lights!) wore stained-glass shades as exquisite as cathedral rose windows.

A painting of Christ in the Garden of Gethsemane was framed in gold on one brocaded wall, and a scent of candle wax wafted from somewhere not seen.

Irene arrayed herself on a black horsehair settee that gleamed like satin. Then she set her parasol ferrule into the deep carpet as if planting a lance outside a jousting tent. I couldn't help thinking of the Widow of Windsor. Irene resembled an extremely youthful and comely Queen Victoria sitting in state to greet her ministers.

Only this minister was a bishop.

It would be interesting to see how Irene, ordinarily as irreligious as a pagan child, would handle a prince of the Church. And vice versa. I occupied myself with removing the small pencil from my handsome silver chatelaine and producing my petite notebook from the pocket of my faux riding habit.

"Oh," I whispered to Irene. "I just remembered. She rode."

Irene darted me an alarmed but incomprehensible glance.

"Lola. She learned in India when she was a child. Rode like an Amazon, they said."

"Not a recommendation to me, who does not ride at all," Irene assured me.

As the door creaked preparatory to opening, we resumed our spine-stiff tea party postures.

A man on the weathered side of fifty entered, attired in a dark gray suit, with a circle of white collar at his neck. Only a trifle of gray threaded his hair, and the wrinkles on his face were the sort left by smiles rather than frowns.

"How good to see you," he said. "Mrs. Norton?"

Irene nodded and smiled. He then turned to me. "And Miss Huxleigh. May I offer some refreshment?"

"Tea would be wonderful," I said.

"Alas, Miss Huxleigh, we are a morning-coffee and afternoon-sherry-drinking set." Amazingly, he must have detected my slight moue at the mention of sherry, for he next offered "Lemonade? And ginger snaps. We have very fine ginger snaps."

I didn't know what ginger snaps were (they sounded rather aggressive), but this unassuming bishop seemed so pleased to offer them that I knew I would have to consume at least one to be polite. Being polite is a burden that I find harder to justify as I get older.

The bishop seated himself on a tapestry-upholstered armchair under the familiar image of Our Lord on his knees by the altar of a large rock. This presented an uneasy contrast between the roots of religious belief and the modern-day ease of following it.

"I understand," he said, "that you are the source of a generous donation, Mrs. Norton."

"The generosity is all yours," Irene answered. "My donation is not so grand as to merit an appointment, I know, but I sought some information in turn, if I may put it so bluntly."

"Feel free to put it any way you like. You would be amazed at what strings come attached to donations."

"Mine is not a string, Bishop Potter, but a mere thread. We . . . I . . . had thought to support a Magdalen refuge, but then wondered if such a thing still existed."

"It does, though not by that name any longer, which was found in more recent times to be a bit prejudicial. Is there some reason you wish to support this particular institution?"

Irene allowed her gloved hands to fidget with the closure on her reticule. Nerves were unknown to every fiber of her being, at least visibly, but she found it useful to ape the mannerisms of less doughty sisters on certain social occasions. Worming information out of unsuspecting bishops was one of those occasions.

"I am on a quest to discover who my mother might have been, and it's possible that she was a Mrs. Eliza Gilbert."

The bishop started slightly, which I took for a hopeful sign.

Irene was no less observant than I. "You know that name? I confess that I didn't, at first."

The bishop turned (with relief?) as a serving maid entered with a silver tray.

In moments she was filling tall frosted glasses with lemonade. The bishop declined one, but given the warm day outside and the heavy draperies swathing the windows, the room was a bit stifling so I accepted.

"Most refreshing," Irene said, setting down her glass with a final gesture after taking a first sip. "I am right in suspecting that you are familiar with the name of Eliza Gilbert?"

"Indeed." The bishop folded his arms and smiled ruefully. "In fact I heard it again after a long while only a few weeks ago. How did you arrive at the notion that this Mrs. Gilbert was your mother?"

"First," said Irene, "you must understand that no mother reared me. I had in fact become quite accustomed to the idea that I not only had no mother but no chance of learning to whom I had been born, when a rather noted New Yorker known as Nellie Bly cabled me in Paris that she thought she might know who my mother was. After much investigation, it was suggested to me that the apparent candidate can be found under a tombstone in Green-Wood Cemetery under the name of Eliza Gilbert."

"*Mrs.* Eliza Gilbert," I put in. It would not do for a churchman to think needlessly that Irene was less than a legal offspring.

Bishop Potter nodded thoughtfully. "If you know of the Magdalen Asylum, then you know of the other name this woman went by, shall I say?"

"Lola Montez." Irene let the name roll off her tongue like a fanfare.

"It is 'Mrs. Norton?' " he said, leaning in.

"Yes."

"You are married."

"Indeed. To an English barrister living abroad. Quite respectably."

I saw her fairly bite her tongue to keep from adding that this was the only respectable thing about her.

"A barrister." His repetition implied approval. "Perhaps your barrister husband, Mrs. Norton, were he here, would urge you to forgo this search for a never-known mother. It is hard to be an orphan. It may be even harder to be the daughter of a woman as internationally notorious as Lola Montez."

"A mother," Irene said, quite reversing her opinion of weeks ago, or perhaps merely pretending to, "is a mother, and worth knowing about."

The bishop regarded her intently for moments that quickly became awkward.

"You are a remarkably beautiful woman, Mrs. Norton. So was Lola Montez. I can detect no resemblance."

"You saw her, then?" Irene sat forward eagerly.

"And heard her."

"Heard her? She danced, not sang."

"When she lived in New York in the late '50s—this became her home city in what would be the last few years of her life—she no longer danced. But she did lecture, and quite impressively. I was just a young man, freshly ordained and freshly rector of a Pennsylvania church. I had been elected provincial bishop of New York, so I came to the city occasionally. I admit that I publicly objected to a woman of her reputation lecturing at Hope Chapel, but I was won over completely when Miss Lola Montez's lecture on the Catholic Church caught my eye and I attended. She was quite incensed about my previous position on her, but forgave me, and the lecture was held in the Episcopal Church."

"I understand her dancing was laughable."

"I can only speak to her elocution, Mrs. Norton. She spoke eloquently enough to give a preacher a blush of envy. Her health had not yet begun to fail, at least visibly, and she utterly commanded the podium and that audience. I recall a slender figure with curling dark hair gathered behind her ears, expressive features, and the most unworldly dark blue eyes that radiated light and life. I was, I admit, far more captivated than a cleric should have been."

Irene frowned. This was not the image of Lola Montez the books had painted, although we had not read our way through all of them.

"Your eyes," the bishop pointed out, "are quite lively and vivid as well, but are decidedly brown."

"There was a father involved in the process of my being here," Irene said.

"Are you searching for his identity, is that it? You expect some inheritance perhaps?"

"No. I prefer to owe nothing to any man."

The bishop's eyebrow's lifted with surprise and a bit of personal insult.

"But of course I realize that the assistance of men in the business of this world is invaluable." Irene's most winning smile immediately won over the bishop again. "I am amazed that you found Lola Montez so substantial. I expected, frankly, to trace the path of a trivial, shallow woman given to impetuous affairs and fits of childish temper."

"She spoke well and made good sense, what can I say? That's why I've never quite believed the reports of her excesses. They seem more scandal-ridden than one woman could amass in one fairly brief lifetime, for she was not forty when she died."

"The tombstone," I interjected, "indicated she was forty-two."

"It was wrong, Miss Huxleigh. Father Hawks attended her and fussed mightily about the error. You see how even the most trivial facts can be engraved for eternity. I am no apologist for Lola Montez," he said, turning to Irene again, "but from what I saw of her, once, on a lecture stage, when I was a callow youth of twenty-seven, you should not be ashamed to call her mother."

Irene was stunned. It was as if the bishop had spoken to some hidden fear she had not expressed even to herself.

"Of course . . ." The bishop repressed a smile of recollection. "My uncle regrettably objected to her speaking at the Church of the Good Shepherd, despite my support of the idea, and she was most exercised with indignation at that turn of events. However, when she was mortally ill two years later, it did not stop her in the least from seeking solace from Father Hawks, and she died a member in good standing of the Episcopal Church. Even my uncle was touched by her passing."

"Would you have forbidden her that pulpit if you had been bishop then?"

He gave the question a good minute's consideration. "Probably. The papers can be scurrilous, and one must consider the reputation of the Church. We could welcome her as a member, but not as a cause célèbre, hmmm?"

"And some say the churches are hypocritical."

"You have a bit of fire and brimstone about you also, Mrs. Norton. Let us call it politics rather than hypocrisy."

"You are in good company then. But I don't wish to argue with what happened thirty years ago, I wish to understand it. Do you think it possible she had a child no one knew about, in '58, say?"

"She traveled a good deal, had spent several years in California, then went to and fro from Europe and Australia. Women have their ways of concealing these things. It's possible. Yet she made no mention, no provision, on her deathbed."

"I know. She left twelve hundred dollars—"

"Not a mean sum in those days."

"I know. All of it to charity and the Church. None to her mother."

"It was not a happy connection from very early, I understand."

"None to any of the reputed men in her life."

"None survived her, except her first husband, Lieutenant James, who was utterly estranged. He not only charged her with adultery after they separated but when he sued her for divorce later, he ensured that neither of them was allowed to remarry. Ever. Father Hawks dutifully inquired, you see, who might be her heir, but her first husband obviously had no claims on her. Father Hawks was loath to let her leave all to the Church without due consideration."

"And you know this for a fact?"

"We have talked about it, Father Hawks and I, and . . . I was much taken with her lecture. When she was shortly after leveled by a stroke, I took a personal interest."

This time Irene lifted skeptical eyebrows.

"It shook me. That vibrant personality I witnessed at the lecture podium so soon having that wonderful voice stilled, those expressive limbs fettered, that mind imprisoned. I was young. I didn't yet know the bitter paradoxes of life and death."

"I am strangely impressed by how much she impressed you in so short a time, Bishop. It is not what I expected to learn of her."

"We none of us are always what we are expected to be, I hope."

"No. Not even bishops."

He hesitated before speaking again. "I don't wish to mislead you. She herself felt she had sinned much. Her last few years were spent in good works, and her penitence as death neared so touched Father Hawks that he, well, as he aged he became a bit undone by it."

"What do you mean?"

"He has the notion that her religious repentance at the end was almost . . . saintly."

"St. Lola?!"

"Exactly. You have it, Mrs. Norton. You've heard how even to this day her evil reputation follows her. Almost no one knows of her last months, of her honest religious fervor. So I told Father Hawks, but he was adamant not only on the genuineness of her conversion but insisted that she had amassed jewels from her many admirers that she intended to leave to the Church. He believed they had been stolen after her stroke, and hidden by those greedy enough to counter a dying woman's last wishes. These twin convictions, her saintliness and her lost jewels, became a mania with the poor soul, particularly after age forced him to retire from active service."

"He is alive?" Irene was standing, no longer bothering to soften her commanding personality, blazing like some avenging angel herself.

"Well, yes. Quite elderly, even tetched a bit perhaps, but . . . yes. He was here last week, pestering the members about her beatification, querying them about those people who took her in during her last illness."

"I must see him, meet with him."

"Certainly." Her conviction had drawn the bishop to his feet as well, and he turned to delve in the top drawer of a nearby desk. "Here is his carte de visite, which we clergy leave with congregation members."

I crowded over Irene's shoulder to view the simple rectangle of white the bishop had handed her.

How newfangled everything was becoming. This card included a photograph of its bearer as well as an address and a telephone number for the club.

Irene wove slightly on her feet. I felt it because I stood so close to her. Her face had gone as white as the paper of the carte de visite.

"Thank you, Bishop," she murmured. "This is a most valuable referral. Now we must . . ."

"Go," I said, taking her firmly by the elbow. "Thank you for your courtesy and the, er, ginger snaps."

I led her out of the chamber and down the short hallway to the door. Once we stood at the top of the usual flight of steps, breathing the warm, heavy air of late summer in the city, she shook me off.

"What is the matter, Irene? You looked as if you had seen a ghost."

"I had, Nell, most unfortunately."

"Unfortunate for the ghost, I presume."

"For him, and for our quest." She glanced at me, totally restored to her usual sardonic metal. "And for your peace of mind, I fear. Father Hawks is the poor tortured shell of a man whose body I saw on the Vanderbilt billiard table, with Sherlock Holmes himself in attendance."

"No!"

"Yes. How dreadfully distressing. I'm afraid, in good conscience, we must let Mr. Holmes know immediately. Get a grip on yourself, Nell! You don't wish to swoon at the top of a flight of stairs, not with all the summertime offal of the city of New York awaiting you at the bottom. And while wearing your brand-new ready-made ensemble from B. Altman's. Before Quentin has seen you in it."

Sometimes Irene could outdo a long sniff of smelling salts for bracing effect.

24

Missed Fortune

~~~

"You do realize, Nell, the key piece of information Bishop Potter revealed among the cornucopia of possibilities he presented?"

"Besides the utterly odious fact that the dead man in Mr. Vanderbilt's billiard room was poor Father Hawks?"

"Yes, besides that. And I believe that your use of the extreme
expression 'utterly odious' refers more to the fact that Sherlock Holmes was
present at that scene than to the inhumane condition of Father Hawks's
body."

I held my tongue for a count of twenty before I spoke again. (Conversing
with Irene always took more self-control on my part than with anyone else on
the planet.)

"From our selfish point of view," I admitted, "it's extremely frustrating
that the one man who could shed light on your possible mother's last weeks on
earth has died just one step ahead of us."

"That fact is frustrating, yes, but it also is highly suggestive, and, I must say, extremely sinister."

"I do not like you to use that word."

"Which word? Suggestive?"

"Sinister. You know that you can't resist the sinister."

Irene was lounging on the sofa, a wisp of smoke from the little cigar in her serpent-wrapped mother-of-pearl holder haloing her pompadour, looking like a femme fatale in the Sarah Bernhardt School.

"Blame it on my theatrical upbringing," she said. "You haven't mentioned the key fact we learned, beyond the obvious shock regarding the identity of the victim on the billiard table. Poor Mr. Holmes! I doubt he has a prayer of tracing that ravaged shell to Father Francis Lister Hawks."

"He has proven himself quite the match for you in previous encounters."

"No need to speak so sharply, Nell. I realize you don't want me getting ahead of myself. You know, this game of one-up really doesn't matter. Stopping these criminals is what the true 'game' is about, and this is a particularly gruesome and confounding one."

I took a deep breath. "I find it most provocative that Father Hawks was proposing sainthood for the late Eliza Gilbert. It strikes me that any sensible prince of the Church might commit any number of sins to prevent that outrageous notion from even becoming public knowledge, much less being acted upon."

" 'St. Lola' does have a gloriously contradictory ring. I can quite envision a play of her life. It would be a stunning role, to say the least."

"There *is* a play of her life; she wrote it and performed in it."

"But the last, most poignant act was missing. Also any mention of issue, such as myself." Irene bestirred herself to extinguish the cigarette, then shook her head. "You're quite right, Nell, that a churchly body might recoil from attempts to establish a world-famous sinner as an inspiring example of eleventh-hour salvation. Still, I doubt today's hierarchy would resort to such medieval solutions for disagreements in doctrine as torture and murder."

"Who better?" I put in, "especially as the Catholics may be involved, given Lola's loathing of the Jesuits. I must say that I do find her sensible in that one regard. You do recall the Inquisition?"

"I also recall the witch hunts. They were a nondenominational persecution, you will admit."

I nodded as I shivered in my summer weight gown. "This death at the Vanderbilt house sounds that medieval."

"And it smacks of the churchly," she admitted at last, sitting back again. "I must take credit for pointing out to Mr. Holmes that the body bore the marks of crucifixion. However, the key fact for me yesterday was Bishop Potter mentioning that Father Hawks believed Lola Montez had been robbed of her jewels. From what little we read, they were plentiful and spectacular. Even as early as the mid-'40s, she traveled with one entire trunk holding her 'capital' and jewels. And that was before King Ludwig lavished more gems upon her. One does wonder what has become of them. Wealth is a more universal motive for misdeeds nowadays than religious differences."

"And if you really are her daughter, her only daughter, you would be the natural heir of such wealth."

"Two large 'ifs,' Nell. While I am never one to scorn rightful endowments, I'm far more concerned about the jewels and what religious opinions of a long-dead adventuress would lead to the death of a humble retired priest in New York City this summer."

"Obviously, he knew something others killed him to keep anyone from finding out."

"No . . . I'm afraid someone killed him to find out *what* he knew, specifically. I suspect his death was accidental, in that such brutal treatment of one his age had an unexpected result. Not that his tormentor, or tormentors, would have freed him afterward anyway."

"What difference does it make? His death was horrible beyond imagining. I wish we could go home and forget about it."

"So do I, Nell." Irene stood and went to the window overlooking Broadway. "I can't believe that in this day and age someone would so abuse an old man, or any human soul. But, then, we had ample evidence in Paris of what still goes on, this globe over, that one would think had been eradicated from the earth with the Huns. That's why I shall have to let Sherlock Holmes know of this development."

"I knew it! Any excuse to intrude on his investigation."

"*Our* investigation has intruded for us. And I'm not willing to let Father Hawk's death go unsolved or unpunished, are you?"

"No, of course not. I merely . . . dislike that man."

Irene left the window and came to me. "Nell, you are loyal beyond belief, but you must forget the minor role he played in the King of Bohemia's pursuit of me two years ago. You yourself remained in St. John's Wood to 'welcome' the hunting party after Godfrey and I had made our predawn escape. You yourself reported what the king, Mr. Holmes, and Dr. Watson said. You admit that Mr. Holmes obviously regretted working for the king. By your account, he even rejected a costly jewel in exchange for the portrait of myself I'd left as a memento for the king."

"Yes, but have you ever thought why he did so, Irene?"

Bemusement was not a common expression with her, but I had evoked it now. "Why, to express his contempt for the king, of course. After all, I'd left my portrait in exchange for the formal photograph of the king and myself posed together, which Willie was so anxious to reclaim. How indiscreet of him to allow me to wear the Crown Jewels, even for a private occasion, when he had never intended to marry me. I've seen enough of Mr. Holmes to know that he doesn't suffer fools gladly."

"Irene, he was the fool! He refused a huge emerald-and-gold ring and accepted only your portrait instead!"

She thought for a bit, then wrinkled her nose. "I should have done the same. King Willie has rather Teutonic taste. Emeralds are often flawed and quite fragile and, I think, too gaudy for the well-tailored man, especially an Englishman and a no-nonsense Englishman like Mr. Holmes. I myself prefer sapphires and rubies, as a matter of fact. Perhaps Mr. Holmes does too."

"Irene, you are being deliberately obtuse."

"Thank you, Nell, for implying I have to make an effort to be obtuse."

She was smiling as she sat beside me and took my hand, a gesture rare between us, perhaps more because of my natural reserve than hers.

"My dear, dear Nell. I know what you fear, and must say that you have been too good a student of the fears instilled in women rather than the freedoms available to them."

"Women have no freedoms," I objected without thinking.

"Exactly. Not unless they take them. I learned early that some unknown fairy godmother—perhaps even Lola Montez, who knows?—had bestowed upon me the curse and the blessing of a comely face. I am well aware of the effect it has on people. With strangers it may grant me a wider berth and some small favors. With those I associate with more closely, it has brought me envy from many women, and false regard from many men. It has brought me more tears than smiles, because I have not known whom to trust. As you saw in Bohemia."

I gazed at her, and swallowed.

"I tell you that if Mr. Holmes holds any special regard for me, it is not because of my face or form. He is simply not a man to be swayed by such sur-face considerations."

"He is a man," I argued.

"He is a man of the mind, first and foremost, and that sort of admiration I will accept gladly. You mustn't worry, Nell." She shook my hand with a fond, governesslike admonition I well recognized. "I am not susceptible to admirers, even ones who treasure my brain rather than my beauty. It's you I worry about."

"Me?"

"You are susceptible to hasty judgments that spring from fear. It's not your fault. It's how you were born and bred to be. But, have faith, Nell! The world will not bite you, and if it does, my goodness, you can always bite it back!"

"I can?"

"Indeed, and you have already taken a nip or two out of it on occasion. You must relish the chance to dance near your fears, for that's how you conquer them."

"So nothing I can say or do will keep you from bearing the tale of Father Hawks's identity directly to Sherlock Holmes?"

"No. It is the right thing, the only thing, to do."

There was such conviction in her tone, and a mute echo of agreement in my heart, that I argued no more.

25
A Footnote to a Foolish Time

_{∿∾}

On arriving in this country she found that the same terrible power which had pursued her in Europe . . . held even here the means to fill the American press with a thousand anecdotes and rumors. Among other things, she had had the honor of horsewhipping hundreds of men whom she never knew, and never saw. But there is one comfort in all these falsehoods, which is, that these men very likely would have deserved horsewhipping, if she had only known them.

—LOLA MONTEZ, *AUTOBIOGRAPHY*, 1858

 Irene's note of that very afternoon was returned by evening.

"Tea at four P.M. You know my location."

I studied the unadorned black penmanship. "No salutation, no polite phrases. It could be a telegram. He didn't even bother to sign it."

"I'm sure," Irene said over my shoulder, "he is more used to telegrams than notes."

"It doesn't even indicate if we are to meet him in the hotel dining room or . . . elsewhere."

"Tea will be served in his rooms. He would not care to have us overheard."

"What did you say in your note?

She smiled and stood in the middle of the room, hands clasped before her, while she recited like a schoolgirl: " 'Dear Mr. Holmes. Miss Huxleigh and myself have learned some shocking information relating to the Vanderbilt incident that we felt obliged to convey to you at your earliest convenience. Most sincerely yours, Irene Adler Norton.'"

She eyed me. "Was that proper form, Nell?"

"Far too genteel for the likes of a consulting detective. Do we really want to discuss this gruesome news over tea?"

"Mr. Holmes was no doubt thinking that you would be missing that lovely English habit in New York."

I snorted, rude as such a thing was. Obviously I'd spent too long in America already. "Mr. Holmes would no more think of my entertainment than of the man in the moon's."

Irene shrugged. "I did make it plain that you were a party to the meeting."

"And must we wait until tomorrow afternoon? The matter seems more urgent than that."

"Mr. Holmes may be attending to urgent matters on other fronts. I imagine he has a far harder task than we do in tracking the past of Lola Montez."

"How so?" I was unwilling to grant *the* man any quarter.

"We trace but one woman, and a woman who cut an incredibly wide swath through her times and climes. He must unravel the entire Vanderbilt family. The founding father, called the Commodore, though he was no such thing, had twelve children, Nell, ten of whom lived. Can you imagine the next generation, of which Mr. Willie Vanderbilt is the prime heir? And the number of their offspring? Quite a tangle, I'm thinking."

"Gracious! American millionaires are as zealous about making families as making money, it seems."

"When I was living in New York years ago, I remember much public speculation on how the Commodore would divide his millions. He had just died as I left for England and he was lamentably unimaginative about the process."

"How so?"

"He left the bulk to his eldest surviving son, who did likewise. There was enough that the other offspring did not fare badly, but hard feelings might have resulted. So there's a surfeit of heirs, some of whom might be disgruntled."

"Not to mention," I added, "*unsuspected* heirs of the sort in Madame Restell's little book. Do we tell Mr. Holmes about that, by the way?"

"No." Irene snapped out the answer. "I don't want him delving any further than necessary into that particular part of my own history."

"But he might be ever so much better than I at deciphering codes and such."

"Do not play the disingenuous miss with me, Nell. I visit Mr. Holmes from a sense of duty in the matter of the identity of the dead man found on Vanderbilt's billiard table, not to make his investigation, whatever it is in the larger picture, easier."

I was well satisfied. The book would stay in my hands, along with its secrets, and along with the possibility of my using it to deflect Pink from prolonging any contact with Quentin Stanhope. It might be Quentin's duty to "ride herd" on Nellie Bly's discretion, but it wasn't mine. Anything I could do to extricate him from her was to the good. One might interpret my desires as selfish and beneath me. Or one might interpret them as assisting a friend in discharging a tiresome obligation that kept him tied to the New World and a bossy, difficult stunt reporter, when he longed to be . . . in the Old World, pursuing life in the mysterious East.

We presented ourselves at the hotel at quarter to four, then made our way by elevator to the floor where Mr. Holmes had rooms.

It was our second visit to his headquarters here in New York, and likewise his second opportunity to serve as host.

I mused on Godfrey's annoying absence at the opposite side of the world. Surely bucolic Bavaria could not have matters so absorbing that he must remain there for more endless weeks? Then again, I recalled the revolution of 1848, some say caused by La Lola. That resulted in poor King Ludwig abdicating his throne in favor of a son who soon died, leaving his grandson in his place, his decidedly odd grandson. Not that Ludwig himself was not decidedly odd, with his portrait hall of great beauties and his passionate, so-called platonic, two-year association with Lola that nearly cost both of their lives.

"We are here, Nell."

I was startled to look up and see Irene's parasol handle poised after rapping on the closed door before us. I dimly remembered the sound.

"Whatever were you daydreaming of?" she asked. "You didn't even make a fuss about the elevator."

"Oh, a woman with a past."

"Not myself, I hope."

"Not you. You have the most elusive past of anyone I know."

The door opened suddenly it seemed, filled with far too much of Mr. Sherlock Holmes: tall, dapper in his careless yet precise way, examining us as a hawk would a pair of peahens.

"Ladies." He stepped back to allow us entry.

A round table near the window already bore a tea tray.

"Oh," I said, "I hope the water is still hot."

"The hotel has learned to deliver it scalding," he said, doing us the courtesy of pulling out first one chair and then the other over the heavy carpet.

Irene ignored the first chair and sat in the position with her back to the window. "I have seen enough of Fifth Avenue this trip," she murmured.

I took the chair offered, and Mr. Holmes settled next to me, looking amused.

"Perhaps," he told Irene, "you have tired of having the footlights in your face."

I immediately did what I did best: began tinkering with the tea things so that we should each have a cup of properly prepared tea as soon as possible.

I remembered that Mr. Holmes took nothing in it. In some ways he was a perfect monk. Irene abjured milk but liked lemon. I took mine with milk but not sugar.

While I was dispensing my domestic duties, Irene helped herself to some of these hard, crumbly, indigestible American biscuits.

Mr. Holmes and I refrained, which left him free to speak.

"Your note was most provocative."

"So I intended," Irene said. "I have it on good authority from Brigid, lately the Vanderbilt housemaid, that there can be no question about the identity of the man on the billiard table."

"The devil you say!"

He had leaped up like Punch in a park puppet show.

"I take it you had not yet determined his name or state in life?" Irene sipped tea in a missish way most unlike herself. She was toying with him.

"Not a bit," Mr. Holmes admitted, pacing as if two ladies were not sitting at tea but three feet away. "The case is aggravatingly unmotivated, a form of blackmail and intimidation without any clearly stated ransom. The perpetrators believe that the victim understands the import of this death."

"And Mr. Vanderbilt doesn't?"

"Nor do any of his household." He stopped to regard Irene sternly. "How do you come by this so-called knowledge?"

"By accident," I put in, "believe me. If Irene were not troubled by a most admirable sense of obligation, we should not be here."

"Obligation?" His gray eyes were all steely interrogation.

"I intruded myself into the house and thereby saw the murdered man," Irene said. "How can I rest content to leave him there unnamed, unmourned, when I know who he was?"

She reached into her reticule and extracted the carte de visite. "I saw his features in a dreadful flash. They will never fade, even as disfigured as they were." She laid the card faceup on the tablecloth and pushed it toward Mr. Holmes.

He regarded its slow approach much as Messalina the mongoose would watch a garden snake slithering into her range of combat.

He snatched it up as quickly as Messy at her most lethal. "'Father Francis Lister Hawks.' How did you come by this?"

I had to say, with some niggling bit of smugness, "We received it from the Episcopal bishop of New York, whom we visited yesterday."

"Why?"

I glanced, penitent, at Irene. She may not have wished Mr. Holmes to know our source. My moment of lording it over him was dear-bought.

She, however, appeared unflappable, a vestige of her stage career that was most useful in real life, even if often it was only a pose.

"I had a donation to offer for a good cause," she answered piously, taking my lead.

By now Mr. Holmes was tapping the card on his opposite thumb.

"Come now," he said, "you can't expect me to believe you would cross the Atlantic to make donations to churchmen you had never seen nor heard of before. You must have been—"

"Ah, caught out," she cried in mockery. "We were, of course, following the trail you set us upon. Which makes one wonder, has that path always been as useful to you as to me?"

"No." He paced again and when he turned the full light of day bared his features. He was exactly where Irene had wished him to be: surprised and in no position to conceal it.

"I had hoped, if I may speak bluntly to ladies who have insisted in the past that they need not be spared the harsher realities—"

"Go on, Mr. Holmes," Irene said, "but, pray, when have you ever not been blunt?"

"I had hoped," and his tone showed that hope was now as dead as Father

Hawks, "that the search for your ancestress would permit me the freedom of the city in any matters that I'm investigating."

"That is why you bothered to wave the name of Mrs. Eliza Gilbert at us in Green-Wood Cemetery. You had hoped we'd go on a wild-goose chase for this figment of a woman buried under a name she never bore in life. Did you know then who she really was?"

"Of course. She wouldn't have made a good diversion if there weren't grounds for her to be the Woman in Black. I saw Professor Marvel's wall of beauties when I investigated the previous case."

"You really think that Montez woman was my mother?"

"There is small resemblance, but stranger things have happened. My brother, Mycroft, and myself are seldom taken for brothers, for instance."

This made me madly speculate how his mysterious brother—the man Quentin had said *was* the Foreign Office—differed from him. Was Mycroft Holmes short? Stout? Fair? With a beard and mustache?

Irene was not so easily diverted. "That was not kind of you, Mr. Holmes, to toy with a woman's search for her mother."

"Kind is not what you expect from me."

"I didn't think I expected anything from you."

"But you do." He smiled. "And right now you expect the 'passkey' of this card to buy you information about how this man came to be on the Vanderbilt billiard table. I'm afraid I can't tell you."

"Won't tell me."

"Can't. And wouldn't if I could. This case is confidential."

"You don't believe that Lola Montez could be at the bottom of it?"

"Ha! The stage has lost a playwright as well as a performer, I see." He laughed, an annoyingly short and sharp reaction, a private kind of mirth. "I keep a commonplace book at Baker Street, an index of biographies of persons of possibly criminal or merely passing interest. Unfortunately I can't consult it from here, but Lola Montez is in it, as are you."

"Am I? Is the entry . . . actionable?"

"My dear Mrs. Norton, the entry is impeccable. You are—were, I should say—a supreme performing artist of the operatic stage. Despite the . . . smudged reputation that attaches to the performing sisterhood, I know for a fact that your personal and professional conduct has always been beyond reproach, if a bit misguided in the matter of foreign noblemen. After all, I investigated the matter myself.

"Lola Montez, on the other hand, was a traveling gypsy curse. She agitated against the state and church powers in Bavaria for libertarian reforms that brought down her sponsor, King Ludwig. She married early and often, and all too often did not marry. She did not divorce when she should have, the first time, and married when she should not have. That made her a bigamist. Her third husband was a Californian. She courted a possible fourth on a ship returning from Australia, but he fell, or jumped, overboard. She blazed a trail across the inhabited world, madam, that a blind man couldn't miss. But she was known more for the noted men she briefly bewitched than any accomplishment of her own. A misguided force who ultimately destroyed herself, she could hold no interest for future generations other than as a laughable oddity, a scandalous footnote to a foolish time."

Irene had gone very quiet during this speech, which had begun by complimenting her at the expense of a woman she despised on principle. Yet something had happened in the past few days as we unearthed bits and pieces of Lola's admittedly tempestuous life, especially as we had read of her lonely and obscure death. And I felt it now too. We had begun to see her as less of a caricature from a newspaper cartoon and more as a real person, as young Eliza Gilbert fleeing an impossibly unsuitable marriage for one no better, then turning the only career she could manage, and herself, into a global sensation.

Irene reached out to collect the card and draw it slowly back across the table to her reticule.

Silence held.

"I beg to disagree," she at last told our host, "at least in your conclusions about my possible and not very distinguished forebear. A woman on her own must do what she can to survive, and all too often she is abused for achieving that survival."

I stood along with Irene.

Mr. Holmes looked off-balance, as if what he'd said had the opposite effect to what he'd intended. And in such cases, there is no use saying more.

No farewells were given and he did not escort us to the door.

We rustled down the hall in silence, and had to wait for a long time after Irene pushed the mother-of-pearl button to call the elevated car.

She bit her lip. "You're right, Nell," she told me, "reputation is far too easily lost."

"But you don't even like her yourself, Irene."

"That's not the point. The point is that the world will paint what picture its own low mind imagines no matter the facts. The Lola Montez who pasted sayings from the Bible around her deathbed was not the same woman who eloped with a captain when she was fourteen."

"You don't much believe in religion."

"What I believe or don't doesn't matter. If Father Hawks was so impressed by her religious conversion that thirty years later he was agitating his bishop to have her considered for sainthood, she had changed. Or she had never been what the world said she was."

"Mr. Holmes was actually complimenting you by the contrast. I admit he was clumsy and rather dismissive, but—"

"I will not rise because another woman falls, and that's all there is to it. If there is a redeemable side to Lola Montez, and I'm beginning to suspect there is, I will find it."

"And then what?"

"And then I'll know. We'll know."

"And if Father Hawks's death is part of some awful contemporary conspiracy that could endanger us?"

She glanced at me, a look of mischief only underlining the determination in her expression. "Then we will be well ahead of Mr. Sherlock Holmes on detecting it, won't we?"

I reflected on the notion of a crucified man deposited on a billiard table in a Fifth Avenue mansion and decided that being well ahead of Mr. Sherlock Holmes, in this instance, was not necessarily a good thing.

26

The Last of Lola Montez

~◦~

Lola sat in a pretty garden, her hollow cheeks, sunken eyes, and cadaverous complexion forming a remarkable contrast to the gay flowers. . . . In fact, she had the strange wild appearance and behavior of a quiet idiot, and is evidently lost to all further interest in the world around her or its affairs. And so ends her eventful history!

—MRS. BUCHANAN, AUGUST 1860, TWO MONTHS AFTER LOLA'S STROKE

Alas, Irene reacted as she always did when Mr. Holmes proved to be intractable: she charged ahead on her own investigations even more fiercely.

"You are right, Nell," she told me in the cab on the way home from his hotel, "that is a singularly annoying man. One would think having provided the name of the victim in a case he is handling for the wealthiest man in America would have merited at least a polite round of applause."

"Unless he really already knew the victim's identity."

"Bother! I suppose he could have, and might have chosen not to tell us, thus we were peddling yesterday's newspapers. Or he simply wished to discourage us. Well, that has not worked."

"I am quite discouraged."

"You must stop that at once! This search for the last of Lola Montez is becoming quite intriguing, now that murder has entered the picture. Why would anyone slay such a saintly old cleric in that manner?"

"Someone who did not want Lola elevated to the ranks of Episcopal

Church saints at any cost, I would imagine. I would number myself among that honorable society."

"People no longer murder for theological issues, at least not in America, I hope."

"Wasn't Lola herself the object of what she called religious persecution?"

"Yes. She was dead set against the Jesuits, or, rather, they were dead set against her. She even claimed that they had followed her to America to bedevil her."

"That I can believe, Irene, whatever else of her personal testimony might be self-serving, or, in the way of theatrical personalities, wildly exaggerated."

"I have taken note of your slur upon theatrical personalities."

"Ah, but you will not remodel yourself as a result. I must say that we in England are not enamored of the Jesuits. In fact, we executed a great number of them during the Reformation years, when they were sneaking into our shires and cities weaving plots against our king and country."

"So Lola perhaps was not imagining things when she accused them of conspiracies to undermine her libertarian influence on King Ludwig."

"Most likely not! I have grown up on tales of Jesuit spies and their treachery in my own land for decades, even centuries. They masquerade as missionaries, but are highly educated and wily, and always scheming to bring down our government. In fact, I find it disturbing that the notorious fallen woman Lola Montez was so politically astute on this issue. If the Jesuits were plotting in Bavaria as they had been for generations in England, she was indeed a national heroine and a stout friend to the king for opposing them."

"Religion and politics, I confess, are two subjects that bore me to tears, but I see I have neglected too much of my education on this score." Irene gazed out the window at the passing congestion of Broadway. "Still, why would such very European matters have emigrated to America now? Our form of government is both too secular and too multifaceted to topple with such denominational schemes. The strict separation of church and state does not lend itself to mischief from treacherous clerics. We have no one man to dethrone, like a king, as in England or Bavaria."

"No, but England still has its queen and Bavaria a king who is descended from Lola's Ludwig. I can't imagine anyone bothering to unseat a cipher like President Buchanan, though."

"Buchanan. That reminds me. That old school friend of the young Eliza Rosana Gilbert who reunited with Lola in America shortly before her illness and death. I wonder if she or any descendants remain in New York. She would only be seventy today."

"And how shall you find specific Buchanans among this noisy, crowded, teeming populace?"

"I see you're regarding the passersby with disapproval, Nell, but the vitality of even the meanest of these streets below Washington Square encourages me. Perhaps our best path is to follow Lola's final addresses as so kindly listed in the books about her. Someone in the neighborhoods may remember her or Mrs. Buchanan."

I said no more, for I did not wish to lose my composure in public.

The next morning we set out again for the Episcopal Club.

Irene had telephoned the previous afternoon and I'm sorry to say the bishop extended her every courtesy. I suppose there is no end to what $300 may buy under the guise of charity.

We were received in the same somber chamber in which the bishop had seen us, but he had sent an emissary. This was a young cleric whose prominent ears bore a striking resemblance to those of the freckle-faced curate who had inspired my youthful admiration long before I'd left my parson father's home in Shropshire. I hadn't thought of Jasper Higgenbottom in years, but doing so now, in this context, brought me to the brink of a blush.

I fidgeted while he handed Irene a list and explained its contents. His youth and unprepossessing appearance did not contrast well with Quentin's seasoned dash. How could I have ever deceived myself that a country parson's daughter was any match for such a gentleman of good family and global travels?

Meanwhile, young Father Edmonds was warning Irene that the areas we proposed to visit were not fit for ladies.

"Poor Father Hawks," he said, "kept ample files on Miss Montez. He listed some of her latter-day addresses in New York, but these areas have changed much in almost thirty years, and I can't guarantee that even the street names remain."

"Information is valued for what it may reveal, not guarantees," Irene said.

"In the late '50s, she had rented a flat on Clinton Place north of Washington Square in Greenwich Village," he said. "That is still a respectable neighborhood.

Father Hawks notes that at this time she was living as Mrs. Heald, so she would hardly be remembered in that neighborhood as anyone special. After her stroke in June of 1860, she was taken by her childhood friend, Mrs. Buchanan, to a summer place in Astoria, opposite Eighty-sixth Street. That October, she was moved to a boardinghouse at One-ninety-four West Seventeenth Street, only three blocks from the Buchanan home on the same street, which was just off Broadway. And there Father Hawks ministered to her until the day of her death on January seventeenth of the new year. I can't speak to these addresses being respectable today, or even how respectable they were in Miss Montez's day."

Finishing this speech, he handed the paper to Irene and directed to me a broad smile.

"That is quite a becoming hat, madam."

"Miss," I corrected.

He lifted a skimpy eyebrow and his ears turned red. "Is it possible I have met you somewhere before, Miss—?"

"Huxleigh. And no. I am British and Anglican."

"Then we are cousins."

"I am quite alone in the world, without relations of any sort."

"I was speaking metaphorically, of the common communion of our churches."

"Common indeed, I fear."

Irene regarded this exchange with polite amusement, then stood to thank the young man again, and we left.

"I believe you have made a conquest, Nell," she told me when we had regained the street.

"I can't imagine why. I said not a word the entire time until he began badgering me."

"No doubt he was smitten with your looks and manner."

"Ridiculous! There is nothing special about either."

Her laughter rang out so merrily it attracted quite of lot of unwanted attention from the men in the street. "You must not expect everyone to agree with you there, Nell. I suspect he recognized a kindred soul, modest, devout, eligible. . . ."

"I will not be discussed in this manner."

"It would not hurt to make Quentin a little jealous."

"What a devious and immature notion."

"Nevertheless, it's tried and true. Jealousy is both a symptom of deeper regard and a goad to it."

"Really?" I contemplated that in silence, for I certainly felt embarrassingly jealous of Pink. I was wise not to express this to Irene, for she would have insisted that it was a symptom of my deep regard for Quentin, and then I should look like the fool I knew I was to the one person whose regard meant the most.

Irene already had forgotten my potential swain and was studying the list he had given her.

"Let us begin where she ended, the boardinghouse where she died. People tend to remember death chambers, and perhaps there was talk about who she really was in the neighborhood at the time."

"I doubt anyone even noticed, Irene. If she was calling herself Mrs. Heald and was buried as Mrs. Eliza Gilbert, Lola Montez truly ran against all her previous history: she slipped off the final stage of her life quietly and anonymously."

"Hmmm. A sad ending to one of the most dramatic sagas of midcentury. I wonder, given the fate of Father Hawks, if she slipped off the planet unaided."

"Irene! You think she was murdered?"

"She was not yet forty, Nell, despite the inaccurate date on her tombstone. Purportedly, she caught a chill by taking a walk, her condition having improved enough to permit it. She was speaking again, and writing a journal. To some all those signs of recovery might have made her a dangerous woman."

"Irene, she was a dangerous woman all her life."

"Exactly my point. If these 'Ultramontanes' she mentions and the vengeful Jesuits from Bavaria had followed her to America, as she maintained frequently and publicly, they might have hastened her end. She was lecturing often on Romanism as well as the British and women's fashion."

"It is idiotic to think that a scandalous and mediocre Spanish dancer would be worth assassinating."

"You forget the furor she spawned in Bavaria. The mobs nearly killed her more than once."

"The mobs, not individuals."

"But we all know that hirelings are paid to stir up such mobs and raise a ruckus. Then it's reported in the newspapers and a tempest in a teapot can overthrow a monarch."

"Lola Montez was far more than a tempest in a teapot!"

"I'm glad you agree."

"I refer to her childish tantrums, which clearly could have benefited from an association with a good governess. She was spoiled, wild, willful, and sometimes possessed by such fits of temper that I'm amazed she was not imprisoned."

"Men like to believe that women are weak little things requiring their protection. Prosecuting Lola for being a wildcat quick to raise a whip, dagger, or pistol in her own defense would have made them look mice instead of men indeed. So she was safe to carry on. I don't doubt that she meant every word and deed, either."

We took a hansom to Broadway and Seventeenth Street, then walked the few blocks to Lola Montez's final residence.

The day was warm and the street was lined with four- and five-story brownstone buildings. Tall wooden poles surmounted by dozens of electric wires defaced an already dreary prospect.

I can't say that I was impressed by New York City's domestic side. Paris was far airier and more interesting, even in the poorer quarters.

We reached 194 West Seventeenth Street to find a building as alike to its neighbors as one berry to another in a patch.

Irene seemed almost intimidated as we studied that soot-stained facade. Not even a personality as fiery as Lola Montez's could have made much of an impression on its stolid ordinariness, even at the end of her life.

"We must go in," she said, "and ask after residents of thirty years."

"Irene, this is a boardinghouse. New York is stuffed full with ones just like it. The very point of a boardinghouse is that the residents come, and go. There is no chance."

"There was no chance that I would find a link to my mother, and here I am on the trail of Lola Montez. We can but try."

I gazed into her eyes, wishing I could see the fabled blue orbs of La Lola. I believe they would have echoed the stubborn set of Irene's expression and the determined fire of her glance.

"We can settle it one way or the other," I agreed.

Up the exterior stairs and in we went, to imbibe the eternal reek of the boiled corned beef and cabbage the immigrant Irish imported to New York City along with counties' worth of red hair.

"The smell alone must have been Parma violets to an Irish girl," I noted as we paused in the narrow, dark hallway.

Irene turned to me, her eyes warm with some unnamed emotion.

"She ended with her own, with her school friend and Irish neighbors. There are worse ways to die."

I thought of pitiful Father Hawks, and could only nod agreement.

A parlor was to our left, a dining room to our right, both empty. Both rooms were also dingy, shabby, and smelled none too clean. Irene walked through the dining room to the kitchen area beyond it, and there we found a plump woman in a plaid cotton house dress and apron pummeling a mound of dough on a floured tabletop.

Her sleeves were rolled up to her elbows and tendrils of her gray hair clung damply to her reddened face. No wonder so many children and even adults lolled idly on the tenement steps; the summer heat made the building interiors into furnaces. I felt my cotton blouse wilting against my skin and my cheeks growing feverish.

"Is it rooms you'd be wantin'?" The woman brushed her wet tendrils off her face with one bare wrist, leaving a swath of white flour in her hair.

She also managed to eye us up and down in a swift assessment. "Quarters here are plain." Her tone implied that she had judged us "fancy."

"We seek information about a . . . relation," Irene said.

"You're lookin' for relatives? There are some here who don't much want to be found, I'll bet. I ask their names and take their money and have me husband throw them out if they don't pay, and that's all I know about them."

"Have you been landlady here long?"

"What do you think?" The woman almost snorted her disbelief at the question. "I didn't go gray performin' in Mr. Barnum's circus first, now did I? Me man Kelly and I arrived on these golden shores when our countryfolk were too weak from starvin' to do much, but we scraped enough togither to get this building, and here we have been since, cookin' an' cleanin' for strangers, and all our young ones scattered hither and yon to earn what they can."

Irene picked up a bowl of flour from the washstand and moved it closer to our cook at the table.

"Then you were here in '59?"

"For sure. In New York City, but not at this place. I've not got all day to be standin' here tellin' strangers my business."

"That's just it," Irene, putting her hand out to the woman's arm. "We may not be strangers. I'm searching for my mother, and have information that she had lived here."

"Irish, was she?"

Irene's glance to me was rueful. Eliza Gilbert was Irish, all right (not that accident of birth is any recommendation to me), later claimed to have Spanish blood and even later became a Bavarian countess.

"That she was," Irene said at once. "Limerick born, although some say Sligo. Either way, she didn't stay long. I'm told she died in this building."

"Not recently." The landlady looked affronted at the very idea, although death must visit Seventeenth Street as often as it did any address in Manhattan.

"No," Irene admitted, "it will be thirty years ago next January."

"Thirty years?" The woman brushed her palms on her apron. "Why didn't you say so at the first? As it happens you are not the first to inquire about this lady."

"We aren't?" I asked, speaking for the first time.

"No, ma'am," she answered me, looking from one to the other of us. "Why, what a coincidence. The good father was here inquirin' not a week or two ago."

" 'The good father'?" Irene's facile voice held a controlled note of excitement, or perhaps anxiety.

"Yes. Of course I told him all I could, which was little, but he interviewed all the current boarders in one evening. So very tiring for a man his age. In fact he took a little whiskey before he left. I couldn't let him leave without something to restore his strength."

"Was his search successful?" Irene wondered.

"I don't know. He said it was church business, very important church business."

"Indeed it is," Irene said, assuming a tone I could only describe as suddenly sanctimonious. "Miss Huxleigh and I are here on church business as well. I have approached the bishop wishing to make a substantial donation in the name of my late mother. He directed me to the good father, who has apparently been . . . led into another place by his mission, and is not available, alas, to consult with us right now.

"What is this about?"

Irene edged closer. "I'm not at liberty to say, but the bishop mentioned the process of evidence-gathering. For sainthood."

"Holy Mither o' God! The good father mentioned the lady in question had been most devoted to her prayers, but nothing of this. A saint in the building? No wonder he was searchin' for the room she occupied, died in. A shrine. I have a shrine in me house."

"Quite likely, but you must say nothing to anyone until it becomes a fact."

"And this lady was your mother?"

"It's possible. We were separated at my birth. The Troubles, you know."

"Indeed, and a brutal time it was back in the '40s and '50s when the people of Ireland were reduced to eating the furze in the ditches like sheep, thanks to the murderous English. 'Tis no wonder a saint would come out of that heinous time."

I was suddenly glad I had only spoken once, and too briefly for my accent to register. Besides, this entire spurious discussion of the late Lola Montez as a candidate for sainthood was so outrageous I was too furious to speak anyway. Irene was exploiting this poor woman's superstitions as heartlessly as a confidence man.

"Do you know," Irene was asking now, "which chamber was so blessed? Whether the good father found what he sought?"

"I believe it is the ground floor room at the right rear. There have been some alterations to the ground floor rooms throughout the years. The dining room was expanded and we added gaslights."

"May we see this chamber? I have been searching for my mother my whole life."

"Why, of course, madam. And what would be the name of this holy lady?"

Irene stood flummoxed for a moment, then resorted to the string of Spanish names Eliza had tacked onto her birth name. "Maria. Dolores."

Mrs. Kelly shut her eyes in awe. "Maria. Dolores. The Holy Virgin Mary, Our Lady of Sorrows. She was well named."

"By herself," I almost snapped, but of course I could not reveal my kinship to the "bloody English."

"I'll take you to the room. The current resident is a traveling button salesman, but now that I know the import of the chamber's long-previous resident, I will move him to another room at once, and keep this one vacant. How soon will the Church know its decision on Maria Dolores?"

"These things take much time and testimony," Irene answered gently. "Meanwhile, if we may—?"

"Of course. Of course." She wiped, then wrung her hands in her apron. "The room has not been tidied as it should be, I didn't know, God have mercy. . . ."

We followed her out through the dining room into the hallway and then back in the dimness to some doors tucked behind the stairway.

The landlady's keys chimed with our steps, and she darted ahead to unlock the door on the right.

"Mr. Burnside is an old bachelor, don't you know? Not the tidiest soul perhaps, but good-natured and prompt with his rent. I can't speak to the condition of the premises."

I was struck first by the bareness, and saw only the wide-planked wooden floor, the roughly-plastered walls whose pale paint had weathered with time and dust into the color of cardboard. An odor of old tobacco was the only incense to be found in this so-called sainted room.

Furniture was spare: a narrow cot, an old oaken armchair upholstered in worn carpet tapestry, a wooden chair, a table with a basin, towel, and small round mirror above it. A battered bureau whose drawers did not quite close, and a wardrobe that sagged against one wall.

One window looked out on . . . I had wandered over to see the view, and regretted it. I saw an alleyway lined with trash buckets facing rows of back stoops and not an inch of sod anywhere, or a flower, only the effluvia of city life, papers. Above us were strung not the ugly electric and telephone wires that plagued even Fifth Avenue but lines of laundry flapping in the contained winds of the inner courtyard.

"It's gaslit," Mrs. Fenster noted with pride, going to one wall and holding her hand up to the level of a crude metal fixture.

"Wonderful," Irene said. "But we don't need it now. If we may spend some time alone in this chamber." She bowed her head. At least she was not enough of a hypocrite to say what her posture implied: that we would be praying.

"Of course, my dear lady. The place is yours for as long as you like, as it was for your dear, sainted mither. Me own mither was God's own emissary, but she died in the Famine."

I bit my lip. I'd heard of the Famine, of course, but it seemed some dry fact of ancient history having to do with that unruly island to the west of the "sceptered isle" I and William Shakespeare had been fortunate to call home in vastly different eras. To see an Irishwoman standing before me whose mother had been lost to hunger and hunger alone in these modern times made my soul shrivel. Perhaps the French were not completely wrong to disdain the English on some issues.

In fact, the moment the poor woman had left us alone, I rounded on Irene, perhaps because I could not turn on myself.

"How could you deceive that poor, unlettered woman, Irene, and mouth churchy sentiments you don't believe a jot of?" I whispered.

But Irene hardly heard me. She was standing by the big, bare window coated in dried raindrops of dust, staring at the grim, monotone scene beyond, and the ragamuffin children playing under the dingy laundry lines above.

Their childish cries came faintly through the glass and brick that separated us, and they sounded as happy as children in Hyde Park, though they looked nothing like them at all.

Irene stretched out first one arm, then the other, to the filthy walls of the room, unaware how her figure made the shape of a cross against the bright white light of daylight beyond.

She turned slowly, studying this bare, naked, empty room in utter silence. She paced its length, then width, touching each wall with the same slow wonder.

Irene almost resembled a ballet dancer, in her grace, her aloofness, her silence.

She trailed a hand along each wall as she made a circuit of the room, stepping back when she encountered the interruption of furniture pieces as if they were clumsy dance partners she avoided rather than embraced.

At one particularly dingy spot on the wall, she stopped and pressed close to examine the variations in texture and color with her fingers as well as her eyes. I was reminded of a blind person, attempting to read what was unseen with fingertips alone.

This room was indeed a shrine for Irene, far more than it ever could be for me, and I was ashamed that I had doubted her.

What had stuck me as facile was, I saw, genuine. The worldly cynicism I both deplored and envied actually was no more than a key to Irene. Her feelings ran far deeper than she allowed anyone to suspect.

"Some say she had become a fanatic," Irene said, rather dreamily. She touched the wall again. "She pasted religious sayings all around the room. She read the Bible over and over, particularly the New Testament story of Mary Magdalene. What had she come to, this rebel, this revolutionary, this intense lover and hater, this spider dancer? In this room. Was she mad? Was she saved? Was she pathetic? Or triumphant?"

"I think . . . she was sincere."

"Sincere." Irene turned to smile at me. "I knew you would find the perfect word, Nell. If we can all end at least sincere, then we have accomplished something, and the rest doesn't matter, does it?"

"Well . . ." I was not quite ready to say that penitence erases all, although parts of the Scriptures might. I was not quite ready to be as magnanimous as the Scriptures.

"Father Hawks described her as at peace. She died with her hand on the Bible and him at her side. She rejected the Catholic faith she was born to. She called upon an Episcopal priest and bishop at the end. If she is a saint, Nell, she is an Anglican one."

I opened my mouth, speechless, when I saw in Irene's eyes that fond twinkle with which she liked to tweak my deepest sensibilities.

"This particular sainthood has only one advocate, and he is dead."

"Yes." She made a circuit of the room again, this time at a brisk, businesslike pace. "One wonders if that is *why* he is dead."

"Martyred," I couldn't help saying with a shudder.

"Martyred. He was indeed." Irene had grown grim again. "Eliza Gilbert, or Maria Dolores, or Lola Montez may or may not have merited sainthood, but that old man, that old priest, did not deserve to die as he did in any world I would care to claim." She surprised me by shuddering herself. "That was an evil worse than Jack the Ripper's, because it was done not out of madness but in the cold-blooded service of an ignoble goal."

"You know the reason?"

"No. Only that nothing on earth, or in heaven, can justify it. Now. We don't have forever."

"No one does, but what do you mean?"

"We must search the room."

"Why? Nothing of Lola remains."

"Ah, I do believe that spirits leave their impressions on places, or vice versa. I sense her in this room. I understand nothing about her earlier life yet. The facts and the contradictory reports leave that all a mysterious swirl, like the spider dancer's petticoats. But here, I find her. Sure of herself at last. I do not much like the word and concept 'humble.' "

"That is obvious," I said, but she ignored my interjection.

"It strikes me as an insincere stance, like Dickens's awful 'umble' Uriah Heap. But I think Lola Montez had found her humble self here in this room, and it was not defeat but triumph. And to that extent I think that Father Hawks was not wrong. I think he died to protect that belief, in her and in himself."

"How awful, if true!"

"How remarkable. He may have converted her, in the conventional sense, but she also converted him." Irene sighed. "I almost feel regret for what we must do next."

"Which is?"

"We must search this room, Nell, from stem to stern and back again."

"There is nothing here!"

"There is everything here, only we have not found it yet. I doubt Father Hawks did either. At least that is my humble hope."

"Another man lives here now. We would violate his occupancy."

"In a good cause, Nell."

And so I joined her in the rough work of turning a simple room upside down. We moved the cot and searched under the supportive struts. We pummeled the mattress. We pushed the wardrobe away from the wall, and explored its every corner, filled mostly with mouse-eaten crumbles of wood and dustballs.

We looked under and behind the bureau drawers, on the chance that it had been there when Lola was in residence. We turned the chairs upside down.

Finally, there was no piece of furniture left to manhandle. We stood in the middle of the room, sneezing from the dust, perspiring like farm laborers, red-eyed and worn.

Irene eyed the blocked up fireplace behind the wardrobe, for a small stove now sat near the window for winter uses.

"Oh, Irene, no!"

For answer she went to the stove and found a coal shovel beside it.

"Lola was in this place from fall through Christmas and into January. I would venture to say the fireplace was unblocked and useful then."

She rammed the shovel lip into the dry mortar between two bricks. It crumbled.

We took turns banging away at the bricks. Finally one consented to being pushed and pried and levered loose.

Then another.

"How will we ever restore this? What will we tell the landlady?" I wailed, surveying the mess that was beyond concealing.

"Looking for relics of the sainted Maria Dolores, which is the absolute truth."

"What relics?" I cried.

"This." Irene sat back on her heels, withdrawing yet another brick from the ghastly hole we had gouged out of the wall.

A brick of oilcloth covering.

My heart began to pound with the possibility of discovery.

Irene delicately pulled back the filthy, aged-stiffened cloth. It was the color of diseased dirt, and I myself would be hard put to touch it, even with gloves on.

Irene, however, regarded it with the silent awe reserved for holy relics.

"Nell. I think . . . I think it is her last diary."

I stared at the much-folded lump of thick papers. Could it be?

Irene was ruffling up her skirt and baring her petticoat pocket. The filthy burden, oilcloth and all, was slipped inside. Her petticoat would do well not to sag and split with such an uncomely burden.

"Quick!" Irene began pulling the chipped bricks back into a pile. "We must restore this wall to its earlier semblance. At least the wardrobe hides it. It's a miracle that Father Hawks didn't find this, for clearly this is what he sought here. Lola has left this for us."

"For you."

She paused to regard me with utter seriousness. "I do believe so. For me."

It took nearly half an hour by my lapel watch to jam the crumbled mortar and brick back into some imitation of a wall.

We pushed the wardrobe over the fireplace again, grunting like longshore-men.

Irene hiked her petticoat up at the waist by a foot, expecting the weighty parcel in it to inexorably draw it back down as we made our way home.

At the door she turned to regard the room one last time.

Again I sensed that strange presence and absence, both one and the same thing, with which Irene communed.

Then we shut the door and bustled down the hall to the parlor, where our hostess was waiting. Oddly, she never noted our disheveled appearance, or if she did, she may have attributed it to religious ecstasy. These Roman Catholics are an emotional lot.

"And—?" she asked, breathless.

"You are wise," said Irene, "to reserve the room for higher purposes. I'll tell the bishop of your cooperation. And I'm sure Father Hawks, when he is com-municating again, will be most grateful."

The landlady's generously hopeful smile faded toward the end of Irene's comment into confusion.

"Father Hawks?" she asked. "Who is Father Hawks?"

In the street outside, Irene took my elbow in a death grip.

I spoke like a doll with a button that makes it cry. "The 'good father.' If that wasn't Father Hawks, Irene, who on earth was it?"

"I don't know. Possibly no one Episcopal, or Anglican, after all." Irene gazed at the teeming street, seeing nothing. "And most probably, no one up to any good at all," she added.

Memoirs of a Dangerous Woman:

Motherhood

*She came back to London and made her debut at her Majesty's
Theatre. When news of this event reached her mother she put on
mourning as though her child was dead, and sent out to all her friends
the customary funeral letters.*

—*AUTOBIOGRAPHY,* LOLA MONTEZ

She had named me after herself: Eliza. I often had cause in later years to
wonder why.

Now that she has come all the way to New York City to see me as I
lie ill in this autumn of 1860, I have to wonder why a woman who as
good as disowned me should wish to claim me at what most likely is
the end of my life, though not hers.

Call me cynical, but I think she wonders how much money and jewels I
have to leave her.

My humble surroundings will certainly disabuse her of any ambitions in
that direction, and I could not be happier about that.

What will she say for herself when there is nothing to be gained? That
should be interesting!

How sad that I don't expect her to bring me anything but an open palm.
Father Hawks would chide me for lack of charity, but I cannot forgive the

woman whose cold heart set me on the wayward path of my life. Whatever they may say of me, no one can deny that I was charitable to others, and that my feelings ran as deep and open as the great Mississippi River.

I dread seeing her again. Or, rather, I dread her seeing me in this state. I wish my left arm could still lift a castanet, that I did not need to use my right to wipe the drool from my stroke-slack mouth.

She comes at last when I am truly humbled. I suppose it's a good exercise for the spirit, even if I can't bring myself to forgive her, no, not even after all these years. . . .

Some things are expected of a mother, and she gave me none of them but only grief.

She was considered a beauty and married a soldier. When he died, she married a soldier of higher rank. By then I had been born, Mr. Gilbert's only daughter. We were living in India at the time of his death.

How a little child could learn from India, and how I loved it! In India I began what would become my legendary mastery of foreign language and horses. Horses have their own mute dialect and I rode them with abandon at an early age, safer on those broad, jolting backs dark with sweat than I have ever found myself on Mother Earth.

My mother packed me off to England twice, both against my will. Once I was but seven, a half-orphan, and hardly understood why I should be wrested from all I loved to be cared for, or not, by strangers in that damp, chilly land that never called to me.

My stepfather, Colonel Craigie, had some care of me, more than she. I sensed that even then.

When I returned to India I had been well-served by an education most girls of my day never had, but was no more welcome to my mother. She was quite the belle of Delhi by then, and I was on the brink of womanhood. Already people praised my white skin, my deep blue eyes, and curling black hair, but even more, my poise and wit.

In no time we were bound for England again, all three.

I have confessed to Father Hawks, along with the more notorious of my sins, my lack of feelings for my mother, and why.

Her desire to be rid of me when I was seven, and my helplessness to prevent her from tearing me from everything I loved, perhaps made me willful.

She brought me back to England herself the second time, and she still desired to be rid of me, but in a new way. I was a pawn for her ambition for her new husband, which was at bottom ambition for herself. Like all women of her time, she lived to rule through others.

She wanted to trade me in marriage to my stepfather's commanding officer, a man past sixty when I was not yet fifteen. I used to lie abed at night and count the decades between myself and this old man: twenty-five made one; thirty-five two, forty-five three, fifty-five four, sixty-something, almost five. Almost fifty years. One might as well have told me to wed the mummy of an Egyptian pharaoh!

Can anyone imagine how a spirited child, one reared in the exotic freedoms of India, would have regarded such a cold marital bargain? How my flesh and imagination both shriveled at the very thought?

So when Lieutenant James informed me of this master plan, an elopement with a handsome, thirty-year-old lieutenant seemed the only answer. Better the devil you know than the devil you don't know.

What did I know at fourteen, except that I wouldn't be sold by anyone, even my own mother.

Later, when I understood the range of feminine powers, I realized why I had been destined to be shuffled off to an old man's boudoir. My mother did not need a blooming rose of youth in her own garden.

Now that I no longer bloom, but wilt like damp tobacco leaves, it's safe for her to approach me again and feel superior. Everything I had is wasted, including my body, if not quite my mind.

27

Untold Tales

~∞∞~

[Mrs. Eliza Craigie was] a cold, passionless woman, who greeted and said adieu to her daughter, much as she might have made a fashionable call. She was greatly disappointed at finding Eliza without worldly wealth and visited her only twice, if I remember correctly, during her stay of two or three weeks.

—A WITNESS

We had late tea in our rooms, huddling over the musty, much folded and cracked wad of writing paper.

I peered at the faded ink in the lamplight, although the hour was only 4:00 P.M. and daylight still filled the window frames. With more and more ridiculously high buildings going up all over New York City, however, soon the streets would be forever shadowed no matter the time of day.

So I predicted to Irene.

"You must remember that New York City sits atop Manhattan Island, Nell. There is more room here to go up than out."

"London and Paris have managed to keep to a decorous four or five stories," I pointed out.

"Maybe the Eiffel Tower will change that," she suggested, knowing it was my least favorite monument in the world.

" 'The new cathedral,' of our age," I said. "Towers of Babel erected to industry."

"I for one like an eagle's-eye view, but we are concerned here and now with the mite's-eye view. Can you make anything of the writing on these papers?" Irene asked, refusing to debate slackening modern standards any further.

"The handwriting style is bold, although the execution is weak, as one would expect from an invalid. Time has sadly faded the ink. Nothing in the penmanship is the least like yours."

"Why would it be? She and I attended quite different schools."

"You went to no school at all!! At least Eliza Gilbert had a thorough education for her time, although it seemed to have made little impression on her."

"I graduated from the University of Varietal Knowledge," Irene said with mock indignation. "I'll have you know I was taught calligraphy by the Amazing Annabel, a lady who simultaneously wrote with her hands, feet, and mouth to the astonishment of all Europe and the eastern half of the United States. She was quite a taxing teacher and fiercely demanded proper-shaped letters. She always said that I should be ashamed to do not as well with my hands as she could do with her feet."

"Your penmanship is admirably clear," I admitted, "if extravagant. I fear these new papers will be nearly as hard to decipher as Madame Restell's code-book, but I see some references to Scripture as well as other matters, so it may be helpful if I pore over it long enough."

"Imagine." Irene rose to reclaim her teacup, which no doubt was cold from neglect. We had kept the tea things well away from the table on which we laid our hard-won documents. "These sheets of paper, combined with Madame Restell's code book, must contain the untold tales of many unhappy women's lives three decades ago. And only you can interpret these remnants."

"They are hardly Holy Scripture, Irene. I expect to find a good deal of sin in these pages."

"And so one does in Scripture, I am told. I hope you discover some good, Nell. No one is irredeemable."

"No," I admitted reluctantly. Not even Pink, I supposed. "How, or why," I asked, "did Eliza-Maria-Lola-Mrs. James-Mrs. Heald-Mrs. Hull-Mrs. Gilbert conceal her last papers in the fireplace bricks?"

"A good question. She knew she was dying. She had seen and rejected her mother. She had signed a document leaving anything that came to her via Bavaria after her death to Mrs. Buchanan, thus forestalling her mother from any future windfall inheritance."

"How she must have hated her mother!"

"Why not? Lola blamed her mother's neglect and ill use for forcing her into an unwise elopement and then onto the stage to support herself as a result. I am not a great believer of 'forgive and forget' either, but Lola had gone so far as to embrace the Church and leave a sizable donation to a group for fallen women. With the rest of her means, she paid the debts for her care. She would seem to have had her house in order, what was left of it. Why hide her spiritual diary?"

"Indeed, it could have inspired others like herself to repent."

Irene paced around the room, consuming American "cookies" and cold tea. At least she had so far refrained from smoking.

She paused at the window, gazed out, then whirled to face me.

"I submit, Nell, that Lola Montez did *not* conceal these papers."

I looked up from my close work, my eyes blinking in puzzlement and at the swift change of focus. "Who else would have done it?"

"Father Hawks. He was there at the last. During the hasty arrangements for her burial and resulting chaos, he could easily have dislodged a few bricks in the fireplace and concealed the papers. The use of oilcloth suggests he wanted to preserve them and he anticipated some long period of concealment."

"Wouldn't the fires have destroyed them?"

"The niche was far enough behind the surface bricks to protect them. What he didn't anticipate was that time would render the fireplace redundant."

"Then he had expected to use them sooner."

"Perhaps."

"He wanted to preserve evidence of Lola's conversion, to make a case for her sainthood."

"Possibly. Since he is dead, Nell, we can't know. But we have to wonder if he died preserving the secret resting place of these very papers."

"No!" I lifted my hands away from the worn pages under my care. "Father Hawks was the saint, then, a martyr certainly. What could be in here worth suffering such a brutal death to protect?"

"We won't know until we study them, or find whoever wanted to possess them so badly."

"Or they find us." I shivered at the idea of facing the unknown monsters who had so maltreated the good father. Then I frowned. "Who is this false father who searched the room before us?"

" 'False father.' Interesting turn of phrase, Nell. It does occur to one, that, embarked on a search for a long-lost mother, one should wonder about a long-lost father."

I had not thought of that! I had not foreseen that our search for Irene's mother could turn up a father, but of course it might . . . would. If Lola Montez had been such an unpleasant surprise for us both, what would a father be?

I looked over at Madame Restell's book, which shared the table and might hold much information of concealed mothers, and fathers. Could it be that Irene's father was an even more unlikely, or key, figure than her purportedly notorious mother? For instance, the king of Bavaria, which would make Irene a princess, albeit an illegitimate one? Oh, my goodness, she did not need any more encouragement to royalty than she had flirted with in the past!

"When do you think you will ferret out the mysteries in those two most different but interesting documents, Nell?" Irene asked from the window.

I looked up to see that she had at last lit one of her small cigars. Smoke was curling past her silhouetted shoulder at the window like steam from rolls fresh from the oven.

"I have no idea, Irene. One was designed to frustrate all interpretation, and the other is in a such sorry state of preservation that it is virtually unreadable."

"Well. Then I propose we seek out a source that is in a better state of preservation, and readable. As to whether it will frustrate all interpretation, I can't say until we try."

"A source?"

"Someone who knew Lola."

"Mrs. Buchanan, but she may be very hard to find, or even dead."

"That's why I suggest another source first, one very much alive."

"Who on earth—?"

Irene swept past the desk to pluck from the sofa a newspaper section of that day's *Times,* in fact, and showed me the quarter page folded to be showcased.

"Irene, this is the theatrical advertisement section."

"Indeed, and you will note one Lotta Crabtree is featured in a play."

"Lotta Crabtree? Why is that name familiar?"

"Remember Lola's sojourn in the '50s near the California gold fields, in Grass Valley?"

"I do. Most atypical for her, except for marrying another man she wasn't entitled to. Grass Valley was a retreat for her. She ran a salon, such as it could be in the unsettled West, kept a tame bear . . . oh, and tutored a small child who was already performing."

"Yes. Lotta Crabtree, who is now the flirtatious queen of the American stage and a ripe forty-two, by my calculations."

"What would a child know of Lola Montez?"

"What she thought of Lola during this very unusual, and serene, time of her life."

"Yes, for the flame of three continents, Lola did rather bury herself in that tiny town out West for several years."

"She did other things in Grass Valley atypical of her; for instance, playing with children as well as bears, and taking little Lotta Crabtree under her rather tarnished wing."

"Ha! You admit at last that she was a Tarnished Woman!"

"What woman who achieves notice is not tarnished in these benighted times, Nell?"

"And what times have not tarnished women who achieve anything?" I riposted. Then paused to examine what I had said.

"Exactly, my dear Nell. We will make a suffragist of you yet."

"Over my dead . . . mongoose. You are hardly a suffragist yourself."

"True. Perhaps it is the 'suffer' part of the role that makes it unsuitable to me. I don't think Lola much believed in suffering either, until the end at least, and she must have been quite worn by then, poor thing."

"You don't doubt the sincerity of her conversion."

"Not at all. I doubt its necessity.

"Now," she added to this astounding statement, "how to approach the most highly paid performer on the Broadway stage?" Irene paced, puffing and tapping off ashes in scattered crystal trays as she went. "Finding her residence will be difficult, for the gentlemen admirers are so ardent they detach the coursers from her carriage and draw her to the theater themselves. She will be sure to keep a secret domicile."

Irene sighed. "Had I been allowed to perform a while longer, I might have had gentleman-steeds at my disposal."

"And you would have relished that, I suppose."

"No. It's rather silly, but still a great sop to the performer's self-esteem, something Sarah Bernhardt much enjoys. However, in my case, I don't think even Godfrey would approve."

"Since when do you worry about what Godfrey would approve of?"

"Since I married him, dear Nell. Luckily"—Irene smiled and screwed another slim cigar into her holder—"Godfrey approves of more than you would imagine."

She blew out a thin veil of blue smoke. "I'm afraid I'll have to resurrect Irene

Adler the prima donna for the occasion. Even adored American comediennes are impressed by opera singers. So I'll need a truly elegant ensemble, as will you."

"Why?" I demanded.

"And Quentin, of course."

"Quentin?"

"There is nothing like a presentable Englishmen for opening American doors, and Quentin is *très* presentable, is he not?"

To this string of improbabilities, I could only sputter.

"Good. I'm glad you agree. Tomorrow night should do nicely. I'll write Miss Crabtree at her theater and Quentin at his hotel tonight. I do hope the dear fellow has brought black tie and tails on this trip. It will save valuable time. What do you think, Nell?"

"I'm sure I know nothing about the state of Quentin's wardrobe."

"Ah, but you will, my dear. Very shortly. Won't that be exciting?"

28

Ungovernable

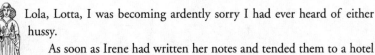

I found the gentle Lola in the back garden, having a little game with a couple of pet bears, with whom she seemed to be on terms of playful and endearing familiarity. She was bareheaded, sunburnt almost to the color of a Mexican, and with her hair hanging in rich profusion over her graceful shoulders. Her dress was of the simplest make and of the coarsest material, a common frock. . . .

—CHARLES WARWICK, AN ACTOR VISITING GRASS VALLEY

Lola, Lotta, I was becoming ardently sorry I had ever heard of either hussy.

As soon as Irene had written her notes and tended them to a hotel messenger boy to deliver, along with enough funds to buy an imperial elephant's howdah, we hied again to Brentano's Literary Emporium, fountain of all things theatrical.

Biographies of Lotta Crabtree were a dime a dozen, and appeared to read like dime novels. Again we left laden with parcels of books, along with the script of La Lotta's latest play.

The young male clerk, emboldened by a second visit, now displayed an absurd partiality to me.

"Alas," Irene mock-complained on our exit, "I am wholly a matron now, a married woman, which must somehow show, for it's you who are collecting all the tender young swains. So passeth prima donnahood."

"Nonsense!" I retorted, though I couldn't deny that the clerk had displayed an unusual solicitude for my opinion and wants.

We returned to the hotel for an exercise I pretended to chafe about, but which secretly pleased me enormously. We settled down like schoolgirls again to read our heads off, nibbling on tea-table sweets until our teeth and foreheads ached.

The foreheads especially ached after Irene imported the sherry decanter to our indoor picnic table and insisted I have some "for thy stomach's sake."

This routine reminded me so much of that first interior "picnic" with Irene and Godfrey and Quentin and myself in London—shortly after Quentin's and my dramatically unexpected reunion outside Notre Dame in Paris—that I could hardly resist her. So I didn't.

We read simultaneously through the various pasteboard-covered books until I was as familiar with this precocious child called Lotta Crabtree from San Francisco of forty years ago as I now was with Irene's own precocious and bizarre childhood from the New York City of a quarter century ago.

Lotta, I learned, was short for the more conventional Charlotte. Mignon was her middle name.

"Goodness," said I as I read, "her mother was English-born, as was Madame Restell, and even Lola Montez was almost English-born—though she did her a-borning in Ireland, benighted country that we own and now deeply regret it. Is everyone in America originally from England?"

"You did own *us* for a while, you know."

"You Americans are rebel Englishmen and women, yes, but you have been through your own bloody Civil War. I would think by now you would grow your own leading ladies."

"Ah, Nell, we can grow apart, but we can never quite lose our British roots."

I refrained from comment. I confess I was coming to envy the uniquely American energy and cheek I encountered all too often nowadays. I wondered, oddly enough, how Sherlock Holmes was surviving his similar encounters here.

Little Lotta Crabtree, performing at the age of six, was dubbed La Petite Lotta of the gold fields. Apparently child performers were the rage in the almost womanless mining towns. So both Lola and Lotta made their very different sort of conquests, Lotta being roughly twenty-six years younger than Lola. Being, in fact, young enough to be her daughter. Hmmm.

I read the passages about Lola's tutoring of Lotta with the insight and interest of a former governess. As much as I wished to totally disown Lola Montez as a candidate for the role of Irene's lost mother, I admit my eyes teared over as I read.

Never and nowhere else had the creature who had recreated herself into Lola Montez been as happy, productive, and beneficial to others as in Grass Valley, California, in the years 1853–56.

This crude town, far from the rude urban overindulgences of Gold Rush San Francisco, was a place of flora and fauna, of such constitutional opposites and yet natural allies as flowers and dogs and bears, of adventuresses and servants and children in happy, egalitarian collaboration.

Liberté, soeurité, egalité?

Little Lotta, the daughter of a doughty English mother and a self-serving American father whom the mother met in New York City (where else), was set dancing on the stage at as early an age as Irene herself.

Little Lotta, it appeared, when Irene filled me in on her history and career, had indeed studied at the literal, adorably tiny feet of Lola Montez.

Now considered New York's leading comedienne, she was a strawberry-curled, coy, flirtatious piece who was adept, as Irene put it, at the 'strategically inciting wiggle.' "

"Her act," Irene said, "will not last much longer, for at past forty she outgrows both it and the boyish trouser roles that have been her bread-and-butter . . . and caviar."

(This last proved prophetic, I add as I censor . . . er, amend these diaries: three years after we saw her, Lotta Crabtree retired from the stage to a quiet life of artistic self-improvement, charity, and animal advocacy in New Jersey. So much for having one's carriage pulled by adoring young men. One wonders if she would show them as much charity as she did to the hardworking street horses she went around putting hats upon in later years. I myself find hats a sufficient indignity to humans that horses should be spared them, come to think of it.)

Our early morning outing to B. Altman's the next day produced ready-made evening gowns in pastel shades dripping with lace and flounces and diamanté. This was not sufficient for Irene, who next proceeded to the Twenty-sixth Street flea market, where she scooped up great quantities of plumage and jet beading.

"Monsieur Worth's trick," she explained. "The brunette colors in evening dress imply richness and sophistication."

We set about sewing the new frivolities into place. By the time Quentin called upon us in the early evening, in black tie and tails as Irene had hoped, we were ready for the Diamond Horseshoe.

Our seats were in the finest boxes overlooking the stage, courtesy of the phantom Mr. Belmont, whose praises Irene sang in ever increasing arpeggios.

Quentin looked beyond dashing in his formal garb. For some reason the starched white collar and shirtfront against his adventure-tanned face provided a stunning contrast that had women in neighboring boxes nearly jerking their heads off their necks to further appreciate.

Irene had decreed that Quentin and I must make a pair, and she led.

I had been allowed to maintain what she called my "demure English charm." However, my cheeks had been pinked, my hair padded with "rats" and crimped on hot irons, and my eyelashes darkened by various items in her traveling case of actress's allure, including burnt cork.

I had also insisted that she lace me within an inch of my life to Nellie Bly's strict eighteen inches.

Quentin quite adeptly played the role of swain to us both, which made me wonder how often in real life he had mastered the same role.

The play was loud, saucy, and somewhat amusing. Lotta Crabtree, a curly-haired imp, cavorted boyishly in trousers or girlishly short skirts. I could see why critics hailed her as "the eternal child" and "the nation's darling."

Were such a little charmer under my charge, I should have made her march to the tune of discipline, which had obviously never entered the life of a girl who'd had gold nuggets thrown at her feet since the age of five or six.

That her own father had run off to England with a trunkful of her hard-gotten gains when she had been only six might have had something to do with her refusal to outgrow her childish onstage roles. Who would want to grow up in such a world?

At the end of the play we stood with the rest of the audience and applauded until our glove palms overheated.

Irene hastened us from the box before the rest of the throng was moving. She swiftly led us down the side aisles to the back of the theater, and then even farther down into the bowels of the backstage area by a narrow, dark stairway.

Quentin took my elbow. (I was garbed in gloves past that point, but still I felt the residual heat of his hands through the two layers of fine cotton.)

"Step carefully," he whispered to me. "Irene knows backstage mazes the way a snake knows its burrow, but we poor mongooses could trip and break something."

"Messalina is fine," I said, rather sharply, aware only that we were alone in the dark and he had me very firmly in hand.

"Delighted to hear it. You are looking exceptionally charming tonight."

"How can you see, in the dark?"

"I noted that fact much earlier."

"Do you have any idea why we are here tonight?"

"I imagine for the usual reasons, to play supporting characters to Irene's leading role. Do you know what she wants of Lotta Crabtree?"

"A possible connection to Irene's own mother."

He held me back from moving, halfway down the stair. In the dark.

"Poor Irene."

"Few would consider her so."

"We know our mothers, and she doesn't."

"Our mothers are . . . were, in my case, from vastly different classes."

"But we are in America now, where class doesn't matter."

"Of course it does! It always matters. It merely goes under different names in America."

"And what name do you go under in America? Nell."

I felt his breath on my bare neck agitating the slim satin ribbons that tied on a cameo from Irene's jewel box. I also felt, though barely through the whalebones and thick sateen, his hands circle my triumphantly narrow waist.

Oh, dear. I hadn't really imagined the consequences.

He had, however, and applied them. Thoroughly.

I admit I felt much vindicated, vis-à-vis Pink, also known as Nellie Bly.

A theatrical hiss from below interrupted the histrionics above. Quentin ebbed away from me, reluctantly I thought. Or perhaps hoped.

"Nell! Quentin? What's keeping you?"

Neither of us answered, although we tripped down the stairs hand in hand.

Here, on this level, the need for darkness to safeguard the theatrical set above from too-obvious observation, was over.

Electrical lights lit our way down a wide, long hall lined on either side with racks of costumes.

This aisle gave way at last to various doors, and finally, to one marked with a star. A name was embossed within that golden shape: Lotta Crabtree.

A dapper man of medium height in the finest evening broadcloth I had ever seen, as silken as a wet otter, bowed to Irene. His dark eyes and classically cut profile gave him an elegance I'd seldom seen in an American man, though he must be near sixty years of age.

"August Belmont at your service, madam. I trust the seats were acceptable."

"Impeccable, my dear Mr. Belmont. Baron Alphonse could not recommend you enough," Irene added. "These are my friends, Miss Huxleigh, and Mr. Stanhope."

"Ah, Stanhope, at last we meet." He shook hands with Quentin with an odd air of relief. "I trust your American assignment is proving tractable. Miss Huxleigh, you are most welcome."

In fact, I did feel so after being the recipient of his most graceful bow.

"Miss Crabtree is waiting for you." Mr. Belmont opened the door and bowed us into the inner sanctum like a butler.

And that is when his name finally impressed itself upon me: one of the banking Belmonts of New York City. Baron Alphonse did not associate with the lower levels.

The dressing room proved similar to the many in which I had visited Irene: amazingly small, considering, equipped with a mirror flanked by gaslights. The performer herself sat front and center in that mirror on a nondescript chair.

A piquant face peeped from under fountains of red-gold hair and gazed back at me in the mirror. Here was Sarah Bernhardt at age twelve, uncorrupted. Here was meat for an English governess.

I smiled at Lotta Crabtree's reflection as if she were my very own charge. She smiled back, a trifle less collected than before.

It was a promising start.

29

Lotta and Lolitta

~ole~

The face of a beautiful doll and the ways of a playful kitten.
—THE NEW YORK TIMES, 1883

"My dear Madame Irene Adler Norton!"

Lotta Crabtree greeted Irene as the French do (most excessively), with barely touching kisses upon both cheeks.

(Quentin, I am happy to say, appeared not to have mastered the affectation.)

"I have heard of your European triumphs," Lotta added, showing adorable dimples. She stood barely over five feet tall, and her curled masses of hair were light red, although glints of darker crimson caught even the dimmer lights of the dressing room.

"Exaggerations, no doubt," Irene said. "And I have heard of your American triumphs." Irene delicately did not say for how long. "How charmingly you keep! You are still the elfin child prodigy you were in Grass Valley."

Lotta sat, her long strawberry-blond tresses and the flounces of her short skirts bouncing with equal vigor.

"Oh, I am a long way from Grass Valley. How did you hear of that?"

"First," said Irene, "I have followed your career with admiration. Alas, I left New York as you arrived."

"You left for Europe. Of course you are a prima donna, and I a mere coquette and songstress."

"'Mere' does not adequately describe your talents," Irene returned.

Lotta eyed Quentin in the mirror. "And this is your husband. I heard you had married a prince."

"Mr. Stanhope is a prince among men, and among Englishmen, but not my husband, who is in Bavaria at the moment."

"No! I had heard you'd married the king of Bohemia, but now you say it is the king of Bavaria. I hear . . . what can I say? . . . that he is quite mad . . . not for marrying you, I'm sure."

"No, not for marrying me, for he has not. King Ludwig the Second of Bavaria died three years ago, and his brother, Otto, assumed the throne. He is mad, that is certain. I am not married to either the past or present king of Bavaria, alas. I am wed to an Englishman."

"Not this Englishman, though," she said, studying Quentin.

He bowed. "Alas, not. I am unwed. So far."

He had not let loose of my left hand, which twitched in his light custody.

Lotta shook her head at all this intricacy of who was and was not married to whom. "I've never married," she announced in her merry, piping voice, "and never will, any more than I shall ever sing grand opera." Her eyes returned, fascinated to Irene. "You sang at Milan and, and . . . someplace German."

"That was Prague, in Bohemia. The rulership is German."

"Ah, the king you did not marry. But you wore a fabulous spray of jewels somewhere, I saw in the newspapers here."

"The Tiffany corsage of diamonds," Irene admitted. "I wore it for my debut as Cinderella at La Scala in Milan."

"Yes! I drooled over that sketch for days. I even looked into purchasing the piece, but was told the Rothschilds had scooped it up."

Irene only nodded, not volunteering that the priceless necklace was in her custody in France, a gift from Baron Alphonse de Rothschild for services rendered and to be rendered. Indeed, Godfrey was laboring on behalf of the Rothschild interests in Bavaria even now.

"Of course," Lotta went on, bending toward the mirror to powder her hair with some red powder or another, "I had made my fortune playing merry little boys, so I have little call for such imposing pieces on stage. And I do not have your stature to wear it."

"Great jewels become whomever they deck."

"I would not care to compete with them for attention, I suppose." She saw me watching her powder her hair. "Paprika," she explained.

"Isn't that a pepper?"

"A spice made from a very hot pepper, but I don't have to eat it. It adds a lovely sparkle to my hair onstage and off. Now, Madame Norton and company, is there anything I can do for you?"

"There is indeed," Irene said promptly, "but perhaps we could adjourn to Delmonico's for supper first?"

"Oh, no. I prefer to head home directly after a performance, but pull up some chairs and we can visit awhile."

Quentin promptly did the pulling up so Irene and I could do the sitting and visiting.

"I don't know quite how to broach the matter," said Irene, who could, and did, broach the Prince of Wales on the subject of his rakish ways. "I'm searching for my mother, you see."

"Is she lost? Mine is at home, waiting for me. She has been a stalwart support during my entire career."

"We were separated at birth, my birth," Irene explained.

"Oh, how tragic! I don't know what I would have done without my mother. She would sew my costumes when I was just a tiny thing, and before you knew it the miners were throwing golden nuggets at my dancing little feet. Can't your father help you find her?"

"I never knew him either."

"I'd be sorry for you," Lotta said, "but if I had never seen my father, my mother and I would be richer for the trunk of gold he ran off with when I was six. As much of my earnings as he could carry. I hear he went to England and lived like a gentleman on it."

"I can't believe your own father robbed you!" I expressed my outrage.

"Quite thoroughly, Miss . . . Huxleigh, isn't it? Well, my mother had come to this country by way of India and met up with John Crabtree in New York City. 'Twas he wanted to go west and find gold, but my mother and I were most successful in mining the camps via my feet. I suppose he left me with a memorable last name that looks well on a marquee, and the sense to invest my money wisely.

"But—" She turned to Irene again. "I sympathize with your lack of a mother. Mine has been a foundation to me all my life."

"That's why I've sought you out. I'm told, by some, that you might have known my mother years ago, when you were a mere child, and I was a mere mote in the future's eye."

Irene had been as delicate as possible in softening the years that lay between them, her being the younger by eleven years, yet Lotta Crabtree was tressed and dressed like a girl many years Irene's junior.

"Knew your mother? Really?"

"I refer to . . . Lola Montez."

This was the second living person who had actually met Lola, and the first woman, though she had been but a child.

Lotta perked her lively eyebrows, and whistled through her tiny teeth, a boyish whistle she must have employed in her trouser roles.

"The Countess of Landsfeld. Land o' Goshen! I haven't thought of her in years, nor anyone much else from Grass Valley either. Oh, she was a human hurricane, Lola Montez, impossible to ignore when present, but, like all forces of nature, easy to forget when gone."

"A rather tragic epitaph," Irene noted.

"Oh, but she had fun when she was here!" Lotta's laugh rang out sweet and loud. "Smoked like a gold-camp chimney! Always had her pouch of tobacco by her side, the way other ladies had their fancywork. She would roll one of her smokes, inhale like a fire breather, and after four or five puffs, dampen it and roll another and smoke that."

Lotta's child-size hand reached for a case on her dressing table and opened it. "I suppose these are my legacy from Lola. Care to try one, Madame Norton?"

"Don't mind if I do." Irene took one of the thin, dark cigars, as did Quentin!

I shook my head and the box never even came within sniffing distance.

Quentin took Lotta's matches and lit first hers, then Irene's, and finally his own smoke.

I watched aghast as smoke and memory silently filled the small dressing room, and I "smoked" by proxy, simply by continuing to breathe. And cough. Why is it that smokers believe all around them inhale the same clouded air and enjoy it as much?

As if reading my thoughts, Irene laid down her cigar after two or three puffs. And Quentin excused himself and retreated to the hall.

Lotta Crabtree, however, went on smoking as if every inhalation retrieved a memory.

"She charmed all the gentlemen, of course. Gracious, she had married and divorced a San Francisco businessman named Patrick Hull before he quite comprehended either state. She horsewhipped the editor of one newspaper and challenged the other to a duel over critical reviews of her dancing. But mostly she retired to Grass Valley and held a sort of salon where anyone of note or artistic leanings eventually showed up."

Irene kept nodding at each of these bits of scandalous information, as if begging for more . . . and she got it.

"What a horsewoman she was! She taught me to ride. And insisted on teaching me the fandango and the Highland fling. She wasn't the best dancer, to be frank. I had better rhythm and grace at six than she did at . . . what?"

"Thirty-six, she would have been then," Irene said quickly. Without calculation. She had been reading long and thinking hard about Lola Montez.

Lotta shook her abundant curls. "She went later to Australia, I think, and finally back to New York, where she died, right here, wasn't it?"

"Very near here," Irene said.

"I'd bet she left her heart in Grass Valley."

"With that man she married, Hull?"

"Him? No. Men were fancies with her. She liked the gender, and always imagined that the Grand Passion was only one man away, yet she always found him wanting. Even when she was married to Hull she took up with a charming German baron. He called himself Dr. Adler, dispensing with his title in the West, and relishing such homely tasks as building Lola a wine cellar and fencing her property. They'd hunt together in the mountains, although she never shot game. Their forays were really nature expeditions. He knew the name of every flower. I suppose there are mountains in Germany. Anyway, I well remember the day Lola found it too cold to accompany him, and he never returned. Someone said an 'accident' was the cause, but no one learned much about it. And I was just a child, so no one bothered telling me."

Adler. Irene and I exchanged glances. Was it possible?

"Did Lola take his death well?"

"Now that I think of it, Lola retreated from society after he was gone. Eventually she hired a French chef and began holding soirees at her home filled with all her European treasures. Dr. Adler's wine cellar with the bottles chilled by an underground spring got constant use. He must have been a clever man."

Lotta frowned as she drew slowly on her cigar. How bizarre it was to see that dark roll of tobacco visiting that cherubic little girl's face . . . and shook her head.

"Lola often brooded in those days, wanting to be alone, though she was invariably generous to the beggars who came to her door. Still, her spirit was legendary. Once, when her Indian servant boy was shoved and called a 'damned nigger' by no less than the editor of the *Grass Valley Telegraph,* Lola seized her riding crop and went to the store where it happened. The editor fled the premises, and Lola stood guard over the boy, whip tucked beneath her arm, while he finished shopping. That was when I decided to make her acquaintance, for my mother could never stand up to my father. Lola liked to watch us arriving at the School for Young Children near her house. I was only seven, but one day I marched into her yard to pay her a social call. She adored my imitations of personalities in the town and began to tutor me. It was a wonderful apprenticeship; really renowned performers were always stopping at Lola's house, the Booths, Ole Bull the violinist, Laura Keene, the actress of the day.

"What a house! Crammed with precious goods. She sold most of her marvelous furnishing and property before she left Grass Valley. I was only a child, but I'd seen much of life from the lip of a stage, and raw, gold-field life at that. She seemed to be unburdening herself of things. I felt a change in her, that she was fading . . . not just leaving. I knew I'd never see her again. I knew she'd never dance again, and that I would, for a good long time."

"And so you still do today," Irene said, "the most popular and highly paid star on Broadway."

"I won't die in New York City, though," Lotta said, stubbing out her ugly little cigar. "I've places in New Jersey and Boston. I've donated a fountain to San Francisco. I intend to live for a good long while longer, and I don't intend to fade."

She reached for the powder puff and dusted her red-gold curls with more paprika, until a shimmering red glitter fell upon her blond, baby curls in the gaslight.

Irene snuffed the slow-burning cigar in the tray beside her.

"Thank you for that last portrait of Lola; only you could have painted it."

"Do you think she was really your mother?"

"What do you think?"

Lotta grew unusually sober. "She loved teaching me and urged my mother to take me to Paris. There was no envy in her, of my youth or my talent. She was a second mother to me." Lotta stood, a childlike figure with her skirts above her ankles. "Whether she was a mother to you or not, I couldn't say."

As I gazed at them, it would have been easy to mistake Irene for the mother, Lotta for the eternal child.

"I'm sure," Irene said, glancing about the dressing room filled with flowers, "she would have been very proud of you."

And so we left that room of full-blown blossoms and cigar smoke and joined Quentin in the hall outside.

Memoirs of a Dangerous Woman:

Grass Valley

❧

I recall Madam Lola ... riding many miles over the hills to carry food and medicine to a poor miner, and more than once watching all night at the bedside of a child whose mother could not afford to hire a nurse.

—RUFUS SHOEMAKER, EDITOR, THE *GRASS VALLEY NATIONAL*

I might as well confess the worst first. When I came to California, I only horsewhipped one newspaper editor, challenged another to a duel, and married a third. I repented posthaste of my most grievous mistake, the marriage, and divorced him. (Some would say I shouldn't have either wed or shed him, as my first husband was still alive and our divorce had never been sanctioned. Yet I can swear that I did both marry and divorce that charming but impossible Irishman Patrick Hull, according to the laws of the place.)

I did all this in San Francisco, where five thousand cheering men greeted my arrival, drawing my carriage on their backs through the streets. I danced. I argued with the editors who printed the lies that had followed me from the Old World, though the Jesuits had not penetrated the American continent as far as this, its extreme western end.

And then I went inland to live in my beloved Grass Valley, where I spent the happiest days and years of my life before then, and after. And there, isolated in the wildest part of this unspeakably large land, America, at the age of . . . hmmm, past thirty, shall we say? . . . I found myself becoming teacher and mentor to the many adorable children entertaining the miners, and longed to be a mother at long last.

What has worked this great change in Lola? For one thing, child entertainers were worth their weight in gold in California, a rough-and-ready—a town near Grass Valley was actually named that: Rough and Ready—area of men mostly without women, unless they were Chinese seamstresses. Or whores.

So these astounding, prancing tiny tots brought gentler memories of home and hearth to the miners' rude hearts, who threw gold coins and nuggets onto their stages as wildly as San Francisco had accepted and feted your own Lola.

Every Christmas in Grass Valley I held a party for the little girls, so few and yet so precious (as I had never felt precious, but only a burden to be sent away from my own mother).

There was little Matilda Uphoff, all of three, whose parents ran a bakery. And Susan Robinson—La Petite Susan or the California Fairy Star. Her family of traveling players had settled, as had I, in Grass Valley. Ah, only eight years old, and already able to twirl the banjo, dance the clog, and sing "Black-Eyed Susan," not to mention doing the Shawl Dance, a far cry from my own Spider Dance. A golden shower of dollars greeted her petite toes whenever they touched stage, even in the primitive areas far from San Francisco.

Ah, my gifted fairy girl, my black-eyed Susan! One dreadful June day in '54 her skirt caught fire from the footlights in El Dorado County. So the gold and the glimmer ended, though she survived her severe burns to perform again. But some things do not survive such tragedy, and she never found the path to greater fame.

I remembered all the times I had flirted with the footlights, stamping the flowers thrown to the stage as if they were attacking spiders, my hems foaming like shore-tossed waves. . . . I have started many conflagrations in my life, but I have never been burned.

And then there was Lotta, six years old, a gamine with bright red hair. What a born minx! I took her immediately under my wing, of course, and taught her the fandango and the Irish jig.

I well remember the day I brought this tiny tot to a blacksmith shop in nearby Rough and Ready. My horse needed shoeing, so we fetched up at the smithy of W. H. Flippens. The big burly man set about to enchant the red-haired elf by showing her how his hammer could play a tune on his anvil.

It was then that I lifted Lotta onto the anvil itself, where her wee feet matched the strike of his hammer until a crowd gathered to laugh and applaud.

Oh, if only I had been granted a guide when I took the momentous step of supporting myself by dancing on the stage. The whole valley talked of the red-haired mite dancing on an anvil.

Lotta. Her family name was Crabtree. Of all the Grass Valley girls, she alone was destined for greatness. I urged the mother to take her to Paris, but California was a world away from the Continent, and the idea was too bold for Mary Ann Crabtree. Instead she took Lotta away from me to tour the mining towns.

She ultimately guided her daughter to Broadway, and there little Lotta grew older but not up and reigned while I took New York's lecture circuit by storm and then . . . now my role is offstage, and the footlights fade for me, but not for darling little Lotta, long may she reign.

I've come across a letter from Ludwig, King of Bavaria, dated 1853. He wrote and spoke English, but not easily. Reading again his words returns me to that country that I loved better than India.

My Lollita:

I am glad the gold comb in the shape of a crown is favorable to you in California, the place of gold lying on and inside the ground. I am glad that you have your swan bed with its curtains of silk and the ebony-and-pearl furniture and the nine-foot mirrors and gilt and the pearwood table with ormolu and most of all the love seat upon which you look so beautiful. I see all these things I keep as you left them and I see you. Now they are all in that rustic world of California, where you have bears for pets, and I am not amazed that tame them you will.

It is with sadness, much, I did as you write two, three month ago: pack things you so favored during your stay in Munich, in the palace I fitted for you as if a queen.

It is with great happy that I know you to be peaceful at last in this place of California. I am remembering of the mountains in my own land, and the simple folk who there dwell.

I see you there in your white silk gown, wearing the rubies that speak for your heart of great feeling, among the bears and the men who mine, yet an island of beauty and the stateliness of Europe.

Then I hear word here from the castle at Aschaffenburg, where Theresa my queen keeps. My two nephew saw a lady dressed all in black, her face veiled so as to be unseen. They spoke, but she did not answer. She passed them into the servants' quarters.

The princes followed, they are good boys, curious. The servants had seen no one. So all, servant and prince, went to Queen Theresa and asked if she had seen this dark lady.

Her face went white, they say, as if a specter she had see. She said the Black Lady who appeared foretold the death of a member of the royal family.

I thought of you, my Lollita, when I heard this story as I worked in Munich to ship to you those pieces of your time here in Bavaria you longed for. I remember then the tale of the Black Lady, a princess of my house who has been dead for a century, or more. Once, like you, she danced at a ball, and after her death was often glimpsed dancing among the living, years later. Immediately, a member of the royal house of Wittelsbach had died.

Is she an omen, this Black Lady? I look upon the things we shared and loved, and think of death. Mine? Yours? My Maximilian, who now reigns in my place while I am a packing agent?

No, my Lollita, that was all months ago, numbering two. Now I can tell whom the Lady in Black was seeking. And it was not I, not you. It was Theresa. She had died of the cholera. I am what you call 'a free man' now, so much as any man who has been a king may be.

Sad days have come to Grass Valley. Hull and I are done. He shot and killed Major for being a bear. Lotta is gone. Her mother, Mary Ann, followed her delinquent husband, the former bookseller, to Rabbit Creek, where she will run a boardinghouse and Lotta will enrich the father's coffers.

Even my dear maid, Periwinkle, is unhappy. She tells others she wants to return to New Orleans. I found her brooding on the porch, and when I asked why, she said, "I'm in a brown study on a deep subject."

So I told her this: When I lived in India as a child I learned that when a man died his soul housed itself in a star.

Periwinkle lifted her eyes to the heavens, as I had intended. I told her of Paris and Alexandre Dujarier, a brilliant literary critic and editor of *La Presse,* a liberal Republican newspaper. What a perfect match we were, both still in our twenties. And I told her how perhaps the only man I truly loved had been drawn into a duel and an early death. I pointed to the sky, awash in stars.

"There he is," I said. "And if I am still and alone in the woods, and wait for him to come to me, he does."

"Who do I await to come to me?" Periwinkle asked in her low voice. "No one should live only with the dead."

"No one," I said. "We will make this house ring with merriment again, and drink Champagne and eat cake. And perhaps soon, we'll go where the stars twinkle for all, somewhere far and wonderful."

I missed the stage. I had lost too much in the mountains. My agent arranged a tour of another rough-and-ready land I hadn't yet seen. Australia. I could form whatever company I wished. We first would play San Francisco for two months, then embark for another and I hoped kinder continent. Australia!

I mounted my horse and rode to Rabbit Creek. Mrs. Crabtree was running a second boarding house, and had a second child. The husband was nowhere useful to be seen. He was away scouring the goldfields, I was told.

I explained that I was forming a company for a world tour, and offered to take Lotta with me.

Mary Ann Crabtree told me she was relinquishing the boarding house. Her absent husband had been singing Lotta's praises to the starry sky, and they would tour the mining camps, performing in smoke-filled rooms on crude stages with candles for footlights.

I was hardly one to object to smoke-filled rooms, but I pled for a wider world stage for Lotta. Mary Ann would hear none of it. I hid my disappointment in a last embrace with the heartbroken child, and left Grass Valley, forever.

Much later, I heard that Jack Crabtree's daughter had thousands of gold coins thrown at her tiny dancing feet in the camps, and one night the failed prospector who was her father filled a trunk with her earnings, and left both wife and daughter far behind.

By then I had been to Australia and back, and my own life had changed . . . oh, so irrevocably.

30
Shadows of Lola

～✦～

"What an impertinent snip," Irene said in the hall when we three reunited.

"What, Lotta?" I asked, incredulous. She was such an endearing child . . . for forty-two.

"I well know," Irene said, leading us along the passage to a broad stairway to the street, "how precocious a child performer may be. The mind and the body at five and six is a learning machine. There was nothing I couldn't attempt, and master in my childish hubris, at that age: dance steps, songs, pistol target shooting. Nothing inhibits one. Anything is possible."

She stopped to address Quentin and me, blocking our way. "Lola, on the other hand, was well past that age of innocence when she found her only future was to go upon the stage. She was almost eighteen. That is an ocean of difference. How dare that stunted Lilliputian ridicule Lola's abilities in her thirties when she was attempting to pass what she had learned on to a promising student? How many veteran performers would sabotage rather than encourage a young pretender? I owe everything I am, and was, to those seasoned troupers who took me under their wings."

Quentin and I eyed each other. We stood upon the same mined battleground.

"You're saying," I suggested to Irene, "that Lotta has some reason to denigrate the memory of Lola Montez."

"Doesn't everyone?" she retorted. "You've read those endless vilifications as well as the paeans of praise. There is no getting at the truth in such a situation. I myself have been bitterly misjudged, in public and in private, and there is no undoing such damage. You know that, Nell."

I did indeed.

Quentin stepped in, offering an escort's arm to both of us. "May I suggest supper at"—he glanced at me, all apology and persuasion—"Delmonico's?"

Even I had realized that there was no more impressive after-theater venue to be seen in New York than Delmonico's.

Irene seemed to have turned some personal corner. I understood that criticism of Lola Montez would not be welcomed. She had identified utterly with this woman almost forty years her elder, whose only course had been, apparently, infamy or destruction. Whether the creature was Irene's mother or not had become moot. Irene saw one whom the fates had conspired against, and her operatic soul was committed, as well as her instinctive defense of the underdog.

At Delmonico's we ordered oysters and Champagne . . . well, Irene and Quentin did. I cared for neither of those, but I cared for Irene and Quentin, so didn't say so.

"She left California," Irene summed up over the oysters. "She divested herself of her investments, her goods, her admirers, and her friends, her young protégée, and made arrangements for the care of her animals and her latest bear."

We nodded.

"She embarked from San Francisco to tour Australia. The return voyage saw the tragic overboard loss of another of her 'true loves.'"

I nodded. Quentin could say nothing. He had not steeped himself in the irregular lives and loves of Lola Montez for three days straight.

He could, however, put his ungloved hand over mine on the tabletop, as if he understood we were on a sick watch over Irene.

I thought of my dead-at-childbirth mother, an utter cipher. Was she good? Bad? Neither? I knew not. She had died before I could form any opinion of her.

For the first time I saw that as a deprivation.

Irene went on. "She lectured, with perhaps the greatest success at anything she had done in her life. Then, suddenly, on December twelfth she sailed for England, to wed yet again, this time a member of minor European royalty, although her first husband had never been officially declared her ex-husband. This Germanic princeling proved to be a—what is the word from the last century?—a poltroon. A fraud with five children and a wife, here in America, no less. But then Lola was a fraud with no children and possibly four 'husbands.'"

Irene put her hands to her head, while Quentin ordered tutti fruttis all round.

"It seems," Irene said when she had recovered from her amazement at Lola's amatory adventures, "that Lola recognized she had lost her last cast of the dice. She came back to New York, resumed her lecture tour in the New Year, and was . . . a triumph. The question is, was this last, sudden whimsy to wed in England real, or was it because of me?"

For a moment I sat dazed, so caught up in the drama of Irene's account that I could not see where it was leading.

Quentin could, however. "You mean she left New York long enough to give birth to you, then returned and resumed her usual life?"

Irene shrugged expressively, a gesture she had probably learned at La Scala in Milan. The Italians are even more accomplished shruggers than the French.

"What would she have done with the, er, child?" I asked.

"A nursemaid brought it back on the steamer and it was given to Madame Restell to place."

"With itinerant performers, not a respectable family? I find that hard to believe, Irene."

"Lola had been an itinerant performer. Perhaps she wanted the child where she could be easily seen, without a frowning respectable family wanting to know what lady desired to see the child."

"But—" I was seeking any objection that would bury this fancy once and for all. "She left you nothing. In her will. She had some means, and she left you nothing."

Quentin chose to intervene, and to contradict me. "She could have left funds for the child with the theatrical people, before she died, before she was even ill."

"And," Irene said mysteriously, lighting the petite cigarette she had installed in her mother-of-pearl holder, "she may indeed have left me something. We just don't know what, or where, it is at the moment."

"Ah!" I was in fine fettle myself. "Now we chase the Lost Treasure of Lola Montez! We are all to be headlines in an illustrated tabloid paper!"

Irene shrugged ever so slightly. "She had collected fabulous jewels and trophies and treasures during her travels. You read of them yourself, Nell. Such things don't vanish into London fogs. Such things are difficult to sell in the wilds of California or even in New York. That she left the last of her bank account to the Magdalen Asylum, a home for fallen women, says a great deal. But where are the ruby parure, and the gold and diamonds from the Indian prince, and the twenty-thousand-dollar diamond necklace and other jewels from Ludwig the First?"

"Pawned, sold, stolen, or lost," Quentin suggested, earning my rigorous and approving nod.

"Perhaps." Irene smiled and blew smoke toward the lighting fixture high above, another of those annoyingly steady electric lights. "Or perhaps they were hidden for just the right person to find."

31

The Dockside

Oh, Lola is an untamed woman a lion would be afraid to pet.
—A PARIS WIT ABOUT LOLA MONTEZ STOPPING TO PET A TAME LION IN THE STREET

⊰FROM THE CASE NOTES OF SHERLOCK HOLMES⊱

The dark-clothed man who had watched the rear of the Vanderbilt residence could have been some holy mendicant, I suppose.

I don't know much about holy mendicants, but the manner of the dead man's death had put me in mind of religious matters despite myself.

A family like the Vanderbilts would be subject to many calls upon its charity. It's possible the churchly beggars wished to study the habits of the household to determine whether they could ask aid—approaching disgraced maids, for instance, or unemployed stablemen, if the Vanderbilts had recently turned out any servants.

Such a surreptitious act doesn't speak well of the holiness of the mendicants, but I suppose holiness is not what it used to be nowadays.

I decided to watch the Episcopal Club of New York and moved my cart to the street across from it.

Hacks came and went, and the occasional carriage. The churchmen who went in and out were indeed a dark-clad lot, mostly clean-shaven, somewhat portly, and none reminded me of the lean, cloaked figure that had glided into the club in the wee hours of last night.

My presence attracted other local loungers and peddlers, and we engaged in a lively conversation on whether churchmen were more or less free with a coin to the working poor.

It soon became clear that the Episcopal Club of New York was a favored daytime refuge of the local clergy, but also functioned, as some London clubs did, as a convenient place for out-of-town members to bunk overnight on occasion.

So some members were resident, some transient, and all appeared to be respectable to the point of inspiring total despair that my watch duty would be anything but stuporous.

I missed London's concealing fogs. I was forever having to hide my presence or produce some make-work reason for it after dark, such as repairing a broken wheel on my cart.

At least I was off the overlit thoroughfares blazing with that accursed innovation of Edison's, electric lamps. Both the criminal and the detective have reason to abhor this latest invention.

The street had emptied by midnight. I had lit my pipe and was wistfully regarding its thin blue haze in the light of a distant gas lamp as some wisp of fog when three men on foot came hastily down the street.

The pipe was smoldering in my pocket, and I was enfolded against the inset doorway in an instant.

Like my thin cloaked man, these fellows were overdressed for a summer night. They wore long ulsters and wide-brimmed soft felt hats.

And they avoided the club's front entrance for a side approach. All sight and sound of them melted inside before I could ascertain their exact means of entry.

I had hardly bestirred myself to find out when I heard the soft twitch of a hinge, and the muffled noises of many men.

My doorway remained my bulwark as I saw four men exit the building for the street. My hand went to the pocket sheltering not a warm pipe bowl but cold steel with a checkered walnut butt: my Webley Metropolitan Police pistol.

Watson knew I seldom carried this weapon. Indeed, I find weapons a bother, so Watson is only too happy to unearth in my service the Adams six-shot revolver, a souvenir of his time in the Second Afghan War. Here, abroad,

I must equip myself for all eventualities. This was indeed one, for the fourth figure in the men's midst was hooded and bound and being rushed from the sedate environs of the Episcopal Club of New York to God only knew where.

I followed, my shoes soled with silence, my pipe growing as cold as my pistol, and my will hardening as well. At last I was on the trail of the villains who had slaughtered the old man. I am never surprised by the monstrosity of man, but now I was eager to know how and why these particular men had come across Europe, apparently, to invade the castle of an American millionaire.

I had, of course, studied a map of Manhattan Island. On foreign ground, I was as obligated as an invading general to know the lay of the land. Call me Cornwallis.

Here, in New York, I followed a fretwork of streets. We headed south, toward the tangled area comprising Greenwich Village (amazing how these Yanks memorialized British place names right and left).

Beyond this lay the industrial areas reaching toward the docks and all the warehouses, gin mills and doss joints that plague every port city throughout the world.

I must tread as close on my prey's toes as possible without alerting them to my presence. The thrill of the hunt is like none other I have known. While I would never slay a dumb brute in its tracks, be it bird or beast, I find man the most subtle and rewarding game. One can never underestimate the prey's ability to turn and fight, to defeat my simple object of finding where he goes to ground.

My every sense and all the faculties I had spent a lifetime honing were at fever pitch. I sensed each sound and smell in front of and behind this party. I was Toby, the tracking hound, only I had a secondary charge: to remain invisible and undetected, even as I hunted the unseen spoor of unknown men abroad for an undisclosed purpose.

That the ground was not familiar added a certain challenge in the blood.

Ah! They had vanished into a row of warehouses. The reek of salt and fish enveloped all. Lights? No electricity here near these docks.

I could sense the oily water washing against ancient rotting wood only a few hundred feet away. Miss my prey, and they could be afloat on those soiled waves, striking for some steamship or boat.

No. Their business was here. With Vanderbilt. And myself.

I began to breach each apparently abandoned building, testing doors, peering into the deeper darkness, scenting oil and tar and rotting rope.

These men knew where they went. I had to find out where that was. I feared for the muffled form in their midst. If I took too long, came too late . . . another body for the billiard table.

Of course she had been absolutely right, coming on the scene, knowing nothing about the history of it. *The* woman. As always, as Eve in Eden, deceptive but perceptive in equal measure. Immediately reacting in character, like the superb actress she was. Is. And perhaps superb in another area. *Holy Mither of God!* No cheap stage accent, but the genuine rhythm and lilt of Mother Ireland. Otherwise I would have been alerted to the impersonation. What a woman! *Crucified.* A word not bandied about at the end of the nineteenth century, by God. In an instant she had transfixed what I had not yet seen.

I . . . am an idiot Apostle, and she is the Magdalen on Resurrection Day. She saw, she was first. I know that much.

I would not be here but for her.

So where am I? Thrown off the trail, frantically hunting men who mean no good. When have men ever meant good if they were not forced to it?

Ah. This door opens on an oiled hinge.

I cling to the wall. Waiting, sensing. I do not think, I feel, the only time I allow passion to overcome reason, and only now because it alone works.

The air is still. Yet . . . someone has passed. There is a scent of . . . sealing wax. Ink. Fear.

Here! I open another door, cross vast expanses of piled crates and machine oil.

Oil. I withdraw the small pocket lantern, cast a narrow beam on footprints through the slick surface of the floor.

We are all snails, in our way, and as simple to track.

Even now, at midnight, I hear great winches whining and creaking, lading on crates of goods bound for Singapore and Queensland and South America's many soiled cities.

The oil tracks fade, but I have another clue to follow.

A screech, sharp as an owl's in this vast, high warehouse where no bird has perched.

A scream, unmistakably a man's.

No time for secrecy, I must race to the rescue before it's too late—

I clamber up rough stairs, around a blind corner, the pistol out of my pocket. . . .

Nothing stealthy about my charge . . . oh, for Watson at the rear!

I have reached a bridge of iron, high above the warehouse floor. Some overseer's office, halfway to heaven.

Men scatter like spiders, to the side, below, down stairs, suspended from railings.

My pistol marks them and holds silent. They slither away. They are prey now. I must find their own victim.

I open a door, half frosted glass, onto some cat's cradle of an office strung far above the warehouse floor.

Cramped, dirty, hardly more than a hole, occupied by a battered desk.

On that desk, a man.

With his hands transfixed to the old, oily wood with the sharp impaling spikes of . . . letter openers.

The man's eyes roll in his head as he swoons with pain. He is alive and can speak, can I but . . . unpin him and take him away from this mad, mercantile torture chamber.

I do, but he swoons nonetheless.

One man I can carry.

I watch all the way for those who have done this, but they have melted away like spiderwebs in the rain. I know, can I but return to a civilized street in this city of devils, that I have captured a witness.

32

Helter-Shelter

❧

The [newspaper] boys called him a great fake, but they were hardly just to him in that. I should rather call him a great actor, and without being that no man can be a great detective.

—JACOB RIIS, THE RECORDER OF LATE NINETEENTH-CENTURY NEW YORK CITY
POVERTY, ABOUT INSPECTOR THOMAS BYRNES, NYC CHIEF OF DETECTIVES
AND INVENTOR OF THE THIRD DEGREE

⊰FROM THE CASE NOTES OF SHERLOCK HOLMES⊱

In London I know every crevice where vice and venality might be found, where petty criminals go to ground.

Here, in New York, I am in a new world.

I stowed my rescued man in the capacious bottom of my peddler's cart, unconscious, and set out to find my new friends, Hungry Joe and Mother Hubbard.

In the middle of night the city shivers with skittering life forms. Like cockroaches, the criminal element scuttles over the empty streets, either celebrating successful felonies or in the process of robbing, killing, devouring.

In London, I had a half dozen hidey-holes where I could don a disguise or wait like a spider until the web of my weaving trembled with the touch of my prey upon the silk.

Not in New York.

Everything was new, and forbidding. I needed allies, and quickly.

Hungry Joe I finally found in a saloon not too far from the Vanderbilt mansion on Fifth Avenue. Great wealth always sits cheek-by-jowl with great larceny.

"Oh, yeah! The peddler from Vanderbilt Row. Whatcha want, fellow? I'm off for the day, drinkin' my profits away."

"I need a safe place to go to ground. I've a near-dead man to tend."

"Do you, now?" He whistled sharp over the foamy head of his beer. "Why should I help you?"

I showed him.

"Well, that's damn patriotic of you! My pocket's never offered a warm nest for a gold eagle before. We none of us have a place to call our own but the streets and the alleys. 'Cept Mother Hubbard. She's got a crib, if'n you can pay the rent. Down lower town way, where the swells don't go 'cept to get late-night ladies."

I waved the ten-dollar piece in front of his nose, and soon we were lurching along the darkened streets, he pulling my cart, I pushing. The sum was princely, but Vanderbilt could afford it and the case was dire.

Watson is wrong. I have a heart. It was beating hard for the cause of the wounded man in my charge. My witness. If he lived.

The place stank of beer and urine, no worse than any Whitechapel doss house or opium den. I could have used the calming effects of my 7 percent solution, but not here, where I controlled nothing.

Mother Hubbard eyed, then acknowledged me, then demanded five dollars. I felt like a character in a Dickens novel, but I paid.

I was shown to a somewhat sheltered corner, with a blanket in a crumpled heap. There I laid my charge, and dosed him with cheap whiskey for his wounds, and cheaper bread for his sustenance.

Not for some time had I found occasion to go to ground so far on the selvage edge of a society. I was reminded of camping out on Grimpen Mire, unsuspected. Save now I was in the middle of a great metropolis, yet in a place somehow as wild as any moor in England.

The man I tended raved in his sleep. I heard talk of giant spiders, and Ultramontanes, and the approaching hot irons. I felt transported to an earlier, viler age, to the Inquisition, when each man's inviolable conscience was an invitation for torment and unimaginable torture.

Crucifixion.

A barbaric concept. The stuff of ancient history, and yet . . . relevant to the Vanderbilt case.

I bandaged my charge's wounds, wishing Watson were here to explain their extent.

The poor youth caught my coat collar in his mutilated hands, and sang my praises, thanked me. In my own terms, I've done nothing. The overall pattern still eludes me. His suffering is a slap in the face. Yes, I've saved him from further torment, but until I know everything, that means nothing.

He raves. Speaks in tongues. Spanish. French, which I know. He finally mutters a word. A word I know so well my blood chills. A name. Irene. *The* woman. I'd made certain that she remained far from my Vanderbilt investigation, and now I hear her name mentioned by the second victim of this shadowy conspiracy. I can't doubt that she has somehow become *the* target of these pitiless villains.

"Irene Norton," he murmurs again. *"No. No. No!"* he screams.

33

Dining at Delmonico's

~∪∪~

*I used to wonder what disguise you would come in, but I never thought
I would see you as Nellie Bly.*

—THE MATRON AT NEW YORK CITY POLICE HEADQUARTERS, 1889

⊰ F R O M   N E L L I E   B L Y ' S   J O U R N A L ⊱

Of course I asked Quentin Stanhope to lunch at Delmonico's.

Already he was squirming, no doubt remembering the disaster that
had transpired the last time we two had dined at Delmonico's.

I wanted him to remember that awkward occasion. A man not at
ease is a man I can bend to my own purposes, even a self-assured Englishman.

For a wild moment, it occurred to me that I could try to enroll Sherlock
Holmes in my quest . . . but, no, he had no such gentlemanly strictures piled
upon him as Quentin. Nor had he the normal gentleman's reluctance to treat
a woman harshly. Only one woman might command extraordinary patience
from him, and I was not she.

I wondered briefly what Irene and her henchwoman Nell might be up to.
Surely nothing as interesting, as scandalous, as bloody awful as the Affair at
Noll Cottage. At last I could put to use the information on Madame Restell I
had gleaned during the previous month!

Nothing was wasted in the inventive reporter's experience.

I made sure that the maître d'hôtel at Delmonico's seated Quentin and myself in the fenced outdoor portion of the restaurant, where we could be seen by all comers.

"Wouldn't you rather lunch inside?" he inquired with a divinely attractive frown when we were led to a prized public table his English accent had commanded. "It's beastly hot outside."

"You've survived the beastly heat of India," I pointed out, "and I prefer a natural breeze."

At this he frowned further, for not a breath of wind was stirring.

"You said you had an investigative matter to consult me upon," he noted as soon as we had been seated.

"Hold your horses, Mr. Stanhope. We haven't even read the menu. It's bad for the digestion to rush into lunch on a hot day."

So we ordered, I an iced tea, he a lemonade, not iced. The British abhor ice, except in their manner at times.

Quentin's manner was becoming frosty, if not ice-cold.

"This meeting smacks of an attempted bribery," he said. "You know I can't help you reveal the Ripper."

"You'd be bribed by a lunch at Delmonico's?"

"You have more on your mind than lunch."

"Why, Mr. Stanhope, you can't be implying that I would resort to . . . seduction to get a story."

The dull flush beneath his sunburned skin was even more attractive. Perhaps I *would* resort to seduction to get a story, though I never had before. Silly Nell was not injudicious where she cast her girlish affections. . . .

"I am obligated to deal with you politely," he snapped out as sharply as Sherlock Holmes might have, "but you are mistaken to think that because I wear kid gloves on occasion I don't have access to iron fists. You treat matters of the greatest international gravity as a joke, or worse, grist for your personal glory mill. I won't have it."

"My, the heat does make you testy!" I dropped my coy manner and leaned over the table. "Listen, Quentin. I'm on the trail of a really juicy story. A domestic story. Set here in the good old U.S. of A. If I get this story, and you help me, you can keep your nasty old Ripper and all those funny foreign place names. This story will rock New York City, and the whole country!"

"What do I have to do?"

"Ever the cynic, Quentin."

"Ever the news-hungry hound, Pink."

The waiter came with our beverages. I admit that I had worked up a thirst. Englishmen are never easy. I would swear I will never marry one, but then I'd already sworn I'd never marry, so the oath was redundant.

The ice clicking against my teeth as I sipped the tea made Quentin set his jaw as he lifted his lemonade glass to his lips. I suppose iced teeth are anathema to an Englishman, the way smothered news stories were an affront to me.

"You don't have to do anything," I told him, "except trot around New York City with me and claim to be my husband."

That Delmonico's lemonade must be strong stuff, for I watched his expression grow as sour as his drink when he heard my words.

34
What the Nursemaid Saw

One of the most astounding stories of conspiracy, of turpitude, of plot and counter-plot, ever revealed outside the realms of improbable fiction.
—*The World*

FROM NELLIE BLY'S JOURNAL

Although I didn't need Quentin Stanhope for my earliest investigations, it tickled me no end to insist he come along.

Maybe I wanted to a get a midge up Miss Nell's corset. Maybe I wanted to make the ones who had gagged me after the Ripper hunt pay, and Quentin was the nearest representative.

Maybe I liked to be seen in his company. Certainly the boyos at the paper sat up and snapped their suspenders when he showed up at the *World* on my instructions . . . or at my insistent invitation, shall we say?

"Mr. Quentin Stanhope," I introduced him around the office. "Of London."

Talk about killing two birds with one stone! The office gossips had a new target for their suspicions, and I was putting Quentin through hoops for the sin of trying to shush me like an unruly child.

He took being paraded through the offices with good grace, and even shook hands with Mr. Pulitzer, impressing the boss with my taste in men.

Hah! No one knew or guessed my taste in men except myself, and there it would stay until I said differently. It's amazing how men in the working world want a woman hooked up to some other man so she will stay out of their hair . . . if they have any left.

So Quentin was the perfect shill for the office gossips—I could cite my undying devotion to my absent Englishman for years after this—and he also would prove necessary on my quest.

He seemed to sense my goals, for as we left the building he took my arm like a considerate swain, rather than a husband.

"It must have galled you to the bone, Pink, to agree to keep the Ripper story quiet."

"Yes," was all I answered.

"It wasn't because anyone underestimated you as a journalist, it was because they knew all too well your effectiveness."

"So I'm to be a happy eunuch?"

He winced, and not from the strong sunlight in the street. "I'll aid you as you wish, but you might consider telling me what the object is. It's possible I might have some insight to contribute."

"A modest Englishman! All right. We're going to see a nursemaid at Bellevue."

"A nursemaid in hospital?"

"In *the* hospital. That's the way we say it here. She was stabbed."

"Who would stab a nursemaid?"

"How about her employer?"

This he mulled. In fact, he said nothing more until we arrived, which is most unusual for a man. Usually they insist on knowing where they are going, or pretend to.

"Mrs. Mary Donnelly," the nurse said, nodding to the figure lying halfway down a stark row of iron cots. The smell of carbolic acid tainted the air.

She was wan but she had the Irish mouth: a thin determined slash above her overlong chin, which denoted stubbornness.

"Are you feeling better?" I asked, taking the sole chair near the bed.

Quentin Stanhope stood at my shoulder, pale summer straw hat in hand.

"They tell me I'll survive, no thanks to that lying Mrs. Hamilton. A common whore. God knows what happened to the babes they sold her."

"My name is Nellie Bly. I—"

"Miss Bly! Really? 'Tis Irish you must be, you've got such a heart for the poor and downtrodden. Excuse me drizzlin'. Such a bad time 'tis been. 'Twas no way I could allow that poor man to be diddled about the nature of his own so-called child. And what happened to the previous babe, I ask you? My God, what these people were up to! I only tried to warn the mister! And she stabbed me like a pig at the marketplace! What would she have done to the babe . . . the babies? She didn't care, that harlot, except for diddling a rich man of his money."

I was taking notes as fast as I could scribble. "You were so brave."

"Not really. I denounced her in front of her husband. Who else could make things right for the poor babe in her clutches? I never expected her to have a knife, or to try to cut the throat out of me. She was mad. And he didn't understand, he could hardly move for the shock of it. Poor man. His babe not his own? His wife a baby-buyer and worse? Why would he believe me? But I had to tell! I couldn't let her kill another babe and then find another to take *its* place. Mayhap to a man they all look alike, but to me each is its own angel and I could not be fooled."

Silence held at this, then Quentin spoke for the first time. I had told him the facts of the case en route to Bellevue.

"Was Mrs. Hamilton accustomed to carrying a dagger?"

"No, sir! I had no idea that lying whore would attack like a wolf! I only knew that the child they brought back from California was not the child they took. Men are such fools! A woman is a woman to them, a babe a babe. Ye cannot fool a nursemaid who has cradled a child at her breast. The little faces are hairless mostly, and all ears and no nose, but they are as different as one rosebud from another. If you haven't looked at a bush in full bloom, you wouldna know! But I know. 'Tis my job, my curse to know. No child is the spittin' image of another, no matter how young. No woman with the instincts of a mother would say such is so. Ah, she was a demon mother, who would sell herself and all those other mothers' children so! I would denounce her again, her and all her heartless kin. Poor Mr. Hamilton. D'ye know how he keeps himself now? And what has become of that poor babe? Where is he?"

She asked good questions, the kind I was wont to ask. I blushed to realize I hadn't answered them before I came to her.

Quentin Stanhope took my elbow and drew me to my feet.

"We're looking into it," he assured her. "We shall find and account for both of the babies this gang presented as Mr. Hamilton's child in turn. And when we find them, they shall have the homes they deserve."

I turned to stare. I knew better than to offer such unlikely guarantees. His hand on my elbow pinched a good deal. I realized then that I also would have to offer these guarantees.

"That's right, Mrs. Donnelly. We're here to set things straight."

Her hand caught my sleeve. "I would take that second-to-last dear boy, if anyone would allow it. I loved him dearly, and it pierced my heart when I saw he did not come back from California."

We left the ward, and Quentin's hand never left my elbow.

"What of the boy," he asked, "Eva Hamilton took to California and didn't bring back?"

"She gave him away, because he didn't look enough like the first baby who died."

"Can we find him?"

"If someone in California can."

"I suggest you wire that you have found a fine mother for the lad."

"Who are you to tell me what to do?"

"Your unwilling confederate. If you need money, the Rothschild coffers will pay."

"Can you be sure of that?"

"In this instance, yes. The Jews have suffered savagely for centuries from being falsely accused of killing Christian babies. This one will be saved."

"Two died," I admitted. "The first baby Eva obtained, after only a few days. She got another, and it died. The third did not resemble the previous two enough, and even Mr. Hamilton would have noticed that. Thus this last one."

He shook my arm. "Any living babies of this atrocious string of fraud and deception must be found and provided for, especially this third baby who was lucky enough not to resemble the debased people in this matter. He must be found and delivered to Mary Donnelly, who has a deep and self-sacrificing attachment to him. That woman is worth three times any who have been involved in this tragedy."

"Agreed. But, Quentin, let go of my arm. I'm not the baby-dealer. I want to expose this hideous traffic. Will you join me willingly?"

"More willingly than you wish," he said.

That is the trouble with unwilling tools. They soon develop a mind, and heart, of their own.

I couldn't help smiling. I had a most unexpected partner in daredevil reporting, one Quentin Stanhope, gentleman and spy, and Miss Nell's errant swain.

What would Irene Adler Norton make of this?

35

Paying Tribute to Venus

❦

The fearful constitutional consequences which may result from this affection . . . the fear of which may haunt the mind for years, which may taint the whole springs of health, and be transmitted to circulate in the young blood of innocent offspring are indeed terrible. . . .
—DR. SPENCER THOMSON, 1856

 "Are we on the hunt for your family tree or for the family jewels?" I asked Irene the next day.

"I thought Quentin looked exceedingly well last night."

"He always looks well."

"I should have been more specific. I mean handsome."

"I suppose so. You're evading my question."

"America appears to agree with him. Or perhaps it was your company."

"Irene, I doubt my company has ever made a particle of difference to anyone but you."

"Are you forgetting your Coney Island expedition with Quentin?"

I could feel my cheeks heating up. "No. That was . . . Quentin being thoughtful enough to take me off your hands for a while."

"Really? I thought I glimpsed Quentin having difficulty taking his hands off of you."

"Irene!"

"I'm sorry, Nell. To answer your question, it may be that Lola Montez's treasure has a good deal to do with her manner and place of death. In that case, it doesn't really matter if she was my mother or not. I want to know how this woman ended her life in such reduced and forgotten circumstances. She had always mastered every situation before that, from Bavaria to California to Australia to this very New York City on more than one occasion."

"She was deathly ill from a stroke, Irene. Even the strongest will quails before that, and this new humility led her to seek forgiveness of God. Quite an inspiring story, really."

"Accounts differ," Irene said sharply. "Some say Mrs. Buchanan exploited her when the stroke had weakened her. That Lola was neglected and even abused during her last weeks, that her money and jewels were signed over to Mrs. Buchanan when she no longer had her wits about her."

"Gracious! You needn't sound so fierce! I wasn't there."

"No, you weren't. Nor was I. More than one helpless invalid dies leaving all the goods divided between the Church and a final caretaker. Suspicion always arises in such cases. Even Lola's own mother—whose marital machinations she'd fled, not wisely but well, twenty-some years before and never laid eyes on again—even she made a long and costly pilgrimage to America to, what . . . find out how much of Lola's fabled wealth remained? Maybe Lola hadn't been already hoodwinked out of it. Maybe she'd hidden it, anticipating just such greedy forays."

"What an odiously negative view of humanity, Irene! You would have poor Father Hawks, who later sought sainthood for Lola Montez, certainly the most publicized sinner of her day, conspiring to bilk her at the end?"

"His search for saintly recommendations could have covered a hunt for her money and jewels."

"Irene, do you regard no one as safe from suspicion, including the clergy?"

"Now you have it, Nell! Oh, I would trust Parson Huxleigh, were he alive and here, but that is about all. You witnessed my kindness to the poor clergyman who fell injured outside our house in St. John's Wood two years ago . . . and how that act of charity would have been rewarded by the masquerading Sherlock Holmes had I not seen through his scheme and fled. Father Hawks was tormented to death, Nell, as men have not been since the Inquisition or women since the witch hunts. He must have known something crucial to someone very implacable. A humble priest? Tortured to death in this day and age. Why?"

I frowned, for I couldn't dispute her, however much I wished to.

"People commit such atrocities, Nell—at least in human history as we know it—for only two reasons: fanatical religious conviction or maniacal personal gain."

I wrung my hands. Father Hawks was to be deeply pitied, even revered for his death that so mimicked Christ's, not viewed with suspicion.

"What gain could be great enough to merit such atrocious acts?" I demanded.

Irene's eyes flashed with conviction. "You have asked the crucial question. Exactly: why and who? Only something . . . paramount, something . . . legendary, could evoke such extreme measures. I am not a religious woman, Nell, which you know and lament. But the instant I saw that poor, abused body on the billiard table I . . . I found myself making the sign of the cross. Yes, it was in my character as an Irish housemaid, and yes, I am actress enough to reach for the facile gesture. And, no, I am not a Roman Catholic, and I realize you Church of England folk have no time for such, but the gesture was sincere. It surprised me. I truly felt myself in the presence of such an enormity of human misbehavior that only an appeal to a higher force would answer. Perhaps it was because of all the evil we encountered during our last . . . travail. Sherlock Holmes felt that awful awe as well. I realized that also. Otherwise he would have seen through my stage colleen, but he didn't until he too reassembled his composure.

"I would think that man did not have a religious bone in his body."

"No, he is reason personified. But what we saw defied reason. I think that even his ardent agnosticism is lit by the occasional flash of what he would officially dismiss as mere superstition."

"Why do we care what he thinks or feels?"

"Because if anyone will solve that crime, it will be he."

"Good! Let him do it.

"So he will. Meanwhile, we must recognize that our examination of Lola Montez may take us in directions far removed from the mere sentimentality of motherhood."

"Such as?"

"Fatherhood. I must have had one. Still, I remain unconvinced that parents are essential, especially at my age."

"Gracious!" The forgotten men. "Given Lola's reputation, your father could be anyone!"

"Anyone on three continents, for Lola traveled between Europe, Australia, and the U.S. during the crucial time period I was told I was born. And her habit of wearing shawls could have easily concealed a delicate condition."

"Wouldn't you like to know who your father was, as well?"

"No!" Irene bounded out of her chair, agitated. "I'm finding one delinquent parent heartache enough," she burst out, her strength of feeling surprising me. "None of the men in Lola's life are ones I'd care to call father."

"But he could be a prince or a millionaire," or this mysterious Dr. Adler.

"Or a newspaper publisher or an itinerant actor. Whoever he was, he wouldn't have remained with Lola even if she'd had a child."

I, reared by a father only, was loath to relinquish Irene's. "He could have been somebody like Godfrey."

Mentioning her absent husband had an instant soothing effect. "Well, if he was like Godfrey I'd look for him straightaway. But who is like Godfrey?" She sighed, and settled back in her chair again. "If only he were here! Godfrey lends a clarity to my mind that is like bright north light to a painter. And he had less than conventional parents as well. I wish I'd followed my instincts and had never sought my so-called mother."

"Oh, Irene, motherhood is a supposed to be a sacred state. This should all be so simple and innocent."

She eyed me askance, as if she were a governess and I still a child. "Nothing is ever either of those things, Nell. You'd do well to keep that in mind."

"I? I'm not searching for a lost mother."

"No." Irene smiled, withdrew a cigarette, then paused. "Speaking of innocence, or lack of it, some later biographies of Lola hinted she might have died not from a stroke but from the wages of her presumed sins."

I didn't know what to say.

"Syphilis, Nell, is the disease one gets from a life such as Lola is reputed to have lived."

My face reddened truly, for I had heard whispers of such an unmentionable thing, "a delicate disease," it was called. I'd never heard any specific word attached to it until now. Syphilis. It sounded like the name of a Greek deity. Or was I thinking of the wretch who had to roll a boulder up a hill, and forever fell back and had to start again? Rather like our current quest.

She hesitated before speaking again. "Usually such things are passed from the man to the woman."

"Except in marriage," I said quickly. Moral distinctions must be made.

"Marriage is no exception. The man passes on the condition because men far more often than women break marriage vows. It's the way of the world. Such diseases are a matter of—" I watched Irene search for a delicate way to put it. She shrugged, having found none. "Of having numerous lovers.

If Lola did suffer from a venereal disease," Irene added, finally lighting her cigarette and shaking out the lucifer that had achieved that task, "such a condition is inherited. By any offspring. And it often leads to madness and death even in the second generation."

It took a moment for her implication to become clear. If Lola Montez was truly Irene's mother, and had suffered from "a delicate disease . . ." I do believe I almost made the sign of the cross myself, King Henry the VIII forgive me.

I didn't sleep a wink or a blink that night.

I'd heard whispers, of course, about certain dissolute noblemen behaving madly. I suppose I knew why, but I never admitted it.

Now that awful ghost was hovering over my own house.

Irene's eyes had darkened to an onyx glitter as she pointed out this unwholesome fact. I realized that this worry had absorbed her from the moment we received the many biographies of Lola Montez. With her more worldly outlook, it must have occurred to her far earlier than when she had finally told me.

We must determine if Lola was her mother, or neither of us would sleep a wink again . . . and Godfrey! Oh, I missed him too, and his ever-so-tactful way of explaining to me confusing worldly matters. Was it not possible, even likely, that if such evil was transmitted to the younger generation it could be transmitted to whomever one . . . um, whomever?

Was it possible that . . . unsanctioned kissing could transmit the curse? Was that why religions were so strict about such matters?

Had Quentin . . . no, I would not think about it. Quentin would never do anything to harm me, and surely, like Irene, was worldly enough to know how to ensure that.

But Irene could not help who her mother was . . . or what she had died from.

I tossed and turned, furious at my own ignorance and yet tortured by my speculations. My hair matted against my sopping scalp and face. And then I shivered as the cool air in the room attacked my feverish body.

Madness and death.

Already the unfriendly accounts made Lola look a bit mad. But then, she'd always behaved like a woman who recognized no limits, and that is considered madness in many circles.

Only one course would answer this dreadful uncertainty. We must discover whether Lola was Irene's mother, or not. And then we must know how Lola had died and what part this pretty word *syphilis* that signified such disaster might have played in that ending.

I saw now that Irene would not, could not, be turned from this investigation in view of the high personal stakes.

I saw now that I could not, would not, be turned from this quest in view of the high personal stakes.

The means most in my power were the two hidden documents from two vastly different sources—and even periods of time—that Irene had unearthed during our three weeks in New York City. One was the faded, almost illegible scrawls presumably written in Lola's hand, found in the modest boardinghouse where she died in early 1861. The other was the coded client book of the society abortionist and secret adoption arranger, Madame Restell, found in the imposing Fifth Avenue mansion she had built across from Vanderbilt Row, where she so spectacularly left this earth in 1877.

I arose, lit my bedside lamp, and studied both documents until my vision blurred. Lola's papers offered some clear passages. The Restell book listed columns and columns of abbreviated words and numbers that seemed vaguely familiar, yet I could still make no sense of them whatsoever. Time and persistence was the only hope here. Meanwhile, I needed my wits for the morning.

I said a quick but fervent prayer that Lola Montez was not the woman she had been reputed to be by her worst enemies.

And then I made a vow that I would find out the truth about Lola, and that not even the beasts who had tormented Father Hawks would stop me.

Oh, and I said a prayer for Quentin, and what it was is not even the business of my own diary.

36

And Baby Makes Three

The notion of combining the exploitation of crime, scandal, or shocking circumstance with the spirit of a crusade, delivered into words by a clever and talented writer who donned disguise to get the story was sensationalist in character and something altogether new in the field.

—BROOKE KROEGER, *NELLIE BLY*

❧ FROM NELLIE BLY'S JOURNAL ❧

I told Quentin to get some new clothes at a department store.

Off he went, whistling.

That man was determined not to writhe under my thumb. I returned and also went shopping, at a street market, where I found a mended wool shawl, once fine, and some slightly worn women's clothing, including the ugliest straw hat I have ever seen. When it comes to women's dress, the hat is the most important piece, for it sits atop the face, and whatever message it gives underlines the veracity of the face beneath. I was going for a "poor but honest" impression.

Quentin, once out of his London-tailored garb and into American department-store goods, would do for my slightly well set-up new husband.

We met at my brownstone on Eighty-sixth Street, under the watchful eye of my mother.

"Mrs. Cochrane," he said with one of those bows the Brits do so well. "I'm delighted to meet the woman who has reared the formidable Nellie Bly."

"Oh, go on, Mr. Stanhope! Pink tells me you are quite the swell fellow, and it's very good of you to aid her in her latest venture. Mind you, not that anyone would be stopping my Pink."

"I have seen her grit and grace exercised on two continents, madam," he said, managing not to sound utterly smarmy, which was a miracle. "It's a privilege to assist her."

So with the maternal blessing we sallied forth on another of my masquerades.

He eyed my attire with a respectful eye. "Quite plain and even frumpy, my dear Pink. You show deep dedication to your work."

I surveyed him back. "The store-bought clothes underline your air of Johnny-come-lately petty bourgeoisie. If only you spoke the president's English."

"But I do, dear heart," said he, immediately assuming a Yankee accent so authentic it had me blinking. "Blending into any environment is the chief virtue of a spy. If I can speak Urdu, I can certainly master the American 'twang.'"

"All right." I would never admit I was pleasantly surprised that my plan to humiliate Nell and her swain would work so well to my own purposes. I stopped and pulled off my darned cotton glove, slightly gray at the fingertips. "You can put on this last prop."

He gazed at the plain gold ring I had bought at the flea market. It was probably ten-karat gold, and much nicked, although it had been sold as fourteen.

Quentin frowned. "I would have done better than this."

"I am a woman who has hooked a man slightly above her station. I'm content with less. The real money will go to buying the infant."

"And how much will that be?" he asked, producing an admirably scarred brown leather wallet. Apparently he had visited his own flea market.

"I won't know until we try."

"And where do we try?"

"The poorer quarters on the Lower East Side. I have some villains' names to bandy about. We'll see where they lead."

"What are the names? I should know them as well as you, perhaps better."

"Joshua Mann and his so-called 'mother,' Mrs. T. Anna Swinton."

"'T. Anna'? What kind of name is that for a woman?"

"Don't know. Don't care. But that was the old harridan who helped Eva

Hamilton produce her rotating cast of infant children. I think her odious son, Joshua, had been Eva's pimp in her early days. They were the 'family' of swindlers, not foolish Robert Roy Hamilton, who was hoodwinked into making an honest woman of his mistress when she started pleading pregnancy."

"He must have been simple-minded."

"Especially since his Eva had several so-called 'husbands' in her past, and stints in brothels in Philadelphia and even New York."

"So the first baby 'produced' died. Why?"

"One would hope little Eva wished her brat to survive."

"And this woman bought another baby, who also died?"

"Again, we come back to a simple-minded Robert Roy." I sighed, not wanting to face more than the bare facts, for the individual fates of the infants were heartbreaking. "I imagine these babies' mothers were poor and desperate, half-starving, and their infants as well. None of them had half a chance."

"Babies are sold the world over," he assured me in acid tones, "and into situations far worse than the Hamilton household."

"The third baby didn't look enough like the first one. That tells me it was bought sight unseen, or by Mann or Swinton."

"And the fourth one?"

"Passed muster with Hamilton, but not the nursemaid."

"She was a brave woman."

"And paid for it."

"Where are the happy couple now . . . meaning this Mann person and his mother, Mrs. Swinton?"

"Out on bail, charged with fraudulent production of an infant under false pretenses. It's so strange, Quentin. I can understand why Hamilton wanted to move his unconventional family away from gossip to California, but they were both unhappy in the West and he moved back East post haste, bringing Mann and Mrs. Swinton along to Atlantic City! Then they again engaged the same nurse who had seen the third child who'd been given away. Why did that obnoxious trio expect to diddle the nurse as well?"

"It might have made the husband suspicious if she had not been rehired. And . . . she counted for nothing. Mere hired help is expected to be invisible. Perhaps the miscreants thought their ploys would be as invisible to her as to her master."

"The wife herself is a maze of contradictions. She goes on trial as Eva Hamilton alias Steele alias Parsons alias Mann—"

"Then this Mann was more than her pimp, he was her husband."

"Among a certain class, that's usually the case."

"It makes one long for uncivilized climes, where slavery is open."

"Pooh, surely you know that the major cities traffic in anything and anybody."

"I do. But I didn't know that you did."

"Do you think that I have made my reputation by blinking at abomination, and swooning?"

"My dear Pink, I don't contemplate your reputation at all."

"Perhaps you should. You might stop underestimating me."

"I doubt it."

I realized that was as much concession as I would ever get from this cucumber-cool Englishman.

"Are you ready to embark on a charade of baby-seeking?"

"As ready as I'll ever be. Where do we go for such a thing?"

"At least we'll avoid an area in the Forties and Sixties on the West Side from Eighth to Twelfth Avenue known as Hell's Kitchen."

"Sounds even hotter than upper Fifth Avenue. And far too close to Millionaires' Row for comfort."

"Oh, it is. But there's another area on the Lower East Side where poor women will do anything for a slab of bread or a cot to sleep on. That's where babies are to be had, by the droves."

He extended his elbow. Trust an Englishman to walk into hell in polite precision.

I took the proffered arm. I was an ordinary wife now, desperate for issue, ready to beg, borrow, or steal the needed infant . . . or to buy it if necessary. A henchman husband only added to the credibility of the masquerade. I was sure Joshua and mother had done the baby-hunting for Eva.

I flexed my ring finger, left hand. It would be a cold day in hell when I would wear such a symbol of submissiveness in real life, but in my quest for justice and front-page news, I would suffer any indignity, even if it came attached with an arrogant, albeit good-looking, Englishman.

37
Mother Hubbard's Cupboard

～✦～

MARGARET BROWN, alias YOUNG,
alias HASKINS, alias OLD MOTHER HUBBARD

Sixty-one years old in 1889. Born in Ireland. Weight, 120 pounds.
Height 5 feet, 3 inches. Gray hair, gray eyes, light complexion.
Generally wears a long cloak when stealing.

—*1886 PROFESSIONAL CRIMINALS OF AMERICA,* INSPECTOR THOMAS BYRNES

❧ FROM NELLIE BLY'S JOURNAL ❧

"Good God," said Quentin Stanhope, "this is as unsettling as parts of Bombay, India."

After dismissing our hack at Broadway in lower Manhattan, we had penetrated darkest New York City on foot. I was interested to hear that one as well traveled as he found the tenement areas as oppressive as any overcrowded, poor quarter on earth.

Odors of food and filth mixed into that peculiar potpourri that grinding daily want produces. I had smelled as bad or worse in the madhouse, but here the inmates were free to run around and populate and they did. The streets rang with the cries of hordes of dirty, ragged, barefoot children, not the happy cries of a park but wails and screams, and even these littlest residents of Tenement Hell preyed on each other in a dozen tongues.

"Do we simply inquire after any spare infants from one of the street peddlers?" Quentin asked.

"I've been given a name by one of my liaisons in the area. We are looking
for Mother Hubbard's Cupboard."

"You're joking!"

"This is another New York here, and certain people are known on the
streets as if they lived in a village instead of a mighty metropolis."

"In that case—" Quentin's arm shot out to snag a youth who was running
by and dragoon him into our service.

Filth and freckles hid most of the skin color on his face. A dingy checked
cap thankfully hid what condition his hair might be in. His fingertips were oily
and raw, and open sores festered on his dingy neck.

"A dime if you tell us what we want to know," Quentin offered in a pass-
able American accent.

The word "dime" caught the ears of several running boys. They surrounded us with the smell of damp cloth and rank sewers.

"We want Mother Hubbard's."

"Coppers?"

"Hardly," said I. "We've . . . lost a child and heard she could help."

"She'll help ya right into Blackwell's Island, all right. A dime?"

"Two!"

"Two."

The boy hitched a shoulder toward the row of soot-darkened brick buildings. "Middle one. Ground floor. Runs a school, she does, so you'd better
mind your p's and q's."

The other boys snickered, so I didn't ask exactly what he meant. Such
boys' mouths were as filthy as their skins. And several were eyeing me with the
hungry looks of wolves, only with a disturbing human hunger.

Quentin tossed the boy his two dimes, something of an overcharge for a location but forty paces away, and threw a handful of nickels at the rest of the mob.

We left them scrambling to rob each other of the coins.

The street din rose with the addition of their squeals and at the second-
story window a woman leaned out and hollered for them to be quiet.

"I've got a colicky baby who needs sleep," she shouted.

But no one heeded, or cared, and she withdrew back into the dark interior.

The heat inside must have been awful, for the cries of irritable infants
streamed from every building.

"What becomes of them?" Quentin asked.

"Who? The children? If they survive the first years and their mother doesn't get sick or the family evicted, they grow up to join the mongrels scrabbling in the street. If they survive that, they grow up to get jobs on the docks. Some get drunk on their pay and kill each other in saloons. A few, I imagine, earn their pay and marry and have children of their own and fight to move into a building a little closer to the respectable parts of the city.

"Maybe their children will get some schooling, and grow up to get better jobs and move out of these slums entirely. But that's the fairy-tale ending doled out only to the exceptional. Most of the girls get pregnant and they never even progress to being tenement shop workers. They bear children till they die of consumption or one cuff too many from a drunken husband."

"There's a tone of personal umbrage in your voice, Nellie Bly."

"I do take it personally. My father was a judge, but my mother was his second wife. When he died she and us kids had to get out with a few goods, and that was it. She married again, a Civil War veteran, but he drank, and was crazy anyway. I finally got my mother free of that brute, and my brothers and sisters too. So I know a bit about what these poor children go through, and that's what I bring to the readers of *The World,* what poor people go through."

"So whether you commit yourself to a madhouse or to finding some poor waif to buy, you really act as a spy, as I do."

"You might say so."

He tipped his hat to me. "Let's find this Mother Hubbard and see what she has hidden in her cupboard."

It turned out that Mother Hubbard ran a school for street thieves, all of them under the age of fifteen.

This New World Fagin had ensconced herself and her larcenous brood in the deserted ground floor of a former factory building.

Quentin and I approached her discreetly, as the only adult in sight, and tendered our cards: two one-dollar bills.

We explained our quandary most piteously, recognizing that we were performing for a mistress of the piteous appeal.

"Mother Hubbard," said I, as if this ridiculous name were an honored one, "we're in terrible trouble and heard you might help."

She was a sharp-featured old dame dressed all in black like a Dickens grandmother. "How'd d'you hear o' me?"

"A friend," I said quickly. "A friend who you helped previously." I wasn't sure if Eva herself had gone baby-shopping, but I was pretty settled that Mrs. T. Anna Swinton had something to do with it. "Mrs. Swinton. An older lady. Quite respectable. She swore . . . oh, dear, perhaps this is the wrong place." I wrung my hands until the gesture burned and brought tears to my eyes.

"Now, Philomena," Quentin said, startling the Hepplewhite out of me. Where'd he get that name? "You mustn't get upset. You know your health is delicate."

"Delicate," I repeated, managing to snivel slightly. "Yes, I . . . I lost our baby. In childbirth. And can never have another, the doctor says. And . . . and Jefferson's parents are coming to New York and expecting to see their grandchild!"

I had now begun to wail like a guttersnipe. Quentin took my wringing hands.

"And my folks were planning to settle a christening gift upon their grandchild. With all the expenses of the laying-in, not to mention the empty cradle and such, we sorely need their support."

"And I want my baby back!" I wailed, quite convincingly, for I had pretended that it was one of my sisters who had died at birth and became quite weepy.

"Can you help us?" Quentin asked. "And what would it cost?"

"Depends." Mother Hubbard was all business, despite her black bonnet and capelet. "What age do you require?"

We exchanged connubial glances. "Under three months," I said. "It must be young enough to look like Grandfather Fettlespeed."

"Girl or boy?"

Again we consulted each other.

"We never said," Quentin explained. "Once the baby, a girl, died, it seemed best not to get my parents' expectations up."

Mother Hubbard nodded. "But you never said it died, either, or your expectations of a settlement would have gone rock-bottom down."

"Well . . . yes," I admitted, trying to sound more bereft about the baby than the money.

"How soon d'you need it?"

We hadn't decided on this.

"Two, three days," Quentin said.

"And you've money on you."

"Some," he admitted stiffly.

"It'll be twenty dollars!"

"Twenty dollars!" The words burst from me unrehearsed. That a child could be bought and sold for little.

Mother Hubbard's shrewd eyes darted from Quentin to myself. "Eighteen dollars and not penny less."

"We can do that, Philomena," he assured me with dramatic anxiety. "It'll be a squeak but—"

I merely nodded miserably and put my handkerchief to my eyes.

"I can't say the gender," she added. "Come back tomorrow with the money and 'tis all yours."

"Will she . . . he . . . it be healthy?"

"You're buying a milk cow, are you? I can't say. I suppose you'll be able to keep it alive if you take decent care. The mothers of these young rapscallions here breed like rabbits and there's always one desperate enough to replace a hungry new mouth with the wherewithal to feed what's already here.

"I tell her a barren couple is desperate to give her babe a good home, and she's quick to believe it's for the best." She eyed us up and down. "You look a respectable sort. I'd not trade a baby to you otherwise, but I won't take a penny less than eighteen."

We nodded eagerly and took our leave.

In the crowded, reeking summer street outside we breathed deeply despite everything and took stock.

"Philomena?" I demanded.

"An unusual name smells authentic. All-purpose names like John and Mary smack of deceit before the syllables peel off our lips." Quentin frowned and spoke again. "And how will we deal with collecting the baby and Mother Hubbard's school for scandal?"

"I'll alert the police. That's all I can do, that and print the truth in the newspaper."

"And the baby she produces?"

"It will go to an orphanage, which may be more merciful than being on the open market."

"But you can't guarantee that?"

"I can guarantee that I will expose a shocking trade in infant lives. I can't guarantee to succor every victim! I have my mother to support, and my idle brothers and their families. I can't do it all."

"Hmmm," was all he said in that irritating British way of his, and of Sherlock Holmes's. And of Nell Huxleigh's.

"Are you willing to abet me further in this investigation or not?"

He nodded.

"We must try another route. I must build a case that infants are easily available on the street to anyone who comes inquiring, no questions asked."

"What will happen to the fourth Hamilton infant?"

"An orphanage, I imagine. Robert Roy certainly won't want it. And can anyone blame him?"

"Life, and death, are cheap all over the globe, Pink. In some places the unwanted newborn are left out to die in the elements. Nature is the chosen form of execution so human hands rest easy. New York City is no worse than anywhere else."

"But why can't it be better?"

"Perhaps it will be, when you publish your story."

"Maybe. For a while. Here. But the world won't change."

"Maybe it will. For a while. Here. And there. That is what we hope for, we spies, knowing we often hope in vain."

Nodding, I felt it was odd to feel triumphant that I'd found Mother Hubbard and her link to infant lives. To do good I had to expose evil. Not change it, just expose it. Perhaps that wasn't enough.

I arranged to meet Quentin again for another foray into the buying of babies.

I needed to show a pattern in order to shock the public into indignation.

I wondered if I was very much different from Jack the Ripper in that.

Memoirs of a Dangerous Woman:

Fields of Gold

∾

I see she's having squabbles in the New World as in the Old. She finds no peace in either. . . . It would be better if she would stay in the fourth or fifth continent. . . . The memory of her stay in Bavaria brings her so much income but . . . gold doesn't stay with her.

—KING LUDWIG I ON HEARING OF LOLA'S AMERICAN ADVENTURES, 1852

Two things had my long tour of Australia taught me: I no longer had the stamina for my brand of tempestuous dance nor for younger lovers.

Perhaps I was prescient when I made a will before I left California, for I'd made a quantity of money in quartz mining and other gold-field enterprises. The legacy of Dujarier's investment on my behalf proved valuable in the long run, though his own run was cut tragically short. I still mourned him.

But I knew none of this and was so in my native good humor when I left Grass Valley and the West for the open Pacific and the new performer's Gold Coast, Australia.

First came the long two months' voyage from San Francisco to Sydney. Then the endless overland treks from town to town in yet another vast and unsettled continent. And the inevitable contentions within the performing company.

Also the inevitable "whipping contests" with my male detractors among the local newspapers and mining towns, for who had not heard of the speed and sting of both my temper and my whip?

And the inevitable romance with my leading actor, a tall and comely comic/romantic lead named Frank Folland. He supported an estranged wife and two children in Cincinnati, but his heart was fancy free, and his fancy soon became me.

Yet something unseen was dragging at my body and spirit. Not only could I not sustain encores during the long Australian tour but on some nights I grew faint both on and off the stage. Headaches fandangoed around my brain like whips.

As in my beloved California, Australia was awash with gold fever. The mining camps clamored for me. I won them over with my plays and the Spider Dance, which they found far less scandalous than reputed, and they ofttimes complained of that fact.

Still, it was a highly lucrative tour. When Frank and I booked the three-masted American schooner *June A. Falkenberg* to return home, I took its Germanic last name as an omen of my changing fortunes, for Bavaria had been both home and cradle and cross for me.

Our ways might part, Frank and I knew. Ambition and something new warred within my bosom. I could tour the exotic Far East. I could retire to Grass Valley again. Frank considered rejoining his family in New York City, or even reconciling with his wife in Cincinnati.

Nothing had been set in stone; we had the endless voyage ahead of us in which to decide.

Then, it was decided for us.

Our alliance was ending. He was twenty-nine to my thirty-five (though of course I said I was but thirty). I no longer quite looked it, said my mirror. Something was draining me.

After a stop in Honolulu on July 7 for a belated Fourth of July celebration, the ship sailed on. A dinner that night honored Frank's twenty-ninth birthday. Champagne flowed like ambrosia on Mount Olympus.

Frank went to the deck to clear his head, a young man in his prime standing under a waning crescent moon, gazing at the myriad moons reflected in the whitecaps, his mind mellow with fine wine and celebration.

The ship lurched in the dancing waves. He was not seen again on that deck or this earth.

I wailed. I raged. I beat my breast until I fell gasping to the floor. So quick. So invisibly done! So unseen. So unthinkable.

Not all the letters to the editor in the world would undo the fatal fact of it. I went quite mad for a while. What else was there to do, cooped up on that endless voyage? I called to God to take me too. He didn't answer. I loathed myself, my selfish self. I had many long days and nights alone to contemplate my failings.

Eighteen days later the Golden Gate came looming out of the San Francisco fog, looking like a prison door opening to swallow my heart.

I could think only of notifying Frank's parents and estranged wife, of providing for that poor woman and her children.

All that I had loved in California and Grass Valley seemed dust in view of the death of this one young, high-hearted man on his very own birthday.

I tried to go on. I rented a house, hired a maid, found my beloved dog Gip and a few other needy ones of his kind. Only the dogs cheered me. How they tilted their heads and gawked at my chatty white cockatoo from Australia, and the gorgeously feathered lyre bird whose tail was a musical instrument complete.

But even my beloved pets couldn't console me. Why was I so shaken, so unhappy with myself?

I performed, as expected, but my heart wasn't in it. My heart wasn't in me any longer. In two weeks, I made more than $4,000. And my heart wasn't in it.

Sacramento clamored for me, heart in it or not. Before I steamed upriver, I hired Duncan and Company, an auction firm. Mr. Duncan had a niece, he told me, who danced a little, named Isadora.

This I considered a happy omen, for I'd always been superstitious, like most theatrical folk.

I consigned all my jewelry, the glittering landmarks of my life and travels and travails, my successes and triumphs, for the benefit of Frank's two young children.

I had no children of my own, save in my heart. Save Lotta and some other young performers.

The power of my name created a sensation. One newspaper said my collection was "probably not surpassed by and possessed by a single individual in the United States." It was expected to bring $20,000 to $30,000. Five thousand souls trooped into the Duncan showrooms to gawk at my diamonds, rubies, and gold.

My heart warmed at what my past could deliver to Frank's children's future, the only children I would ever benefit, besides Lotta, through my tutoring.

Eighty-nine lots of my life went up for auction in San Francisco, yet the proceeds were under $10,000.

Later, it was said to be too rich a bounty for a frontier city.

My entire life seemed to be worthless now, or worth less than it should have been. I opened in Sacramento to sold-out performances, and the first night of the Spider Dance brought the highest receipts in the history of the Forrest Theater.

My body, my jewels seemed cheaply sold. I returned to Grass Valley, but the town had been leveled by fire while I was in Australia. Now it was a-building anew. And I was not. All was changed. All gone. Ashes, ashes, all fall down.

It was there, in Grass Valley, with my beloved house up for sale, that a most extraordinary gentleman called upon me.

He was as tall and powerful as any frontiersman, and rough of manner, but a woman who had toured the mining camps for years was not to be dismayed by that. Besides, I knew him.

He was also filthy rich. And I knew that.

There in my simple house filled with the glories of European decor, he presented me with my auctioned jewels.

While I gaped and stuttered, he told me that he had bought them back for me, that they were going too cheaply, that a woman as beautiful as I should not give up the things that gave her power.

I explained that I aspired to a higher role in life, and always had, than that of merely a beautiful woman.

He nodded as I spoke, not much marking my words. I think he was a man who did not much respect women. But he respected wealth, and he respected what I had amassed from nothing, as he'd also done.

He wanted one favor of me in return for his rescue of my underpriced jewels. If I did him this one simple favor, he would pay Frank's children the $10,000 dollars he'd paid for my jewels and let me keep my "pretty baubles."

It would be a fortune for Frank's children, and no loss to me, but only if I did him one favor.

Although he chuckled and patted my knee, that was not the favor he required (or one that I would have granted).

No, what he wanted was very simple, and fell in perfectly with my current plans. I was to tell no one he had been in California. I was to tell no one what he asked of me. Ever.

I was melancholy in those days, and a bit hopeless for the first time in my life. What he asked didn't violate my newfound conscience. It benefited Frank's children. It preserved the jewels, which had sentimental value far above their monetary worth, from being sold for a song on a tin whistle.

It suited his private purposes very well. And perhaps mine.

I agreed.

He was a major personage in that country and time, and it never hurt to oblige a major personage. As long as one didn't sell one's soul. And my soul was feeling as weak as my body then.

My home in Grass Valley had survived the fire. I sold it. I took one last look at my rosebushes, and left. I'm told it still stands today, but it's far away and I no longer have the heart to chase my own past.

My jewels I still have, thanks to that man's sagacity and generosity, motives that don't always fight each other.

All I have to decide is what to do with them, what worthy soul I should leave them to. A soul, I hope, less willful and wild than my own.

Not long after this remarkable visit, I gave my last performance of the Spider Dance at the Metropolitan Theater in San Francisco, under the invitation of its manager, Junius Booth, of the great acting family that included his brothers, Edwin and John Wilkes Booth.

I took my curtain calls and so danced off the California stages forever.

But not before I read in the newspapers of the passing of my former husband, George Heald, twenty-eight, from the "white death" of tuberculosis.

My lungs had always been weak, so I could imagine his agony. In honor of his passing, I considered myself his widow, and used the name "Mrs. Heald" from then on offstage.

I boarded the Pacific Mail steamship *Orizaba* at San Francisco on November 20, Thanksgiving Day, though I had little to be thankful for except my enterprising benefactor who had settled for squeezing my knee.

The morning paper hailed my departure and estimated that my latest tour had netted $23,000. Money had always been a consequence of what I did, not purely a reason, else I wouldn't have spent it so freely on myself and others.

The many bags and trunks from my long-ago life in Europe that I had imported to California were now being laded aboard the *Orizaba*. This was a long, low two-masted ship, with sails fore and aft. A large wheel on her port side kept the tall black stack amidships billowing forth black smoke at a rate that almost matched my own with a cigar or cigarette. As usual, the lading crew hooted and hollered at the number and weight of my trunks. I could not but agree. My whole life seemed a long train that I was dragging behind me, including the jewels my benefactor had returned to me.

No more Panama for me and mosquitos the size of humming birds. No more mule trains. We were bound for Nicaragua, a country above Panama, where a new railroad built to accommodate gold prospectors would speed passengers across the Central American neck to a steamship waiting on the Atlantic side.

Soldiers of fortune thronged the passenger manifest. Nicaragua was open, unclaimed country. I met a tall, gray-eyed soldier from Tennessee, William Walker, who was determined to rule that land.

Such claims were not unheard of in those days. Once it was bruited about that I was encouraging backers to make me 'Empress of California.' Why not? I was Countess of Landsfeld and uncrowned queen of Bavaria, me, a little, lively Irish girl by way of India.

We landed at San Juan del Sur on Nicaragua's Pacific coast. There New York–bound passengers took a modern coach to Lake Nicaragua and then boats down the San Juan River to the Caribbean coast. All my many, many trunks came with me.

At the coast, the steamship Tennessee awaited at San Juan del Norte. Mr. Walker, the "man of destiny" from Tennessee, stayed behind to conquer Nicaragua.

I moved on, with my trunks and my weight of sorrow. I arrived in New York on December 16, shortly before Christmas, and I wasn't entirely unexpected. Old friends who represented something new for me, Christian spirituality, awaited me. And my gentleman caller from California. And the family of my lost love, Frank Folland.

How famous some of these would become, and rich, though none as notorious as I. At my age, notoriety was no longer a boast but a burden.

I came to visit New York City. I would try to leave it one last time, but the Statue of Liberty had claimed me as her own, and this Sligo girl would never leave her, nor the hundreds of thousands of starving sons and daughters of Ireland who found refuge there, as did I, finally and forever.

38

Forgery Afoot

❧❧

One of the steps which is called death to the tarantula ... is the very poetry of avenging contempt ... The head lifted and thrown back, the flashing eye, the fierce and protruded foot which crushed the insect, make a subject for the painter which would scarcely be easy to forget.
—THE LONDON *MORNING POST* ON LOLA'S DANCING DEBUT, 1843

"It would help to find Mrs. Buchanan," Irene said.

"I presume you are not referring to the former U.S. president's wife."

"No, Nell. I wish I were. It would be easier to lay hands on such a public person."

"And what would you do, could you lay hands on this private Mrs. Buchanan?"

Irene paused in pacing and smoking.

"A fine question. I would like to know if she was a greedy, grasping harpy in the guise of a compassionate friend. Of course it wouldn't gain me a scintilla of knowledge to phrase it that way. So I would say I was compiling a biography of the late Lola Montez, and required her testimony."

"How will you find her?"

"Since she and the Episcopal Church were equally involved with Lola at the very end of her life, I'll see if the bishop can help us again. After all, we are highly valued donors."

"Perhaps you should call on him at his office rather than at the club."

She considered my suggestion with a tilted head. "I think not. I suspect the bishop wishes to keep news of Father Hawks's quest for Lola's sainthood unofficial. I'm sure it was considered the crotchet of an aging man, but tolerated because it was so crackpot."

"You are not inclined to Father Hawks's view of her, then?"

"I believe she became truly contrite for her high-tempered earlier years. She acknowledges that she was a 'wild, willful child' from her youngest days. I think time mellowed her, especially her years in Grass Valley, and then her disastrous trip to England to marry such a fraud. In some ways, she was always searching for a man who could take care of her, even as her fiercely independent ways rebuffed their very solicitude. I would describe her at the end of her life as wiser but not necessarily holier."

An ugly thought reoccurred to me. "Irene, given the fact of her stroke, and the rumors of her neglect and abuse, it would be easy to torment a person in such a weakened state. Do you think someone did, and that's why no trace of her wealth remains?"

"It's possible, as I've suggested, but a stroke wreaks havoc with the victim's reason, and you can't squeeze sense from a stone. I do hope her end was natural, and that the presence of the clergy kept any mischief at bay. The unwelcome visit of her greedy mother seems to have been the worst torture inflicted upon her."

"How sad."

"So, it's settled. We revisit the Episcopal Club."

"I'm not sure I wish to keep on deceiving the clergy."

"We are not so much deceiving them as not fully informing them. And you must go, Nell! That young Father Edmonds who took a shine to you will no doubt be more generous with information than if I go alone."

"That's all nonsense, Irene!"

But I fetched my hat and gloves.

We took a streetcar, I think because Irene wished to salve my penny-pinching nature. While we jolted through the bustle and odor of high summer traffic, I considered the fact that I indeed had become an object of interest to strange young men. Was it the freer social atmosphere of America? The department-store clothing? My new Nellie Bly waist? Or some substantive change in myself? I was not about to ask Irene her theory on the subject, nor would I interrogate the bookstore clerk or Father Edmonds either. And especially not Quentin.

We grew not a little warmer walking the two blocks to the Episcopal Club. When we asked within for Father Edmonds, we were told that he was not available. After Irene introduced us, we were shuttled to the parlor to await the bishop himself again.

"My dear ladies," he greeted us as he turned to close the door behind him. "What can I do for you today?"

"We didn't mean to impose on you personally," Irene said. "We'd asked for Father Edmonds, but he was unavailable."

"It's no imposition," the bishop said with a ready smile. "Please. Ask away."

"I wondered about the Mrs. Buchanan who attended Mrs. Gilbert in her last illness. Would it be possible to find and speak to her?"

"A shame Father Hawks is not available."

"Is he the only priest who was pursuing information about her?"

"Certainly! You must understand that we tolerated his devotion to her memory because of his age. The likelihood of him uncovering any striking information about her was slim. The most he had to offer were reports of occasional strange noises in the room in which she had died when it was empty, reported by the landlady. The building had suffered recent renovation, so the rooms might even be hard to assign with confidence nowadays. As I told the newspaper gentleman who called, Father Hawks is a sincere man who perhaps has been overimpressed by this woman's sad yet repentant death."

"The newspaper gentleman? When did he call?"

"Why, just before you first did, or after. I don't quite recall. Frankly, I wasn't as forthcoming with him as with you. I don't want poor Father Hawks's odd notions paraded in large type before all of New York. Your own inquiries are personal, and I'm sure that you wouldn't wish them to become public."

"Certainly not!" I spoke for the first time, and rather adamantly.

"Exactly, Miss Huxleigh. I could see from the first that you were women of sense and sensibility. As for your quest for Mrs. Buchanan, Mrs. Norton, she would be quite old today, but the family was a solid one. Still, the population of New York City is much greater than it was almost thirty years ago."

He paused to consider. "I can only suggest you inquire at her old neighborhood."

"And will the newspaper gentleman be there before us? How would we know him?"

"Tall, stooped fellow. A bit old for the ink trade, but most avid. A civilized fellow, yet I wasn't inclined to help him, for obvious reasons. The newspapers

chase sheer sensation these days, especially all those muck-raking lady reporters. I don't care to have the Church as a subject of lurid speculation in the
public press, you do understand."

"Of course!" I said. "It is shocking what such ink-stained wretches will do
to get a sensational story these days.'

"Miss Huxleigh, I agree entirely. Is there anything else you wish to know,
Mrs. Norton?"

"Just where Father Edmonds might be. He was so helpful in your absence
during our last call. Miss Huxleigh and I wished to thank him, perhaps to invite him to tea."

"Alas, young priests are called from pillar to post to serve their superiors. I
can't say when he will be available again."

This last sentence he addressed to me with great sympathy, as if I had any
reason to care! Oh, Irene! She was forever pushing people into the most unlikely situations.

"A pity," Irene said, blithely ignoring my unease. "Miss Huxleigh had been
minded to knit some useful article for him in thanks for his previous assistance.
Perhaps *you* shall have to be the recipient."

"I am honored," the bishop said with a bow, smiling as he stood to show us
out.

I was too outraged to speak, which was just as well.

"I cannot believe it!" I told Irene when we stood atop the steps of the Episcopal Club again. "There were women in my father's parish who'd set their
caps at the widowed parson, you may be sure. You made me look like the worst
of those churchgoing hussies. I would never—"

"It gives us another excuse for visiting and asking questions, don't you see,
Nell? If I weren't known to be married, I would have put myself in that role in
a wink."

Before I could summon the outrage to answer this dubious reasoning, she
spoke again.

"The elderly newspaperman disturbs me."

"You think it is Mr. Holmes. You led him to the Episcopal Club, though
he showed scant interest."

"Yes, it could be he, but that wouldn't disturb me."

"Who else would it be?"

"Someone far more sinister."

"Such as—?"

"The older priest who was *not* Father Hawks."

"I had forgotten about him. So what are we to do now?"

"You noticed that 'noises' have been reported in Lola's former room. Not an expression of saintly phenomena, I think, but of repeated searches. The gullible landlady would take each such 'visitation' as a sign."

"Yes, we ourselves have contributed to the phenomenon."

"But I think we are the only searchers to take something away. I doubt the disruptions will stop until something has been found, so we must see to it that something is."

"What are you suggesting?"

"That we unplug the hole in the walled-up fireplace we exposed and 'salt' something provocative in the hidden niche. Then we can watch to see who comes to discover it."

"We can hardly ask to see the room again."

"The landlady had decided to move the occupant."

"We can hardly march in again and take it apart."

"Not by daylight, no."

"By night?"

"The better to observe unobserved."

"And what item will you put the place of Lola's diary?"

"Why, some clever, coded forgery of your own devising, Nell. If you are not going to knit something useful for poor enamored Father Edmonds, you could at least put your skills to excellent use concocting a wonderfully confusing diary for Lola Montez."

"That's fraud, Irene."

"Did poor, dying Lola Montez deserve all the vultures gathering around her then? And now? I doubt it. Who would most appreciate the skill and audacity of a faux diary designed to 'smoke out,' as the dime Western novels say, the tormenters of her loyal and martyred priestly advocate?"

"Somehow you've made deception seem like a noble ploy in a holy war, Irene."

"Exactly."

Whatever disapproval I might have mustered vanished before the challenge of the handiwork in question: forging Lola Montez's diary. What boundless invention was in store. . . .

⚜   ⚜   ⚜

We returned to the Astor House, where Irene pampered me as if I were da Vinci working on the *Last Supper*. I'd always relished the intricacies of the ladylike domestic arts. Now my small helpful sketches had evolved into a masterwork. Studying the worn papers from the actual hand of Lola Montez, I set about fashioning a facsimile that was as authentic looking, but even less readable.

The passages in the actual document I could translate were religious quotes from the New Testament, especially those relating to Mary Magdalen and forgiveness. "I wish to have my terrible and fearful experience given as an awful warning to such natures as my own." I meditated on this passage, wondering what "terrible and fearful experience" she referred to. This seemed more dire than mere illness. I envisioned a deathbed visit from someone more unwelcome than her long-unseen mother . . . the same Ultramontanes she accused of pursuing her everywhere she went, including America, and who were pursuing her after death, older but no less intent, or vicious, as poor Father Hawks would testify. I must mislead them, discourage them from our own trail by dropping feverish hints in this document to convince them that Lola knew and hid nothing in her last days. In her own hand, Lola would possibly help save her own daughter! I began work on my project of deception.

Irene was at my service for once, dashing out to gather what I required as soon as I realized it.

"Paper. Thick, creamy paper," I ordered.

She returned in one hour with four samples, three of which I rejected out of hand. "This one might do."

She was gone to buy more. And black ink.

I rolled up the paper in an apron and crinkled it. By the time she returned, I was in an artistic snit.

"I've tried pressing this paper with your curling iron, I have beaten it with your glove stretcher, and it will not crinkle suitably. This project is not only insane but impossible. I wash my hands of it."

Irene studied the single, abused sheet. It looked decidedly abused, but not aged.

She gazed at me, my haggard expression, my disheveled hairdressing. With one releasing gesture, she let go of the result of two hours' worth of labor. The paper dropped to the carpeted floor.

Her expression became both haughty and commanding. "I believe, Nell," she said, "you need a demonstration of Lola Montez's spider dance, of which we both have read so much."

I admit I was confused.

Irene caught her skirt up on one side and anchored it with her hand on her hip.

Her other hand lifted above her head at a graceful but rather distorted angle.

Her high-heeled embroidered walking boots assumed a balletic position.

"In Spain," she declaimed, "in New York City, spiders are everywhere. Small, unseen, spinning webs. Deadly." She shook her head in a rebellious gesture. Her posture grew instantly vigilant and tempestuous. "I stamp upon them. I shake them loose from their mooring in my petticoats. I crush them beneath my heels."

And thus she began stamping at a furious pace upon my poor paper, twitching her skirts from left to right, her feet thundering until the carpet must have cried out for mercy.

"Irene, what is this madness?"

"It's the Spanish tarantella, Nell, so named after the large and fearsome tarantula spider. I see that my skirts and petticoats are infested with these deadly crawlers, and won't stop shaking them loose until every last spider is . . . as still as death."

I recalled with a shudder the false spiders of cork, rubber, and whalebone Lola would shake from her skirts on occasion.

By now a sea of petticoats and skirt were frothing about Irene's knees. Her toes and heels were hitting carpet in such a thundering rhythm that I feared for the folk below, whose ceiling was our floor.

Stamp, stamp, stamp. *"Estampa, estampa!"* Irene called out. "So Lola Montez would serve the floral bouquets tossed to stage in her honor, stamping them into crushed petals and scent. . . . Andalusia. Barcelona! Carmen! *Olé!*"

Irene stopped, hands akimbo on hips, her hems hiked as high as Lotta Crabtree's, and gazed at the ruin beneath her neat boots. "Is the paper sufficiently aged yet?" she inquired.

I gingerly plucked it out from under her bootheels.

"Thirty years' aged," I said. "Quite impressively scored and torn. I suppose you shall have to subdue every page I manufacture in this way. Wherever, whenever did you learn such a savage dance?"

"Carmen," she said shortly. "An opera by Bizet that's well suited to my dark soprano, which I never had the opportunity to sing. But I learned the dance."

"Perhaps you *are* indeed the bastard daughter of Lola Montez!"

Irene laughed. "This storm of motion was worth it to hear that word from your lips, Nell. And, yes, I understand Lola's art. You see how it must have shocked the Europe of her time, but it is only a folk dance of Spain, that's all."

"It's a fine aging agent for paper," I said, admiring her footwork. "Now I must water down the ink just enough to mimic old age. I'll be sure to request my needed sheets of paper during the midday hours tomorrow, when the guests below are likely to be out and about."

Irene's heels and toes beat a last, scorching drum roll on the floor.

39
Taken by . . .

~~~

*I want to wear boys' clothes, and will as soon as
I can get other women to join me.*
—OLIVE SCHREINER, 1884

By now both Irene and I had read enough about, and by, Lola Montez
that I had no difficulty producing many mock pages in her hand and
style of expression.

"Wonderful, Nell!" Irene slouched in the chair in her walking-out
clothes to study my pages, and hers. When dressed as a man, she
quickly assumed the less precise posture of one. "You could have quite a future
in the forgery way. Such a shame to thrust these away for inconsiderate villains
to find."

"If there are any," I answered. "How can you be sure anyone will find anything?"

"I'll leave a faint trail of soot. Those bricks are still filthy with ashes." She
glanced quickly at me. "You needn't come in while I 'salt' our paper mine, but
you must wear men's garb while you wait in the street for me to rejoin you."

"You have just your own."

"Not anymore." Irene grinned like a newsboy. Something about men's
clothing made even a smile bigger, broader, cruder. "I stopped at a flea market
during one of your requests for paper. If you'll take that parcel into your
room, you'll soon be ready to go."

I had seen the string-wrapped brown paper bundle, but had hesitated to inquire about it.

Irene laughed, lighting up a small cigar, sans holder. "You regard that package as if it were a sack full of spiders! We are done spider dancing around Lola's diary. Tonight we place it, and then stand back to spring the trap!"

I would have begged off, but half suspected that such a move would please Irene. I picked up the parcel and retreated to my bedchamber.

Although she would have been happy to help me dress, as I had often helped her, I was too annoyed to rely on her at the moment. I released my corset by the speedy method of pushing the stays together so the front hooks separated. Ah! How did Pink breathe with such rigorous lacing? I'm ashamed to say that I had worn gentleman's garb on one or two occasions previously, so was able to dress myself in trousers, shirt, and jacket quite quickly. Irene had purchased a billed, checked cap large enough to swallow up my hair like a boa constrictor a rabbit, and had provided a dingy white silk scarf to conceal my feminine throat, especially once I turned up my coat collar.

I had to roll up the trouser legs once, but the area we visited housed laborers, so my dark serge suit was almost too formal for the location. Impromptu cuffs added a nice touch, I thought. My own black walking boots would merely peep out from the long trouser legs and suffice, since we planned our larcenous expedition for the dark of evening.

"Very nice, Nell!" Irene greeted me, rising to adjust the lay of my collar and scarf and cap, nevertheless. "A pity you don't smoke. A pipe would abet the masquerade. But you have quite the jaunty look of a former newsboy about you, so we shall let you play the young gentleman."

We slunk out the back servants' stairs of the hotel, as usual when up to no good.

The alley reeked as badly behind the Astor House as it did on the Lower East Side.

Irene quickly relit her cigar. For once I welcomed the pungent scent of the sulphur on the lucifer, what the Americans call "matches," and the tobacco.

"We'd better walk, but it's only a dozen 'blocks,'" Irene said blithely, and off we set.

My gait was not as practiced as hers, but the trousers pulling at every step forced me to extend my stride. No one gave us a second glance as dusk darkened the city and street lamps came out like large, falling stars someone had stopped only three yards from earth.

Actually, to be abroad at such an hour, ignored, was most refreshing. I almost felt invisible. I almost felt that our bizarre enterprise had a hope of success.

As we turned down Seventeenth Street, the lights became fewer, and I felt an uneasy recall of Whitechapel and what had happened in the dark and murk there less than a year ago.

And yet! We knew the Ripper as no others did, and we knew him to be safely harnessed. He was not here, though others as heartless and vile as he might roam.

I hastened to keep up with Irene by lengthening my stride. And it was odd, these long, loping steps increased my confidence. I felt almost a hound upon a trail, a horse reaching for the end of a race. I had never been one to move at more than a stroll, but suddenly the cooler night air was an intoxicant and I rushed to meet it.

My overlarge leather gloves pinched her rough coat sleeve. "Quentin would have been a better partner tonight."

"Quentin might ask questions I wouldn't want to answer, as Holmes would. I'm not giving up the edge we have in the affairs of Lola Montez unless we have to. She is my mother. Maybe."

With this I couldn't argue. I knew where my mother was buried, as Irene might know, but most of all I knew my mother for a tranquil, loyal, loved parson's wife. As Irene did not. Indeed, it seemed no one had loved Lola Montez as much as she herself had, and therein was truly a tragedy.

After a ten-minute stride (as I thought of our bizarre outing), Irene grabbed my coat sleeve and pulled me into the shelter of a dark doorway. We leaned against some abandoned building, which reminded me that this was a dangerous district.

"Take my cigar," Irene said.

Striding through the streets was one thing; smoking was quite another!

"You don't have to puff upon it. Just hold it. Let the little ember burn. You will look like a loiterer, whom no one will want to approach, and I'll find you easily when I emerge."

My gloved fingers took this loathsome object.

"I'll go in, place the false diary, and hide inside the wardrobe."

"How can you be sure someone will come searching tonight?"

"I can't."

"Then we'll do this again?"

"If we have to."

I had nothing to say to this grim prospect. And so she left me there: lifting my lit cigar before a rickety wooden door. The Statue of Liberty I was not.

While I waited I had much to contemplate. First I watched the shadow that was Irene dart to the side of the boardinghouse and then disappear around the back.

The screaming, milling Street Arabs of the day were at last asleep in their cribs. I suspected they would be up before the dawn, hawking papers, heading for twelve-hour days in the tenement shops and factories, hanging on to their desperate mothers' apron strings if they were less than five or six years old.

As a former governess, I felt the plight of these pathetic creatures as a stab in the heart. It was so easy to view the coddled offspring of the upper classes and dismiss the rest as hopeless guttersnipes. Yet even in the finest houses, a child was expected to answer every adult's need: for quiet, for learning what was desired despite the child's aptitude, for being seen and not heard, as the saying went.

What was one to do? Unguided, the young were little animals. Over-guided, they were little automatons. I decided I was very glad that I was no longer a governess, for I wasn't really good at that.

What was I good at? Assisting others, like my father, and then Irene. Being useful, although I was beginning to suspect that I was being useful at rather useless things. I was, according to Irene, a promising forger. I remember being cast alone together with Sherlock Holmes during the last dangerous times. How he had actually allowed me to assist him. And then called me "Huxleigh," like the lowest servant. Or . . . like—? No. *The* man is too arrogant to give any woman the benefit of the doubt. Except Irene. He has the feet of a chocolate soldier there, all stiff and solid, but that melt at the first lingering touch of sunlight.

I glanced at my leather-gloved hand. The cigar still burned, though I did nothing to encourage it. Its ember was a small red star in the dark, and its scent disguised far more noxious ones.

I stiffened. I'd heard the scrape of shoe leather on stone.

While I watched, a man came down the deserted street.

His strides were long, as mine had been, but his were longer, stronger. And then I saw another man, perhaps twenty feet behind. And a third, another four yards behind the second!

They were strung out, like crows on a fence. Dark of habit, vague of motion. Each moving separately, yet in unison.

My heart began beating, and finding no confining corset to stop it, began thrumming like a Spanish dancer against the false front of my man's jacket.

I sensed the trio noting me.

I didn't move.

They passed on, dismissing me as some midnight lounger, a doorway lurker, an idle smoker.

I watched them take Irene's same path along the side of the boardinghouse.

Despite the cigar, I clasped my gloved hands before me. What should I do? Rush forward to warn her? She was lying in wait for just such a committee. She'd be furious if I disrupted her charade.

But three men. Three dark men striding down the empty street, noticing everything. Had they really dismissed me? Or merely pretended to?

Oh, how I wished for Irene's small lethal pistol . . . and then realized that she must have it with her.

I was so agitated that I actually put the cigar to my lips and breathed in. Nothing happened. Apparently cigars were for Irene and Lola and Godfrey but not for me.

I bit my lip. How long must I wait? If all went well, this villainous trio would depart with my handiwork clutched to their black hearts.

Well, they'd leave with my falsified diary. Perhaps to them their own hearts were merely gray. Ashen. Like the residue in the walled-up fireplace.

I waited. The cigar burned on, very slowly, as if holding its breath, as I did.

I waited. Was it minutes? Half hours?

No one emerged from the small space between the boardinghouses.

I waited.

As I'd been told to.

And then, I could wait no more!

I stroke out from my hiding place, across the damp, faintly lit street smelling of horse manure and human urine.

What wretched place was this? No place to leave a child unattended. No place to leave a friend alone. No place to leave anyone!

I rushed along the building, my gloved hands pulling over each other against the brick like sailors drawing on a line, beyond my control, my hands and not my hands.

The stench of the broad alley between the backs of tenements met me like a wall of revulsion. I felt along the jagged bricks until my leather-padded fingertips found the indentation of a door.

It gave to my impetuous weight like a curtain.

I was inside, and smelled the stale aftertaste of corned beef and cabbage from before.

The room would be to my left now. The sinister side. Did I interrupt the unholy trio? If so, I would stutter an apology in the deepest croak I could manage and ask for Mrs. Kelly. I knew the landlady's name. I could make myself seem a resident of this miserable place. I could make myself seem a resident of hell, if necessary.

The doors gave way before me, all unlocked, unguarded.

What a dire sign this was, but I was too overwrought to realize it.

The room I entered felt familiar, but the gaslights gleamed faintly against the walls. I saw a wardrobe I recognized, thrown half askew. A dark hole that had once been a fireplace.

I rushed to kneel before it on crushed stone, amid scattered bricks. The hiding place that had held Lola's diary was empty. My forged replacement had found a home!

I rose and went to the wardrobe, pulling a twisted door open. Irene's mad plan had worked.

It was empty. Utterly empty.

I was alone in the room. No diary, no three shadowed men. No Irene.

40

Shaken by . . .

~☙~

How nice it would be to be a man. She fancied she was one until she felt her body grow strong and hard. . . . She felt the great freedom opened to her; no place shut off from her, the long chain broken, all work possible for her, no law to say this and this is for woman.

—REBEKAH IN *FROM MAN TO MAN,* BY OLIVE SCHREINER

My pockets were heavy with the coins Irene had insisted I take along. *Weighty pockets,* she had said as we had set out (only hours before!), *are a hallmark of the man at large on a city street. You will walk more convincingly with coins to spend.*

I managed to hail my first cab with an imperious wave and a gold coin pinched between leather-clad thumb and forefinger.

The equipage stopped, to my astonishment. I leaped inside, thanking God that I remembered that name of the hotel to which Irene had sent messages to Quentin. "The Fifth Avenue Hotel at Madison Square, and a dollar tip if you be quick about it."

He lashed the horses, as I cringed inside. I didn't think he'd hurt anything—and then I didn't think, but felt the wind lashing through the open windows I didn't know how to raise. I held my cap down over my ears and thought furiously.

At the hotel, I gave gold for speed and the horses' poor sweating flanks. "Rest them for an hour," I muttered in a croak I regarded as masculine.

Inside the lobby, evening gaslights glared down on my poor figure like disapproving dowagers. I strode forward as best I could, and asked the clerk for Quentin's room.

"Mr. Stanhope is out," he said, with a supercilious glance at the tower of key cubby-holes behind his back. "He has been out all day. And night."

I stared. "He can't be!"

"He is, and it is his business."

"How much his business?" I demanded in my best imitation of Irene out in her walking-out clothes.

"I can't say." A smirk. "A lady was involved."

"Brown hair? Extravagant hat? Tiny waist?"

He smirked again. "The gentleman is correct. I can take a note for Mr. Stanhope and give it to him . . . in the morning."

Who he thought I was I can't say. The lady's brother. A rival. He took me for a man and there was nothing to do but depart in that guise.

I stood on the dark street outside, watching the slower traffic of the city at night clop by.

Irene was gone. Quentin was . . . gone.

My composure was gone. How long I could range the streets in my decidedly pathetic guise, I didn't know.

I thought of Nellie Bly, and wracked my brains to remember the address at which she resided with her mother. Her mother. She had one. I did not. Irene did not.

I lifted a weary arm and waved at a hack. He came over as if I held sugar for his weary horse.

I got in and told him where to go.

Forever after that awful night, the sound of horses' hooves will be linked to the pounding of a Spanish dancer's nail-studded shoe heels and toes in my mind.

My head was an anvil and each sound of the city a hammer that impressed itself upon my beaten brain. I was dazed beyond sleep by then, and stumbled out of the last cab, giving the driver a princely coin.

Another building to broach, another door to push through. An elevator, which I abhorred, to stand in like a corpse. My lapel watch was back at the Astor House, but it felt as though an aeon had passed since Irene had left me behind and blithely entered the stage set of her construction, the empty former room of Lola Montez.

When the elevator jerked to a pause, I shook myself awake.

The operator parted its accordion of metal bars. I stumbled down a passage, searching for doors. I no longer knew whether I expected Irene to be behind one of them or . . . Jack the Ripper.

At last I knocked on something that seemed faintly familiar.

There was no response.

I knocked again. I really didn't want an answer by now.

Again, I knocked.

A neighboring door opened. A woman with her hair in kid-leather curlers looked out, glaring.

"Young man! Stop that racket! This is a respectable establishment."

I shrugged, too tired to lift my hand to mahogany again.

The door leaned in with me, and I stumbled through, utterly off-balance.

A firm hand grabbed my elbow and reversed my momentum.

I was still upright, to my great amazement.

"Good God. What have we here?"

I wasn't sure.

41

Taken by Storm...

~∞~

Holmes had, when he liked, a peculiarly ingratiating way with women.
—WATSON IN "THE GOLDEN PINCE-NEZ"

"Perhaps," said a strangely bracing sardonic voice, "you'd care to explain the burning cigar in your pocket."

I blinked in the light of the paraffin lamp blazing beside me on a side table as I patted my jacket pockets in confusion. My right hand detected a lump. I reached for it dully, like a child roused in the middle of the night whose actions are clumsy and slow.

Another hand pushed mine aside and pulled out . . . not the candy my child self hoped for but Irene's cigar. The lit end still smoldered, a dull red ember.

I regarded it with an odd mixture of disgust and anguish, and then to my eternal shame I burst into tears.

"That will never do," Sherlock Holmes said. "Sit down." He steered me onto the armless chair next to the table that held the lamp. He took several strides away and returned with a glass of water, which I greedily gulped down, only then realizing how terribly thirsty I was from my frantic journey uptown.

Since it was hard to sob and drink at the same time, this act stifled my tears. When I finished the glass, I took off my right glove and wiped at my eyes. All I could see before me was the wavering muted tapestry pattern of the mouse-colored dressing gown Mr. Holmes wore. His voice came from above me, clipped and calm.

"You have been lurking about the lower town area with your partner in crime detection, Madam Irene. You spent some time near the Episcopal Club, and more time in and out of at least two hired hansom cabs on the way here. You stopped at Mr. Stanhope's hotel, but found him out. I'm amazed that you didn't next seek your American ally in dangerous stunts, Miss Nellie Bly."

My sniffles revived at the mere mention of her name.

"Ah, I see," he said after a moment. "The explanation for why you next came to me instead of her is not written on your trouser cuffs but in your face."

"Irene is in terrible danger," I finally managed to say.

"I know." He stepped away again to refill my water glass, which he returned to the table. "Here is a handkerchief. If you can manage to wet your throat and dry your eyes for a few minutes, I shall be ready to return to the Episcopal Club with you."

At that the mouse-colored dressing gown vanished from the outer room's circle of lamplight like a theatrical curtain being drawn away.

I sat and sipped and sniffled as he had recommended. By the time I was composed again, he'd reappeared dressed in a caped ulster and a soft-brimmed city hat, all of it dark.

"You can tell me what happened in the cab," he said, taking my arm to guide me out of the chair and to the door. "Pull your cap down lower and your scarf up higher around your chin. Madam Irene obviously dressed you for the dark. The lights of a hotel lobby will compromise your disguise, which was always unlikely."

I was incapable of taking offense or arguing with him at the moment, so stuffed the handkerchief in the pocket that had held the cigar, which, left behind, now lay in state in a tray next to the paraffin lamp.

"What time did she disappear?" he asked as we awaited the elevator.

"How did you—?"

"It's my profession to draw conclusions, and correct ones. Most unfortunate that Mr. Stanhope was out. Please, dear lady, don't snivel at every mention of his name. He may have been out on Rothschild business. One must never underestimate what a foreign spy might be up to."

"Quentin is not a foreign spy!"

"He is when living on American soil. Obviously the government we all share has set him to ensure that Miss Bly holds her tongue about a certain lurid affair last spring that involves several European countries."

"So you don't think that—?"

He was silent while he eyed what he could see of my face, I imagine a red nose and watery eyes. "Your personal presumptions may not be entirely wrong," he admitted, at least refraining from putting my fears that Quentin was out late *with Pink* into so many words.

Still, when even Sherlock Holmes bothered to believe that there might be a *tendresse* between them—so much so that he also most uncharacteristically thought to spare my feelings by not stating that outright . . . well, I could have bawled like a baby again.

But I didn't. And the act of refusing to express my tangled snarl of emotions—dread, disappointment, and chagrin, but mostly dread—served to stop my humiliating self-indulgence. I was dressed as a man; I would not sob like a girl a moment longer. I gave not a whimper as we entered the elevator and kept silent during our plummet to the ground floor.

"Hold your tongue until we are in the cab," he softly advised me as the elevator operator unfastened our iron cage. We stepped out into the lights of the lobby.

Only hotel staff lounged about the scattered furniture and potted plants. I needed all my breath anyway to lengthen my strides to keep pace with his. Not until we reached the door to the street did a returning resident appear. This portly fellow, wearing an askew top hat and straining waistcoat, almost collided with us as he reeled in from a night of food and drink and who knows what other overindulgences and entertainment.

"Watch yerselves, gents," he advised as he bounced off the steel-spring figure of Mr. Holmes.

Holmes didn't bother to answer, and I scuttled through the open door behind him, welcoming the concealing darkness of the street, which was soon the deeper dark to be found inside a hansom cab hurtling along Broadway at a fearsome clip, as instructed to do in no uncertain terms.

I flinched as the whip cracked for the fourth or fifth time.

"They seldom touch horseflesh," he said, pausing in the act of lighting his pipe. "The sound alone is sufficient to encourage speed."

"Those whips must have 'touched horseflesh' once, or the poor creatures would not respond to the noise."

"Well reasoned, but irrelevant now. I gather you are sufficiently restored to tell me what happened."

"What? You can't predict it from my appearance?"

"Miss Huxleigh, I've no doubt that the past hour or so has been exceedingly trying. I am, in fact, fairly amazed that you were able to maintain your guise and your wits to move so far so fast. But try to curtail your congenital annoyance with me. It won't help her."

Underneath the dingy scarf, which smelled of beer and tobacco, my cheeks may have flushed, whether with fugitive pleasure that he approved my recent actions, or sheer fury at his lofty arrogance, I couldn't say then and I can't say now.

What I did say then was, "Irene and I weren't outside the Episcopal Club. We were outside a boardinghouse a few blocks away."

"Which boardinghouse?"

"The one where Lola Montez died almost thirty years ago."

"Ah, one-ninety-four West Seventeenth Street."

"You've been there?"

"No, but I know the addresses associated with her in New York." He rapped on the roof and called out the boardinghouse's address to the driver. "How long did you spend watching the building?" he then asked me.

"Only a few minutes. Then Irene went inside—"

"How?"

"She walked alongside the building to a rear entrance."

"Out of your sight? What was she doing?"

"Inspecting the room."

"What did she expect to find there?"

"She expected to find nothing there. She went to leave something for someone else to find."

He drew deeply on his pipe. The side lamps from a passing carriage cast deep shadow on his craggy face for a moment, making his expression look bleak.

"If she is playing with the people I suspect she is, the danger is of the gravest."

My hands curled into fists inside the thick leather gloves. For a moment I felt a pugilist's fury. "We don't need criticism; we need help."

He glanced at my hands. "I don't suppose you're carrying Mrs. Norton's small pistol?"

"No."

"Was she?"

"I don't . . . know. Perhaps."

"What happened while you waited for her to come back?"

"Three men came down the street."

"Looking—?"

"I don't know! Dressed in dark clothing and hats. Not quite walking together, but strung out in a line. They went down the side of the building where Irene had gone perhaps ten minutes before. And then, nobody came back!"

"How long did you wait?"

"I hadn't brought my watch. Perhaps another ten minutes, and again that."

"Certainly long enough for Madam Irene to have left whatever it was she was leaving."

"Ye-es. She had to disarrange the furniture to do it, though, so I didn't expect her right back."

"Did you follow the men to the rear of the building."

It seemed less a question than an accusation. "No. I didn't. She'd told me to wait for her where I was. I suppose I should have—"

"Absolutely not. You did the right thing. I don't need your footprints in those ladyish boots cluttering up the ground the three villains have trod."

"You think that they are?"

"Are what?"

"Villains."

"I fear they are, villains of the most merciless sort. I have one poor man in Bellevue having his wounds tended even now. He was a frequenter of the Episcopal Club."

"No!"

"How freely have you two come and gone from the premises?"

"Only twice. A few days ago and . . . yesterday.'

"Twice too many times is as bad as thirteen."

"Oh, I tried to restrain Irene from this senseless search, but she would hear nothing of my objections."

"I am sure you did, Miss Huxleigh. I didn't mean that it was your fault."

"And you! If it's anyone's fault, it's yours!"

"I beg your pardon."

"*You* had to coming stalking after us into Green-Wood Cemetery. *You* had to disabuse Irene of the notion that the wicked Madame Restell was her mother. I was actually glad that you had produced the demure-sounding Mrs. Eliza Gilbert as a better candidate. Now we have been delving into the life and death of no one less than Lola Montez, and have paid a dear price for that."

"I had no idea at that time that Lola Montez was at all involved in the matter."

"Which matter?"

"The Vanderbilt case."

"And now you do believe that she is?"

"Perhaps. To what extent isn't clear. The woman has been dead nearly thirty years, after all."

"What is the Vanderbilt case?"

"I don't discuss such things. No doubt your associate has confessed the details of her audacious visit to the Vanderbilt mansion, and what she found there."

"Poor Father Hawks! Yes, I did hear that, although I have no idea why someone would leave such a brutal souvenir at the Vanderbilt home."

"Extortion," he said. "What else can be the motive when a man of such paramount wealth is involved?"

"But how can the death of a lowly Episcopal priest serve to make a millionaire lose heart? Why Father Hawks? He was utterly harmless, save for his silly conviction about Lola."

Holmes inhaled on his pipe, then let the smoke stream out the window. I almost felt that the ghost of Lola was present with us, and was vicariously inhaling the smoke he exhaled.

"What conviction did Father Hawks cherish about Lola Montez?"

"She repented quite dramatically of the excesses of her former life and character."

"Deathbeds have that affect."

"Father Hawks had concluded that she deserved sainthood."

Sherlock Holmes stopped in midinhalation on his pipe. "A saint? Lola Montez?" The incredulous words came out on puffs of smoke. "The old man was clearly cracked. This makes his death even more disturbing."

"That someone would torment a confused old soul like himself?"

"In that the motive becomes even more mysterious. What could he have known that was worth so much?"

"He could have known the location of the lost treasure of Lola Montez."

I hated to arm him with this information Irene and I had picked out of the situation, as Forty-niners must have chipped gold nuggets out of masses of hard, ungiving rock.

He stared at me, then laughed. "More is at stake here than the tawdry jewels amassed during a notorious lifetime."

"You will recall that the Crown Jewels of Bohemia, merely shown in a photograph, nearly toppled the kingdom of Bohemia," I said. Icily. "Lola Montez did topple the kingdom of Bavaria."

"I'm glad to see that you have recovered your composure, and then some, Miss Huxleigh." He ignored my indignation to glance out over the hansom doors. "We are where we asked to be. I suggest we forget recriminations and get to work."

In a mirror of his words, the cab stopped with the forward and backward rock that indicated the journey was at an end.

Mr. Holmes released the doors that boxed in our lower limbs and dismounted. I found that with my walking-out costume I could do so without relying upon the hand he offered for my assistance.

"Thank you, my good man. Here's two dollars."

The driver sputtered his thanks (apparently Irene was not the only one profligate about cab fares), flicked his whip in the air above his steeds' hindquarters, and left us in the same inky and silent street that I had fled only two hours before.

Would that I could turn back the clock and prevent Irene from entering the boardinghouse, or that I had gone with her.

I didn't have long to brood on that, though.

"Come along," Holmes was directing as he pulled a small lantern from one of the capacious pockets in his ulster.

"You want me to accompany you?"

"I need someone to come behind and hold the lantern." The pipe had disappeared, but he lit the lamp with a lucifer, then adjusted its shutters so that only a narrow beam was cast forward. "Do you think you can manage that?"

"Certainly!" I took the lantern and fell into step behind him

Such a funereal pace he set! My task proved to be far more arduous than I had suspected, for he was eternally stopping and bending over, nose nearly to the ground. I, of course, had to mimic his movements, and, further, stretch out my arm so the lantern illuminated his task, whilst remaining strictly behind him.

This is a most taxing posture, and the only thanks I got for maintaining it were brusque instructions.

"Higher, please. Lower. To the left. Right. Don't move!"

Had I wished to be a performing seal in a circus I could not have arranged things better.

However, the more irritated with Holmes I became, the less the gnawing fear for Irene's welfare ate away at my innards.

"Higher, Huxleigh!"

I was jerked out of a sudden image of her figure disappearing into this very dark we were now exploring.

"Have you learned anything?" I whispered, for of course we couldn't converse in normal tones while sneaking past people's bedrooms.

"Three men's footprints—one most intriguing—overlaid a man's shoe tracks, but in a dainty size. I understand Lola Montez possessed an exceptionally petite foot."

"So did Cinderella," I answered sharply. I really didn't wish to encourage this fantasy that Lola Montez was Irene's mother. Nothing good would come of it. Indeed, nothing but bad had come of it so far.

Especially my night duty alongside the boarding house.

When we finally turned the corner to inspect the back of the building, I heaved a sigh of relief.

"A little less windily, Miss Huxleigh. We are closer to the sleepers than ever before."

He followed the trail to the back stoop, where, under the glare of the lantern I held, he plucked several invisible traces from the wooden stairs with a tweezer. They looked like tiny dry blades of grass.

Luckily, the room in question looked out on the back courtyards, and was entered just inside the back door.

After studying and testing the door, he reached to take the lantern into his own custody.

"I have much to study inside that room. Wait here, be quiet, don't move unless absolutely necessary."

"May I at least sit on the stoop?"

He swung the lantern light over the three steps in question.

"Yes," he said, shuttering the lantern so we were completely in the dark.

Then he went into the room Irene and I had so thoroughly searched only days before.

Slowly, I sank into a seated position on the filthy steps, thankful that only flea market clothing would be ruined.

The time was that no-man's-land between midnight and dawn, when decent folk are asleep in their beds and indecent folk are most busy about their evil business.

No one moved in the space between the backs of Boardinghouse Row, but night life made itself known. The trash that had collected here shifted in the sounds of slight chimings of glass or rustles of paper. Mice, rats, insects moved under the cover of refuse, seeking food and shelter.

Above me, the laundry, most of it left out for the night, flapped in the intermittent wind like phantom whiplashes and ships' sails. The shifting white cloths above moved, ghostlike, hiding the dark night sky.

And then came the click of dog nails on the damp pavement. I glimpsed ranging canine figures, some quite large.

I sat as still as still could be, not wanting to attract the beasts' attention, not knowing what Sherlock Holmes was learning inside Lola Montez's last residence, not sure what the morning would bring, hope or despair.

A long time later the door behind me whispered open. Someone bent over me.

"She's not there, of course, although signs of her activities abound. I must follow the trail on foot. Can you get yourself a cab and return to the Astor House?"

I had done something of the sort only hours before. Now it seemed an insurmountable task.

While I remained silent, he leaned closer, bringing an overwhelming scent of tobacco that painfully reminded me of Irene, and her absence.

"I must follow the trail now, unencumbered. I'll let you know what I find in the morning."

Morning. What a bitter, rueful word. I doubted I'd like what I found "in the morning," no matter what Sherlock Holmes did during the rest of this night.

I stood up, my knees creaking like the laundry lines above us.

"I'll be waiting to hear your report." I sounded like a client.

When he said nothing more, I turned to rebuke his silence.

But he was gone, part of the immense dark of which I knew nothing.

I rose to make my way to the street, marveling that I should be abroad at such an hour, alone, and too numb to even fear what I should.

Once I made Broadway and its many streetlamps, I was able to hail a cab. I sank into the boxed-in seat, appreciating springs, and ordered myself returned to the Astor House.

42

Taken by Surprise...

He is dark, handsome, and dashing; never calls less than once a day, and often twice. He is a Mr. Godfrey Norton, of the Inner Temple.
—SHERLOCK HOLMES IN "A SCANDAL IN BOHEMIA"

There is a kind of weariness in which feeling is forgotten. A weariness in which even the most hysterical mind has been too overtaxed to make its frantic mental rounds. That is the state in which I approached the door to Irene's and my rooms. I had the key clutched in my hand, but I wasn't quite sure how to use such an implement.

How I dreaded the emptiness beyond the door, dreaded the absolute reality that Irene was gone. Lost. Perhaps forever.

But I had nowhere else to go.

So I painstakingly pushed the key into its hole by the light of the gaslight on the wall.

I jiggled the key, having forgotten the particular touch of this lock... except I hadn't forgotten it, I'd never known it, for Irene had led, in this as in so much else, and always unlocked the door for me.

Weary tears were gathering in my eyes but I fought them, though there was no one here to hold them back for.

The darkness inside surprised me. The air felt cold, though the outside air had been tepid with leftover summer heat.

I couldn't remember where the gaslight was exactly, for that was another thing Irene had readily rushed to do herself . . . as she had readily rushed to the back of the boardinghouse.

I edged along the wall, hearing my feet shuffling on bare floor, patting the wall at shoulder height. Should I have gone left instead of right from the door?

I shifted to return . . . and a piece of tangible darkness seized upon me!

Instantly I was rolled up in it, like Cleopatra in a rug. This rug was composed of wool and solid stuffing (for I kicked and pummeled in my own silent resistance).

Someone broader and taller, a man, had encompassed me in the dark, and we fought along a good length of the wall. My panic at the memory of the three evil men revived my will. Messalina the mongoose could not have been more intent in her deadly struggles with the cobra.

Cobra! Cobra. I knew that word for a certain British spy's pseudonym in India years before. Was this Quentin then? Come to visit and—finding our rooms suspiciously deserted for so late an hour—deciding to stay?

"Quentin?" I interrogated the dark. All it could do was not answer me.

But it did.

"Nell? Nell! What on earth are you wearing? Where's Irene?"

I gasped, too shocked to answer.

At last one of our flailing hands found and twisted the gaslight key.

The strengthening flame finally revealed the features of the man who held me half-captive, half-embraced.

"Godfrey! Godfrey? Thank God you're here! You are here, aren't you?"

Godfrey was the antithesis of Sherlock Holmes. He didn't bring me water, he brought me brandy.

He also sat me down, but on the sofa in the middle of the room. Then he went around the chamber turning on all the gaslights until the room blazed as if for a ball.

"Irene's work," he said, eyeing my ensemble.

Of course it started me weeping again.

Godfrey sat beside me, his arm around my shoulder. "Just tell me," he said. "Start with the worst and work backwards."

"She's not here! Sherlock Holmes is looking for her. She vanished tonight. I'm to wait here until morning for news. Those three men may be murderous devils! Irene may have had her pistol with her, I don't know. We expected to encounter no more than a deserted room. I was to wait and watch, but I couldn't stay there, not when she never came back. It was but hours ago, Godfrey. If only you had come but a bit sooner, perhaps we'd all be here in this room, together."

"Time is a bawd, Nell," he finally said when I'd run out of all I could manage to say. "It never pays you back for what you lose by it."

We sat silent for a moment, sharing that bitter truth.

Then he spoke again.

"You say Sherlock Holmes is looking for her? Where?"

"He is a human bloodhound. If she has left a trace, he will find and follow it."

"Tell me again," he said.

This time I narrated events in sequence, and then Godfrey cross-examined me in the methodical way of a barrister. Strain had sharpened his features into something resembling Sherlock Holmes's hawkish visage.

"Stanhope knew about your genealogical quest?"

"No. Holmes did, of course. He steered us toward it that day in Green-Wood Cemetery."

"Why did he, do you suppose?"

"I think he wanted Irene otherwise occupied. You know that their paths have intersected before, generally with them both at cross-purposes. And—"

"And what?"

"Perhaps he thought, in his way, he was doing her a service. He'd been drawn into her quest, thanks to the murders of her former theatrical family members, shall we call them? Apparently he'd come across information about Lola Montez that made her a more likely maternal candidate than Madam Restell. Oh, Godfrey, why are we sitting here, exploring old questions? Why aren't we out looking for her?"

He sat back, shaking his head. "As you said, we can do no better than to have Sherlock Holmes on the trail. Rushing out would serve no purpose and would only mean Holmes couldn't find us if . . . when he has news to report. For now, we're best employed unraveling events from here. All we know is that when Holmes entered that boardinghouse two hours after Irene had, no one was there. Not Irene, and not the three men you saw follow her in."

I nodded, ready to choke on sobs again, but dampening the urge.

"Did Holmes mention blood in the rooms?"

"No. Only that there were signs that Irene had done more than merely visit the premises. I didn't tell him about the secret chamber in the hidden fire-place. But, I imagine, with his tricks of observation, he might have noticed that the wardrobe had been moved, or bricks and old crumbling mortar removed."

"So Irene did what she had intended to."

"Perhaps, yes."

"Could she have left before the men arrived?"

"Then why not return to me?"

"Perhaps she was able to slip away just before they came, but had to hide until they left."

"Then why not come back to me?"

"She could have feared leading them to you. She could have"—Godfrey's eyes narrowed with an unhappy thought—"seen an opportunity to turn the tables on them and follow them."

"Leaving me waiting there in the dark, alone?"

"It's not likely, but this sounds like a desperate case—not the matter of Lola Montez but the Vanderbilt investigation Sherlock Holmes pursues. Irene would not hesitate to walk into danger if she thought it was a matter of someone else's life or death. Already a harmless old priest has been slaughtered. His body's appearance on a billiard table at the Vanderbilt mansion forges a clear link between Sherlock Holmes's quest and Irene's, whether we or they like it or not. We can best serve matters by exchanging all the information we each have. That way we'll be informed and ready when Sherlock Holmes returns . . . with Irene or, God forbid, without her."

"Exchange information, Godfrey? What information could you possibly have to offer?"

"You forget where I have been the past several weeks."

I had, in fact, done just that. Not so much as forgot it but dismissed it in the fever of my anxiety about Irene.

"Bavaria," I said slowly, like a child repeating a lesson not quite learned.

"Bavaria. Precisely. The scene of Lola Montez's greatest triumphs and failures."

"How did you know we had turned to investigating this woman?"

"Irene mentioned in a cable that she could use any tidbits about Lola Montez I might run across. Naturally, I read between the lines, gathered as much information I could before I had to take the train to Ostend, and immediately sailed for New York."

"You never got the massive packet that Irene sent, then?"

He shook his head. "She'll have to tell me about that herself."

"And you came all the way here, so quickly, merely because Irene had casually mentioned a name?"

"Irene never casually mentions anything. And what I learned of Lola Montez on my first sweep through the newspapers, histories, and memories of the older foreign office attachés convinced me that coming to New York was not deserting my post but serving the Rothschild interests in the best possible way, as well as my own, of course."

"Lola Montez was a poor dancer, a poorer actress, and an ill-tempered, high-handed woman of no moral standards. What could she possibly have to do with global political affairs today, almost thirty years after her death?"

Godfrey smiled patiently. "Her enemies did a thorough job of discrediting her, with her own able assistance, I admit. But in the late '40s in Bavaria, she was a fiery Republican liberalist who had convinced a monarch to grant unparalleled freedoms of speech to his subjects and the newspapers. She was overturning the tightfisted rule of his religious cadre of advisors. She was encouraging the students to protest and revolt. Remember, France underwent a spasm of reform and revolution again at that same time."

"Yes! That's when Marie Antoinette's Zone of Diamonds, which we found, had been smuggled out of the country to England."

"Exactly. And Irene found the Zone all by herself, by the way. The '40s were a period of great foment in Europe. Lola Montez was at the center of it in Bavaria. Of course she fought fire with fire when her secret foes lashed out at her, and they drove her from the city of Munich and forced the king to abdicate. Ludwig is now, thirty years later and dead, regarded as a benign ruler who meant well for his people, but his ultimate legacy is the madness of his son and grandson, and the notoriety of Lola Montez."

I sat back in the sofa, astounded. "Lola was a serious political force? For good? I thought she had invented that notion, as she had invented herself as a Spanish dancer, from half-truths and sheer audacity."

Godfrey smiled. "The same may be said of her political career, but she was effective enough to be dangerous, and this rouses even more dangerous foes. The Ultramontanes, for instance."

"Ultramontanes! We've heard of these . . . this faction. What on earth are they? Who are they? Are they still . . . practicing?"

Godfrey rose, brought the brandy decanter to the side table, and poured himself a glass. He also lit a cigar, and the scent of it brought Irene back into the room. I cursed every time I had complained of her smoking.

"Steady, Nell. All we can do at the moment is think and compare notes. Otherwise we'll go mad with waiting, and that will help no one, least of all Irene. I can tell you that Sherlock Holmes is considered the best man in Europe when it comes to the practice of private inquiries, which is quite different from espionage in its purest form."

"Should we contact Quentin, though?"

He glanced to the telephone sitting on its lacy doily like a Black Widow spider in the center of its web. "We'll call his hotel first thing in the morning."

"That might be well." I felt my color, and indignation rising. "I called at his hotel last night, as soon as I left the boardinghouse, but he was out."

"What time was this?"

"Perhaps one in the morning. Or so."

"Ah. And then you went to Holmes, as a last resort."

"I don't like the man."

"You don't have to like him, Nell. You only have to rely upon his reputation for unraveling vexing mysteries with amazing results."

Godfrey made a fist, and by the whiteness of his knuckles I saw how much our enforced inaction chafed his instincts, if not his better sense. He loosened his fingers and lifted the brandy glass to his lips, barely wetting them.

"We must strip these events of what you and Irene embarked upon them to determine: whether Lola Montez is her mother. All that is moot now. The question is, what has the late Lola Montez to do with the fresh murders now?"

"The Episcopal Church is in it up to its Romanish collars," I said. Stiffly.

He nodded. "So it seems. I sense we're missing some link, perhaps the one that drew Holmes into the issue. His interest is not political but criminal."

"There is plenty of crime here for him to investigate. First Father Hawks dead, now Irene missing. Wouldn't she be back here by now, Godfrey, if she could?"

"Remember, Nell, how she explored Monaco in men's dress by night? Perhaps you'd better look through her things, see if you can find her pistol. If it's missing that might lighten your mind."

"I don't know where she keeps such a thing, Godfrey! She insists on 'sparing' me knowledge she deems upsetting. Had I not been so easy to upset, I might have known more."

"You know the intricacies of a woman's wardrobe, Nell, far better than I. 'Search and ye shall find.'"

I stood, a bit unsteadily. Apparently six sips of brandy are equal to a few hours on the surging Atlantic.

"I'll look, but I can't be sure I'll look in the right places."

"And you might wish to don your ordinary clothes," he added, "so we'll be ready to go out in the morning if we need to."

I had my assignment, I realized. One, I was to reassemble my ordinary self. Two, I was to discover if Irene had been armed when she disappeared.

An hour later I stepped back again into the parlor. I had been busy. I hated to think what thoughts had occupied Godfrey while I had left him alone.

He still sat on the sofa, his dark head bowed beneath the bright gaslights. The Astor House had no doubt been ultramodern when it had converted to gas, but now electricity was creeping through the city, nudging the gentle flickers of gaslight away.

Godfrey was reading the newspaper, the one Irene had "borrowed" from the *Herald* vault. The one containing the obituary of Lola Montez. Was Irene destined for an American obituary as well? Were Godfrey and I mourners unaware?

I took a deep breath, and reported my findings. "I can't find a pistol anywhere," I told him.

He jumped up as if summoned at the Judgment Day. "No pistol?"

I shook my head. "I've been through everything I can think of."

"Then if she was armed and didn't use the pistol . . . she wasn't personally threatened at the boardinghouse. Excellent news, Nell. It argues for Irene being alerted. It argues for her being the hunter rather than the hunted."

"But wouldn't she have gotten word to us somehow?"

"There is no 'us,' as far as Irene knows. There is only you. I'm almost sure that she expected you to do what you did: rush to find an ally."

"Sherlock Holmes protects the Vanderbilt interests, not Irene's. They are his clients."

"Sherlock Holmes may be considering at this moment, as we are, that he and his graveyard suggestion was the catalyst in drawing Irene and yourself into this farango. He may have meant the opposite, but 'may have' doesn't matter in life-and-death situations. I would rather have a guilty man in my corner than any number of wonder-workers."

"You're saying that Sherlock Holmes is both, in this instance."

Godfrey nodded, then pulled out his pocket watch. "Almost seven A.M., Nell. Morning. I suggest breakfast in the room. We must have the strength to do whatever we're called upon to do today."

"I can't eat with Irene gone!"

Godfrey shrugged, not with indifference but with acceptance, and picked up the telephone.

I'd had no idea that he knew how to use one.

But, then, I'd had no idea about a lot of things before this expedition to America, including a person who'd named herself Lola Montez.

Memoirs of a Dangerous Woman:

The Ultramontanes . . .

Mlle. Lola Montez . . . has left a card at the Shooting Gallery of Lepage . . . entirely perforated with pistol balls, in firing rapid doubt coups. The most famous Parisian shots avow themselves vanquished by the prowess of the fair Andalusian.

—PARIS NEWSPAPER, JULY 1844

The Jesuit party . . . are angry with Lollita, who is Catholic but a sworn enemy of the Jesuit; that's obviously an unforgivable crime. Who knows, if she were doing the opposite and introducing the Jesuits into Bavaria, along with the holy Ignatius Loyola we might get a half-holy Lola. . . ."

—KING LUDWIG I, 1846

Ten years have elapsed since the events with which Lola Montez was connected in Bavaria, and yet the malice of the diffuse and ever vigilant Jesuits is as fresh and as active as it was the first hour it assailed her . . . I was compelled at last to fly before the infuriated bands of the Jesuits of Austria.

—*AUTOBIOGRAPHY*, LOLA MONTEZ

It took ten years and retreat to another continent before I could publicly and frankly address the machinations of the Jesuits and the Ultramontanes in Bavaria.

Those who haven't lived under the thumb of the papacy laugh at the alarms I've sounded. They think my accusations of the Jesuits spreading lies and scandal about me as far as America belong in one of my plays, not real life.

Before I ever went to Bavaria, or knew that I would, I had heard tales of the Jesuits' thirst for power in the governments and royal houses of Europe.

After having been expelled from the cities of Berlin and Warsaw, and the backwaters of Spa, Baden-Baden, and Ebersdorf—once for the mere act of demonstrating my dancing prowess to a gentleman by throwing a leg over his shoulder—I returned to Paris, scene of my doomed romance with Dujarier.

And there is where I first heard of the Society of Jesus and its political machinations that had caused it to be banned in more than one European country. France would have been a Catholic country save that their bloody revolution fifty years before had made them a wholly secular society.

But Catholics and Protestants halved most European countries, and the Reformation was still being fought. In Paris we heard constantly how that battle was being waged. For if the loyalties of Catholic citizens everywhere were first to the pope "beyond the mountains," then no government was secure.

The Jesuits were exposed and excoriated in lectures at the Collège de France. Newspapers across Europe detailed the Jesuits' plans to undermine nations, undo kings and governmental officials, and destroy any brave enough to oppose their secret agenda.

In France, in Spain, in the many German states, the Jesuits were a hidden political force working against the great movements of nationalism and liberalism.

So now, when I'd retreated to the Paris of my lost love, I was secretly approached by members of this very despised society, who wished me to help them convert a Russian nobleman of my close acquaintance to their cause. Spanish noble blood may run in my veins, and I might be expected to sympathize with all Catholic causes, but I refused to be used in this manner. I informed the French foreign minister of their plot to influence Franco-Russian affairs, and for once Jesuits were banned from a place, not Lola.

But, oh, I paid the price for my patriotism to my current country. The

Jesuits swore eternal vengeance, and God knows that the Church of Rome claims to be eternal. . . .

My second stay in Paris wouldn't allow me to forget the tragic ending to my first visit: Dujarier's death.

At the end of March in 1846, I was called to testify in the trial of Beauvallon for the murder of Dujarier.

My dear one's mother and brother-in-law brought the action. Mobs thronged the entrance to the Palais de Justice as Dumas *père et fils* and myself arrived. Since the bloody revolution, Paris has always been a city of mobs.

The case was simple: Dujarier, an innocent in the matters of duels of honor, had been goaded by a superior opponent into a fatal meeting. Dujarier had been too innocent to even choose a weapon that would have given him a chance at life: a sword, rather than a pistol. I testified how I pled with him not to go; I knew that I was the better shot and offered to take his place. He would hear nothing of it. And that awful morning he discharged his pistol, which fired far wide of Beauvallon. And then he stood there as a man of honor while the sharpshooter Beauvallon slowly took his shot, aiming for death, not a shot gone wide, or even a minor wound.

I came forward when called to testify, clad in a black silk dress, a black veil, and a black cashmere shawl. The Woman in Black, as I was ever after.

In the witness box, they handed me Dujarier's bloody clothing and pistols from the duel. Had I worn them, shot them, Beauvallon would be dead, I knew it!

I held the small lead ball that had pierced his face.

The arguments made clear that Beauvallon had goaded Dujarier into the duel, that he was by far the more adept. He had not hesitated to shoot the unarmed man full in the face.

Ranks of gendarmes and soldiers held back thousands of people swarming the Palace of Justice. The jury retired, and in ten minutes had a verdict. Not guilty.

Sick of France, I gathered my trunks of clothing and jewels, my maid and my lapdog, and, some say, a young English lover, and left for the seaside resorts of Belgium, and then traveled into Germany. Heidelberg. Homburg. Stuttgart.

The summer faded, and so did my grief. Fall was coming. The theaters would be reopening. I aimed for Vienna, but my route took me across Bavaria, through Munich.

It would be the most significant detour of my life.

43

Holmes Again

The Countess of Landsfeld would not be welcome anywhere in Prussian territory because her presence might incite public demonstrations by liberals, socialists, and communists.

—BRUCE SEYMOUR, *LOLA MONTEZ: A LIFE*

 Waiting is such a helpless state. I have come to detest it more than anything. While Godfrey and I waited to hear from Mr. Holmes, I found myself jumping up at every muffled sound in the hall.

I hadn't realized I'd become so accustomed to going out and doing things on my own. When I reviewed my actions after Irene had disappeared, I grew quite astounded by my own nerve.

Godfrey had been able to take a room adjoining our suite, so we'd ordered breakfast served in Irene's and my larger parlor. I'd simply rearranged my shirred eggs rather than eating them. Godfrey was, as far as I could see, subsisting on brandy by night and coffee by daylight.

The sight of his fine-featured face taut with unrelenting worry made my heart twist. Surely Irene would have sent us word, were she in any state that would permit it!

A knock on the door sent my eyes to my reinstalled lapel watch—8:45 A.M.—and then to Godfrey.

He leaped up, paused to gather himself, then went to open the door.

Sherlock Holmes shouldered in like a weary pugilist, head lowered, shoulders leading. Seeing Godfrey drew him up short.

"Mr. Norton. This is a timely surprise indeed!"

"Mr. Holmes. What word have you?"

They were both of a height, and both at the end of their tethers. No time for pleasantries.

Holmes answered. "I bring no news, either of hope or despair. The four people I tracked from the boardinghouse retreated in the same direction, but whether together or not, I can't yet say."

"And that direction was?" Godfrey wanted to know.

"The dock and warehouse area near the harbor."

"Will you take coffee, Mr. Holmes?" I asked, merely to break the intolerable tension within, and between, the two men.

"Not ordinarily," he said, "but yes."

He came to stand before me while I poured . . . and while I cogitated as to how to turn the energies and aims of these two motivated but wary men into an asset rather than a competition.

Holmes bolted the hot coffee I handed him as if it were cold milk, while Godfrey watched him. The man who had spent the night assuring me of Holmes's expertise had been replaced by a stern taskmaster.

"You," Godfrey said, his silver-gray eyes hardening into sheer steel, "set Irene on this fool's mission. You directed her attention to Lola Montez. You bear responsibility for her absence now."

Holmes shrugged, a gesture I now recognized as his way of shaking off arguments and concerns he regarded as less than logical. The man lived and breathed logic. Emotional appeals only muddied his mind and wasted his time.

"I pointed out the obvious," he said. "That is my profession."

"My profession is the law," Godfrey replied, "and it's obvious to me that your 'obvious' has led my wife into subtle dangers. Why haven't you found her?"

"Because she doesn't wish to be found, my good man." Sherlock Holmes swallowed the last bitter dregs of coffee. "You underestimate your lady wife. She could lead a bloodhound a tangled trail. Pity rather the three men who sought to contain her. I'm sure you can understand their plight."

Godfrey let out a deep breath. "You say she's in control of herself and her actions and her whereabouts?"

"I say she may be in control of any number of things. I just don't quite know what and where yet."

"I did not," Godfrey said, "come all the way from Bavaria to be put off with vague answers.

"Bavaria?" Mr. Holmes visibly inhaled after saying the word, as if it were redolent of scent. He eyed Godfrey with new attention. "Of course. You have been recently in Bavaria, I perceive."

"How do you perceive that?" I challenged him. "You have already heard where Godfrey has come from."

"I'm afraid I regarded him as a given on this scene and did not give him a second look, once I had adjusted to his sudden presence."

Like a bird he brightly surveyed Godfrey and the entire parlor. "It is perfectly obvious that Mr. Norton has spent some weeks in the country. The sueded velvet hat on the entry table speaks strongly of the Tyrolean. I note a watch chain of German manufacture. It is much more elaborately scrolled than the English or even the French variety one would expect Mr. Norton to use. Items of foreign manufacture on his person indicated an extended stay rather than a mere visit. Also, his footwear is a sturdier sort than one finds in the far western countries."

Godfrey shook his head. "I'm not sure from your clues and conclusions that you aren't a haberdasher rather than a detective, sir."

I held my breath. I knew enough of Sherlock Holmes to realize that he did not accept gently slights to his observational powers.

He suddenly laughed, as if glad for the opportunity.

"Haberdashery is the first refuge of an able investigator, sir. Clothes may not make the man, but they make the man easier to read. I see that you're astute enough to have made yourself available here when needed, on very little evidence. The proof of that is found not in your dress but in your anticipating what has become a very dangerous situation.

"Now." He turned to me. "I'm certain, Miss Huxleigh, you've been diligently aiding and abetting Mrs. Norton in mastering the life and times of the late Lola Montez. We must pool our knowledge. Mr. Norton knows Bavaria, where this current nest of evil had its birth. Miss Huxleigh knows Lola Montez, rather better than she would like to, I believe. I know the Vanderbilt connection. Surely we can conspire to solve this lethal riddle."

I noticed that when in Godfrey's presence Mr. Holmes retreated to the more polite form of Mrs. Norton, rather than his usual more intimate and perhaps more dismissive reference to her as Madam Irene.

"Tell me about this Bavarian business of yours," Holmes added.

"It can't have anything to do with the current crisis. Besides, it's confidential," Godfrey answered reluctantly.

"So are your wife's whereabouts at the moment, all too confidential. I suggest you forget discretion. I assure you that I'm not about to cause my brother, Mycroft, any problems. What you say here will go no further."

"Then we'd all better save our strength and sit down."

"Goodness, Godfrey," I commented as Mr. Holmes complied. "Certainly Bavaria is not large enough to require a long-winded disquisition."

"Bavaria, no." Godfrey settled into a lawyerly explanation; that is: informed, thorough, and a trifle dull. "It's smaller than Bohemia and appears rather less important on the world stage. It occupies a scenic mountainous region in the south of Germany, with Munich its principal city. We all know from our recent adventures the past two years in Bohemia and Transylvania about the tussle such pocket kingdoms have had for years with the encroaching Austrian-Hungarian Empire. As in Bohemia, the line between church and state is muddied and contested by both parties. There is no Jewish question in Bavaria: there it's the ancient struggle of Protestant against Catholic, although the Catholic was in the ascendency at midcentury."

"Which," I asked, "is why Lola Montez was always prattling of enemy Jesuits pursuing her?"

"Yes, and quite accurately, Nell. The Jesuits were entrenched in Ludwig the First's ruling cabinet and all Bavarian institutions . . . until Lola came along and unseated them."

"But," I objected, "she was Irish-born and claimed to be Spanish. Surely she was Roman Catholic herself?"

"From what I have found, Lola had no graven images of any denomination before her, except her own perhaps."

Holmes stirred on his chair. "So she was a political creature after all?"

"She divided in order to unite. I suppose that makes her highly political. You must understand King Ludwig, a dreamy, idealistic man of sixty. Wrote poetry. Poor chap had a perfectly boring queen, and the succession was assured. He kept a portrait hall of the world's most beautiful women. When Lola appeared in his city, and at his court, she rivaled any painting in his private gallery, there in flesh and blood instead of oil and tint. She had by then stormed the Continent's major cities, and beyond, all the way to Russia."

"Just with some Spanish dances?" I asked. Despite the mixed reviews of her performances, I hadn't been convinced that Lola Montez ever had anything special to offer.

"The dances were the least of it. She was, apparently, extraordinarily beautiful in person. I've seen Ludwig's portraits. She strikes me as a bit sharp-featured, but everyone who'd seen her in person spoke of how her eyes mesmerized, and no painting can capture the spell of a living glance."

"No," Holmes said, a bit too fervently for my liking, as if he was thinking of the same compelling living glance that I was.

"No," Godfrey agreed, answering Holmes with a touch of complacency.

Was it possible that these two vastly different men were a bit jealous of each other? Jealousy is a wasted emotion, I decided. It was impossible to imagine that they were. Besides, Holmes had carbolic acid for blood. Sometimes I thought Godfrey had barrister's ink for blood, but from Irene's occasional unguarded comment, I was apparently wrong.

And Quentin, what did he have for blood? Perhaps . . . nitroglycerin.

I was, of course, taking notes in the tiny silver-encased pad on my belt-hung chatelaine during all of this, and many tiny papers it was taking up, despite all my assiduous abbreviations. Foreign diplomacy is always so taxing.

"So," Holmes summed up, "Lola's beauty, and politics, bewitched the king. That seems an unlikely combination of attributes for a femme fatale."

"It's not that laughable," Godfrey said earnestly, sitting forward. "She had a knack for befriending powerful men, whether the relationship ever became romantic or not. She'd entertained some of the most advanced artistic rebels and political thinkers in Europe. She'd become their equal and convert, and a passionate one. She was a dangerous woman by the time she came to Bavaria and met its impressionable king. The Jesuits were right to fear her, and they did."

"Ludwig is dead, and so is Lola," Holmes said over the familiar bowl of his pipe.

Trust him to force Godfrey to a quick summation.

"Their names and their very different influences live on in Bavaria to this day," Godfrey warned him. "They can't be dismissed as overripe historical anomalies. Ludwig stood by Lola, and her political principle, until revolution, stirred up by the disenfranchised Jesuits, threatened. She was forced to flee, almost over her own dead body, and Ludwig the First had to abdicate his throne in favor of his son, Maximilian the Second. Lola Montez did unseat some prominent Jesuits, earning the powerful international religious order's undying enmity, but it was the liberal revolutions sweeping all of Europe in 1848 that unseated Ludwig. The Ultramontanes—"

"Yes, Godfrey," I interjected. "What are these? Irene and I ran across that word many times."

"Not what but who, Nell. The word means 'over the mountains' and it referred to influence of Catholic Rome from beyond the Alps in the Italian states."

"So Lola was against the Roman Catholic influence."

"And especially the power of the Jesuits in Bavaria in restricting freedom of the press and suppressing free speech. Indeed, Lola's influence on the king made Bavaria a leader in the move for conservative monarchies to make concessions to liberal parliaments. Yet it couldn't forestall civil upheaval in Bavaria. Lola was an excuse for it. She was easily slandered, a woman bold about her love life and fiery in her political beliefs. Now Ludwig's grandson, Otto, is shut away in a madhouse while a regent sits the throne. He's quietly mad, with no notorious foreign woman to blame for the loss of his kingdom."

"Godfrey!" I gazed at him sternly. "You rather admire that scandalous woman."

"Indeed. Had Ludwig the First half the starch in his spine that Lola Montez had in her dancing petticoats, he would have hung on to his throne and provided the model of a modern liberalized monarchy."

Holmes, for once, seemed to take my side. " 'The past is prologue,' " he said through the smoke he recycled from his pipe. "What is Lola to Otto, and Otto to her?"

"Very little," Godfrey said. "Otto is the son of a man who'd become known as Mad King Ludwig, Ludwig the Second, grandson of Lola's Ludwig. It's rumored that young Ludwig's wet nurse had syphilis, explaining his mania for building extravagant palaces like Neuschwanstein."

I swallowed a gasp of recognition, for I didn't want to indicate that I had ever heard the dread word "syphilis." To hear it said so cavalierly by Godfrey, and to know Irene's secret fear that if her mother was Lola Montez and if Lola Montez had died of syphilis . . . It was all too dreadful to even think, much less say out loud. So I didn't.

"What is recorded," Godfrey went on, "was that Ludwig the Second was utterly indifferent to his own mother. The syphilis rumor may have been manufactured to explain his supposed 'madness.' "

"His mother, Queen Marie, was so averse to the word 'love' that she attempted to have her husband, Maximilian, replace the word with the term 'friendship' in all poetry published in the realm."

"Now that is truly mad!" I exclaimed.

Godfrey smiled conspiratorially. "You have put your finger upon it, Nell. Love and friendship are both powerful forces in our lives but one can't usurp the other."

"Can't they exist in tandem?" I asked.

"Sometimes," he said with a smile. "Sometimes not."

"Ludwig the Second died three years ago," Holmes noted from his corner.

"Exactly," Godfrey conceded, "but not before beginning a building spree that is still the wonder of that part of the world. Ludwig was a lonely, isolated boy, reared by a father with very queer ideas and a mother who couldn't love him. He became enchanted by the composer Richard Wagner. I find it fascinating that the dancer and Bavarian liberator Lola Montez died in January of 1861, while young Ludwig, Crown Prince of Bavaria, at the age of fifteen heard his first Wagnerian opera, *Lohengrin,* in February of that very year."

"Nothing good will come of hearing Wagnerian operas," Holmes declaimed through the pipe stem in his teeth, "but go on. In the stuff of legend lies the seed of truth."

"Truth is very hard to find in Bavaria," Godfrey said, wincing. "The larger-than-life tales of the two ruling Ludwigs is like marzipan on pound cake: it hides the serious political maneuverings behind the Spanish dancer and fairy-tale castles. Bavaria had led the other German states in resisting unification, That role was weakened by the civil strife in the first Ludwig's time. The second Ludwig's obsession with Wagner's operas and building grandiose palaces that bankrupted the kingdom ended Bavaria's power, even though his mother had converted from the Protestant to Catholic faith in an attempt to unite the country. After the Franco-Prussian War in the early '70s, Ludwig the Second invited King Wilhelm the First of Prussia to become the first emperor of a new united German state. Thus the most liberal German principality led them all into the highly conservative control of Prussia. This is amazing, given that the man was an eccentric recluse who amused himself rowing his seashell-shaped boat around an electrically lit grotto. He was declared insane and kept imprisoned, but three years ago was found drowned in the lake near his castle prison, along with his alienist. Of course the deaths were highly suspicious. With his brother Prince Otto just as mad, their uncle became regent. You can imagine the state the country is in to this day."

"A sensational story indeed, but what does all this matter?" I asked.

Holmes answered me instead of Godfrey.

"Normally nothing, Miss Huxleigh. However, the most recent succession in Bavaria is tainted by madness, machinations, and a mysterious royal death. No doubt that's why the Rothschild interests wanted you there," he said to Godfrey.

"Yes. The regency of Prince Luitpold these past three years has threatened stability in the region. Bavaria had acted as a damper on the increasing militarism of Prussia. Now with the royal succession history, all sorts of political schemers are stirring up things in Bavaria. The Rothschilds's supreme aim is peace in Europe. They've had admirable success, considering the endless outbreaks of revolution and war this century."

"Why, Godfrey," I said with some surprise and even wonder. "You are acting for the Rothschilds more in the way of a diplomat than a lawyer."

Godfrey shrugged wearily. "A lawyer is a negotiator, Nell, and God knows these times require negotiations."

"Or," Sherlock Holmes suggested from his smoke-filled corner, "a spy, like our acquaintance Mr. Stanhope."

I glanced at Godfrey, hoping for a denial, which was not forthcoming.

All he said was a lawyerly aphorism: "Complex political situations require complex approaches."

"But what has all this to do with Irene and where she is now!?" I burst out. "The political history of Bavaria may be endlessly interesting to gentlemen who sit around fires and smoke cigars and drink brandy older than they are, but I want to know where Irene is, and why! I want to know what is happening here and now, not there and then! What on earth could . . . immoral Irish Spanish dancers and drowned kings and disenfranchised Jesuits have to do with it?"

Sherlock Holmes finally took the pipe stem from his mouth to favor me with a direct, and devastating, look.

"Everything, my dear Miss Huxleigh. Absolutely everything."

For a full minute I could say nothing in answer, which must be a record for me. "Then Irene is in . . . extreme danger."

"She is mortal," Godfrey added, reluctantly.

"Indeed. As are we," Homes noted. "Miss Huxleigh!"

I bolted to my feet, like one of Mr. Kipling's subalterns.

"We will need your knowledge of Mrs. Norton's state of mind and also of what trail she pursued that brought her to the attention of this sinister cadre."

"Her state of mind? For one thing, she was determined not to impinge on your investigation involving the Vanderbilts."

"Intentions are admirable, but she could no more do that than fly away from that boardinghouse. It's clear that these two investigations are one. She suspected that, of course."

"She never said anything—" I hesitated. "Irene is a woman of her word. She would do as she said: focus only on the trail of Lola Montez, her possible mother."

"What?" Godfrey had not heard of this supposed relationship, for he stood frozen. "She cabled for information on Lola Montez, but I thought it had to do with the Restell woman from a recent murder case, not her own origins."

"And," I realized, "you left Bavaria before the mountain of letters she wrote you about the entire Restell affair had arrived. It's clear we know nothing about what each other has been doing, or why."

And so we adjourned to the round table at which Irene and I had spent hours poring over the works of Lola, which still littered the surface.

Godfrey's flicking glance dismissed the collected books, articles, and illustrations. "I find it impossible to believe that Irene should be the offspring of such a disreputable hoyden."

"The actuality of the connection is moot at this point," Mr. Holmes said crisply. "It is what others believe to be so. Miss Huxleigh, I could use another bracing infusion of that acrid ambrosia called coffee."

I rolled my eyes, quite within his view, but fetched refilled cups for both men.

"Quentin," I said suddenly, after performing my maid's duties.

Two sets of gray eyes regarded me, blank as schoolroom slates.

"He's a spy," I explained, "used to mastering foreign territory. He should join us."

Both men nodded brusquely, so I felt released to fly to the telephone to call his hotel. Again.

But Quentin was still "not in." I had to disconnect, unhappy and in no position to show it. What on earth could Quentin Stanhope be doing that kept him away from his hotel day and night?

I had the most dreadful sinking feeling that I wouldn't want to know.

⚜   ⚜   ⚜

When I returned to the table Mr. Holmes was moving the books and papers on Lola Montez around the table. "Norton," he asked idly, "could there be a plot afoot in Bavaria to overthrow the regency?"

"There are always rumors, but that's impossible! No progeny of the two demonstrably mad brothers would be tolerated. The Wittalsbach line ends with them."

Holmes lifted the cartoon of Lola springing nimbly from Europe to the New World in a swan-prowed little boat.

"Unless King Ludwig the First had a third child, an unsuspected third child by a woman with untainted royal blood. Perhaps that's why someone is so interested in Madam Norton's inquiries and also why the same forces might wish to abstract gold and gems from the Vanderbilts."

"But what would the Vanderbilts have to do with Bavaria, or Lola, for that matter?" Godfrey wondered.

"I don't see that thread of the web clearly yet," Holmes admitted. "Perhaps it's not Lola that these schemers are interested in but the offspring of Lola. Perhaps they seek a puppet of their own to replace the incarcerated Otto and his regent, Luitpold."

"That would mean a lost heir," I said, "possibly morganatic."

"Or," said Holmes, elevating another image of Lola, "an heiress."

Oh, my sainted father! Then Irene might indeed be a candidate for queen of a European principality. Queen of Bavaria!

I wondered how the king of Bohemia would like that!?

44

Babes in Arms

~ole~

I could still hear Nellie Bly, who had accompanied him during the last leg of the rescue mission, calling him "my dear Quentin" not an hour after our disastrous reunion, a reunion that was only disastrous after certain, unforgettable . . . passages between us.

—PENELOPE HUXLEIGH, 1889 DIARY, IN *FEMME FATALE*, CAROLE NELSON DOUGLAS

How interesting it is to watch a foreign agent become a domestic spy.

"Why is it necessary," Quentin asked, "for us to 'buy' so many babies?"

"I need to demonstrate how shockingly easy such an act is, and that anyone can acquire unwanted infants, for any purpose."

"This has not been an 'easy' assignment," he pointed out.

Dawn was just now warming the East River as we watched from the Battery.

"We pursued the rumor of an available infant from tenement to saloon to brothel to tenement," he said.

"But this last one was just ten dollars, an even more shocking sum. Don't worry, Quentin. I'll have someone from the foundling home meet us there later today when we finish the deal. Even an orphanage would be better than the conditions that poor baby has the ill luck to be born into."

"No doubt you see why two of the Hamilton infants died. Most of these children are already ill. I suppose the more misery you can document, the more shocking your story will be."

"And the more likely to raise public indignation so something is done about this shameless trade in babies. I must look for more available infants because I hope to find where all four Hamilton babies came from. Surely we may cross the path of someone who had been contacted previously by the lovely Mrs. T. Anna Swinton and her son, Joshua Mann. Only one person may have sold them all four infants. These wretched mothers are too sick or deprived to keep their children."

"Your own mother might have resorted to such a thing, after your father died and his first wife's children inherited everything but some furniture and a cow."

"We were never that badly off. I saw to that."

"You began supporting your family at an early age?"

"And why not? I was in my later teens. No one else would. My older brothers thought only about establishing new families for themselves."

"Is that why you aren't married, but live with your mother?"

"No. I'm not married because I have no need to be. And I live with my mother because she is a more interesting and less taxing companion than any man I have met so far."

"How are we men so taxing?"

"You won't let us women be. Be free, be what we want to be, which is not wives, if all of us would think about it. Not even Nell Huxleigh wants to be a wife."

"Why do you say 'even?' "

"Well, she is horribly traditional, isn't she?"

"Hardly. You don't know her at all."

"Do you?"

He paused to consider it, then smiled. A most irritating sort of smile. "Not really."

"It's the unknowability of Nell that attracts you," I said.

"Did I say I was attracted?"

"Well, you're not attracted to me."

"Ergo, I must be attracted to someone else. You're an odd contradiction, Nellie Bly. Half suffragist, half flirt. All reporter."

"Aren't you 'all spy?' "

He bowed his head in acknowledgment of my thrust.

Still, I felt I hadn't touched him at all. Oh, these Englishmen! So self-sure, so remote. Such challenges.

"What will you do about the infants we're offered after the story has appeared in the paper?" he asked next.

"My job is to reveal, not to heal. If I took personal responsibility for every poor soul I discovered on the streets of the city, I'd soon go mad. I do hope that the revelation of their plight will encourage some of the public to seek to adopt them. What I'd really like, what would end this story with a fine fillip—"

"Yes?"

"—would be to find an adult child that was farmed out by Madame Restell to a new family decades ago."

"Nell's told me about Madam Restell and her thriving abortion enterprise for women rich and poor, which also included finding new homes for inconvenient babies too advanced to be aborted."

"Nell told you all that!?"

"Not in so many blunt words."

"I'll be hornswaggled! I thought Miss Mealymouth was far too refined to deal with real life."

"Not when it touches on her loyalty to Irene." He turned from watching the water lighten to reflect the forest of masts in the river. "What you really want, Nellie Bly, is to reveal who Irene's mother was."

"That's impossible. This trip abroad by our Parisian duo has revealed one thing: that Irene Adler was born in a trunk, as they say in theatrical circles, and reared by a committee of freakish but kindly variety performers. I've met some of them myself."

He just smiled and said nothing.

"Damn it, Quentin! Do you know something I don't? You want to keep me quiet about Jack the Ripper. Now you want me to keep quiet about Irene Adler's origins. Madame Restell's history is too old to retell, but not if someone sensational is a graduate of her replaced-waif efforts."

"Irene is hardly sensational. She doesn't even perform publicly anymore. There's more to it than what you say, Pink. You're irritated with Irene for being first to see and pursue the Ripper, and then the Restell mystery. You want your front-page headlines, all right, and you want to benefit society. But most of all, you want to one-up Irene Adler. I'll help you with the Hamilton story, gladly, for it's appalling the way these newborn infants are bought and sold.

But I won't help you embarrass Irene, especially by making public revelations about her personal life."

I said nothing. There was enough truth in his annoying little speech that I chose not to answer it. For now.

"And," he added, "you do like to irritate Nell by monopolizing my attention." He smiled his charming smile again. "Not that the pleasure of your company is not engaging, as well as very informative."

A new, unwelcome thought stole into my mind with the dawn.

Why was Quentin Stanhope being so congenial about accompanying me day and night through the worst sections of New York?

Was he keeping *me* occupied, so I couldn't keep an eye on Irene?

"You are truly devious," I told him. "Now I can't tell whether you are accommodating me with your company or misleading me."

He bowed. "I have never received a more welcome compliment."

45

A Flock of Fathers

~~⚬❧⚬~~

*For I am a stranger with thee, and a sojourner,
as all my fathers were.*
—PSALM 39

Sherlock Holmes's astounding theory about Irene's parenthood involved the one forgotten figure in this imbroglio. Her father.

Could she indeed be the lost daughter of Ludwig the First? Why
did such a thing never occur to me? Of course I'd been trained to shy
away from scandal.

I shuffled madly through the piles of material Irene and I had studied.

"It's true," I said as I searched, "that the miserable Lola gadded about the
globe, and back and forth between Europe and America. She was rumored to
have met King Ludwig secretly, especially just after his abdication. And with
her penchant for wearing shawls, and black, she could have concealed a . . . a
certain delicate condition. But to have borne Ludwig's child? And left it to a
troupe of performers?"

"Where better to hide an heir who might be in danger?" Holmes pointed
out.

"All rank supposition," Godfrey objected at last. "We can't sit here scouring these books of dubious history while Irene is missing. It's fine to theorize
about the past, but we must act in the present, and quickly."

I nodded my agreement. Whether Irene was a pretender to the throne of Bavaria was far less vital than where she was now.

"We have one incontrovertible clue to the matters behind these events," Holmes summarized.

Godfrey and I waited, with bated breath. Breaths.

"The man who was kidnapped from the Episcopal Club by the same villains who were following Mrs. Norton has been raving with fever since I brought him to Bellevue. Some decent medical attention may have cooled his brain. It was he who alerted me to the fact of your wife's involvement, Mr. Norton."

"How?"

"He mentioned her name, as if he had been trying to keep it from his tormenters. Don't bestir yourself; I believe he was successful, partly because I interrupted them before they could work the same deviltry they did on poor Father Hawks."

Godfrey was standing despite the detective's reassurances.

"We must see him at once." Godfrey checked his watch. "Nine A.M., soon enough for a hospital staff to be stirring." He turned toward the table by the door that bore his hat, stick, and gloves, as well as Mr. Holmes's.

"Coming, Nell?" Godfrey asked.

I hesitated, glancing at the telephone despite myself.

The man Holmes leaped into the gap provided by my missish hesitation.

"Miss Huxleigh should remain here, for the man's physical state is gruesome. In this instance, she'll be here in case word comes, or if Mr. Stanhope finally decides to make himself available."

That last phrase stiffened my spine as no whalebone appliance ever made could have.

"I'll go!" I dashed to the table to retrieve my hat. I pinned it on so swiftly that I nearly pierced two fingertips with six inches of steel hatpin.

Waiting was no longer a chore I was willing to perform, for anyone.

Mr. Holmes shrugged, but Godfrey reached out and squeezed my fingers before I could don my gloves. He understood my need for action after a long night of waiting up and wondering.

And . . . I had seen the poor victim of the Ripper at St. Sulpice Hospital in Paris last spring. Surely this man could not be in a more shocking state of mutilation than that pathetic woman!

Mr. Holmes strode ahead of us out of the elevator and was soon in the street whistling up a hansom with the confidence of a native.

I wondered what Godfrey thought about the detective's leading role in the search for Irene, but there was no time for us to confer.

The lumbering coach drawn by two horses, called a gurney, that the detective hailed held all three of us handily. Soon we were jostling toward Bellevue amid the crash and clop and infernal jangle of early-morning New York City traffic. The peddlers' cries keened like the seagulls wheeling eternally near the port.

"What do you think of the city?" I asked Godfrey.

"I've not had a moment to notice." He surveyed the street through the window. "I see that buildings reach higher here than in London or Paris."

"Indeed, we've read of edifices as high as fifteen or even twenty-some stories being constructed."

Of course saying "we" brought everyone's mind back to the one of our party who was missing. Mr. Holmes slouched against his side of the carriage, packing his pipe with fresh tobacco and scowling at the street.

"What a contrast in elements this case offers," he murmured as much to himself as to us. "Old World. New World. Old World jewels. New World gold. Events as fresh as last week, and as stale as forty years ago. Matters of church and state, united by violence and, presumably, greed. Victims in America, violators from Bavaria. And then there is the matter of the Red Indians."

Godfrey and I exchanged glances. Mr. Holmes appeared to be raving as senselessly as the man he had placed in Bellevue.

Our conveyance stopped before an assemblage of buildings numerous and stately enough to be a university.

Mr. Holmes bounded out of the carriage, leaving Godfrey to assist me down and pay the driver.

I looked after Holmes's vanishing figure, the ulster's shoulder cape hem flapping like gull wings in the haste of his progress.

Godfrey took my elbow and we hurried after him into a building with bars on the windows. This, I feared, was the dreaded mental facility into which Nellie Bly had committed herself last year to get her most famous story, an exposé on how harshly the mad were treated in America. And everywhere else, I would guess.

"*Ten Days in a Mad-House,*" I muttered under my breath.

"What?" Godfrey asked.

"Nellie Bly has been here before us. She had herself committed for a newspaper story, then wrote a book about it."

"I doubt we're visiting the madhouse section. Holmes's man is wounded and fevered, not insane."

"I hope."

When we caught up with Holmes, it was inside the facility, where he was arguing with a middled-aged woman in a blue-and-white apron and cap.

"The attending physician is not here," she said as firmly as I had ever heard a woman address Sherlock Holmes, "I can't allow you to see the patient without him. You are not kin."

"My good woman, I'm the man who brought him here."

"That may be, Mr.—"

"Holmes."

"That may be, Mr. Holmes, but I am the day nurse in charge and I can't have strangers cluttering up my ward."

"I'm English, as you may note."

"Yes, sir. Indeed so."

"And I've brought a noted British consulting surgeon to see the patient, Dr. Norton."

She gazed at Godfrey and myself with a skepticism I couldn't blame her for, although Godfrey looked extremely Harley Street in his silk top hat and striped trousers.

"And also with us is Dr. Norton's nurse, Miss Huxleigh," Mr. Holmes went on. "She is a latter-day graduate of Miss Nightingale's nursing corps, you know."

"Miss Nightingale! Well, we are the result of Dr. Elizabeth Blackwell's efforts to advance women in the medical arts here in the United States. Perhaps you've heard of her?"

"Indeed. My medical friends would consider it a great honor if we were permitted to see the patient we are so concerned about; not in the quality of care he has, obviously, but as to his mysterious condition."

"Dr. Norton, is it? Miss Poxleigh? Do come along. We welcome inspection by visiting physicians."

Well. It was certainly incumbent upon me to display no queasy tendencies now!

We clattered down the stone-floored passages, inhaling carbolic acid and other strong odors of medical purification.

The ward was half filled, and our quarry lay three-quarters of the way down the dreary rows.

We all approached with brusque efficiency, none of us as brisk or efficient as Sherlock Holmes. I wonder what the blue-striped nurse would think if I told her she was following the lead of a human bloodhound, not a man.

So we gathered around the plainly covered bed: two men, two women; three imposters, one actual nurse.

I gazed at the linen-pale face on the flat pillow, and felt the huge room spin, felt my senses reeling in a very unnurselike manner.

Apparently both men detected my suddenly vaporish state, for a strong hand on either elbow held me upright.

"Thank you, Sister," Holmes said, though why he had addressed a nurse as one would an Anglican nun, I can't say. And I didn't much care at that chaotic moment. "We'll examine the patient in our own way."

Somehow his high, commanding tone drove her away after a few attempted demurring noises.

"Nell! What is it?" Godfrey hissed in my ear.

I had the pleasure of seeing Sherlock Holmes's complete attention focused on me.

I inhaled deeply of the attar of carbolic acid and ammonia, which acted as smelling salts to a sensitive nose.

"I've seen this wretched fellow before," I said.

"You know his name?" Mr. Holmes's face was as close to mine as a Mesmerist's, and as commanding.

"Not his first name—"

"Not needed."

"It's . . . Father Edmonds, who received Irene and myself in the bishop's stead at the Episcopal Club not two days ago. What has happened to his hands? They were quite . . . graceful when he met with us."

Mr. Holmes raised his eyebrows more than half-mast. That was the sole satisfaction I had of my surprising statement.

I did not require actual smelling salts, although I had some in a silver container on the chatelaine that hung around my waist.

The shock of recognizing Mr. Holmes's "victim" as someone Irene and I had met by daylight in quite ordinary circumstances wore off as if one veil after another were lifted from before my eyes.

Now that I had recovered from the shock of unwelcome recognition, Godfrey suggested that I near the poor man's bed. We would get better testimony if the man saw someone . . . anyone . . . he knew, however slightly. Who can argue with a barrister on such a matter?

As he awoke, however, Father Edmonds appeared to know me far more than slightly.

"Oh, dear God," he murmured devoutly. "I've died in your service and now meet you and your angel in heaven. You sent her to pave the way, as so often you did in the Old Testament. I tried to keep her face before me during the most arduous of my trials, and to keep the name of your fellow angel from my lips, no matter what the emissaries of Satan demanded, or did."

I was struck dumb with pity, guilt, and humility.

The man's bandaged hands twitched on the plain coverlet. I remembered Holmes's terse description of how he'd found him: pinned by the hands to a table, daggers through the palms.

Had any modern man suffered so?

"You are not dead, man," Holmes said, "but I plucked you away from the hounds of hell. They now seek this . . . angel's companion. You mentioned her name when I found you. Irene."

Godfrey twitched beside me, but managed to keep silent.

Father Edmonds, perhaps prone to sermons from his calling, answered in another rush of words. His captors must have been most annoyed with him. "In pagan times," he said, "to the Greeks, Irene was the goddess of peace. I remember her appearing before me, as beautiful as God's shining sword, but her handmaiden shone softer before my eyes, a modest violet amidst a bouquet of tiger lilies."

"I did say he raved," Sherlock Holmes murmured to no one in particular.

I recognized my role when it was named: modest violet.

"My dear Father Edmonds," I said, stepping to the bedside, and taking one of his mangled, gauze-wrapped hands in my own. "We had no idea the Evil One was so swift behind our steps. You are not the only man of God to have suffered at His"—ah, "hands" did not seem to be a useful figure of speech in this instance—"behest. You have withstood the worst admirably. But you must tell us everything, so we may end this villainy."

"They wanted to know . . . it was Father Hawks this, and Father Hawks that. And the Magdalen. The Magdalen Society, and a woman named Lola. And a woman named Irene, who I of course recognized as God's messenger."

I doubt that Irene would ever be granted a more celestial role in her life, excepting the part of "heavenly Aida," as the aria from Verdi's opera put it.

Mr. Holmes would tolerate the patient's delusions only so far as they would feed his inquiries. "What did they want with 'Irene?'"

"Merely to know where she came from and had gone. I said 'Heaven,' of course, and they became most vicious."

"And Lola?"

"They wanted to know what Father Hawks knew of her. I was unable to satisfy them on either issue. And then God's archangel came screaming down from above and scattered them."

I lifted my eyebrows at Sherlock Holmes, who shrugged modestly.

"How will his hands do?" I whispered to Holmes, for the poor man would not let go of mine.

Godfrey leaned in to hear the verdict.

"The doctor here says they'll heal well," Holmes said softly, "though with some loss of dexterity. The physician is most interested to study a very uncommon case, and will no doubt be diligent in the extreme."

Godfrey leaned in to present the patient with a question. "Could you recognize any of them?"

"They were hooded. Cloaked. Like monks, I suppose. I thought I was having a nightmare of the Inquisition. Dark men, and I could see no eyes, but I knew there would be no pity in them. They seemed . . . devoted . . . to their fiendish quest. I pity any woman or angel who would fall into their hands."

We all winced at that assessment, even though Father Edmonds seemed to equate women and angels.

"Miss Violet," he said, his pale, haunted eyes finding mine. "Say you are all right. Say your friend is all right."

"We are all right," I said, patting his bandages. "You must concentrate on your own healing. We . . . angels will attend to those evildoers."

He nodded, gazing up at us. "I see halos about all your heads."

On that note we left him, although Mr. Holmes could not help noting that the electric lights above the beds had produced the effects of holiness, not our natures.

"Irene," Godfrey noted glumly as we stood in the warm summer air and inhaled the smell of manure instead of cleansing chemicals. "And Father Hawks. And Lola Montez. Two are dead, one missing."

"As pretty a puzzle as Watson ever attempted to record. Ah. My pardon. Watson is a physician and my self-appointed biographer."

"We know who Dr. Watson is," Godfrey said shortly. "What we don't know is who this devil's nest of torturers are. You forget, Holmes, that Nell and I have faced the Ripper without your assistance. If you can't produce any clues to Irene's whereabouts, we'll find these monsters on our own."

Holmes regarded us with an eye as cold as a cobra's. "I doubt it. If anything is clear, it's that your wife's quest and mine are one in the minds of these villains. Like it or not, we three are allies . . . or losers. Together. I will lose only a client. You and Miss Huxleigh will lose far more. Perhaps it's time to meet these shadows face-to-face."

"How?" I demanded.

"Offer them what they want."

"What?" Godfrey asked.

Holmes studied his own long, narrow, violin-playing fingers. "I might do, in a pinch."

46

Rescue Party

> ⇜∽∾⇝

How long and terrifying was that dark and endless upward sweep ...
of this long and terrifying staircase ... leaving below the light and its
comforting rays. For in that penumbra there were spirits lurking to
destroy me. ...

—CONSUELO VANDERBILT BALSAN, THE GLITTER AND THE GOLD, 1952

"Quentin Stanhope," Mr. Holmes said in the carriage as we progressed toward the main part of Manhattan. "Which hotel does he stay at?"

"The Fifth Avenue," I replied, then blushed as I felt Godfrey's gaze linger upon me.

Holmes still directed this interrogation, except that it had moved locations and victims. "Did you leave him a message on any of your various visits?"

"No." I avoided Godfrey's ever more curious gaze.

"Then we'll call on him directly. Miss Huxleigh is right that we could use an ally of his talents in the forthcoming search. The man must return to his hotel sometime."

Not if he was welcome elsewhere, such as at Pink's place uptown, as they called it.

Once again we stood supplicant at the hotel's registration desk, but this time Quentin was reported to be in.

"Mr. Stanhope came in quite early this morning," the clerk mentioned with a carefully blank expression. "He may not wish to be disturbed."

"Nonsense," Holmes said. "He would be more aggravated should he miss our call." He eyed me and I nodded.

I knew the room number, even if the clerk refused to reveal it.

We marched next to the elevator. I hoped that the warmth I felt in my face was purely imaginary as we wafted upward four floors.

Godfrey nodded thanks to the elevator operator as we left it and moved down the dim hall, which was carpeted in a dark maroon pattern.

When I paused by the right room number, Godfrey lifted his stick to knock, but Mr. Holmes nodded at me.

"You must be our spokesman."

I opened my mouth to protest, but after two more raps, Quentin's annoyed voice came from beyond the heavy walnut door.

"Yes? Who is it? I told the desk clerk I didn't want to be disturbed."

It suddenly dawned on me that he might not be alone behind that door, but Mr. Holmes prodded me with a short irritated nod, and I certainly didn't want to seem timid in his eyes.

So I answered.

"It's me. Nell. Quentin, something has—"

The door jerked open wide.

Quentin stood there, unshaven and uncombed, in a hastily tied garnet silk robe.

My face seemed to be changing to that lurid color.

"Nell! What are you doing here? What's wrong?"

I was solely the object of his regard, which no doubt Mr. Holmes intended, for he took my arm.

Quentin blinked with the bleary surprise of a child hauled from bed at an ungodly hour.

"Holmes? Godfrey?" He turned to me again, as if for explanation. "Nell? Is this something to do with the strange young man who called for me at the hotel very early this morning? I can't begin to imagine who that could have been. Certainly neither of you two," he added, surveying the tall, grim figures of Mr. Holmes and Godfrey.

"You would certainly never imagine, Stanhope," Holmes said crisply. "That was Miss Huxleigh in a walking-out costume devised by Mrs. Norton."

"Nell!?"

It was flattering how repetitively he turned to me for explanation, but I wouldn't be allowed to play spokesman here.

"May we come in and sit down?" Holmes demanded more than asked. "We've had a long night of it ourselves."

I held my breath, not eager to cross the threshold.

May we come in indeed? Not if a lady in deshabille also occupied the room. I knew Quentin was too much the gentleman to permit that. What I didn't know, and most certainly did not want to know, was if this was indeed the case, and if that lady might possibly be someone I knew.

Quentin stepped back from the door like a polite host. "Come in, certainly, though I am in no state to receive a lady. I apologize."

I breezed past him on winged feet. The chamber, a bed-sitting room suite, was deliriously empty. "That doesn't matter, Quentin. Our business is far too urgent for anyone to stand on ceremony."

A round table by the window was hemmed in by three light chairs. Quentin lifted an armchair over to it, and ushered me onto its heavy upholstery, and then there were four.

"What's happened?" he asked, alert all at once as the men took their seats. "Godfrey, a pleasure to see you here, but weren't you on Rothschild business in Europe? And Holmes—"

"Irene's missing," I said, keeping my voice steady and still sounding as if I were hiccoughing walnuts.

"Missing? When? Where?"

"Last night." Holmes was surgically precise. "Around midnight. From a boardinghouse at Seventeenth near Broadway. Miss Huxleigh was awaiting her across the street, but Mrs. Norton never came back."

"Awaiting her in the garb of a young man?" Quentin asked me.

Holmes answered before I could, impatiently. "Miss Huxleigh had been got up by Mrs. Norton to pass as such in the dark. When Mrs. Norton failed to return to their watching post, Miss Huxleigh investigated and found Mrs. Norton, and the three dark-clothed men who had followed her, gone."

"Nell!" Quentin viewed me with sympathy and alarm.

Holmes was summing up, and he did not stop. "Miss Huxleigh came first to your hotel, but you were out. She then came to my hotel, where I was able to put an end to her rather feeble impersonation. We returned to the boardinghouse to examine the area, and then I sent her back to the Hotel Astor, while I trailed whatever signs I could find. When I returned at dawn to report to Miss Huxleigh, Mr. Norton had arrived from Europe and was awaiting me."

"What did you find?" Quentin asked Holmes, finally ignoring me, and Godfrey.

"Three men followed Mrs. Norton into the boardinghouse, and one particular room. Four sets of footsteps left the building. Mrs. Norton doesn't seem to have been a prisoner. One would wish to assume that she had evolved from hunted to hunter."

"She left Nell standing across the street, not knowing what to think?" Quentin sounded unconvinced.

"And wouldn't you have done the same, if opportunity to track an enemy spy had so suddenly offered itself?"

"Yes, but—" He glanced at me, and I thrilled to see that he was not so sure in my case.

Godfrey spoke. Gravely. "It's a better thing to suppose than some other outcome."

"What do you want of me?" Quentin asked. "I'll do anything. Now. Whenever."

At this Mr. Holmes managed to summarize the events of both his and Irene's separate investigations into threats and extortion against the Vanderbilt fortune and the amazing history of Lola Montez and the even more amazing possibility that this notorious figure might have some intimate connection to Irene.

"So," said Quentin after Holmes had delivered himself of two paragraphs of rapid summation. Godfrey was regarding him with some fresh respect. "Two Episcopal priests have been abducted and tortured, one to death, one for an interest in the late Lola Montez, the other for having assisted Irene in looking into the life of Lola Montez. And this Episcopal Club is where?"

"Near Broadway and Eighteenth," Holmes said, "where I'm shortly going to create quite a stir in visibly inquiring about, er, Miss Montez and Mrs. Norton. I'll also revisit the boardinghouse, but with much more visible effects."

Quentin nodded. "You need me to follow you, unseen, and be on hand, hopefully, when the villains of the piece abduct you."

"You and Mr. Norton," Holmes said. "I trust you to be invisible, Stanhope, as it is your profession. I expect Mr. Norton to be implacable, as it is his wife."

"And me?" I demanded.

The men regarded me as if they had forgotten my presence, as indeed they had.

Holmes had an answer at the ready. "You'll remain at the Astor House, in case any one of us needs to leave information for the others."

"No! I know both sites well, the Episcopal Club and the boardinghouse. I won't be left at the hotel to worry and stew."

Godfrey eyed Holmes. "She accompanied Irene to the Episcopal Club twice," he said, "and knew Father Edmonds. If you appear there with Nell in tow, you'll seem to be following up on Irene's disappearance, and two will attract more attention than one. In fact, you mean nothing to these villains, but Nell has already been seen in Irene's company."

"Exactly," Quentin said heatedly, "why she should not be risked further."

Holmes, though, was nodding sagaciously.

Did the man ever nod in any other mode?

"Mr. Norton is right. It must look as if Miss Huxleigh has engaged a Pinkerton to assist in a search for her friend."

"You will never pass as Pinkerton," Quentin said hotly.

"I will by the time Miss Huxleigh and I venture forth this afternoon. I will then," he said, eyeing Quentin, "return Miss Huxleigh to her hotel and make myself annoying visible at both the Episcopal Club and the boardinghouse as dark descends. That's when you and Mr. Norton will pick up my trail, in guises of your own. As I recall from certain Monte Carlo adventures, Mr. Norton has the usual dramatic tendencies of a barrister."

Godfrey nodded. "I'll manage a disguise, though no one in this affair has reason to know me. If you are accosted, Holmes, you'll let them overpower you and take you—"

"Wherever they took or intended to take Mrs. Norton. Or where she followed them."

"And," Quentin said, "we shall follow you."

"And so shall I," I added.

Three sets of eyes gave my brave assertion the lie.

"It's bad enough," Holmes said, "that you are exposed by accompanying me by daylight. That is sufficient risk. We can't have our roles compromised by looking out for you."

"Then don't look out for me! If you work by dark, I can don the walking-out clothes Irene gave me. No one will notice me."

"You are not," Holmes said, "Mrs. Norton. Your male costume would never fool me for a minute, as hers did once, and only once, I might add."

"I don't need to fool the great Mr. Holmes, only a few shadowy men who were stupid enough to kidnap an innocent priest who knew nothing that would serve them."

"Holmes is right, Nell," Quentin said. "We've all been up and awake and agitated for hours now, and by sunset it'll be twenty-four hours. We can't afford to dilute our effectiveness by worrying about you."

"Then don't," said a voice that wasn't mine. "She can accompany me," Godfrey went on, "as she so often has. We are the amateurs. Perhaps we need reinforcements." He smiled at me, which was reinforcement enough.

"You'll carry a pistol?" Holmes asked him.

"If you'll provide one."

Quentin nodded. "Yes, but I don't like it, Nell being out and at risk."

I sniffed. "Irene never objected to my company on many a dangerous jaunt. I won't be left behind to be told what happens. I want to know. I want to be there."

Quentin rubbed a hand over his weary face. "So do we, Nell, so do we. I only hope we lure the villains into the open."

"I work alone," Holmes said. "Except for Dr. Watson on occasion. One couldn't ask for a more stout-hearted fellow. However, he isn't here."

"But you are," I said, suddenly inspired. "You all are. Irene couldn't ask for finer champions. You are the three musketeers."

They did not seem impressed by my literary allusion.

"And who are you, dear Nell?" Godfrey asked with a glint of fond humor amidst the anxiety.

I thought. "D'Artagnan," I said boldly, invoking the young swordsman from the provinces. After all, I had something that they didn't have, firearms or not.

I had a foot-long steel hatpin. *En garde!*

While Godfrey, Quentin, and I exchanged notes at the Astor House, Sherlock Holmes returned to his hotel to costume himself as the character in which he would make the best target for the mysterious men who were dogging Lola Montez's long-dead footsteps.

But Mr. Holmes did not return to the Astor House as agreed.

About two hours later, just as we were getting restive at his overlong absence, a knock on the door had us all rushing to answer.

The young hotel messenger boy blinked at our united front.

"Urgent telephone message for Mr. Stanhope," he said, holding up a folded sheet of paper.

Quentin snatched it, Godfrey tipped the boy, and I began to read its tele-graphic phrases aloud over Quentin's shoulder as Godfrey closed the door.

" 'Disastrous turn of events at Six-sixty Fifth. Come at once. Present Stan-hope as agent of Her Majesty's foreign service, Norton as Rothschild agent. I don't know what they'll make of Miss Huxleigh, but bring her anyway. This supercedes any current concerns. Stop for nothing. Holmes.' "

"Surely," Godfrey objected, "Irene's disappearance supercedes any new mischief at the Vanderbilt mansion."

Quentin frowned. "One would think so. As least *we* would. Holmes is em-ployed by the Vanderbilts, not us, and his first obligation is to them, of course."

"A pity he must go haring off after his own business just now," Godfrey said. "I for one am going down to the area where Irene was last seen, by God."

"Agreed." Quentin sounded like a second Musketeer chiming in.

It was all very blood-stirring and gallant, but . . .

"No," said I.

They both stared at me as if I were mad.

"I wish Irene safely recovered as fervently as you," I told Godfrey. "But I have known Mr. Holmes—if anyone indeed may know such a man—longer than you. He revels in working alone and needing no one. He wouldn't sum-mon us unless the disaster at the Vanderbilt house involves Irene's disappear-ance. We must go."

"And waste more precious minutes," Godfrey said, "in which Irene may be subjected to unthinkable torments? No!"

"Then I'll go alone, though I am the least wanted or useful person on his list."

"Nell! Make sense," Godfrey pled. "We can't worry about you dashing off on your own when Irene is already missing from just such an intemperate action."

"I'll accompany Nell," Quentin offered. "Once she's safe with Holmes, I'll join you at the Episcopal Club."

Much as I hated to discourage Quentin from any course that involved our mutual participation, I quickly pointed out an objection. "Quentin has been in New York City longer and knows it better," I told Godfrey. "You would be lost on your own."

"Then I'll go to the damned Vanderbilts with you, Nell. Quentin, you can explore the area Holmes was discussing."

"I don't care for us separating like this," Quentin said. "That's how Irene disappeared in the first place."

"All for one and one for all," I said. "Has it been lost upon you that Mr. Holmes requested that you represent yourselves in the most impressive professional terms, as agents of the two most potent powers in European affairs today?"

"We are hardly such elevated figures," Godfrey said with his usual modesty.

I could hardly keep myself from stamping my foot. "But you will be useful in that guise, Holmes says. He even thinks *I* may be useful, which will give you some idea of how truly desperate the situation is. And it involves Irene's . . . disappearance"—I would not say kidnapping—"or he wouldn't presume upon us. I know *the* man. I may detest him, but I don't underestimate him, and neither should you."

Godfrey shook his head as if to dislodge the awful fears that must be buzzing around his brain like gnats, invisible but inescapable.

"If we find the situation unproductive for our first concern," Quentin said, "we can leave directly. Another hour—"

"Another hour." Godfrey's voice was grim, and his hands had curled into fists.

"Irene," I told him, reminded him, "was not beaten by the Ripper. We have to believe that she can survive another brush with the unthinkable."

Godfrey nodded.

I snatched my hat and steel pin from the table as they, now utterly converted, rushed me out the door.

I installed the hat once we were ensconced in the Gurney Quentin had run into the middle of the street to engage. I thought for a moment he would have to vault upon the lead horse's back to dragoon it, but flashing a two-dollar half eagle gold piece worked wonders.

Certainly it encouraged the current passengers to get out then and there, and he tossed a second such coin up to the driver.

I rather would have liked to see him vault upon a Gurney horse in the middle of Fifth Avenue, but had to admit that gold was just as quick and effective in this instance.

"What can have happened?" Godfrey speculated as we rattled along at that smart equine pace that is faster than a trot and just below a canter.

"It is only ten-thirty in the morning," I noted, consulting my lapel watch. "What so dire can have happened?"

Quentin, sitting on my side of the facing seats, touched his finger to my small timepiece. "It was clever of you to have loosened this pin to leave a trail of your own kidnapping last spring," he said. "I'm glad we recovered your bauble, but you deserve a finer one for your travails."

"This has served me well for many years."

"Perhaps an outing to Tiffany's with Irene when we reunite with her—?"

I caught my breath. Not at the promise of Tiffany's but at the assumption of a reunion with Irene.

"You really think so, Stanhope?" Godfrey asked.

"You remember that Holmes suggested Irene was not a captive but a hunter. I would bet upon it."

I bit my lip and nodded to encourage Godfrey, but still couldn't explain why she would not at least find a way to send us a message, were that the case.

Quentin squeezed my elbow in acknowledgment that he knew my anxiety. There are a great many liberties the truly ingenious gentleman may take in even the most public circumstance.

Godfrey, his dear forehead a roadmap of worry lines, didn't notice this by-play. He sat slapping his undonned leather gloves on his palm, as if they were reins exhorting the horses's back to further speed.

The springs jerked back and forth as we stopped, and we three stormed the white stone steps to 660 Fifth Avenue in a solid line, myself whisked up the stairs with boot barely touching stone, my elbows in close custody between my two escorts.

It occurred to me that neither man was eager to lose a woman under his protection.

Quentin thumped the huge knocker like a blacksmith.

The white-faced butler who answered merely had to raise his eyebrows.

"Mssrs. Stanhope and Norton," Godfrey said, "calling at Mr. Holmes's request, with Miss Huxleigh."

"Gentlemen, yes. And Miss. I'll take your things, then this way, please. Right here. The master and Mr. Holmes are in here."

He opened a door that was but twenty steps past the huge entry hall.

I was dazzled by the sight of huge expanses of pale stone carved with medieval intricacy. Had I not been so worried, I might have been impressed by the surrounding magnificence. Yet all I longed to see was Irene's familiar and dear face.

It was not within the rich library into which we were ushered. Smoke wafted upward like incense. My first sight was Mr. Holmes pacing, pipe cradled in his palm, thinking furiously and smoking to match the physical and mental motions he made.

"Ah!" He turned on our entrance. "Mr. William Kissam Vanderbilt, may I present Mr. Quentin Stanhope of Her Majesty's foreign service, on assignment in New York City. Mr. Godfrey Norton, international barrister and key agent for the Rothschild interests in Europe. Miss Nell Huxleigh, their associate. Gentleman and lady, Mr. William K. Vanderbilt, the wealthiest man in America."

"And now the poorest," Mr. Vanderbilt said sadly. He eyed Godfrey hopefully. "You are acquainted with August Belmont, the Rothschild emissary in America?"

"Not yet, sir. I just arrived from Bavaria, but I carry letters of introductions to Mr. Belmont, and others."

Mr. Vanderbilt nodded, obviously impressed (although anyone who saw or heard Godfrey would have been impressed no matter what letters he bore).

"I'm most grateful that gentlemen of your position and experience are here in the city to advise in this most . . . tragic circumstance."

We directed expressions of polite, if urgent, inquiry to Holmes, who immediately complied with one of his thorough, if unemotional, précis.

"Mr. Vanderbilt has been receiving extortion notes from unnamed parties regarding the personages we've already discussed," Mr. Holmes restated to us for our host's benefit. "These allies are aware," he added, turning back to the millionaire, "of the atrocious death your blackmailers have engineered in your own home."

"Therefore," Mr. Holmes went on quickly, as if racing to apprise us of the situation before we should unwittingly make some awkward comment, "it will not surprise you, my colleagues, to learn that Mr. Vanderbilt's only daughter, a child of twelve named Consuelo, has been kidnapped by these dastardly schemers."

We stood stunned.

Each of us imagined a child of tender years in the hands of this band of proven monsters.

It didn't matter that young Consuelo was a millionaire's daughter. We'd have felt the same to learn that the most anonymous Street Arab had fallen into such brutal hands.

"When?" Godfrey asked in the sharp inquiring fashion of a barrister.

Mr. Vanderbilt answered in the dead tones of one who had pushed the incredible facts through his mind again and again.

"Her absence was discovered first thing this morning, by her deportment tutor."

"If you wouldn't mind," Holmes suggested, "it would help if those involved reported to my associates, who have various areas of expertise and knowledge on such matters."

"Even Miss Huxleigh?" the millionaire asked doubtingly.

"She is associated with the Pinkertons in America, Mr. Vanderbilt, yet last spring was instrumental in bringing down a cadre of international spies that threatened the crowned heads of several smaller but vital European kingdoms, which remain on the map today almost solely due to her efforts."

Well! Irene Adler was not the only one to twist facts into fancy to support a position.

As Mr. Vanderbilt left the room to summon his witnesses among the family and staff, he left me with the memory of his awed departing regard.

"I glimpsed the child," Holmes said the moment Mr. Vanderbilt exited the library. "A waif as thin-faced as any London Street Arab, though a million times more privileged. She was peering pensively down through the balustrade of the grand stone staircase as her mother left the house. Now. Listen to the testimony of the household, including the child's mother."

Godfrey seemed about to speak, but Mr. Holmes forestalled him.

"This incident has the most appalling reference to your closest personal concerns, Mr. Norton, rest assured. I would that it did not."

So we waited, we three, in considerable anxiety and confusion. Dreadful as the abduction of a child was, given what we knew of these men, it shed little light on the issue dearest to our hearts, our own abducted, or at least vanished, Irene.

47

The Governess's Tale

How do you think I learned the gentle art of Mesmerism, Nell?
He hypnotized me, to free my voice of my conscious control, and he
taught me to do the same to myself, and, incidentally, others.
It has proved a most useful skill, as you may remember from
an adventure or two we have shared.

—IRENE ADLER NORTON IN *FEMME FATALE* BY CAROLE NELSON DOUGLAS

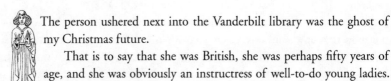

The person ushered next into the Vanderbilt library was the ghost of my Christmas future.

That is to say that she was British, she was perhaps fifty years of age, and she was obviously an instructress of well-to-do young ladies. Such I would have been someday had I not encountered Irene on the streets of London in 1881.

"Miss Bristol was present," the millionaire said, sitting after ushering her into the room, "when my daughter was abducted."

He did not invite Miss Bristol to sit, and indeed I was familiar with such treatment. One always reports on one's feet, as one's charges always recite on theirs, while the pater familias listens and nods from the depths of a luxurious easy chair.

I must admit that Mr. Vanderbilt, though seated, was not at ease in his luxurious leather chair at all.

Mr. Holmes had already heard the governess's tale; I could tell that by the way he lingered on the room's fringes to watch us all as if we were performers for his private entertainment.

"We'd had our morning ablutions and breakfast," Miss Bristol said, "during which we'd conversed in French, as required."

Quentin interrupted. "Miss Vanderbilt has a speaking command of French?"

"Indeed yes, sir. She has spoken three languages since the age of eight. Her mother has seen to her education here at home. She expects Miss Consuelo to be as perfectly at ease on the Continent as in England and the United States. I was, in fact, expecting Miss Consuelo's dancing teacher when the most extraordinary woman appeared in the third-floor gymnasium. My little miss was as entranced as if the Sugar Plum Fairy had paid her a visit."

Godfrey and Quentin and I exchanged glances, for this was not the preface for a violent abduction by the sort of men responsible for the death of Father Hawks and the abuse of Father Edmonds.

Holmes remained content and silent in the background, watching us observing the child's governess.

"How extraordinary was this women?" I asked, speaking for the first time. My English accent put the governess at instant ease.

"Oh, miss, I have never seen the like! She was dressed like a young master, yet her long hair tumbled all around her face and shoulders. And such a face! Quite the most comely face I have ever seen."

"How beautiful?" Godfrey asked, steeling himself visibly even as he spoke.

"Why, such beauty is hard to describe, sir. And it's odd, I remember her well, but not very precisely, after all. As if some veil were put between her and the world. Her face was . . . sweet and dainty of feature. Her hair was chestnut, yet with gleaming strands of red and gold, her eyes a deep, warm bronze, like a statue made flesh. Her expression, benign in the extreme.

"Consuelo is a slim, delicate child, quite . . . sensitive. At the age of six, she was terrified to leave the lights below and climb that immense white stone staircase to the upper chambers. She's twelve now, but still quite timorous. Yet when this woman extended a gloved hand, my miss put her pale palm in hers.

" 'We will tread a quadrille, Miss Vanderbilt,' the woman said, almost like someone from another century, 'that will make you the envy of Paris and Paraballa Land. We will dance away on a moonbeam to Cinderella's palace in Pichu Machu.' "

" 'Are you a new dancing teacher?' " I asked.

"'Indeed I am,'" she said in that same paralyzing, Mesmerizing tone. "'And now, my dear woman, if you will leave us to do our steps, we'll astound you with our progress in an hour hence.'"

The governess shook her head as she reported this exchange. "I can't say why, but I did as this extraordinary woman said. I suppose I expected a dancing instructor to be a bit strange. M'sieur Reynard was."

Miss Bristol hung her head. "I deserve to be dismissed. When I came back in an hour, they were gone, pupil and instructor."

A silence held in the room, while Quentin and Godfrey and I eyed each other in turn.

At last Godfrey turned to Mr. Vanderbilt. "No one saw either one, your daughter or the unannounced dancing teacher, after that?"

"No. I suppose if a man is to mislay a daughter, he'd rather it be to this charming apparition rather than to thugs from the docks, but . . . gone is gone. My wife is inconsolable. And I—am more so. Consuelo is a gentle, docile child, obedient to an extreme. That someone would take advantage of such virtues to wrest her away from us—! If you can't find her and find an answer to my troubles soon, I will tear this city apart."

"That won't be necessary, Mr. Vanderbilt." Holmes sounded quite definite. "First, let's hear from your wife, then I'll examine the gymnasium where the abduction occurred and proceed from there."

Mr. Vanderbilt's pleasant face went from worried to haunted on hearing Holmes's plan, but went to the door and asked the waiting butler to fetch his wife.

"Alva is distraught," he said on returning to his desk, "to say the least. Consuelo is our only daughter, named for her mother's closest friend. Alva has . . . great hopes for her."

As a former governess, I was delighted to hear of a mother who was as ambitious for her daughter's development as well as her sons. So often the girls were slighted in favor of the boys. Even I had to admit that Eliza Gilbert's good education made it possible for Lola Montez to hobnob on equal terms with the leading men of her day.

So I awaited Alva Vanderbilt with some sympathy. The men had all risen even before she entered the room.

When she did, I saw a woman with a soft, square face flushed with emotion. I barely more than noted her elaborate Worth gown, although Irene's acquaintance with the famed "man milliner" of Paris had forever made me aware of overexpensive clothing on other women, even in the most trying circumstances. I suppose I was as expert on that subject as Mr. Holmes was on more homely matters of calluses and cork fragments.

Alva Vanderbilt stood panting softly as the introductions were made: Mr. Holmes, Godfrey, Quentin. I rose when my own forged qualifications rolled off Mr. Vanderbilt's tongue, but his wife's gaze barely flicked over me.

"I've heard of Mr. Holmes from Mrs. Astor," she said. "If you can do as well by us as you did by the Astors, we shall be all right. But you must understand: Consuelo is not any ordinary millionaire's daughter."

"I would not presume to think any millionaire's daughter ordinary, madam," Holmes said with an ironic bow.

Irony was lost on this lady. "Consuelo has been tutored in all the gracious arts. She is destined to be a great lady in your own native land, sir." Her glance raked us all, for we were all British. "She will marry a duke."

I couldn't restrain myself. "The child is twelve?"

"Little time left for her training. She must make her debut here in five years and must be introduced quickly in England. She is an heiress unparalleled. She'll be snapped up at her fresh peak by the most titled man in England, save the royal family, of course. I do recognize that an American will never wear the crown."

"Can you speak of her character?" I pressed on, for the men in the room appeared reluctant to address this lady for some reason. I'm only a humble former governess, but I am never too intimidated to speak up in the cause of a child, and in this case, a puzzled, frightened child surely, even if in Irene's company, for Irene did not sound herself at all. "Can you say how she would respond to confusion and fear?"

"She will do as she is told. I provide a strict daily routine of self-improvement for her. She wears a steel brace, for instance, for several hours a day to improve posture."

Here I felt my spine stiffening more in outrage than in sympathy.

"What sort of . . . appliance is this?"

"A rod up the spine, affixed by a bracket to the temples and chest."

And we were worried about Consuelo in the hands of foreign torturers! "Was she wearing this, this Iron Maiden when she disappeared?"

"Yes. But she didn't disappear. She was taken." Alva, who had been addressing the mounted head of an African antelope on the wall behind me, snapped her gaze of agate to Mr. Holmes.

"Surely you will serve the Vanderbilts with more zeal and dispatch in the matter of a missing heiress than you did the Astors in the trifling forgery of a chess set."

"I will bend my every asset to it. First, I must see the gymnasium where Miss Vanderbilt was accosted and taken."

"Reede will show you upstairs, and Miss Bristol will answer all your questions, even if she can't satisfy mine as to why she left Consuelo to the care of this extremely odd creature. When you are done with her, she may leave with your party. Her employment here is over."

Miss Bristol in her corner started. "My things—"

"Will be found packed on the servant's back entrance stairs." Alva looked last to her husband. "I suppose you're to be congratulated for having been so swift in procuring the services of this English snoop. He apparently has some little reputation. I want my Consuelo back within hours. Her reputation must not be compromised."

I couldn't remain silent, though all reason demanded it.

"Surely the woman who took her wouldn't betray a child to such a fate."

"Children are sold every day on the streets of New York. Don't you read the newspapers? Haven't your heard of the Hamilton case? It's imperative that no hint of scandal attaches to my daughter. I will give my diamond-and-pearl parure to the one of you who claims credit for her swift, safe, and discreet return. Otherwise, none of you will see a penny of Vanderbilt money."

At his desk, Mr. Vanderbilt's face turned ashen, which was a good indication of just how costly his wife's pearl parure was.

48

What the Gymnasium Revealed

Our mother dominated our upbringing, our education, our recreation and our thoughts.
—CONSUELO VANDERBILT BALSAN, *THE GLITTER AND THE GOLD*, 1952

It was swiftly decided, after Mrs. Vanderbilt left, that Quentin would interrogate the servants (and see to the worldly goods of poor Miss Bristol, who was trembling on the brink of tears). Godfrey remained to discuss financial matters, i.e., ransom, with Mr. Vanderbilt, and Holmes would see the gymnasium and trace the path from there to outside the house.

"Miss Bristol, you will assist," he said, fixing the poor woman with a gaze at least as stony as Mrs. Vanderbilt's. "Along with Miss Huxleigh."

I cast appealing glances to Quentin and Godfrey, but they were already turning away on their separate quests.

I can't say why Mr. Holmes desired my company, except perhaps to keep Miss Bristol from the brink of hysteria on which she teetered. So I took her arm and we both led him up the grand white stone staircase to the house's upper regions.

Halfway up this mountain of laddered stone, he stopped to regard Miss Bristol.

"The first day I visited this house," he said, "I glimpsed a dark-eyed nymph at the top, peering down at me. She seemed quite . . . shy."

Miss Bristol spread her fingers on her no doubt palpitating breast. "Oh, sir, she is the sweetest, most docile child. She had a terrible fear of this very staircase. It's so wide and long. From the top, it looks like a mountain slope."

"Quite so," said Holmes, taking us both by the elbow to hurry us up the steep expanse.

There were no handrails to hold on to, and I suddenly saw this great house as the glass mountain from the fairy tale, all slick surfaces that no one could climb with any certainty.

The stair to the third floor was far less grand. We almost immediately encountered the door to the so-called gymnasium. Although the shining wood floor offered opportunity of all sorts of endeavors from fencing to games, and even roller skating, it would also serve well as a ballroom, I noted.

The sharp scent of wax and polish was like a refreshing whiff of hot tea to my nose. I resolved to remain alert, for Irene had been here, incontrovertibly. Why and how? And in what state? Why would she abduct this docile child of privilege . . . unless that child were in worse danger where she was than where Irene would take her?

"Where did you stand, Miss Bristol, and your charge, and the new dancing instructor?"

Holmes didn't cross the threshold, so neither did I.

Miss Bristol pattered to a place near the door. "Here was I. Conseulo beside me. We had just donned our brace, for it was paramount to wear it during dance and deportment instruction. Only instead of M'sieur, this woman appeared in the doorway."

"The woman dressed as a man," he said.

"It didn't seem as strange as that. She seemed like something . . . oh, out of a Punch and Judy play in the park. Which of course Miss Consuelo would never have seen, never have being allowed out to see such a thing."

"And the woman allayed your fears, dismissed you?"

Miss Bristol frowned. "No, I didn't leave. I just didn't see much after she appeared. She had . . . a watch. A round gold watch like a little sun, and it spun so. Her voice was sweet, mellow. I was reminded of a cello. I was reminded of honey in my tea, this afternoon at four, when all my duties are done until five. Consuelo seemed quite enchanted by her. They went off, and I remained. It all seemed quite natural."

I sighed and shut my eyes.

"Yes?" Holmes asked.

The admission stuck in my throat, like a bit of bread that will not go down, or back up again.

"Irene has hypnotized," I admitted, "Irene has been hypnotized."

"Some regard that as fraud and delusion."

"I hypnotized her once."

"Did you? Quite a bold step, Miss Huxleigh. Quite a responsibility."

"I suppose," I said, meeting his glance, "the hypnotic state might be considered similar to that of deliberately taking an opiate drug, as the writer De Quincey did. Only, with hypnotism, no opium, no poppy flower, no cocaine would be required. There are some, nursemaids, who doctor infants so, with cocaine."

"Ha! You waste your breath, and not for the first time. I believe in Mesmerism as a science, and an art. We in our benighted day don't understand its full usage. Not at all. So I'm not surprised Madam Irene is not unfamiliar with its uses. You, however—"

What he was about to say, I never heard, for Miss Bristol gave out a keening wail.

"I thought I saw them leave, sir, hand in hand, as happy as water-babies on a wave. I never thought any harm would come to Miss Consuelo. I'd never seen her face as open, like a flower. I never thought that strange lady would harm her, or I'd have given my life to stop her, save her."

Holmes lowered his head and frowned. "Shades of the Hamilton case. How many dramas in upper rooms can New York society stand in a single season?"

"Hamilton case?"

"Ask your Mr. Stanhope, when we have a moment, which we won't for many weary hours. Now." He bowed to inspect the floor, then produced thick magnifying glass and suddenly stretched himself full length—which was considerable—on the polished wooden floor.

Miss Bristol's eyes met mine. I shrugged. *Mon Dieu!* I was becoming French!

We gazed down upon Holmes's outstretched six-foot-plus frame, two governesses observing an eternal boy at his eternal boy pursuits: making the world into a scientific puzzle for the human brain instead of a conundrum for the human heart.

We smiled thinly at each other, as women who don't count often do.

"Where will I go?" Miss Bristol murmured.

"I have friends who will find you a place."

Her usual modestly lowered gaze suddenly fixed on me with raw intuition. "One of these friends is the woman who took my Consuelo."

"Yes. I hope so. I hope we find them both."

"I trusted her. Otherwise I would have never stood there silent, whatever strange aura I felt."

I nodded. "I trust her too. Even when she is not quite herself."

"This man," Miss Bristol said, nodding toward Holmes. "Should I trust him?"

A good question. He had been hired to work for the Astors, then the Vanderbilts. He hadn't wanted to cross Irene's path, nor had she intended to cross his.

Yet now they were on the opposite sides of a shocking abduction.

"Tell him all that you know," I finally advised her.

And I will listen to every word.

By the time Miss Bristol and I had descended to the back stoop at the rear of the Vanderbilt "castle," Sherlock Holmes had crawled every step of the way.

Never would I make light of his investigative zeal again. That man had examined every shred and splinter and dust mote en route. Needless to say, by now his attire was no better than any Street Arab's when it came to dirt and disarray.

Thus he could pronounce from the back stoop, to an audience of Godfrey, Quentin, myself, and Miss Bristol, that Irene and Consuelo had exited the house by this very route. That Irene had worn men's clothing. That her boots bore traces of—his eyes flicked away from us—interesting, even telltale—substances. That Consuelo had gone willingly, under her own power, and perhaps the lulling power of hypnotism.

And that sixty feet from the house, in the forecourt to the stables area, they had both been picked up by a hansom cab.

"A cab?" Godfrey repeated.

"These villains have discovered that the bold approach is the least observed, something Mrs. Norton mastered in her teens."

"You're not saying—" I began.

"No." He had whirled and struck out at me like a poisonous snake. "Nothing is as it seems. Nothing in this entire case."

He straightened and pocketed the magnifying glass in his ulster, which reminded me of Professor Marvel's coat of many calling cards for the large number of items it could conceal.

"Enough of crawling around the haunts of the rich and infamous," Holmes said. "We'll find what we seek in less elevated locations. Miss Bristol—?"

"I'll arrange a room at your hotel," Quentin said quickly.

Holmes nodded. He looked at me, and Godfrey. "We'll need to dress for the occasion. Not well. Tonight will determine the fate of everyone we know, and a good many we don't know. Miss Huxleigh and I will tackle the Episcopal Club late this afternoon, just as the city fills with evening shadows. Mr. Norton, you will rendezvous with Mr. Stanhope and precede us to the club. Establish yourselves to watch the premises and those who enter and leave it."

"And what will this expedition gain us?" Godfrey demanded.

"An answer to a great many questions, and your wife back, along with little Miss Vanderbilt."

Who could argue with that?

49

In the Pinkerton

⚬⚬⚬

It was not that Holmes merely changed his costume.
His expression, his manner, his very soul seemed to vary with
every fresh part that he assumed.

—DR. WATSON IN "A SCANDAL IN BOHEMIA"

Of course, as all men know, brave talk is one thing. Brave action is another.

By an hour past teatime, I was in a tizzy. I was "walking out" not in men's clothing but in my feminine self, with Sherlock Holmes, who would no doubt be judging each move and syllable of my performance as I introduced him to Bishop Potter and the environs of the Episcopal Club.

Neatly attired in my new checked coat-dress, I was ready at the hotel when he knocked upon the door.

Godfrey answered, for he knew my nerves were as frayed as a ball of yarn Lucifer the cat had mauled. Oh, dear. Can nerves be both frayed and fevered? My cotton gloves touched my face, and came away warmed.

Well!

Here was my escort: a "gent" wearing a bowler hat and a checkered suit, neither new, with a cigar rampant on a field of teeth.

"'Afternoon, ma'am," this lanky fellow greeted me. "I'm fresh from the Windy City of Chicago and eager to see that a lady like you gets the answers she deserves. Mr. Artemis Conklin, at your service, but you can call me Artie."

Godfrey laughed. "Your American accent is astounding. Pinkertons are respected here, no matter their tailoring. Nothing could be more natural than that Nell should employ a private detective to trace her missing friend. Have you a pistol?"

Holmes revealed a large wooden-handled gun.

"These American inquiry agents," he said, "may be effective, but they're not gents of the old school. I'm sure Miss Huxleigh appreciates the difference between her homeland and the Colonies. There we go, ma'am, ahead of me out the door, for a gentleman I am when it suits me."

I sallied out as he suggested, amazed by the just-right blend of crude courtesy he exuded.

In fact, the American Sherlock Holmes was a far more palatable escort than any version I had met before.

Quite a revelation it was. As long as Sherlock Holmes was playing a part— in this case the Pinkerton operative obliging a lady client—he was quite the gallant, if clumsy, escort.

"Irene always said that your profession was half acting and half deduction," I told him on the horse car we took to the lower area of Manhattan.

"She is mighty generous, ma'am," he answered in that amazing Yankee twang.

"Not really. Irene is merely exacting. She's a seasoned stage artist. She doesn't bestow praise lightly."

At that he gave a potbellied Yankee chuckle.

"And I am a 'miss,' " I added. Purely in character.

"I could hardly miss that," he retorted. "Now pay attention. I'll say what I need to alert any loitering observers that I might know more about the events than we do. You must play the naive innocent, no matter what I say."

The "naive innocent"? "That will be a 'stretch,' " I told him, "but Irene has often discussed the necessity of playing against type."

"Has she? Let's hope that she finds us up to her standards, when we in turn find her."

"Will we find her?"

"You may not, but I will. I don't approve of Norton's insistence on involving you tonight. I doubt Mrs. Norton would approve. Try to remember that the well-being of both your friend, Madam Irene, and the Vanderbilt girl depend on your being coolheaded."

"This is not my first time for such concerns, Mr. . . . . Pinkerton."

"Good. Just be yourself and stay out of my way, and all will be well."

This was the last time during that journey that the usual Sherlock Holmes arrogance peeped out of his new Pinkerton persona.

As we alighted on Broadway, the streets still thronged with conveyances. The electric streetlights were just coming on, but not quite needed as we walked the short distance to the club. Yet I thought we would never get there!

Mr. Artemis Conklin had to stop every few yards to gawk about like a country bumpkin. Then he had to search his pockets, pull out a large cigar, and light it.

He again peered intently around the neighborhood, which was decorated with the usual peddlers and loungers. Then he ostentatiously took my arm (it was all I could do not to unceremoniously jerk it away), and said loudly, "So you last saw this Father Edwards at the club, you say."

"Edmonds!" I corrected before I could stop myself.

"Don't worry, miss, we Pinkertons always get our man. Or woman."

At this he chuckled and we again preceded toward the club.

I heard a furtive jingle, like coins, and jerked around to look behind us. But the street was quiet. The loiterers were growing invisible in the shadows of the looming six- and seven-story offices. Night was falling with a thud here, along this narrow street hemmed in by these towering buildings.

Again the clinking sound. I observed a peddler's cart across the street, attended by a man slouched against the wall as if asleep. Somehow the wind must be moving among the clutter of goods.

A gas lantern glowed alongside the steps ahead on our left. The farther one got from Broadway, the more old-fashioned gaslights were still in use. Once again I broached the doors of the Episcopal Club. I was beginning to feel like an American member of the congregation!

Despite my unlikely escort, I was recognized by the attendant and we were allowed in.

The dinner hour found Bishop Potter in. He greeted us in the parlor, listening with a kind, worried face as I explained the disappearance of my friend, and implored him to assist this fine detective, Mr. Conklin of the Pinkertons, in finding her.

"Such a shock, Miss Huxleigh," the bishop said. "Do you know we haven't been able to find Father Hawks? And Father Edmonds, such a fine young priest, has also gone missing. Now you say our revered donor, Mrs. Norton is not to be found. Appalling! Of course I will do anything, Mr.—?"

"Conklin, sir. Father. Bishop, that is. I guess yer kissin' cousins to the high clergy of me own Catholic faith."

Here the bishop's genial expression curdled somewhat. What could he do? More than half the population of New York was Irish Roman Catholic these days. They were tenement shop workers, domestics, laborers, bartenders, and policemen. Even private policemen.

"I need information on the good fathers," said Holmes, taking out a tiny stub of pencil, licking the lead and applying the blunted point to a smudged and crinkled notebook. "Where were they last seen?"

"Why, here, I suppose. Both had official positions at the club, and therefore roomed here. We also have a library and club rooms and direct our charities to the poor from here as well."

"You don't room here?"

"No. No, of course not. I have the official residence."

"Then why do ye spend so much time here?"

"To dine, of course, in a more communal atmosphere. The cook is quite fine. And to escape the pomp of my office."

"I don't suppose you invite any Catholic priests here."

"Prelates, from time to time, but not priests. The large Irish population of New York requires us to set aside denominational differences on occasion. Our congregation, of course, is more . . . stable."

"No Irish need apply, eh, Bishop?" Holmes had strolled insolently to the bay window overlooking the street. "No Jesuits either, I s'pose?"

"Jesuits? No. Hardly. They are the aggressive arm of that ancient religion. Brilliant but doctrinaire. Bishops, on the other hand, well, we all have to be diplomats."

Holmes turned from the window that looked out on absolute blackness now.

"I don't s'pose you allow cigar smokin' inside here?"

"Not in the library. In the club rooms, but—"

"Nothing to it. I'll take meself outside for a think and a smoke. The two often go togither. Maybe Miss Ruxleigh has a question or two to ask you about Father Edmonds. She was much taken with him."

"Huxleigh! And I was no more taken with Father Edmonds than I am with you, Mr., uh, Cronklin."

Holmes had oiled out of the door, the disgusting snuffed cigar already in his hand, ready for a relighting.

Really! I'd never been seen in such debased company before, even if it was a pose, and blushed for the crudity of my companion.

The bishop, being a man of sensibility, immediately sensed my humiliation. "These police types are but a step up from the petty criminals they pursue, my dear," he consoled me with a fineness of feeling I much appreciated.

I glanced out the window to see a bright ember flare against the dark. The revolting cigar. I do wish Irene would stop smoking such things! *Irene . . .* My eyes teared over.

"Please, Miss Huxleigh, do sit down again. Believe me, I'll do all in my power to assist in your search for Mrs. Norton. Such a handsome woman. One hopes that . . . well, much evil happens on the streets of New York. I understand your need to employ an inquiry agent, but perhaps Mr. Conklin is not the best person. He seems eager to be off."

I leaped up from my chair like a fox startled by hounds and whirled to look out the window. No ember glowed in the dark. I had been . . . seduced and abandoned.

Holmes was off on the real business of the night and I was sitting here exchanging inanities with the bishop.

"I must go."

And I did, ignoring the bishop's sputtered objections behind me, prating of dark streets, of Irene's recent fate, promising he would find me an escort. . . .

I had *had* an escort, and he'd quite neatly deluded . . . and eluded me.

I burst out into the street. Night black now, and no one visible there. Not a soul.

Rushing down the stairs, I squinted at the far gaslights, searching for anything moving.

Something tinkled in the sparse summer breeze that crept down this misbegotten street.

Then someone swooped from the dark and captured my arm.

I didn't waste time screaming, but fumbled among the objects on my chatelaine for the sharp, small scissors.

"Nell!"

I paused at hearing Godfrey's voice. "Where's Holmes? Oh, Godfrey, he has slipped us both, as he always intended."

"Perhaps." Godfrey whistled. A clatter of hooves came charging out from the mews behind the Episcopal Club. We were up and into a hansom cab before—as Americans say—I could whistle "Dixie," although why I would do such a vulgar thing, I can't imagine.

"A carriage came past just now," Godfrey said after ordering the driver to make for Broadway as fast as he could. "It paused between the peddler's cart Holmes ordered me to man and the Episcopal Club. When it moved on, Holmes was gone: kidnapped or willingly away. I don't know which. Perhaps we can still catch it."

"What's he up to, Godfrey?"

"Finding Irene and Consuelo Vanderbilt. Without our participation. He's accomplished his goal. He's been taken by the ones who took them, and he left us behind."

"What about Quentin? Where is he?"

"Either duped, as we were, or already on the trail. It could be that Holmes regards you and me as amateurs, as emotionally wrought-up amateurs better left out of the picture. He told me to arrange for the hansom to wait so I could escort you safely back to the Astor House."

"What arrogance!" I sounded like an Amazon. "What shall we do?" I wailed the next moment.

"I for one intend to follow him if I can. This cab will go where I tell it. Unless you object."

"Object? I applaud."

Godfrey was leaning half out of the hansom to see ahead as it turned onto the brightly lit thoroughfare of Broadway.

"There! That Gurney with the two black horses ahead of the horsecar." Godfrey pounded his walking stick on the trapdoor above us. "Follow that Gurney, but at a decent distance."

I heard a grunt in answer.

"Will the driver heed you?"

"A half-eagle gold piece says yes. What did you learn inside the Episcopal Club?"

"Nothing! Holmes engineered this outing merely to attract the wrong attention."

"At which he succeeded brilliantly," Godfrey said with a rueful chortle.

"Godfrey! This entire plan was based on duping us."

"But he hasn't quite, has he?"

I saw Godfrey's keen features illuminated in the flash of a passing electric streetlight. They were as sharp and intent as Holmes on the hunt for scintillas of evidence on a carpet. We were all hurtling toward a way to find and free Irene.

If she needed freeing.

That sober thought I didn't share with Godfrey. Irene was as willful as any wayward child. If she had secret purposes of her own she would think nothing of following them to any extreme required.

50
Sacrificial Goatee

❧❦

The stage lost a fine actor, even as science lost an acute reasoner, when he became a specialist in crime.
—DR. WATSON IN "A SCANDAL IN BOHEMIA"

❧FROM THE CASE NOTES OF SHERLOCK HOLMES❦

My abductors, of course, had to be quite rude about it.

The moment I had been snatched inside their rattling Gurney, I was thrust on the floor at their feet and my hands secured behind me.

I made no resistance. The idea was to remain conscious and hear, see . . . and smell . . . what they were up to. Where they were up to it was no more a mystery after a deep inhale or two of their noxious footwear.

We were headed toward the harbor, naturally, where a rat maze of warehouses permits any manner of concealment.

The one barefoot member of the party, whose tracks I had spied at the boardinghouse the night Madam Irene disappeared, provided the most provocative and chilling aroma. Blood. Fresh blood.

I admit the revelation chilled my own blood. I'd never doubted these were desperate villains willing to commit mayhem in order to gain their ends. I hadn't expected the smell of fresh blood and the fears it gave birth to, for both Irene Adler and for the child she had taken, apparently these . . .

Well, what were they? My bones and head received the endless jolt of the cobblestones, bereft of any softening springs, but I can think in a thunderstorm.

From the shifting bars of gaslight that entered the Gurney windows, I detected thick bull-hide soles and lanolin-soaked uppers. Hardly Regents Street.

Crude men, I decided, from crude climates. As for the unshod one . . . I'd already formed some idea of his origins. In fact, I'd researched the notion a bit. What I found was more disquieting than anything I'd yet seen, including Father Hawks's ravaged body.

Imagination, however, is the great enemy of logical deduction.

Anything I learned now would help me save the Vanderbilt child, and her ambiguous abductress, and myself for that matter, later.

And it was a good deal later, almost half an hour, I should estimate, before the Gurney came to a stop in an area reeking of sea salt, manure, and blood.

Distant ships sounded, mournful as distant whales, while they left and attained the great harbor.

Such lofty matters were remote from the doings here.

I was pulled out of the carriage onto the damp cobblestones, inhaling another dose of salty mist and blood, dragged to my feet between two fellows clad in dark, damp, and cheap wool, and marched into a building as huge and inky as the night around us.

"Hurry!" ordered a voice in English. A voice that had never spoken my language from birth.

The fools had thought binding a man's hands was sufficient. That left his feet, eyes, nose, and brain perfectly free to operate.

I hadn't anticipated brilliant opponents, but madness makes up in power for a great deal of stupidity.

I was half dragged over perhaps forty yards of hard stone floor, glimpsing a roof as high as a cathedral, or more aptly, the wings of a theater, for I saw distant metal mechanisms above, reflecting the light from the bull's-eyes lanterns they bore.

Lanterns indoors indicated a deserted warehouse of sorts.

"Here," cried the one voice that used English.

I was rushed from the dark into a chamber haphazardly lit by paraffin lamps. Their smell mercifully dampened the inescapable odor of new and old blood throughout this echoing building.

I was half sat on a wooden chair placed before a crude wooden table.

"This man came to the club seeking information."

Another man jerked my head back by the hair—my atrociously shaped bowler hat had been left to be windblown about the street in front of the Episcopal Club.

My eyes blinked from the unaccustomed light, but not before they had registered the sight of Madam Irene Adler Norton, smoking a small cigar and standing before me with a pistol akimbo on her hip.

I must admit to being momentarily speechless, but luckily the occasion didn't require comment.

Behind her I noticed the child in her pale lace stockings and frock, half sitting, half reclining on a table, like a nymph in an absinthe advertisement, her thin legs tucked under her. Then I realized the reason for her sitting on a table. Rats.

Even as I thought it, I heard the snakelike rasp of their tails over the stone floor.

"He was going about the club, asking questions about everything," the first man said

"And who are you?" Madam Irene demanded, giving immediate notice that she was playing some role to mislead this gang.

"Artemis Conklin, but I go by Artie."

She lifted the pistol and aimed it at my forehead. "What are you?"

"A Pinkerton by profession, but not for long," I added.

"Pinkerton?" The man behind me sounded confused, and extremely annoyed that he was. I felt his grip on my hair tighten.

Given his barefoot companion, this was not a happy observation.

Madam Irene shrugged. Her hair was down and disarranged, and her trousers stained, but her manner was as calm as if she stood in a chapel instead of a slaughterhouse, for that was what this great empty building had been.

"Pinkertons are a sort of domestic detective," she told the man behind me. I would describe her tone as a dismissive sneer. "They are hired to look into errant spouses and do some antiunion work for the kingpins of commerce, but are otherwise no threat."

"This one was with the woman who earlier was with you."

"No threat also. I had to mount my own inquiries before I, er . . . encountered you and your compatriots. Unimportant tools, my dear Reisling. You can understand my need for them."

"Then you think this man knows nothing?"

She regarded me for a long, torturous moment. It appeared that during her short time with these thugs she had become their leader, or at least their guide.

She blew out a considering stream of smoke that teased my nose like a fresh slipper of shag on Baker Street. Alas, both shag and Baker Street were far from this sink-hole of iniquity.

"I doubt he knows anything worthwhile. You can see by his suit that he's a humbug sort of detective."

"Still, we should let our savage pet have at him. A little manicure job and he will say whatever we want to hear."

At this I was hauled up from behind and slammed facedown of the rough wooden table. My bonds were loosened, but no sooner had my elbows unflexed than two men turned me over and threw their full weight on both my arms.

I saw nothing now but the crude wooden struts of the small chamber's ceiling above my head. I heard, however, the poor child whimper.

My arms were pulled outward and my wrists pinned.

A face from a nightmare . . . dark, painted with the image of bones, raised a knife over me.

I heard a pistol cocked. Another stream of smoke diffused through the lantern light that revealed every fiendish feature of my torturer's face.

"It's him or the Vanderbilt spawn," the English speaker said. "One or the other will make a nice donation to the decor on Fifth Avenue. Vanderbilt needs another warning."

"A waste of time," Irene Adler Norton said with studied ennui, "but you'll do what you will do."

I bunched every muscle in my body for resistance . . . or endurance.

51

Abbot Noir Redux

But the inspector and Irene had not been speaking of my mythical head monk at all. Not Abbot Noir, but abattoir, a word I did know even if I did not expect to hear it spoken in polite society. Slaughterhouse.

—NELL HUXLEIGH IN *CHAPEL NOIR* BY CAROLE NELSON DOUGLAS

Soon our horse's clopping hooves were no longer part of the constant equine drumbeat along Broadway but became a singular effect. Godfrey's and my hansom turned down darker and even darker streets.

We'd borne west, not east. I'd assumed the slums of the East Side, teeming with tenements, would be the destination of so dangerous a criminal element desiring to hide.

But our hansom was slowing to navigate the damp, salty air of the docks. There was no way to muffle the horses's hooves. Both Godfrey and I felt as if our presence were announced with every step as definitely as by a footman pounding a staff at a royal reception to shout out the name of each arriving guest.

The rank odor of wet wood and dead fish was mild compared to another reek that hit us in the open hansom like a slap across the face.

"Godfrey—?"

He thumped on the trapdoor until the driver's top hat was visible, if not his face beneath the ragged brim.

"Where are we, man?"

"Holding pens," was the muffled answer. And another word.

"The Gurney?" Godfrey asked.

"Turned down this alleyway. I don't see or hear it, sir."

"Then stop at once. We'll get out here."

"But, sir, 'sno place to take a lady."

Godfrey released us both from the hansom. We stood on damp cobble-stones shining faintly from some unseen light.

I glimpsed another gold coin handed up to the driver.

"Wait for us."

The top hat nodded, even as the gold piece disappeared. I wasn't sure he'd wait, but then, I didn't care. If we weren't successful in finding Irene tonight, no ride back to Broadway would bring the light back into my life, or Godfrey's, again.

"That odor!" I said as we walked away. "It's like a barn, but a thousand times worse."

"That's because these barns house thousands of farm animals."

"Thousands? This is a—"

"An area of slaughterhouses, I think."

I stopped dead in my tracks. "An *abattoir*." Of course I was familiar with the French word for slaughterhouse. I had, in fact, once visited the great Paris open market of Les Halles, where butchered meat hung on hooks and passersby had to be wary of slipping on the odd misplaced entrail. . . . One visit had been more than enough.

I also recalled once mistaking the word *abattoir* for a personage: Abbot Noir. This had been on the scene of the worst human slaughter Irene and I had ever encountered, only last spring.

"You can return to the hansom and wait." Godfrey seemed to sense my internal recoil. "In fact, I'd like some extra assurance that the driver will wait."

"No. If Irene and Consuelo are in this terrible place they'll need us both."

We resumed walking without more debate, each of us listening, but hearing only the muffled bawls of penned animals awaiting brutal death.

"Perhaps," I told Godfrey as we pushed as quietly as we could farther into the silent dark, "we are in the way."

"Perhaps. But I can't let Irene's fate rest in another's hands, no matter how expert, any more than you can. We must be discreet, Nell. If it appears that our presence will interfere with Holmes's scheme, we must defer."

For a moment, I said nothing. I recognized that *the* man had put himself in danger to resolve this mystery. That he had intended to risk himself and only himself. And perhaps Quentin.

I also recognized that Godfrey's and my claim upon Irene superceded any intent Sherlock Holmes might harbor. Besides, Holmes's first professional obligation was to poor little Consuelo Vanderbilt. Not Irene. No matter how personally he might wish to save her, he was committed to Consuelo. No one else. And certainly not to Godfrey and myself, whom he'd left flailing about in front of the Episcopal Club like a prize pair of turkeys!

Here, near the harbor, one could hear the eternal slap of waves against hull and piling and smell the sea in all its rank, commercial stink. Another scent was beginning to drown that out, and I recognized it. Blood.

In the occasional glimmer of moonlight between the hulking warehouses, I saw that Godfrey was attired in a midnight peacoat like Black Otto, a former personage of his on an earlier, less dire adventure in Monte Carlo.

I didn't doubt that his hand in his right coat pocket held pistol, or dagger, or blackjack.

I myself was ill accoutered for such a desperate expedition, save for the many useful articles on my chatelaine. But now I had to muffle this useful accessory with my hand to keep it from chiming our approach.

A horse snorted in the distance.

Godfrey stopped me with a hand on my wrist. We waited. Then moved forward.

A Gurney and two horses had been pulled close to a building.

We came near . . . and Godfrey bent over a bundle on the wet ground. The driver.

"Dead?" I asked.

"Perhaps. Certainly not likely to rouse until dawn."

We slipped past the horses, standing patiently in the way forced upon their kind, each with a forefoot lifted to ease the waiting.

The sight of these beasts of burden with one foot lifted against their wearisome fate always stirred my heart. My ire against those who had raced this Gurney here, to what dire purpose, rose like a fire in my throat. That they had also abused the two priests only increased my fury. That Irene and Consuelo were even now at their mercy . . . I suddenly knew the fiery heart of Lola Montez, and deemed no weapon—pistol, whip, or dagger—beyond my just and present use.

Godfrey's cautionary hand on my forearm almost spurred a striking out. "Inside here," he whispered in my ear.

I was back, again—as in my dreams, my nightmares—in that ancient, crumbling maze in Transylvania, where creatures and rituals and rites unthinkable had required the utmost of my endurance. And resistance.

Somehow, Irene and I had now stumbled into a new variety of atrocity.

I breathed as deep as a well, inhaling all the brutal stench and stiffening against it. Then Godfrey cracked some unseen portal, and we eeled into a deeper, oily dark, a darkness silent and yet echoing with the drip of saltwater. Perhaps tears?

We moved forward together, on tiptoe, as we had before, and stronger for the first trial.

His fingers tightened on my wrist. My hand made a fist. And we stole further into the heart of darkness.

Some interior light leaked into the scene ahead of us.

I made out a high empty space, long steel tables, pulleys and huge hanging hooks. Scaffolding ahead, reaching up two stories. The smell here was as rank, but stale somehow.

"A deserted slaughterhouse." Godfrey's whisper danced against my ear like a moth dying in the light.

I nodded, not sure that he would detect such a feeble gesture.

We paused again. And heard faint sounds ahead.

So we moved on, sliding our feet along the rough floor, careful to keep from slipping or making any untoward sound that should betray our presence.

Surprise was our only real weapon.

The sounds became sharper, resolved into voices. Arguing voices.

We saw a sort of interior office ahead against one of the towering brick walls. Just a lean-to of wood, with a door and windows with glass panes inset. An overseer's office, I thought.

And from it came the voices.

We inched forward, stopping in tandem when a deep soprano joined the basso chorus. We clutched at each other in the dark. No words were discernible, but the tonal quality of Irene's voice was as unmistakable as a cello among bass fiddles.

I could hear the poor dumb beasts moaning and shifting in distant holding pens. The smell of their thousands and thousands of predecessors soaked this empty building with the metallic tang of spilled blood. This was an animal morgue, far cruder but no less brutal than the famous institution of Paris that attracted goggling crowds.

Would it become a usual kind of morgue before the night was done?

I noticed a glint in Godfrey's hand. Black Otto's businesslike dagger.

By now we were near enough for the light that leaked through the filthy glass to wash our own figures. We dared not go much closer without alerting those inside the office.

We hesitated. I glimpsed a motion atop the office structure, and pulled on Godfrey's rough sleeve.

He glanced up to see what I saw. A dark, hunched figure like a sort of giant monkey, with a crest upon its head like some tropical bird.

To such an apparition, we would be as visible as statues in a museum.

While we braced ourselves for the next move, something rose up behind the shadow and merged with it.

A beast with two backs and four pummeling arms plunged to the floor.

Godfrey sprang to the office door, not to rush through it but to wait and listen.

Then the glass on the three visible office windows exploded outwards, a rushing figure at the center of each halo of breaking splinters. Glass flew like daggers of ice.

One shadow sprinted through the door. Godfrey brought his conjoined fists down on its neck, and the creature rolled to the floor.

Men, or beasts, came pouring out of the small structure, not counting the Quasimodo on the floor still contending with someone . . . one, two, three, four, five.

A pistol shot fired and the bullet whined off some distant slab of metal.

I crouched back, no match for any of the strivings before me, but perhaps able to startle or surprise at a later moment.

For all the gentlemen's vaunted desire to spare and protect me, at this moment, when my friends and foes were contending in a pitched battle for life and death, I mattered not a smidgeon. The first wrestlers rolled toward me, caught my skirt hem under their twisting bodies and nearly pulled me into their brutal wake.

Then the battle shifted and they rolled away.

I felt the floor around me. My hands shaped some mass of abandoned metal, heavy and so rusted I almost sneezed from the powder it left on my gloves as I lifted it. I struggled upright, the weight in my hands, and then staggered against the office wall.

In the uncertain light within figures were writhing like demons on Judgment Day. I thought of Mary Jane Kelly's cramped, vile room in Whitechapel and what slaughter had transpired there. I cowered, yes, cowered against the flimsy wooden wall.

A high thin scream came from inside the office. I'd heard wounded animals and infants scream so, and hurtled through the open door despite myself.

Then I stopped and blinked, blinded, in the light from an unshuttered lantern.

When I could finally see past that brutal fist of artificial sunlight I saw Irene holding a pistol far bigger than the petite one she was prone to carry. A dark-haired child in a pale dress and stockings clung to her trouser legs. And a hulking male figure was before them, frozen like a statue.

"Nell, behind you!" Irene called, raising the pistol to shoulder height.

I spun, the weight in my arms lifting and spinning me faster and harder than even I had thought.

I hit him in the stomach, some looming man with angry eyes and reaching fists.

And continued spinning around, barely keeping my feet . . .

. . . just in time to meet another man head-on as he charged out, brushing me aside. I fell like a sack of rocks.

The impact dazed me. Before I could recover, Irene rushed past me, her pistol aimed as she discharged it.

The sound exploded in the empty slaughterhouse.

A pair of black satin slippers stopped by my nose.

"Oh," came a small, fearful voice. "Are you all right?"

I sat up. "You're all right, that's what matters," I told the slender child, smiling at her despite my sudden, pounding headache. "My, what a lovely frock."

She was an achingly thin willow of a girl, with a small trembling mouth and great dark lonely eyes. I hugged her, no longer worried. If Irene and her pistol were ahead of me, nothing fearful could lie behind me . . . except little Consuelo, who said: "That was a very good discus throw. I've been studying the Olympic Games of the Greeks, you know. Do you dance? Miss Irene said she would teach me."

I looked around, though the open door. In the vast, black empty chamber, figures even darker were scurrying away like monsters in a dissipating bad dream.

Some of the figures came to the doorway and turned out to be Godfrey. Sherlock Holmes. Quentin. And Irene, looking royally annoyed.

In fact, they all looked royally annoyed with me.

Except for Consuelo. Children are often so much wiser than adults.

52

Tall, Dark, and Holmes?

~⊰⊱~

Energy rightly applied and directed will accomplish anything.
—MAXIM OF NELLIE BLY

⊰FROM NELLIE BLY'S JOURNAL⊱

There is only so far that one may goad an Englishman or a beau.

Quentin Stanhope had done a disappearing act on me.

He wasn't at his hotel, and had left no word as to where he might be. I next tried the hotel of Sherlock Holmes. Presto! Also unavailable.

At last I called at the Astor House Hotel, and found Mrs. Norton and Miss Huxleigh "not in."

Well.

If there's one thing I can smell, besides a Paris perfume, it's a rat.

His name is Quentin, and now I knew my docile English spy-cum-nursemaid had gone rogue. Oh, he was very good at squiring me about the lower quarters in search of baby-sellers. But once he was on a true trail, it was bye-bye, Nellie Bly.

I can't say I was surprised. I always knew he was in America solely to keep me from doing things. This may sound conceited, but I understand I'm a dangerous woman to some, at home and abroad, because I won't leave well enough alone.

Leaving well enough alone is the way women and horses have been kept in harness for generations.

That very first article by Quiet Observer saying girls should stay to home and not intrude on the working world had gotten my ire up at the age of seventeen, and I haven't stopped since then, although I've since made peace with the curmudgeonly old columnist who goes by the coy initials of Q.O.

Any one man may be all right. In a bunch, they're a cowardly nest of naysayers to free women anywhere.

Quentin Stanhope is no different. Nor that hoighty-toighty Sherlock Holmes. As for Irene Adler Norton and Miss Nell, I wouldn't trust them as far as I could toss the trunks they brought to New York.

Bunch of Continental snobs, if you ask me!

Now to my next step.

It came to hand on my exit from the Astor House in the form of a begging Street Arab. I never stint on a source.

"Here's fifty cents, my lad. I wish I knew when a certain lady with a lapel watch left this hotel a few hours ago."

One could count on these street rapscallions to spot and value articles of jewelry faster than a Forty-seventh Street diamond dealer.

"Nothin' simpler," said the filthy-faced lad. "If ye have anither fifty-cent piece."

"I've the fifty cents, but have you the information I want?"

"Love the hat, ma'am. M'name's Archy. It was just a couple hours ago, at dusk. A tall, dark fellow had me watchin' for when a bustlin' lady wearin' a silver belt come out, and where she went."

"Hmmm," I said, recognizing Sherlock Holmes at once. "I suppose you can't tell me."

"The lady took a horsecar with another gennelmen in a checked suit. Fast fellow. And Mr. Mayberry's hack followed with the tall dark fellow. A regular Brit in a top hat. Handsome as the undertaker's horse. It's a regular Madison Square farce."

"Here's a fifty-cent piece that says I want Mr. Mayberry's hack for myself."

"He's just back on his favorite corner, there. Wait! My fifty-cent piece!"

I threw it behind me and bounded into the conveyance in question, beating out a top-hatted swell escorting a Union Square fan dancer.

"Where to, ma'am?" my genteel driver inquired.

"Where you took your last fare."

"It'll be pitch dark with night there by now. You're better off stayin' in the lights of Broadway. That's no fit place for a lady alone."

"I don't expect to be alone long," I told myself, not worrying a whit what he thought about overhearing me.

But my brave words came back to haunt me when the driver began taking darker and sharper turnings into the unsavory area that led to the docks.

I couldn't imagine Nell Huxleigh going here, or Sherlock Holmes permitting her to do so.

Yet if the tall dark man who called upon her hadn't been Holmes, it must have been Quentin. Yes, Quentin would be the more likely candidate to squire Miss Nell around at night . . . but why here?

When the driver stopped near a completely darkened building, I leaned out over the doors that kept me a passenger, reluctant to get out.

The area was utterly deserted, and had that disused atmosphere you find in abandoned buildings.

While a I hesitated, I heard the distant rattle of harnesses and carriage. Shortly after, a Gurney came grinding down the damp cobblestones, its horses straining as if overloaded.

"What on earth can that Gurney be doing here at this hour?" I speculated aloud.

My driver heard me.

"Doin' what I long to do, Miss. Gettin' the hell out of this nasty place."

I still made him drive forward a hundred yards or so, though he swore that where we had stopped had been where he'd left "the gentleman" (that had to be Quentin, not Holmes; Holmes was too brusque to be taken for a gentleman) "and the lady off."

There was obviously nothing here.

No lady, and no gentleman.

No Holmes, no Nell.

No Quentin.

I felt a bit like a jealous spouse trying to trail an illicit couple. Disappointed, and foolish.

I knocked on the trapdoor to let the driver know he could hie for the safe, electrically bright lights of Broadway again.

Whatever anyone had been up to in the dark of night, Quentin would be mine again in the morning.

53

Sulphur and Smoke

Men for a little gain cross the seas, enduring at least as much as we, and shall we not, for God's love do what men do for earthly interest?"
—SAINT ISAAC JOGUES'S LETTER TO HIS MOTHER ON LEAVING FRANCE TO BE
A MISSIONARY TO THE INDIANS IN NEW YORK AND NEW FRANCE (CANADA), 1636

Luckily, the driver of the Gurney used to abduct Holmes had proved to be only stunned. He was groaning and sitting against the front wheel when we recovered our wits and gathered ourselves into a party.

A quite respectable party, if the light didn't blaze upon our disheveled apparel: we were three men, two women, and a child, and could just crowd into the Gurney if Consuelo sat on my lap, and Irene on Godfrey's, which didn't seem to be an imposition to either of them.

First we returned Consuelo to her distraught parents, who had, in the meantime, hired half of the actual Pinkertons in New York to guard her and their house. Mr. Vanderbilt overflowed with thanks and promises of reward. Mrs. Vanderbilt simply snatched the girl's hand from mine and marched her up those long, imposing stairs that so frightened the child. Alva Vanderbilt's promise of an immediate bath sounded like a punishment. The woman knew nothing about cajoling and everything about enforcing.

Poor Consuelo had only been persuaded to return home after promises from Irene and myself to visit. Irene was to teach her to dance, and I was to teach her to discus throw.

Given Consuelo's social-climbing harridan of a mother, I believe that discus throwing would prove to be the more valuable skill.

Mr. Vanderbilt could not quite meet my eyes as I turned them from the staircase after Consuelo and her mother had disappeared.

"Very grateful," he murmured to me personally. "I will show how much later, when things are set to rights here at home." He glanced up the palatial staircase, fit for a Cinderella to flee down, as if he too feared the height.

Then we all five adjourned to the Astor House, where our state of clothing was the centerpiece of every eye in a lobby blazing with electric lights.

Safe and uncommented-upon in the elevator at last, we took final refuge in Irene's and my rooms. Godfrey had ordered brandy as we passed through the lobby, by the bottle. Two of them! The man delivering them almost arrived at our door as soon as we did. He peered inward in rank curiosity while Quentin tipped him and accepted the heavy tray.

I surveyed my male escorts. Sherlock Holmes's previously loud clothing now actually shouted with dirt and rips. Godfrey as Black Otto had apparently been caught in a buzz saw. Quentin, attired in the rags of a street beggar, now beggared description. Irene in men's clothes was beginning to look commonplace to me, except her hair was an unpinned snarl and she looked wan and worn.

I myself was a sight, my hair half-undone, my gloves red with rust.

My weapon, it turned out, had been a disused pulley wheel, round and flat enough to pass for a discus, after all.

"Let go of that heavy, cumbersome thing, Nell," Irene urged after we'd assembled in our hotel parlor.

"No. I . . . rather fancy it. One never knows what will come plunging down from the ceiling in New York City these days."

"What was that thing on the office roof?" Godfrey asked Quentin from his position presiding over the brandy. "Some sort of orangutang?"

"Slippery enough to finally elude me in the dark," Quentin complained. "Perhaps a thing half-eel and half-man."

"Nothing so exotic." Holmes was seated in the damask chair, puffing away on his disgusting pipe like a London chimney. "Although his barefoot state was rather apelike. Let Mrs. Norton tell us about him."

"I think you know." Irene told him as her filthy fingers screwed a cigarette into her elegant enamel-and-diamond holder.

In fact, they all resembled a lot of chimney sweeps, a state I could hardly hold against them or savor, for I had the same, smudged appearance. And the odors that clung to us all from that unused slaughterhouse! For once I welcomed the stink of sulphur and smoke.

Godfrey brought Irene the first glass of brandy. She sipped, then set it aside. She had lost her man's fedora somewhere, and her hairpins, tresses flowing like a girl's, as Miss Bristol had described her. Nor had she been wearing gloves.

"I suppose I should explain myself," Irene agreed.

"You could start with the hypnotism." Holmes's tone treaded on a sneer.

How nice, actually, to see him back in fine form. I'd guessed that his situation had been dire before Quentin and Godfrey forced his captors to turn their attention elsewhere.

"Hypnotism?" Irene shrugged. "No, more a pretense of hypnotism than the real thing. Those of us versed in stage illusions know how to appear as if from nowhere." She eyed Holmes significantly. "We know how to command attention, and how to put people off guard with the startling things we might say." Her eyes never left him. "So I wouldn't call it hypnotism, would you, Mr. Holmes?"

He refused to rise to her bait and answer, so I did.

"You charmed them. Like a . . . lady leprechaun."

"I may be Irish by birth, after all," she said, pleating the folds of her skirt in the manner of a schoolroom miss who has been up to mischief and is not one bit sorry.

Godfrey looked a bit alarmed by the declaration, and sat up in the armchair where he had lounged to cosset his brandy glass.

Holmes, I noticed, still left his glass untouched, as I had mine. At least he was abstemious with spirits.

"Irene," Godfrey said. "Is it true? You've discovered your family origins?"

Her hand extended across the small space that separated their chairs and Godfrey met it with his own.

"Who knows?" Irene told him, and only him. "I've discovered a great deal, but nothing is certain when it comes to my family tree."

I looked away. In all the rush and excitement, Irene and Godfrey hadn't had time or privacy for a marital reunion. This reaching of their hands seemed to bridge an ocean and several weeks, as well as the few feet in a room.

So I looked away, and found myself looking at Sherlock Holmes looking away also. He appeared as I'd never seen him before, embarrassed.

"I suppose you know everything that's about to be revealed," I told him. Tartly.

This stirred up his annoying arrogance. "Indeed. But you might be better amused if the stage performer among us tells it in her own melodramatic way."

Irene roused herself and took another sip of brandy.

"Let's see. We leave our heroine on a surreptitious mission to visit an empty room, unaware of three sinister men on her trail."

"Were you really unaware of them, Irene?" I asked.

"Absolutely. However, I'd finished my mission in the room and was on the back steps when I heard the terrible trio coming along the side of the boardinghouse."

"Were they tenors?" Holmes asked suddenly.

"Tenors?" Even Irene was surprised by the question.

"If we're to make a grand opera of it, I'd like the voices assigned, at least."

She laughed. "Two bass baritones and a . . . basso. Hearing their approach, I flattened myself against a convenient arras—the other side of the boardinghouse to you who don't know opera."

"Naturally you overheard them," Holmes pressed.

"Naturally."

"And followed them. I saw the footprints."

"And followed them. They were expecting to follow, which makes one careless about being followed."

"Yes," Holmes said, puffing away like a steamship stack, "I recall that error."

Irene didn't press her advantage in evoking the time when she had followed him home in man's guise and he had been in such single-minded pursuit of her that he hadn't realized that until it was too late.

Instead she smiled at Godfrey.

"They walked back to Broadway, during which time I overheard their plans to abduct the young Vanderbilt girl."

"And?" Godfrey asked. "I'm afraid I know your conclusion."

Irene nodded. "I suspected that they were the creatures responsible for the torment and death of poor Father Hawks. I couldn't stop them alone. So—"

"You joined them!" Holmes summarized, triumphant.

He had always said that the signs showed Irene in command of herself, and apparently her would-be kidnappers also.

"Oh, I didn't go along without a struggle, but I convinced them eventually that I had motives that made us allies, not antagonists."

"Which were?" I asked.

Irene sighed and leaned forward to address me. "You have to understand who these men were, Nell. You have to understand that I'd encountered Lola Montez's worst nightmare."

"Ultramontanes?" I asked, to Godfrey's and Holmes's mystification. How pleasant to be keeping up with Irene when neither man could.

"In a way," she answered me, "but that's a geographical and political description of thirty years ago. It always only meant 'those from over the mountains,' from the south of southern Germany, from the Italian and Catholic city states."

"Jesuits!" I suggested next.

Irene nodded slowly, inhaling on her elegant cigarette holder. She exhaled with the relief of one who is home again.

"Perhaps. Perhaps not quite."

"Who else," I demanded, "save Ulramontanes and Jesuits would care about pursuing Lola Montez thirty years after her death?"

"Not to mention," Holmes noted from his own smoky-pipe corner of the room, "Red Indians."

"*A* Red Indian," Irene corrected him. "How did you know?"

"I saw the bare footprints at the boardinghouse. Of course they were all over the slaughterhouse. I imagine such a one would go unnoticed during the hot August weather of a New York summer. All the street urchins are barefoot, and some of the more destitute adults."

I was aghast. "An Indian? Like Red Tomahawk? An Indian was among these Ultramontanes and Jesuits?"

Quentin, who'd been watching us with sleepy eyes, stirred on the sofa.

"Not so amazing, Nell. I've learned something of the entire globe and its peoples in my vagabond existence as an imperial diplomat. The Jesuits have always been the Vatican's spies and secret agents, boldly going where their Catholic kind faced burning at the stake, from England after Henry the Eighth to a holding action in European principalities like Bohemia and Bavaria. But they've also been dedicated and courageous missionaries. They came to America more than two centuries ago to seek converts among the native tribes."

"Iroquois, Huron, and Mohawk," Holmes said. "All fierce North American tribes before there was a United States of anything. The Jesuit missionaries were mercilessly tortured for their pains. Martyred."

"Crucified?" Irene asked, sitting up.

"In a way. The savagery of the West is only equaled by the savagery of the East."

"And the savagery of the middle, known as the Inquisition," Godfrey put in, his eyes glittering with courtroom indignation.

"The most savage man I knew," Holmes put in, "was a butterfly collector. One who would catch, kill, and pin beauty can never be trusted."

"What do you know about savages?" Irene asked him suspiciously.

Holmes smiled faintly. "I cabled your friend Buffalo Bill in Paris, where his Wild West Show still enchants visitors to the ongoing World's Fair there. He and I are fellow 'campaigners' now, after the events of last spring. He and his able aide, Red Tomahawk, have answered my question about any links between eastern North American tribes and the Jesuits. As it happens, eight French Jesuits were tormented and ultimately murdered by the tribes they went to convert in the early seventeenth century. The most famous of these was the sainted Isaac Jogues, a French literature student turned Jesuit who had been savagely tortured. His fingers had been literally hacked and chewed off among other gruesome tortures."

Irene was stunned, but not convinced. "The Indians tortured and killed those long-ago Jesuits. Why should one now do the same in the name of the Jesuits and the Ultramontanes?"

"Reparation for the sins of the fathers," Holmes answered. "This modern savage is likely a devout convert, seeking to atone for his people's past."

"But he repeated it!" Quentin said. "Good God! He ended up torturing priests to death again. For what? Gold, not God."

Holmes shook his head. "He believes what he's told. I don't know how or where these renegades found him, but they've made good use of him. The Indians called those early Jesuits Blackrobes. You've seen for yourself that this shadowy group has adopted that dress. This Indian may take them for ghosts of the eight martyred Jesuits. Religious belief is a strange, almost hypnotic condition."

"We humans can be an angry, vicious lot," Quentin said, "no matter the clime or the breed. So what were these men really, Irene? Savage-masters? Political malcontents? Murderers? Thieves? And how could you persuade them to trust you?"

"A bit of all that, I think. They wanted to know what I knew. All about Lola. All of this is about Lola, really."

"She's dead, Irene!" I objected.

"Dead, but not forgotten. Isn't that what we'd all want to happen to us?"

"Not I," said I.

"Nor I," Godfrey added.

Irene and Mr. Holmes kept amazingly quiet on the subject, and Quentin was too distracted to notice the byplay, perhaps by memories of Pink and her mysterious mission!

"So," I asked, "who, exactly, were these men who fought so savagely in the slaughterhouse?"

Irene thought for a long while, a purely dramatic effect, I believe. "The heirs of the Ultramontanes, and the Jesuits, and Lola Montez."

"Now," said Godfrey, "there's a union made in hell."

"How," Sherlock Holmes asked her, "were you able to communicate with them?"

Irene tapped the ash off her cigarette into a crystal bowl. "In German. Nell will recall that was the court language of Bohemia, if not the native one. It was also the language of Bavaria. I've sung in German and can speak it, not beautifully, but sufficiently well."

"These were Bavarians?" Godfrey asked with some incredulity.

Irene nodded.

He paused to consider. "The current state of Bavaria is delicate, and the country is in great financial and political peril of being utterly consumed by the Austrian Empire. King Otto is confined to a madhouse. Prince Luitpold, the regent, sits uneasily on the throne in Otto's stead. People respect the late King Ludwig the First, despite his long-ago dalliance with Lola. In fact, they're quite sentimental about his reign now, more than twenty years after his abdication. Yet the house of Wittalsbach is debased by the latter generations' madness: Ludwig the Second's castle-building mania, for instance, and rumors of syphilis behind the insanity. Some Bavarians recall Lola Montez as a liberating force. Others would burn her at the stake as a seductive sorceress. Still, her name has power. What did these so-called Ultramontanes want of her?"

"Money," Irene said shortly. "They want the wealth they believe she took out of Bavaria and, ultimately, California: jewels and gold. I tried to convince them that the record shows that she auctioned off her jewels before leaving California. As for the gold they're obsessed about reclaiming, they must mean the money she made in California with what they consider Bavarian capital. But who knows what became of it? Alva Vanderbilt with her balls and Fifth Avenue palaces had nothing on Lola. She spent like a sultan when she had the means, and more so when she didn't."

"Jewels and gold." Sherlock Holmes made a great show of tapping the used tobacco from the bowl of his pipe into a crystal bowl.

Even I could see that something in this recital had struck a chord with him.

"And," Irene added, "after speaking long with me and learning of my own quest, they were not averse to returning to Bavaria with an untainted heir. Or heiress, rather. One could argue paternal claims on the now-revered Ludwig the First, even if the maternal claims were on the notorious Lola Montez. An honest opera singer, an artiste even, rather than a faux Spanish dancer, held some appeal. The Bavarians were ever a musical people, and perhaps Lola's lack of talent as much as her lack of morals enraged them."

I sat bolt upright. "Irene! You let them think you were that heir? You let them think you were the daughter of Lola and Ludwig? That you could produce the jewels and gold of Lola Montez?"

"Neither jewels," Sherlock Holmes said, "nor gold. Isn't that right, Mrs. Norton?"

"The jewels were sold—for a song, unfortunately. I found that fact during Nell's and my day of reading about the many Lives—I should say Lies—of Lola. I can't go to California and reclaim them from their buyers, even if I could prove a legitimate interest in them. Gold is even more of a challenge. It's heavy and bulky. It doesn't travel well. Not by sea, without notice. From California to the East? How? Robbery was a constant threat along the routes to and from California. So. How was all this gold brought out, even presuming Lola had it? These pseudo-Ultramontanes are not Jesuits, from what I learned, but from among the college students who railed against King Ludwig the First and Lola for their liberalizing ways thirty years ago. They're now latter-day dreamers. That doesn't make them any less demented or lethal. They aspire to impose their old, long-lost order on today's Bavaria. Assuredly, they're responsible for the death of Father Hawks and the torture of Father Edmonds."

Holmes nodded and exhaled smoke. "Father Hawks, as her deathbed confessor, was the last man alive to share the final moments of Lola Montez. He would be expected to know something of her 'lost treasure.'"

"How awful!" I said with a shudder. "Innocents tormented for information they never knew."

"Or perhaps never knew they had," Holmes said. "Lola may have had more means remaining to her than anyone suspected."

"Possibly," Irene said. "She reportedly was eager to keep her mother from claiming any future inheritance. So Lola signed any other future income, beyond the twelve hundred dollars she left to settle debts and to the Magdalen Asylum, to the people of Bavaria."

Godfrey shook his head. "Too vague to stand up in court."

"So," I realized, "these fiends aren't completely mad to dream of finding or claiming something. Still, to drive dagger blades through men's hands—"

"Speaking of such horrors," Irene said to Holmes, "how did you intend to avoid the fate of the fathers?"

I glanced at her, horrified. "They were going to torture a Pinkerton?"

"Indeed. Had you and Godfrey not arrived so fortuitously, and so noisily, we might even now be discussing this with Mr. Holmes in Bellevue."

I stared aghast at the man serenely puffing away on a pipe. "But . . . you play the violin—though poorly, in my opinion. How could you risk your hands?"

"Apparently such a tragedy would have been a boon to amateur music critics everywhere." He glanced at Irene. "I was assuming that Mrs. Norton would abandon her impersonation of a greedy pretender to the Bavarian throne in time to avert such an incident."

"And if she had not?" I demanded.

"I assume you lack faith in me, not your boon companion. I also had a trick or two up my sleeves, being alerted early to these madmen's favorite form of persuasion."

At that he made the gesture of a gentleman shaking his jacket sleeves down to expose the fineness of his cuffs, a strange act of vanity in one whose thoughts were always so lofty.

His action revealed two sharp steel blades on springs.

Irene laughed and clapped her hands. "You have borrowed a trick from my old tutors the card sharps. And I would have intervened, but was hoping I wouldn't have to. As long as I appeared to have an interest in being one of them, Consuelo was safe."

"How so?" I asked.

Irene shrugged modestly, always a dangerous sign. "Once I was accepted as the lost ruler of Bavaria, I told them, I would reveal Consuelo as my daughter, given at birth by Madame Restell to the Vanderbilts. Thus Bavaria would have a legitimately illegitimate claim on the Vanderbilt millions."

"That's impossible!" I said.

"Is it, Nell? Madame Restell committed 'suicide' in 1877, the year Consuelo was born. Who's to say madame's brutal death wasn't murder, timed to conceal the fact that an infant was sold to the wealthiest family in New York at the same time."

"Even more preposterous!" I continued.

"Yes," Irene agreed, "but the mad Bavarian Ultramontanes believed it." She sighed. "Haven't we learned, Nell, in our recent investigations, that parenthood is an easy thing to feign?"

"Amen," Quentin said. "Babies can be bought on the streets of New York for ten dollars and up. When one looks at the mental and moral state of first families here and abroad, one becomes certain that more among us are changelings than we might think."

"How do you know this, Quentin?" I asked, but Godfrey answered for him.

"Look at Bavaria, Nell, with its reigning family gone to seed and a regent on the throne. Natural decay has brought on this insane attempt to reclaim glory days of three decades ago."

"Mr. Holmes!" I never dreamed I would be appealing to him. "Surely all this can't be so?"

"No, it cannot, Miss Huxleigh." He stood, ready to take his leave. "I will shortly be able to tell you all just how much of it is so.

"Mrs. Norton." He bowed in Irene's direction. "It's pleasing to learn that you'd rather shoot revolutionaries than see my humble self mutilated. I regret that your innate humanity cost you the throne of Bavaria."

"Ah," Irene said, waving her cigarette holder like a scepter, "I'd already lost Bohemia. What is one more minuscule European principality?"

He smiled. Tightly.

"I may call upon you all again, but this time it will be for the denouement rather than the climax."

"Will you expect us to applaud?" I asked.

"No, Miss Huxleigh, I will expect you to be surprised."

54

Shocking Connections

~~~~~

*The character of the Spanish dancer, whose pas and pose have been
more than a match for a Ministry, upheld by all the influence of the
Jesuit, is better known than her history.... Wherever she appears,
she is in the midst of an imbroglio.*

—*ILLUSTRATED LONDON NEWS,* 1847

Godfrey, of course, retired that evening to Irene's bedroom.

They rose very late the next morning.

By then I'd already availed myself of the hotel's bathing facilities
adjacent to our rooms.

Irene ordered hot coffee, tea, and pastries, then assigned me to accept them while she and Godfrey attended to their morning ablutions.

This left me fretting over cooling pots of coffee and hot water until they
deigned to stroll back into our common parlor sometime after noon, both still
wearing their dressing gowns.

Irene's snarled locks, however, were one smooth dark river again, and their
recently smudged skins were pink with cleansing and contentment.

While I had my suspicions, as a former governess I couldn't but be cheered
to consider that cleanliness was indeed cheek by jowl with godliness.

"And what did you do all morning, Nell?" Irene asked as she sipped her
cooling coffee.

I could hardly admit I'd spend the morning, and most of the night before it, trying to translate Madame Restell's diary to prove that Irene did not have an illegitimate connection to the Vanderbilt clan and that Consuelo had only a legitimate claim on the same family. I had determined very little.

"Was Lola acquainted with the Commodore?" Irene asked next, as if recognizing the source of my silence.

I tried to leap ahead of her agile brain. "As you pointed out, he died in '77, the same year that Madame Restell perished."

"And that Consuelo was born."

"And that Consuelo was born. But that can't mean anything."

Godfrey begged to differ with me in his polite way. "We like to say in court that there are no coincidences, Nell, just evidence that hasn't yet been properly linked. It's suggestive that 1877 was such a busy year of death and birth among these key figures."

Before I could open my mouth to object to such blatant speculation, someone knocked on the door.

Since my friends had full cups and saucers in their hands, I rose to answer.

I had been hoping for Quentin. I would have been resigned to see Mr. Holmes.

Instead I faced Nellie Bly, as fresh as the daisy nodding over the brim of her yellow straw hat.

"'Morning." She gazed keenly into the room, then her blue-gray eyes widened. "I see another Norton has honored the U.S. with his presence. Welcome to the New World, Godfrey."

He was up, politely bowing to the intruder. "You must forgive us, Pink. Irene—"

"Rises late. I know. A theatrical habit." Pink strolled in past me. "I myself was out late last night, so understand your disinclination to bustle out early this morning. Unfortunately, I have work to do."

"That can't be visiting us," Irene said, smiling to soften the sting.

"Actually, yes." Pink turned around to survey me as well as the Nortons. "I'm surprised your cohorts aren't here."

"Cohorts?" Irene asked.

"Sherlock Holmes, for one, but I'd expect him to be out and about early no matter the case." She glanced at me. "And Quentin. I'd hoped to catch him here. He's doing some work for me and we need to finish our investigation."

"What work?" I demanded.

"Oh, Nell. It's a secret, of course. He hasn't gone and hinted anything to you, now, has he?"

"Quentin is discreet." My answer sounded hedging, but I wasn't about to admit I had no idea what Quentin would be doing in the company of Pink, or her pseudonym Nellie Bly.

"Glad to hear that we agree about Quentin's discretion. Well, if he's not here, I'll call at his hotel. I can use him on a story I'm doing, if you don't need him for whatever vague and dark business you're engaged upon."

I was quick to retort. "No, he better serves us attending to whatever vague and dark business *you* are engaged upon."

Pink only laughed. "All I can say is, Nell, that we make a most convincing man and wife."

Quentin in thrall to Nellie Bly! Quentin at the beck and call of Nellie Bly! Quentin . . . courting Nellie Bly!

Those thoughts sat on the back of my neck like a great, black vulture that afternoon as I moved the papers and books about Lola Montez and Madame Restell's cryptic diary around the surface of the round table, desperately seeking inspiration.

Godfrey, a man of supernatural good sense, had betaken himself away from our rooms on some such feeble excuse as needing shaving cream because he'd left Bavaria in such a hurry.

What he was in haste to do was escape my black mood, brought on by the shocking audacity of Pink entering our lions' den to flaunt her claims on Quentin's time, energy, and attention.

Once already Quentin had been lured from the toils of Pink back into our camp. I must provide reason for him to make that change in obligations permanent!

Irene came over to gaze down upon the pile of confusing documents, then rested an encouraging hand on my shoulder.

I pushed the papers away in a rare fit of temper.

"I can make no sense of it! Lola Montez could have been, or have gone, or have done anything, anywhere. The woman was beyond amazing. An expert shot. Utterly fearless to the point of facing off a maddened mob. A femme fatale. A political idealist. A dreadful dancer. An amazing 'artiste.' A harlot. A heroine. She may be the mother of Queen Victoria, or Tiny Tim, for all I know, and for all she claims in her astounding autobiography."

Irene's hand never left my right shoulder, which forced the vulture claws to edge a bit to the left.

"She's a legend; face it, Nell. We'll never know the entire truth. And I don't think she would have wanted us to."

"What would she have wanted!?"

"The peace that she indeed found at the end, and the fight she waged getting there. Take either one away from her, and she is not a whole woman."

I braced my face on my fists, like a spoiled child. "Call me not a whole woman, but I can't stand Pink lording it over us, and Quentin."

"She's had a bitter pill to swallow: smothering a story of international sensation. It goes against her grain."

"Pink goes against *my* grain."

"Quentin chafes as much. Why do you think he was so eager to join in our risky expedition to the slaughter yards in search of rogue Jesuits?"

"That's another thing! Even Lola's invective against the Jesuits rings false. Yes, they were a force in Europe thirty years ago, but nowadays—?"

"Quite true. These greedy, brutal creatures here in New York seem to be the demented remnants of men fighting a long-lost cause. All of those whose faces I saw—and there were more whose faces I didn't see, for they weren't all at the slaughterhouse that night—were sixty years old or more."

"Goodness, they were doddering!"

"No, these men were quite vigorous still, Nell, and possessed of feverish political passion. Remember, King Ludwig was sixty when he met Lola, and she not yet thirty."

"He was behaving badly for a man of his maturity as well. Didn't you learn anything specific about these creatures, during your time among them?"

"Like all conspirators, they'd adapted noms de guerre. They referred to each other by the names of professions or crafts. One was called Woodcutter, another Baker. And one was called Doctor."

"He must have been an elevated type!" I said derisively, for none of these pseudonyms struck me as apropos. "Butcher," would have been more like it."

"Of course," Irene said slowly, "all these names were used in their German form, not English. I found that jogging my memory. It reminded me of someone we'd read or heard about in connection with Lola's California stay."

"We heard of dozens such people. I'll give Lola Montez one thing: she knew everybody there was to know in her day."

"Something . . . Lotta said."

"About a woodcutter, a butcher, a baker; they all sound like they're out of a fairy tale."

"I was thinking of the Doktor. 'Herr Doktor,' they said."

"Any doctor involved in such atrocities is not worthy of the title!" I was about to fulminate further when I remembered what Irene was trying to recall. "Oh." Then I had to decide if I wanted to say it, given the awful ramifications.

"What is it, Nell. You've remembered something."

Of course she'd ask until I said something, and I'm not adept at falsehoods.

"Lola's friend in Grass Valley, after she'd divorced Patrick Hull," I said sullenly.

"Friend?"

"Well, probably more than that, to be frank! The man she rode into the mountains with, who never came back. Wasn't he a German doctor?"

"No!" Irene straightened up. "No. He was German, but he allowed himself to be called Doctor, instead of by his inherited title of baron, which of course meant nothing in American society, especially in the gold fields." Her voice deepened. "You remember what family name he went by there?"

"Adler," I admitted. "It's a stupid coincidence."

Irene sat down, slowly, in an empty chair at the table.

"She seemed to mourn his death, Lotta said, and left Grass Valley not long after. But then I would have been born sooner than I was told. . . . I'm not sure I'm any more ready to admit to my real age than Lola was, if that's the case."

"Irene, this is ridiculous! If that man Adler was your father and if the Ultramontanes here in New York are following a leader who goes by the same professional title he used then, he'd have to be . . . oh, my, at least sixty years old."

"I could have been 'betraying' my own father."

"Did he look anything like you? For you certainly don't resemble Lola."

"I don't know, Nell. Those men wore slouch hats and high-collared long coats. I never bothered trying to see or remember their faces, because they were always obscured . . . by the dark of night, or inside the slaughterhouse."

She turned to me, her features alight with a flood of new speculations. "If he was the same 'Dr. Adler' from Grass Valley, forget the issue of whether he could have fathered me. The fact is, he vanished, supposedly in a hunting accident, was never seen again in Grass Valley. You know what that means?"

"That he didn't necessarily have to be dead at all. He may have deserted Lola and she reported his 'accident' to save face."

"Exactly. And . . . he may have deserted her because he had followed her there from Germany and had learned what he wished to know, or he could no longer spend the time in such an obscure outpost. If he was indeed a German baron, he might have been needed back in Bavaria attempting to rein in Ludwig's errant heir to the throne."

"He was a spy even then!"

Irene nodded, her lips a thin grim line.

"But what did they want?"

"I said that I think their cause is deluded. That doesn't mean that what they seek isn't real, though."

"What? Lola's gold and jewels?"

Irene sat opposite me, then nodded seriously.

"Gold and jewels." The words lingered on her tongue. "Lola's gold and jewels, all gathered from her time with the king and from the money she made off that notorious liaison for the rest of her life. Where did they go? The jewels sold for nothing in California, say several accounts. But where were Lola's considerable gold-field investment profits by the end of her life? The biographies are vague, and you haven't made much headway deciphering Lola's lost papers. Was the money also gone and lost, worth nothing? Value shifts with time. What's priceless in one era is pathetic in the next. Yet—could she have invested her holdings through a friend?"

"Friend?"

"She had many prominent and wealthy friends in New York during her glory days, even if they were utterly absent at her end."

I sat up as if suddenly deposited on a hat pin. "Vanderbilt. The Commodore. The old man. Didn't he know her?"

"Yes. And that might be what made the Ultramontanes fix their sights on Six-sixty Fifth Avenue and its residents. I have an idea. I only hope Mr. Gordon is still in New York."

"Mr. Gordon? The absentee owner of the *New York Herald,* a rival paper to Pink's precious *World?*"

Irene nodded. "Exactly the one. Thank God it isn't Pink's paper. We must try to see him again at once."

"On our own?"

"What else? Would you want Pink along?"

I shook my head.

"Quentin?"

I paused. Not right now. I shook my head.

"Godfrey?"

"Maybe—"

"I agree. He is the most agreeable partner of the lot at the moment. God-frey, however, being so agreeable, wouldn't wish to intrude on the investigation we've begun, but not finished. However . . . Sherlock Holmes would."

"Not him, either!"

"Then it is you and me, Nell. I think we can solve this riddle before Holmes reaches his promised and 'surprising' denouement. What do you think?"

I gazed at the snarl of papers that encompassed a peripatetic life of forty years and more mysteries and recent gore than would furnish a collection of Edgar Allen Poe tales.

"I think that we have to try."

55

Of Commodores and Queens

✦

Washington, D.C., November 3, 1854
My Dear Lola, Since our last meeting in San Francisco,
I have been most actively engaged in securing aid from wealthy
Southern gentlemen in our project.... When we succeed, and we will,
remember you are to be Empress of California. Have sent by the
Steamer $50,000 to San Francisco.
—LETTER FOUND IN 1914 AMONG THREE NEEDLEWORK SAMPLERS BELIEVED TO HAVE
BEEN DONE BY LOLA

Mr. James Gordon Bennett was still in New York, though not for much longer, we were warned. He was only too glad to receive Mrs. Irene Adler Norton. And myself, as an afterthought.

This time we sat down in that busy office off the madhouse room of shirtsleeved men spitting streams of liquid tobacco into brass vases on the floor.

"Paris?" He eyed Irene as if she did the cancan there. "You reside near Paris? You didn't mention that before. I do as well."

"Perhaps we're neighbors," Irene suggested, just what such a lascivious man liked to hear, and didn't she know it!

"I run the paper from Paris proper or from my yacht."

"Then we can't possibly be neighbors."

"We still might be. My yacht is three hundred feet long. You only have to bring your own sweet little yacht alongside and drop anchor."

"I don't like getting my feet wet." Irene refrained from the Lola trick of flouncing up the hems of her skirts, although Mr. Bennett obviously would have enjoyed it. "My current interests don't involve Paris, however, but New York City. Have you heard of a woman named Lola Montez?"

"Heard of her? I'd give my right . . . elbow to have known her. What a pistol! Unfortunately, I was off at school in France when Lola took New York by storm, so my father had that honor."

"What did he think of her?" I asked, for surely a newspaperman would be a reliable source.

"He dined out on stories about Lola for years. Some lads like to hear tales about giant-slayers, but I preferred the works of Lola. My father met her in Paris in the early '50s, where she was queen for a season, just after the Jockey Club gave her a splendid dinner where she was the only woman among a hundred fifty men. He went to one of her Saturday night soirees. How I longed to be among the East Indian princes, Russian officers, French and Spanish noblemen and diplomats that my father described."

"She ran a salon?" Irene asked.

"She ran a circus. She was showing off her pair of inch-and-half-long pistols that evening. I'd give a lot to have that souvenir. A jeweled box to keep them in, complete with tiny bullet molds, ramrods, cap and ball box. The young East Indian princes shot them off at a wax candle the whole night. There was a German pianist and a Neapolitan vocalist, and Lola herself singing and playing the piano when she wasn't smoking one cigarette after another and casting it away after a few puffs. Apparently her habit with men as well."

"I wonder," Irene said, "given the lung ailment and pneumonia that killed her, which was the most dangerous, men or tobacco?"

"Men, madam, always men."

"Did your father say anything else about her?"

"Oh course. At length. Let's see. He said she spoke seven languages that night, including Persian, that she was a dainty lady to her fingertips, even when smoking. That her knowledge of human nature and politics would provide her keep if she simply lectured on European affairs, in any language.

"Her beauty and air of camaraderie rendered her 'irresistible.' He praised the 'startling brilliancy' of her eyes, the grace of her motions, and the harmonic proportions of her form. I tell you, I dreamed of her many a night. My father was quite the booster of La Lola, although after she came to New York she managed to irritate him at times. Still, the *New York Herald* usually treated her right. Father had an eye for the comely ankle himself. Why are you interested?"

"We're thinking of writing a new biography."

The "we're" caused him to glance in my direction, then quickly away again. I suspect I was not a candidate for the cancan in his mind.

He chuckled and leaned back in his chair. "Lola Montez. Now, there's a woman who couldn't have too many biographies. As if taking old New York by storm in the early '50s wasn't enough, she had to dash off to the gold fields of California, and later Australia."

"The gold fields offered many opportunities to entertainers in those days," Irene said. "The exclusively male society of miners made for a rough, violent life. Many longed for influences of the softer sort. I hear they threw bags of gold dust and nuggets at the performers' feet, especially the children."

"There was plenty of gold to throw around in those days. But New York is not the place to inquire into Gold Rush Days."

"No," Irene agreed. "I just wondered if when Lola first hit New York . . . first appeared here, if she encountered other prominent men of your father's era."

"Lord, yes!" He leaned back in his golden oak office chair, grinning. "All of 'em. Meeting prominent men was her God-given talent."

"And was the Commodore among them?"

"The Commodore? You mean old Cornelius the First? Of course. He was of my father's generation. Rich as Croesus, whoever that was, and a randy old goat with pockets lined in solid gold. The old fellow was not one to miss pinching a garter of Miss Lola's."

The word "randy" was unknown to me, but it didn't make Irene blink an eyelash. She stood hastily, though, as Mr. Bennett's hands edged across the desk towards hers.

"Thank you so much, Mr. Bennett. Biography is such a demanding art form. I appreciate your candor."

"And I appreciate your . . . interest."

He would have risen to see us out, but Irene left in a whirlwind of skirts and hat brim, with me fast on her retreat.

"What a strange, oblique man," I said when were we once again in the smoke-choked outer office. "Yet this is the second time we've encountered a second-generation heir of a family tradition here. The other was the second Bishop Potter."

"This is the second Mr. Bennett the newspaper man, all right, and not an improvement on the first. A playboy," Irene declared. "Why do you think he lives in Europe? Too hot for New York. And despite what he implies, far more profligate than his upright founding father or even the Commodore, who I imagine was more inference than action."

"Oh. I read in one of the news articles about a Bennett who drove a coach and four, well, naked up Riverside Drive and was horsewhipped on the steps of the public library."

"Were the four horses naked, or Mr. Bennett? It makes quite a difference." Irene smiled. "And one wonders if the whipper was Lola. I suppose not. Those incidents might have done to send him abroad, all right. But it's not *his* father I'm interested in."

"If it's Commodore Vanderbilt, he sounds almost as bad as Bennett the Younger."

"The Vanderbilt founding father was a crude old coot, as we say in America."

"That doesn't sound at all respectful, Irene."

"Why do you think it took until the third Vanderbilt generation and daughter-in-law Alva, that steely southern belle, to make the family socially acceptable to the New York Four Hundred? But I rather relish the honest frontier flint of the Commodore that refused to bow to pretension. And so, I think, did Lola Montez."

"They knew each other well?"

"Evidently. And I believe that they served each other well."

"She was his mistress . . . and you think you're their daughter!?"

"No. Even better! I think she was his means, and that I shall be their unexpected progeny of opportunity. They both would love it, I'm sure."

Irene winked at me as we waited for the cab she'd "whistled up" to reach the curb.

"We must stop at Brentano's again, Nell, and read up on the late Commodore Cornelius Vanderbilt. You *will* be kind to the young clerk who was so taken with you the other day? I know you pooh-pooh such advantages, but I'm never one to let a promising lead slip past me. . . ."

Irene continued to muse about these unpleasant subjects without consulting my state of mind as we established ourselves in the hansom's cozy boxed compartment.

"Ah, Nell," she said finally with a sigh as she settled in. "Pink will be purple with jealousy when she learns the truth of the story we've been pursuing without her. And without Quentin."

"Perhaps," I said, "but what has *she* been pursuing *with* Quentin?"

56

The Bartered Baby

※

Bly, in the meantime, was back from her summer of playful reporting and ready to claim her piece of the juiciest scandal yet ... with a harrowing report on the baby-buying trade in New York. ... Bly posed as a would-be mother ... found in at least four locations that she could buy a newborn from a broker for anywhere from ten to twenty-five dollars with no questions asked.

—BROOK KROEGER, NELLIE BLY: A LIFE

⊰ FROM NELLIE BLY'S JOURNAL ⊱

"You seem tired," I commented to Quentin as we took a horsecar to the bottom of the island to finish our loathsome transactions.

"In the service of milady," he answered with a little ironic bow.

We again wore the cheap wedding rings I'd found, but I felt no more sure of him than any wise bride should be of a real bridegroom.

What grim business, buying babies. Quentin's face matched the enterprise.

"You'll have people from the foundling home there to meet us when we purchase each one?" he asked.

"Don't worry. You won't be required to handle even one infant. Just dole out the money."

"I suppose that's what many a real husband is told on receiving custody of an infant he has no idea is a bartered baby. You have to admit that the unfortunate Hamilton is to be commended for at least attempting to do the right thing."

"Perhaps. Yet how could he have accepted his harlot of a mistress as a wife?"

"He meant well, Pink. He tried to be honorable. Few gentlemen of his class would have even considered that. Don't ridicule him for being deceived. Perhaps he saw this as his last chance at fatherhood."

"That is so untypical."

"What? That women can be bad mothers, and men good fathers?"

"That isn't the way I've experienced it."

Quentin shook his head. "I wonder when you'll see that all your campaigns for stories are an attempt to redeem your personal past."

"What a strange thing to say! I've never been an overworked shopgirl, or mad, or abducted into white slavery. I've never sold a child."

"But you could have been any of those." His eyes softened for the first time as he regarded me. "That you aren't is purely to your credit alone."

"Alone. I've been alone, yes."

After that, there didn't seem to be much more to say, or to be said.

But I thought over his words, and wondered if the ills I chased on the streets of New York could be the phantoms of the downtrodden past I'd almost had.

Mother Hubbard held out a scrap of tattered yellow blanket and the red-faced scrap of humanity bawling inside it. Poor mite, the weave was rough on that as-yet-unblemished skin.

Mother Hubbard in her black bonnet and cape seemed a grandmother born, smiling under her white waves of hair.

"That'll be twelve dollars and not a penny less."

A wave of strange nausea prevented me from speaking for an instant.

During that moment, Quentin counted out the price in two-dollar bills.

The child bawled, sputtered, and coughed in my arms, until I feared it would expire on the spot.

I was aware of an alien helpless feeling. Not that I hadn't tended and held my several younger siblings, but none had seemed as scrawny and demanding as this.

Quentin surprised me by lifting the featherweight burden from my arms.

"You'd better have your hands free for making notes," he said softly as we left Mother Hubbard's crib.

Children . . . dirty, barefoot, rag-clad children, screamed and ran rings around us, reclaiming each cobblestone of the street we left vacant behind us for their crude playground.

"Where are the foundling-home people?" Quentin asked.

I looked around. That eternal screaming and the incessant barking dogs were bringing on the headache.

After we passed the intersection, I recognized a bonneted face quite like Mother Hubbard's: old, wrinkled, dressed in the fashions of a decade or more past.

"Miss Bly?" she asked, hurrying to relieve Quentin of his ridiculously small burden. "This is one of the sold ones? We'll keep track of the lot, so you may write of their progress."

"Write of their progress?" I asked, confused.

This elderly angel in widow's black smiled. Sadly. "Whether they live or not."

I gazed at the worn cloth and the already-worn little bud of a face inside it. Red, bawling. Hungry? Or dying?

Quentin pressed a bill into her gloved hand, the face of Franklin. Fifty dollars. "For the child's care."

Would it make a difference, that princely donation? Neither of us would likely know.

As the good woman left, I leaned against the dusty red brick of a tenement. "Three more to buy."

"It's not the buying," he said. "It's the cost of selling. If it's any comfort, it's done all over the world."

It was no comfort.

57

The Belmont Stakes

~∾⊱∽~

[The widowed Kate Warne was] a slender, brown-haired woman, graceful in her movements and self-possessed. Her features, although not what could be called handsome, were decidedly of an intellectual cast . . . her face was honest, which would cause one in distress instinctively to select her as a confidante.

—AMERICA'S FIRST FEMALE DETECTIVE, 1856, ALLEN PINKERTON, *REMINISCENCES*

"Godfrey," Irene welcomed her spouse when he returned to our suite late that afternoon. "Nell and I are so cross and cross-eyed from reading about people long dead. Where can you take us to dine tonight that will be fresh and interesting?"

"Where can I best win your favor . . . so that you two will ask the favor of me that you have in mind, after your cross afternoon of reading about people long dead?"

Irene's delighted laughter echoed up to the electric light chandelier.

"Always one step ahead of us poor plodding females. What do you have in mind, husband, dear? After all, it's *your* brain we'll be picking at, even if it isn't on the menu."

"Irene!" I remonstrated, but I was ignored.

"You aren't strangers to Delmonico's, I gather," he said, including me in the glance he cast around. "I've had a talk with Belmont this afternoon. What about the Maison D'Orée? It's not as famed as Delmonico's, but more elegant."

"Whatever you say," Irene said.

Hmmm.

So I found myself considering B. Altman's best ready-made tea gown for dinner that night. We would be a foursome: Irene and Godfrey, and myself. And this Belmont man.

I now realized he was the Rothschild agent here in New York, and thus a colleague of Godfrey's. I also realized that I was the odd woman out, and would have to serve as Mr. Belmont's . . . dinner partner.

Ordinarily, I'd have been quite undone by having to make small talk with a figure of old New York society, one of the enormously wealthy Belmonts.

However, tonight I felt more than up to it. In fact, I asked Irene to lend me, for the occasion the one Worth gown she had brought on this voyage, despite my earnest arguments against it.

If Pink wouldn't stop at luring Quentin to aid her in journalistic enterprises of a mysterious nature, who was I to snub a Belmont?

The gown was fashioned in a spectacular lavender–light green shot silk, velvet-dotted with lilac, with falls of blond lace at the three-quarter-length sleeves and the V-shaped low bodice. Since I had deigned to wear Worth, Irene decided that I must live up to my gown. She lavished all her theatrical effects upon my coiffure and accessories, so I returned to the parlor as Cinderella with a fairy godmother who had an open account at Maison Worth in Paris.

"My goodness, Nell," Godfrey said, rising in his city-formal black lounge suit at my entrance.

"Your goodness had nothing to do with it," I sniffed. "I owe it all to Irene's good credit at Maison Worth."

He smiled ruefully. "And her good credit it is. Repeatedly. My dear."

He kissed her cheek as Irene appeared in my blue Liberty of London gown, which she had bought for me.

Irene looked charming in the flowing girlish elegance of a Liberty gown, which relied more on fabric than corseted fit for its effect, rather like a Kate Greenaway drawing of children's dress. I, however, looked . . . goodness . . . formidable. At least I was debauched enough to notice.

Irene laid her swansdown cape over my puff-sleeved shoulders. "Mr. Belmont is the key, Nell," she whispered. "Only he can overcome the advantage Sherlock Holmes has in this situation. He must become sympathetic to our cause. Godfrey he already has much in common with. A feminine persuasion may make all the difference in the rest."

Perhaps I'd been reading too much about Lola Montez.

I'd actually come to think I possessed a bit of feminine persuasion myself.

This was a night made in fairy land. Godfrey had a Gurney waiting for us: two seats facing each other. We rattled off under the festive line of electric lights bracketing Broadway.

By the time we picked up Mr. Belmont on Fifth Avenue, we had been chattering like children, catching up on each other's adventures worlds apart.

We grew sober when Mr. Belmont joined us, but by the time we reached Maison D'Orée, we were a festive party again. He was such an urbane and amusing man, though old enough to be my father. Indeed, his son Oliver Hazard Perry Belmont was the man about town in the family now, he said, and quite the favorite at all the society balls and soirees.

He naturally attended to me as we left the carriage for the restaurant, with such discreet aplomb that I was at once both completely at ease and completely myself.

The dining room gleamed like a cabochon ruby. Polished exotic woods of red and purple hue, damask tablecloths, candlelight everywhere. And the food, though exceedingly strange to me, was also wonderfully flavored. Quentin was right. American cuisine surpassed the English and, in my lone and lowly opinion, the French.

After dinner there were exquisite ices. My dining partners resorted to coffee, brandy, and cigars to ruin the enchanting aftertaste, but I was used to such silliness.

Mr. Belmont frowned for the first time that night as he exhaled a stream of cigar smoke toward the candlelit chandelier above us.

"It's good that you were here, Godfrey, during that nasty business involving little Miss Vanderbilt." He glanced at Irene. "And one might even say providential that your wife was responsible for foiling the abduction."

"Well, obviously," I said. "It was intolerable that a child be subjected to such an ordeal."

He smiled at me. "Your protective zeal does you much honor, Miss Huxleigh, but, less obviously, you and your friends' role in this affair also enhances the Rothschild interests we all have served in our time."

I was not used to being put on an equal footing with Godfrey and Irene in their Rothschild assignments . . . and with a man like August Belmont! So I said nothing, as I was quite speechless.

"How so, Mr. Belmont?" Irene asked, tapping the ash from the end of her petite cigar with a gesture of exquisite delicacy. "I can't see that we've done anything out of the usual here."

He laughed at that. "Of course not. Nothing unusual for you! That's the wonder of it. Many's the time in Paris I've heard Baron Alphonse boast over a glass of brandy, extolling his foresight in winning you three to his service. He is always relating some amazing escapade that you have engineered."

Irene and Godfrey and I exchanged glances. We had no idea we had so entertained the Baron de Rothschild.

"And now I see why," Mr. Belmont said, leaning forward. "It's quite amazing. Mrs. Norton and Miss Huxleigh are in New York and happen to stumble upon a plot to kidnap the daughter of the wealthiest man in America. And you, Godfrey, assigned to godforsaken Bavaria on a matter of necessary but tedious political fence-mending . . . you sense at once—at once!—that you are needed in America and arrive in the nick of time to convince Vanderbilt to trust the matter of his daughter's kidnapping to you and yours. And then you promptly rescue her. If I hadn't seen it, I wouldn't have believed it." He eyed us all, eyes brimming with bemusement and laughter. "And the most astounding part is that you think nothing of what you've accomplished."

"We did what we must. . . ." Irene began.

"But it was all unexpected. You are all totally surprising. Baron Alphonse can find a dozen men like myself: astute at business, wealthy, well connected. We serve him, and ourselves, well. We try to keep this fractured old world on an even keel, for the affairs of first families in any part of the world go better without chaos. But we're rather predictable. You, on the other hand, make things happen because you are not. I salute you."

With that he lifted his glass. Godfrey and Irene followed suit, and I quickly seized my water goblet.

"To you all," Mr. Belmont said.

"To the Rothschilds," said Godfrey.

"To the unpredictable," Irene said, predictably.

"To . . . Consuelo," said I.

"Indeed," Mr. Belmont said, and downed a swallow of brandy.

We all drank, and then Irene set down her brandy glass and leaned forward. The candlelight played hide and seek in the highlights of her hair and danced off the diamond pin of a key and a musical clef Godfrey had given her, which nestled as a hair jewel near her temple. She looked beautiful enough to tempt an archangel from heaven, and now was the moment she had waited for during the entire evening.

"There is something we need to know," she told Mr. Belmont.

"Ask anything." He sounded as though he meant it, poor bedazzled man.

"Consuelo's kidnappers wanted something the Vanderbilts have, but we're not sure what. Of course most of their wealth must be in bank vaults, but are you aware of any other places of possible safekeeping?"

He sat back to consider. "Alva has enough jewels to be queen if America ever adopts a royal family. I assume the house Hunt built her on Fifth Avenue must have several internal safes or vaults. One for the silver, of course. And several for her jewels. Is that the kind of thing you meant?"

"Possibly," Irene said. "Do you know of any specifically large private vault?"

"Besides the Vanderbilt bones interred in the family mausoleum built into a hill on Staten Island? Hardly. As for the existence and location of vaults for valuables within another's domicile, that's not the sort of thing one wants known, even among one's own circle. All those Fifth Avenue houses on Vanderbilt Row and surrounding it are palaces and fortresses built by the richest families in the country. Why not just ask Willie Vanderbilt about this?"

"The actual owners take their holdings, and the precautions to safeguard them, for granted," Irene said. "I like testimony from uninvolved sources. Often I glean an intriguing idea."

"Well, all I know is that the Millionaires' Row mansions on Fifth Avenue together must contain dozens of vaults to hold assorted priceless valuables, enough to entice the most accomplished of thieves. You will notice the owners hire security forces to protect their houses."

"Mostly Pinkertons," Godfrey told Irene. "Your former associates."

"Really?" Mr. Belmont looked surprised. "There haven't been any female Pinkertons in ages. That is, you must have been a child when you started, Mrs. Norton. Not that you are old by any means now. . . ."

It was fun to watch a Belmont stutter while an Adler smiled seraphically at his befuddlement.

"I grew up in New York City," she said, releasing him from his faux pas at last. "I started almost everything I've ever done at an early age."

Fortunately, she didn't mention such specifics as target-pistol shooting, jig dancing, and hypnotism.

"You think," Mr. Belmont said, "Consuelo's kidnappers knew about the riches hidden in the house, and wanted them in exchange for the child?"

Irene nodded.

"And that they might make another attempt to take the prize?"

She nodded again. "And I intend to beat them to it."

"I wish you luck," he said.

"Living up to a reputation of being unpredictable isn't a matter of luck," she told him. "It's a matter of expecting the unpredictable in others. But I'll take your wishes and luck, gladly, and you'll soon hear how it all turned out. Or perhaps not."

Mr. Belmont laughed uneasily and caught Godfrey's eye. Godfrey just shrugged, and within minutes the two attempted to debate the disposition of the bill.

"Nonsense," Mr. Belmont said. "Compliments of Baron Alphonse. He'll be most intrigued by your adventures in the New World when next I dine at Ferrières."

We returned to our rooms in a mellow mood, well feted and well fed.

No sooner had the door shut upon us than Irene turned on Godfrey and myself like Messalina the mongoose on an intruding garden snake.

"I hope that Mr. Vanderbilt is as impressed with us as Mr. Belmont, for we must ask him to make a great leap of faith as soon as possible."

"He doesn't seem a man of much faith," I cautioned her.

"We have every possible recommendation," Godfrey pointed out.

Irene stalked around the room, thinking while she removed her white satin gloves, her silver-printed scarf, her black lace cape, and tossed them down on the furniture like sloughed snakeskins.

"Well, I'm soon going to make an impossible recommendation. We'll see what he makes of that."

58

Family Plot

A Romanesque chapel patterned after the Chapel of St. Giles at Arles in the south of France won Mr. Vanderbilt's approval. It would be embedded in the hillside on three sides, with commanding views from the front steps all around Staten Island and of every steamship coming into New York Harbor.

—STATEN ISLAND ADVANCE

I'd now read so much about the Vanderbilts, especially the unpolished Commodore, that associating with his grandson, William Kissam Vanderbilt, was always unnerving.

The so-called Willie was a genteel, even a mild, man.

He met Irene, Godfrey, and me at the rear of his immense Fifth Avenue establishment with nary a demur the next night.

"Mr. Vanderbilt." Godfrey offered his leather-gloved hand.

"Mr. Norton." As Godfrey nodded, the millionaire went on, breathlessly. "The Rothschilds have vouched for you in the most flattering terms possible. Even so, this is quite an . . . unusual request."

"A hidden fortune in gold isn't unearthed every day."

"American gold. Why do the Rothschilds care?"

"This isn't a world of separate continents anymore, Mr. Vanderbilt. What impacts one landmass impacts another, eventually. The roots of this search lie, for instance, in Bavaria."

"I don't see what Vanderbilts have to do with it."

"Yet you contacted the Pinkertons for an extra crew tonight, I hope."

"Yes. Of course. The men I've set to guard the house remain here. Ludicrous as it seems, you indicated the abduction of my daughter was part of this . . . scheme. I'm not sure that we need ladies along on such a midnight expedition on a clearly criminal matter—"

Godfrey couldn't allow the women in his life to be dismissed as mere ladies. "My wife and Miss Huxleigh have assisted on assignments from London to Prague to, er, Transylvania."

"Why have you settled on this particular site?"

Irene spoke up. "Because of the character of your late father, William. He always kept his dealings 'close to the vest,' even in regard to the provisions of his will. I sense that he, like the Commodore, his father, would have kept a secret close to him also."

The current Mr. Vanderbilt frowned. "He indeed did much damage by concealing the division of his wealth through his last will and testament. Why are you so interested in the old Dutch cemetery at New Dorp on Staten Island, where my grandfather is buried?"

"And was only buried there twelve years ago," Irene reminded him. "What is the nature of this plot?"

"The Commodore is buried in the Dutch cemetery at the moment. However, my father, William Henry, had taken me and my brother Cornelius out to Staten Island about, oh, five years ago. He'd told us that, despite the Commodore donating the cemetery fifty adjoining acres and my father himself building a chapel on it, the trustees would only sell several acres for a family mausoleum at 'Vanderbilt prices.'

"My father refused to pay a premium for the land and bought fourteen acres on an adjoining hilltop. He decided to use the architect who had created Alva's . . . our . . . city château here at Six-sixty Fifth Avenue to design a hilltop mausoleum."

Mr. Vanderbilt chuckled.

"What's so funny about the family mausoleum?" Irene inquired with a smile.

Willie K. Vanderbilt shook his head. "My father was something of a sobersides. He and Hunt never did understand each other. Asked to design the mausoleum, Hunt offered a plan as grandly European as the masterpieces he created for Alva."

Mr. Vanderbilt shook his head and lit another cigar. At this rate, the man must consume a box a day!

"Hunt told me my father's reaction to his first plan and we had many a laugh over it. My father wanted something simple. He said we were plain, simple, unostentatious people. This was after Alva had this house built, of course. Do you know how much my father was worth when he died?"

We shook our heads. I personally thought it was none of our business.

"Two hundred million dollars," Mr. Vanderbilt went on. "More than twice what the Commodore had made. My father had been a good shepherd. One of our family bankers explained it by saying that if this sum were converted into gold it would weigh five hundred tons and require five hundred workhorses to pull it from the Grand Central Depot to the subtreasury in Wall Street. If it had all been in gold dollars, it would have taken my father more than thirty years to count it, working eight hours a day."

"And yet your father stinted on a family mausoleum?"

"No. He wanted it 'roomy and solid and rich.' Hunt's second design was built into the hill on three sides overlooking Staten Island."

I've never understood the need to give the dead an earthly view.

"Roomy and solid and rich," Irene repeated. "That sounds quite a bit like your father himself."

The son nodded. "Construction began shortly after he took me and Neily out there, early in '85. He visited in early December to see the twenty tons of bronze grating being installed to keep intruders out. The mausoleum was half-completed. He dropped dead of a stroke on December eighth and on the eleventh was taken down Fifth Avenue in a cortège of a hundred carriages to the old ferryboat at the Forty-second Street wharf. Twelve pallbearers carried his casket up the hill to the vault, where his casket was placed near the Commodore's, until the building was finished."

Silence held among our party, partly in respect for the dead, partly in awe at the tale of so much unthinkable wealth, yet it still all came down to death. Whether William Vanderbilt in his "roomy and solid and rich" mausoleum on a hill overlooking the harbor or Lola Montez with her one small headstone in Green-Wood Cemetery engraved with an almost-anonymous name.

"'Roomy and solid and rich,'" Irene repeated again, like a bell tolling, a passing bell for the dead, making a sustained, lovely note of each word.

59

No Vault of Mine

～✦～

*Oh, no, Mr. Hunt, this will not answer at all.
We are plain, quiet, unostentatious people, and we don't want to be
buried in anything as showy as that would be.*

—WILLIAM VANDERBILT ON SEEING RICHARD MORRIS HUNT'S FIRST DESIGN FOR THE

FAMILY MAUSOLEUM

Had I not already seen Green-Wood Cemetery across the harbor in Brooklyn, I would never have believed that only a bit of water separated New York City, which was Manhattan Island, after all, from such pleasantly bucolic acres.

Our party was even farther south than Brooklyn tonight, on Staten Island, where the land was even more empty and unspoiled. Even in the dark of night . . . even in the true dark of midnight, I could see that.

We'd crossed by private ferry, Quentin standing on deck beside me and pointing out the lights of Coney Island as they twinkled to our left like some constellation fallen from the dark night sky.

I shivered deliciously in the cool breeze that wafted from the direction of the island to agitate the sulky warm night air on deck.

Several coaches were waiting to bear us inland and upland on the winding road to the hill William Vanderbilt had bought so providently near his early death.

The Commodore and William had been here for four years, and so had

Pinkertons on guard twenty-four hours a day, punching a time clock every fifteen minutes.

Half-shuttered lanterns borne by Pinkertons surrounded the shambling bulk of a vast monument crowning the hill.

One might have thought another overbearing temple to the journalistic art and commerce had risen in these fallow fields, but this was a temple to death.

I could barely make out the look of the Vanderbilt family mortuary in the darkness, yet I was able to see stepped wings to either side of some triangular pediment and the rough pyramid shape spoke of unassailable walls and of a city of the dead, much like a necropolis in ancient Egypt.

Irene held a lantern herself, reminding me of Alice Vanderbilt in her signature ball gown as Electric Light from six years earlier, when her sister-in-law, Alva, had challenged Mrs. Astor and the Four Hundred and won. Alva was not here. Only her husband. And myself, Quentin, Irene, and Godfrey, and a dozen Pinkertons.

"If you are right," Mr. Vanderbilt was telling Irene, "no one must ever know of it."

"Including Mr. Holmes?"

"This is quite different from the case he was brought in to solve."

"On the contrary, Mr. Vanderbilt. It's the same case," Irene said. "I require no credit, however, so Mr. Holmes may have it."

"He won't take it!" I objected.

As their gazes focused on me, I added, "He only takes credit where credit is due."

"I'll pay the man," Mr. Vanderbilt said. "I just don't want anyone unnecessary to know about this."

Unnecessary? Holmes? I felt an odd sense of indignation. This midnight expedition seemed secret and underhanded. Before I could express these unfortunate objections, a man cried out from inside the constructed portion of the mausoleum.

We all hastened within, lantern lights converging like falling stars.

By their conjoined light, I saw several large marble slabs and a large bronze grating dislodged from the floor. A dark passage led down into a stone-lined tunnel. I suppose Schliemann at the site of fabled Troy felt his pulse pound as mine did now. Gold. Ancient gold and enmity and legend, all buried in as-yet unhallowed ground.

Pinkertons surrounded us front and back, armed with light and the darker accompaniment of firearms. Irene and Godfrey and I were invited to join Mr. Vanderbilt in leading this descent into what amounted to a hidden mine shaft.

And there, about fifty feet along the lower level, covered in sackcloth, if not ashes, we found bar after bar of gold bullion, gleaming dull ocher in the lantern light, heavy as the weights that lift and lower theatrical curtains across Europe.

Mr. Vanderbilt's face was illuminated with wonder, not greed.

"You were absolutely right, Mrs. Norton. A king's ransom. Or a . . . republic's redemption. How did you know?"

"You owe this unexpected 'gold strike' to your sagacious grandfather, the Commodore, who made the railroad that ran through Nicaragua, making possible the discreet transfer of so much pure gold from California to New York almost thirty-five years ago, without either robbers or robber barons knowing anything of it.

"And," she went on, for once she had the stage she felt unfinished leaving it without delivering an aria or a curtain speech, "you owe that act of legerdemain to a bold and adventuresome woman who called herself Lola Montez. She died virtually penniless in New York City a few years afterward, forgotten and unrewarded, yet in her notoriously excessive number of trunks your grandfather was able to secretly transfer his California investments made solid metal to this spot, the Vanderbilt family 'vault' indeed.

"And you owe it to your harried and underestimated father," she added, "who followed your grandfather's instructions to begin constructing this . . . fort under the guise of a mausoleum, without even knowing about the treasure hidden beneath its foundation."

"I imagine," Godfrey put in, "that the Vanderbilt family architect who created Vanderbilt Row, Richard Morris Hunt, would have been trusted to keep the secret of the gold vault beneath the burial vault."

"My God!" Vanderbilt said. "And Hunt might have thought the secret had been duly passed on to the heirs. No wonder my father ordered the guards around-the-clock. We children thought it was for fear of grave robbers. A few years ago the remains of another business colossus were stolen and returned only after a sizable ransom had been paid. But he really must have been more concerned about this. I can't believe it. For this Consuelo was taken! How did these madmen know? How far does the tunnel extend?"

Not very far, we soon found at Irene's suggestion.

For as we pushed deeper into the unlit byway, we saw a beam of lantern light ahead!

We caught our breath as one to stand stock-still, and listen.

When we heard nothing after several moments, Irene produced her own pistol from a skirt pocket. We moved toward the distant light. I was reminded of Lola leading the miners to the site of the shots in the dark.

Would gunfire greet us when we found whoever had lit that light? Godfrey must have been thinking the same thing, for he'd pushed up alongside Irene.

So we followed that lone light to its source, where we found none other than Sherlock Holmes lounging atop another hoard of gold-stuffed sacks and smoking a pipe like an Irish leprechaun guarding the pot of gold at the end of the rainbow.

Everyone professed astonishment as well as relief, but I wasn't surprised.

The man would not give up a denouement, or a dramatic moment on center stage, any more easily than Irene.

60
Cryptic Matters

It has been my principle to use females for the detection of crime. . . . I can trace it back to the time I first hired Kate Warne . . . and I intend to still use females. . . . I must do it or falsify my theory, practice and truth . . . female detectives must be allowed in my Agency.
—LETTER FROM ALLAN PINKERTON, FIGHTING HIS SON'S AND UNDERLINGS' INTENTIONS TO CLOSE THE "FEMALE DEPARTMENT," 1876

What a merry group of treasure hunters assembled in the library of 660 Fifth Avenue that night!

Champagne flowed, although neither I nor Mr. Holmes partook.

He, however, did accept one of Mr. Vanderbilt's exceedingly long Havana cigars, which also offered an unusually pungent aroma. But how could I complain? All the gentlemen were smoking, including Mr. Belmont, Godfrey, and Quentin.

Irene also restrained herself on this occasion. When I leaned near to inquire why, she merely fanned herself with her fingers and commented that the room contained enough smoke already to hide Jumbo the elephant.

"Now," Mr. Vanderbilt was saying, "I understand why my father insisted I follow my grandfather's wishes in completing the family crypt, post haste. And now I understand why he wanted Pinkertons to guard it night and day."

"Were you never meant to find the gold?" I asked.

"Of course I was. Perhaps the instructions got lost because of my father's unexpected death, or in the drawn-out inheritance process. The Commodore's will was quite nastily contested. The fact and location of so much gold had to be kept secret from all but the principal heir. I'll discreetly question Hunt on the matter."

I had to ask another undoubtedly ignorant question. "And what is the point of hiding it so well? What use would it be?"

Mr. Vanderbilt leaned back in his chair, smiling at me as contentedly as a man asked to tell a story by a favorite grandchild. I suppose that is what you get when you ask a multimillionaire to make something clear about money.

"Miss, uh, Moxleigh, you ask a timely question. Did my father expect his heirs to know of this hoard by instinct? Had he left instructions that were too cryptic? I can't say. I do know that gold is soon bound to become a matter of great national importance. After the silver strike in Colorado followed the Gold Rush in California, a silver standard was adopted as well as a gold one, but that can't last. It always comes down to gold in the end, and the American government has always been narrow-pocketed when it comes to gold."

"Standard?" I asked in all ignorance.

"Simply put," Godfrey said, "it means that a supply of hard gold backs up the government's paper money. Silver certificates are available now too, due to the enormous amount of silver mined from the Rockies, but will likely not last as long as gold."

"So," I said, "for every piece of paper money, some tiny part of an ounce of a hard gold bar lies in a vault somewhere to guarantee its worth."

"Oh, no, Miss Huxleigh," said the other millionaire in the room, Mr. Belmont. I much appreciated his accurate usage of my surname. No doubt my Worth gown at dinner last night was the reason. Clothes may make the man, but they make the woman memorable. "Paper money by nature propagates past the amount of gold behind it. That's when governments falter, and sometimes fail."

I still was not the master of international finance I'd hoped to be. "So everyone wants gold, but settles for paper money?"

The men chuckled in that self-satisfied way a woman less versed in manly matters like money can inspire.

"Amassing and holding such large amounts of gold," Quentin explained, because he had not paused to chuckle, "is beyond the reach of most governments and more so of most individual men."

"I beg to differ," Mr. Vanderbilt said. "Here in the States, more than one millionaire is rumored to have huge stocks of gold. We Vanderbilts were not among them, until now."

"And should never be known as one of that rare company," Quentin said. "I hope our joint descent on the mausoleum didn't alert any persons of ill intention."

"I doubt it." Mr. Belmont sounded certain. "The presence of two women among our party made us look like various Vanderbilt offspring inspecting the family plot. Perhaps we would appear a bit eccentric to do so at midnight, but American millionaires are known to be eccentric."

"I'm glad," Irene said, "that Nell and I proved useful for something."

"More than useful," Mr. Vanderbilt hastened to assure her. His irritated look at Mr. Belmont for the unconscious slight to his family seemed to penetrate deeper than this moment and this issue. "Mrs. Norton solved a riddle she wasn't even invited to investigate in the first place. Perhaps, madam, you'd care to say how you suspected the mausoleum held gold as well the eventual family bones."

Irene hesitated for so long that Mr. Vanderbilt noticed, looked around, and saw his error in etiquette. "But Mr. Holmes was already settled in the crypt when we got there. Quite an amazing feat. How did you manage it?"

"Let the lady tell it," Holmes said, never glancing up at the millionaire. Having exchanged Havana cigar for his humble briarwood pipe, he was now fussing with the pipe's draw and apparently preferred smoking it to taking credit.

"Really," Irene said. "I can't take much credit. It was mere coincidence. My associates and I were unearthing the history of Lola Montez, who of course was a major figure thirty to forty years ago both in New York and in Gold Rush California. The investigation into Lola's enemies turned up a cadre searching for her vanished jewels. Ultimately, I learned from my . . . fellow investigator that the Vanderbilt family was being hounded for 'jewels and gold.' This shadowy gang of men followed and confronted me. I could only pretend we had some common aims. When I overheard their plot to abduct your daughter, I pretended to join them, took Consuelo as gently as possible, and protected her until we both could escape."

"You enchanted her somehow. She seems little harmed by her plight. I'm quite amazed by how you managed to deceive such villains and still prevent my daughter from knowing how dire her situation was."

Holmes spoke for the first time. "Mrs. Norton's Pinkerton experience dates from the time when the founder encouraged the use of a female department. Her role in this delicate matter speaks to the foresight of Allan Pinkerton. Alas, after his death a few years ago, the policy changed and Pinkerton now employs no female agents."

I couldn't believe my ears! Sherlock Holmes espousing women detectives!

"Mrs. Norton," he went on, "did what I and none of her associates, save Miss Huxleigh, had she been there, could do. She kept your daughter from dealing on her own with strange and sinister men until help could, and did, arrive."

Mr. Vanderbilt had withdrawn a fine lawn handkerchief and patted his brow as Holmes restated the dire situation his fragile daughter had faced recently.

"Indeed," he told Irene and me. "I'm most grateful. I, of course, am quite willing to show it. Any sum you'd care to name—"

"Would not be acceptable," Irene said.

The Vanderbilt eyebrows rose, for she had implied that her price was high. While he was about to sputter some reply, she went on. "However, I understand New York City has a splendid new opera house and that your family was instrumental in its construction."

"The Metropolitan, yes." He was frowning at the apparently abrupt change of subject.

"I should like to sing in it," Irene finished. "Someday."

"Sing. Someday. Mrs. Norton, I have some paltry influence, but not over the engagement of artistic personnel."

"My wife," Godfrey said a bit sternly, "is an acclaimed European diva. She was prima donna of the Imperial Opera at Warsaw, and has performed at La Scala in Milan and the Opera House in Prague."

"I didn't know that," Mr. Vanderbilt said quickly, still looking a bit green. I suspected the Cuban cigar.

"Oh, I don't want a role with a company," Irene said. "Just a chance to test my voice against the new house. I only need an orchestra and a few hours, and not now, for I'm out of voice. In the future sometime, perhaps."

"Ah. A private . . . concert. That could be arranged. In fact, it could even be public, given your credentials. European performers do well in New York."

"Yes, I believe it's a family tradition," Irene said, laughing merrily as her eyes met mine and Godfrey's. "But, alas, we must conclude our various affairs here and return to Paris soon."

Did I imagine it, or did Sherlock Holmes's ascetic face relax with relief?

"So." Mr. Vanderbilt eyed all of us in turn. "Your separate investigations intersected and you acted together?"

"Something like that," Godfrey said. "I, of course, as a European representative of the Rothschilds in Bavaria, was also in contact with Mr. Belmont, the Rothschilds' American representative. It's all quite complex, Mr. Vanderbilt. What matters now is that Consuelo is home, unharmed—"

"I'm not so sure of that. She's requesting discus-throwing lessons from Miss Huxleigh."

I laughed lightly, my most unconscionable foray into fiction so far. "The child has quite an imagination. I would suggest drawing lessons. She is a dear girl, Mr. Vanderbilt, and I would, were I her father, endeavor to give her what she *wishes,* since her mother is so concentrated on what she believes Consuelo *needs.*"

He eyed me uneasily, then nodded. Once. Firmly. I believe he knew quite well that the mother's ambitions threatened to overwhelm the child.

I sat back, content to remain silent from now on. If I'd bought poor young Consuelo but a few precious moments' self-satisfaction . . .

Quentin caught my eye, and nodded. Something in his gaze made me look down and avoid all other eyes for the moment.

Irene had interrogated Quentin—there is no other word for it—when our weary but triumphant group, minus Sherlock Holmes, reconvened at the Astor House to discuss our recent adventures and their outcome.

"You're sure," she asked, and asked him again, "that Pink has no suspicions about our latest exploits?"

"None at all. She was absorbed by the society scandal involving bought and sold infants."

"The Hamilton case," I announced. "Something out of Dickens via Newport. I've seen that in all the newspapers."

Irene looked surprised at my familiarity with American scandals, then turned to Quentin again. "This was the story on which you assisted her?"

He nodded. "A truly appalling American situation would keep her satisfied to quash the Jack the Ripper affair in Europe. I must say that Mycroft Holmes was extremely relieved when I wired him that Nellie Bly had found a homegrown cause célèbre."

"Mycroft Holmes?" I was astounded. "You report to him? What does his brother think of that?"

"Nothing." Quentin looked amused. "Because he knows nothing about it. You think Sherlock Holmes is omnipotent, but he suffers as much from tunnel vision as the next man, perhaps more so."

For some reason I flushed. "What did aiding Pink entail?"

"Exploring some of the most debased areas of New York City."

"Is there nowhere that girl won't go in the pursuit of a story?"

"Evidently not," Quentin said, "but I can guarantee that she went nowhere near the Vanderbilts. I saw to that."

"Which of course meant that you had to see to her," I added.

He shrugged. "In my career as a spy I've had to spend time with mountain horsemen who consider chasing a human head around an arid plain fine sport. I've had to mingle with South Sea Islanders who have a taste for shrunken heads and human flesh. However, I've never spent time with anyone more implacable than Nellie Bly, whom we know by the gentle nickname of Pink."

"What exactly did you do to assist this implacable Pink?" I asked, though both Irene and Godfrey were fidgeting in their respective chairs.

"I . . . bought babies."

"For South Sea Islanders with a taste for human flesh?"

"They were mostly Irish babies, so I suppose if we're to subscribe to Jonathan Swift's savagely satirical essay on solving Britain's Irish problem by exporting Irish infants for food, perhaps. But no, these babies were desperately wanted for themselves alone, by childless couples."

"What can be so headline-worthy about such matters?" I asked. Then I added, "Perhaps Consuelo Vanderbilt would have been more fortunate to have been traded at infancy, like a changeling, to a poor family who didn't regard children as stepping-stones to their parents' social standing and pride."

"She might have been," Irene noted from her chair, which was amazingly absent of cigarette smoke. "After what we've learned of Madame Restell and the Hamilton case, who's to say whose parentage is genuine or false? One might need some master Book of Descendency to trace any one of our true origins."

I swallowed and said nothing, for I'd made no headway on deciphering Madame Restell's coded book.

"I suppose," Quentin mused, regarding us all, "Nell and I are the ones surest of our family trees. I'm not at all certain that's any sort of advantage."

"It is to a Vanderbilt," I answered, thinking of the foothills of burlap-wrapped gold in the family crypt.

"And wouldn't you pluck Consuelo from that tyrannical family money-tree in a moment, if you could?"

"That's ridiculous, Irene. A single woman like myself has no right to a child. I have nothing to offer but poverty, as opposed to palaces. But yes."

My final word silenced all my friends. There! I'd said it. Wealth does not make worth.

"Children are worth nothing," Quentin said, "across far too much of the globe, except in certain privileged pockets, where they're worth far too much for anybody's good."

I couldn't say what caused Quentin's disturbing pronouncements, save that he'd relinquished a life of privilege in England to live on the selvage edge of savagery. He must have found some frayed remnant of that brutality here in New York City. With Nellie Bly. Pink. I wanted desperately to know what, and why, but was afraid to ask.

"At any rate," Godfrey said finally to Irene and me, "you've uncovered the many mysteries of Lola Montez, including the gold she transported for the Commodore and his heirs. Is it certain that she's my mother-in-law in absentia?"

Irene and I stared at him, hardly able to believe that extremely round-about lawyerly phrase.

What a way to put it! Well, we could either laugh or cry over all we'd learned about the madcap, sad history of Lola Montez, and Godfrey, bless him, had seen to it that we laughed.

61

A Fond and Frightening Farewell

❧

Mr. Bennett—My enemies—made enemies because I was a proud woman—a self-willed woman—an ambitious woman, if you will, but an honorable woman, who would not become their instrument of wickedness—my enemies by falsehood, and forgery, and every species of crime, have assailed me, and hunted me throughout Europe and Great Britain, and now pursue me to America—but I defy—I proudly defy the Jesuit band and their tribes of tools and instruments.

—LETTER OF LOLA MONTEZ TO THE *NEW YORK HERALD*, 1852

I couldn't believe we were packing to leave the Island of Manhattan far behind us to return to Paris.

How were the animals, I wondered? Had they missed us? Given our Persian cat, parrot, mongoose, and several snakes, perhaps not. One could only hope that they had not consumed each other in our absence.

I was fussing about the fact that our new New York clothes wouldn't fit in our one trunk each, so Irene suggested that we bring them to Anna, formerly known as the Pig Lady.

"I must keep the checkered coatdress," I objected. "It's so like the one that was ruined last spring, and is very practical."

"Wear it aboard the ship, then. And we have more room. Godfrey came over with one large carpetbag, so we can certainly claim room in another trunk and call it his."

"I still can't believe that he realized instantly that he was needed here and came abroad so fast."

"Yes," Irene said, pouting for effect, "he never even got my whole fat packet of letters. They've since been forwarded from Bavaria to Paris."

"So Godfrey won't have to go back to Bavaria?"

"Hardly. Mr. Vanderbilt told Godfrey that Holmes has traced the Bavarian Ultramontanes to a departing ship to Europe yesterday. I imagine the secret services of a number of European nations will be eager to hunt them down. Such remnants of midcentury revolutions are not welcome in any country, including Bavaria."

"I am certainly glad to have seen the last of them. I doubt they took their Indian companion with them."

"It's fearsome what fanatical devotion to a cause, or a religion, can do."

Irene had been busily sorting the clothes to be left behind into Godfrey's large carpetbag.

"Let's take these things to Anna now, before the men return from their last business with August Belmont."

"What about Sherlock Holmes? Will he be returning to England now, as well?"

"I haven't the slightest notion. Our paths have thankfully diverged again. It's good he's a closemouthed man, for I loathe having my private history known by anyone outside my most intimate circle."

"You mean Godfrey and myself."

"Exactly."

"At least Pink has been mostly kept out of it."

"Thank God. Are you ready?"

"Just my hat and gloves." I turned from the mirror near the door. "What was that you just put in the carpetbag?"

"Oh, a small curiosity." She promptly shut and lifted the bag.

My curiosity was hardly small, but I said nothing, even when Irene refused the services of a baggage boy.

A hansom cab waiting outside soon took us the two dozen blocks to the boardinghouse where Irene's childhood theatrical acquaintances, those still living, resided. How rigorously New York City was laid out east and west, north and south, except for the great diagonal line of Broadway. London remained a charming maze dating back in places to Shakespeare's and even Chaucer's day.

Irene knocked at the ground floor room of Professor Marvel. He opened the door and invited us in, but she said she'd take the clothes up to Anna first.

And that she did, though the full carpetbag bounced against the narrow stair walls all the way up.

Anna's daughter, Edith, opened the door.

"Mrs. Norton! Miss Huxleigh! Visitors, Mama!"

By the time we'd negotiated the door into the small set of rooms, Anna had come from the back bedroom where a window made her daily sewing a well-lit chore.

I confess that the huge poke bonnet this soft-spoken woman wore still haunted me. It shadowed her features, and coupled with her old performing name of the Pig Lady made me imagine unthinkable deformities.

Edith had grown up with this unusual headdress, however, and took it for granted.

"Wonderful," Anna exclaimed as she excavated the booty in Irene's carpet bag. "All new! Of course I can make use of it. Thank you so much."

She folded the clothes on a rush-seated chair and invited us to sit on a matching pair of the same humble quality.

"If you want tea," Edith announced, "you'll have to come down with me to the professor's. He has the best jams and jellies."

"I'm sure we can stop there," Irene said, "for we're about to leave for Paris."

"When do you sail?" Anna asked.

"Tomorrow, on the *Alsatia*."

"Oh, Miss Huxleigh!" Edith tugged on my hand. "I'll never see you again."

"Perhaps not." I never lie to children. "But I can write you, and soon you'll be able to write me back."

That seemed to content her. I looked to see that Irene held a small brown book that she'd taken from the now-empty carpetbag.

I knew what the gilt letters on the spine would read: *The Adventures of Lola Montez.* This had been our bible in researching Lola's life, for the volume contained her autobiography and lectures, as well as a long advertising section in the back for various other books, including some that seemed quite inappropriate.

Irene was paging past the few blank pages in the front to the first one that bore any image and type.

Irene leaned forward to put that page in the center of the bonnet's direct regard.

"When I was a child around the theater, Anna, a very young child, did you ever see this woman there?"

The image was an engraving made from a photograph of Lola Montez, probably toward the end of her life.

Like most legendary beauties, images of her existed that made one wonder what everyone had been talking about in her day This profile view showed the head and shoulders of a woman with a strong, straight nose and her hair in a curled bob just at ear level and a bit longer in the back. She wore some shapeless gown with a band of elaborate embroidery at the round neckline, not tight against the throat, but certainly not scandalously low. It resembled nothing so much as a nightshirt.

The large, flowing signature "Lola Montez" was below the portrait, and then the publisher's name in minuscule type. (Perhaps Rudd & Carlton of New York were ashamed of their role in purveying an adventuress's memoirs, although the contents were rather surprisingly learned.)

The bonnet bent over the page until it seemed to consume the image. Then it reared back.

"Her hair was glossy black, and her clothes were black as well, when I saw her."

"This is the Woman in Black who visited me as a child?"

The bonnet nodded. "She did more than visit."

"What more?" Irene asked anxiously.

"Why, she taught you your first dance steps when you were just past being able to walk. She always said you had dancer's legs, though none of us could see it. She took great joy in you, and you in her. Young as you were, you bounced in time to her humming and singing, and stepped forward when you put your tiny hands in hers."

Anna's hand patted the page. "A pity this picture doesn't show her eyes facing forward. She had morning-glory eyes, so blue you blinked.

"She brought you trinkets and ribbons, and I know she left money for your care to the others. Salamandra and her sister. A pity they are no longer alive. They could tell you more."

We all kept silent then, for the women had died tragically just as Irene had come to America in search of her origins, taking untold secrets with them.

"Was she my mother?" Irene asked. "This woman? Do you think?"

"Oh, my dear girl, I can't say. She wished she was someone's mother, that's certain. I could sense her sadness, and that she wanted to pass on some of her musical joy to those younger, like yourself. She could have been a widow who'd never had children, whose husband had died in the Civil conflict then raging."

Anna's blunt fingertip, callused from handling the needle day in and day out, tapped the name under the photo. " 'Lola Montez.' I didn't think she was Spanish."

"You weren't the only one," Irene said with an ironic smile.

Obviously, the name meant nothing to her. Lola's fame was fading, and in a few more decades would be a minor historical curiosity.

Irene rose, and tucked the book back in the empty carpetbag. We embraced Anna farewell. (The bonnet brushed my cheek, fleeting as the brush of a butterfly. I no longer feared it.)

Edith accompanied us downstairs, skipping and chattering. How the child had blossomed once removed from the grim tenement in which we found them!

Professor Marvel was waiting behind his door below. While Edith repaired to the small kitchen to produce her decidedly one-note "tea" (jam and jelly and marmalade on whatever would hold them, including American cookies), Irene wandered to his wall of posters and the like. There we had first learned that Lola Montez might be her mother.

I joined her there.

She stared at the handsome print of the beautiful woman in the Cavalier hat and encompassing black velvet cape. This woman I could see as Irene's mother. The other, not.

"Lola certainly had many faces," I commented, reviewing the array of painting and photographs we had found behind transparent tissue protectors in the books about her.

"I think we all do, Nell. She just showed more of them than most people do."

"I can't say I detect a resemblance."

"No? And who has been twitting me about 'unhappy entanglements' with foreign noblemen, about carrying a pistol and fighting a duel once, about my riding crop incident at the fitting rooms of Worth, or Lola's essay into men's dress when she slipped back into Bavaria to see Ludwig after her expulsion? About my smoking!"

I swallowed, hard. "I meant a physical resemblance. Except for this painting." I indicated the lady in black velvet.

Irene smiled ironically, and I didn't know why. "Do you believe she is . . . was your mother?"

"I still don't know, Nell, but I know that whoever left me with the variety performers did care about me, and that the Woman in Black, who may have been Lola, was kind to me and other children, as Lola was. However mixed the reviews on her dancing, however tempestuous her temper, she had a wild and generous heart. I'd rather claim relation to that than the cold calculation of Lola's own miserable mother. Sometimes we may be better off as orphans."

I didn't know what to say to that harsh judgment, but Irene quickly added, rather briskly, as if closing a book. "It doesn't matter. I'm glad I came to know her better than most of the world ever did. She lived a life she made, as you and I must do today, and in that way she is mother to all women, and men, as she herself said in her rather emphatic dedication to *The Arts of Beauty,* 'who dare to stand up in the might of their own individuality.'"

"Oh. That may apply to you, but I don't know that I quite do that."

"I'm afraid you do, rather emphatically."

Behind us, the professor cleared his throat. "She was a peerless beauty," he noted.

Irene turned, her eyes bright with amusement and something else.

"I hate to disappoint you, Professor," Irene said, "but I've studied images of this woman in many versions, and this lovely, tranquil, genteel work isn't a painting of Lola Montez."

"Ah. No?" He adjusted his spectacles and stepped close, then eyed the cartoon of La Lola in short dancing skirts leaping across the Atlantic from Europe to America. "I suppose any lady pictured carrying a riding crop could have been misidentified as Lola. Still, she is a pretty thing to look at, and I won't take her down from my wall."

He glanced at Irene. "You must send me a photograph of yourself. And Miss Huxleigh."

"Me? Oh, no."

"An excellent idea," Irene said. "We'll have fresh photos made on our return to Paris. Like the late King Ludwig of Bavaria, you'll have your own Gallery of Beauties, of which Lola Montez is the most famous."

"Or was." He took off his spectacles, polished them on a rather grimy handkerchief, and tucked them away. "Fame doesn't hold, nor beauty. I prefer to view the world through a blur these days; it's much kinder to my old eyes that way."

Edith came back with her tiny plates and cups, so the visit finished with us deferring to our hostess and her precocious childish glee.

"If our journey to New York has accomplished one thing worth doing,"

Irene mused as we stood outside the boardinghouse, both feeling, I believe, on the teary verge that farewells threaten to push us over, perhaps even a farewell to the Lola we had found here, despite herself, "it's rescuing Edith and her mother from such dreary poverty."

Edith and the professor waved good-bye from his front bay window as we went down the steps to the street.

I admit that I viewed the world through a wavy surface of glassine, thanks to unshed tears. When, if ever, would I see any of these people again? I don't doubt that Irene was similarly afflicted, for she had some reason to think that she knew the name of her mother at last.

We passed the other pedestrians unseeing, unlooking.

Until two of them barreled right into us—probably our fault—then caught our elbows to steady us . . . and rushed us past the corner of the building down a narrow and refuse-cluttered alleyway!

"No!" Irene was shouting. The tears shook out of my eyes in the rude jostling, and I saw her engaged in a tug of war for the carpetbag with a strange man.

Another man had me by the arm and was pushing me up against the brick wall, keeping me from aiding Irene.

"Let go of me, you cad!" I used my free hand to work loose my steel hat pin. I glanced at Irene. The other man was attempting to hit her with some sort of small club!

I took a deep breath and drove my hat pin into my attacker's serge-covered upper arm.

He screamed and pulled away from me, taking my best jet hat pin with him.

That left me unarmed.

I heard my chatelaine jingle as I rushed toward Irene and the other robber. If she'd just let go of the empty carpetbag, we'd be rid of these thieves.

And then I realized . . . Lola's book was inside. Few copies remained. She'd never relinquish it, and never even stop to think why.

So I fell upon the other villain and kicked him viciously in the ankles. Then I wrenched the small scissors off my chatelaine and began jabbing it into whatever of his skin I could see, which was his hands and neck.

He too began screeching.

Footsteps pounded toward us from the street. Passersby had mistaken the scream of my first victim for a woman's cry.

I glimpsed several men of the business sort and then they surrounded us.

"Ladies! Are you all right?"

"Here's your bag, ma'am."

"The cowardly dastards! They've run right through to the other street."

"We'll fetch a cab."

In five minutes we were ensconced in a hansom, my hat on my lap, for it wouldn't stay on without a pin. Irene had the carpetbag perched on her knees like a child.

Our gallant rescuers had paid the fare back to our hotel.

So many had offered to escort us back in another cab that we would have had a parade arriving at the Astor House Hotel.

The driver slapped his reins and we were trotting back home, which is what one regards a hotel where one has lodged for a matter of weeks rather than days.

"We mustn't tell anyone of this," Irene said grimly as we were under way.

"By 'anyone' you mean—?"

"Especially Godfrey."

"And—?"

"Quentin. Pink. The queen of England. You did hear what they cried out, Nell?"

"No. There was this roaring in my ears. I hardly knew what I heard or did or even saw. Except that my hat pin is gone."

"*Mein Gott!*"

"Irene, are you cursing now. And why in German?"

"'*Mein Gott*' is what my attacker muttered when he couldn't get the carpetbag and you started picking at him with your knitting needle."

"It wasn't a knitting needle. It was an embroidery scissors, and a very feeble weapon indeed. Why couldn't you just let him have the carpetbag?"

"Because it's Godfrey's."

"Godfrey could buy another one at any of these huge department stores that dot New York."

"I don't want Godfrey to know what has just happened, which getting him a new carpetbag would make inevitable."

"Secrets between spouses are the devil's workshop."

"Nell! Do you want Quentin to know that we were assaulted by Ultramontanes on the sidewalks of New York?"

"They left. By ship."

"Apparently not all of them. We shall never be allowed to go anywhere unescorted again if news of this brawl gets back to Godfrey or Quentin."

I considered this, and weighed whether it was such a bad thing, or not. Unlike Irene, I didn't thirst for independence. Then again, I'd never been denied it. Quentin might feel that his duty to protect me outweighed his duty to muzzle Nellie Bly.

I enjoyed that supposition for a few moments, then shrugged it away.

"All right," I agreed, "but we must prepare for further attempts by the Ultramontanes, who obviously believe you have access to the lost treasure of Lola Montez."

"Fine," she said absently, patting inside the open carpetbag to make sure the book of Lola was still safe inside. "We'll buy you a new hat pin, or several, of the best Spanish steel tomorrow before we sail."

62

Leaving Lady Liberty

I am not the wicked woman you have been told.... I have erred in life, often and again—who has not? I have been vain, frivolous, ambitious—proud; but never vicious, never cruel, never unkind. I appeal to a liberal press, and to the intelligent gentlemen who control it, to aid me in my exertions to regain the means of an honorable livelihood.
—LOLA MONTEZ LETTER TO THE *NEW YORK HERALD*, 1852

"How did your mission go?" Godfrey asked when we returned to the hotel, hot and messed in attire, feeling as guilty as children who'd eaten the entire contents of a tea tray in the kitchen.

Yet he looked so obviously relieved, even buoyant, at the idea of leaving America that I understood why Irene didn't want to alarm him further.

Irene opened the empty carpetbag. "Clothing delivered and much appreciated." She had removed the book of Lola in the hansom, and put it in her skirt pocket. "Now you can have this back to fill it with the scandalously scanty number of clothes a gentleman needs to make a transatlantic crossing, compared to a lady."

"Irene," he said, "I've never seen you leave clothing behind, so can certainly offer you the use of my trunk for yours."

He stepped aside to reveal a newly purchased trunk of the proper dimensions. Men can be so very invaluable and surprising.

"So that was your errand!" Irene embraced him rapturously. "Now we can be sure that all Nell's fripperies won't be crushed in transit."

"All *my* fripperies? My dear Irene, you do me an injustice."

"I'm not so sure, Nell." Godfrey stepped to the desk by the door. "This arrived while you were out."

He handed me a handsome flat fruitwood box large enough to hold silverware.

"For me?" I opened the heavy vellum envelope atop it. It contained a folded note and Alva Vanderbilt's calling card (which was not so commercial as to feature her photograph, thank goodness). The note itself was signed by William Kissam Vanderbilt and expressed deep gratitude for saving his "most precious pearl of a daughter, Consuelo."

Within the wooden box was a large clam-shaped box of moss-green velvet, and within that . . . Godfrey held the heavy outer box as I opened the velvet lid and stared at a black silk surface holding Alva's diamond-and-pearl parure, a full parure of long necklace, dog collar, twin bracelets, brooch, earrings.

"Gracious! This can't be for me."

Irene was ogling the contents over my shoulder. "Hmmm. No doubt too modest for Alva, therefore a small loss. At least she's a woman of her word. The diamonds are dainty, merely meant to set off the perfection of the pearls. Therefore ideal for you, Nell, since they will set off your perfect English complexion."

"I can't accept it."

"I kidnapped Consuelo," Irene said. "I can't take a reward for that. But you showed true care for the girl, and I'm sure Mr. Vanderbilt appreciates that."

"It is in unusually good taste for Alva Vanderbilt, from what I've seen."

"Agreed," Godfrey said heartily. "I've plenty of room and my new trunk deserves a worthy passenger."

"Besides," Irene said, then paused. She threaded her arm through Godfrey's, so they faced me as one.

"Think how splendid the pearls will look when you're gowned to sit at the captain's table for dinner after a day of strolling the decks and playing deckside games."

"Irene! Are you mad? I'll be as sick as a seal the entire voyage."

"Oh, Nell, that is too bad. What will we do to entertain Quentin then?" She cast large brown eyes at her beaming spouse.

"Quentin! On shipboard? With us??"

"Yes! Pink is quite occupied with this baby-buying business. Story after story in the *World*. Quentin is free, for now, anyway."

I was speechless. I considered everything, including the weeklong voyage I dreaded to the soles of my feet, and remained . . . speechless. And Quentin would be aboard to see me in such a revolting state?! I think not. I would rather drown. I would rather stay in New York City and become a vaudeville performer: Miss Nell and Her Flying Hat Pins. I would rather go back to London and assist Sherlock Holmes in his investigations. I would rather sit on an Antarctic ice floe and commune with penguins. I would rather . . .

"We must dash out," Irene was saying, leading her husband by the politely crooked arm. "I desperately need a quantity of hat pins and a new shirtwaist. We'll meet again for dinner here."

I never wanted to eat again.

They were gone before I could assemble my senses or my objections.

I sank onto our parlor sofa and tried to assemble myself at least. How could Irene allow me to be thrust into such a humiliating situation? She'd seen me in the throes of mal de mer. She couldn't possibly believe I'd want any other living soul, even Godfrey, to see me thus.

And now, Quentin—?

While my mind erected several atrocious shipboard scenes involving my utter humiliation and despair, some unsuspecting soul was knocking on the door to our room.

A mere hat pin would not do to skewer anyone who dared cross my path at that moment. Were it a mob of Ultramontanes, I would savage them with my bare hands. . . .

I rose and went to the door, eager to dispense my wrath on whoever dared to disturb me at the most dreadful moment of my life, when what should be joy was despair.

The door opened, however, on the very object of my concern.

"Quentin!"

"Didn't Irene and Godfrey tell you I was coming for dinner?"

"No. And they didn't tell me you were coming for dinner for seven more nights in a row until just now."

He grinned, the pitiless demon. "I'm going back with you."

"So I've heard."

His head tilted sideways to study my face, which felt frozen. "You're not pleased?"

"No! Yes! I'm glad you're free of the toils of Nellie Bly, of course. But I shan't see you aboard."

"You're . . . not staying on in New York?"

"Of course not. But I shall be unfit to be seen. I suffer horribly from seasickness."

"Oh." He stepped inside the room, driving me back from my inhospitable position barring the door. "I'd heard something about that."

"Heard? You can't have heard the half of it. Irene can skip all up and down the decks and never turn a hair. I turn several shades of green at the merest waft of motion."

"You were fine on the steamboat to Coney Island."

"That wasn't the Atlantic. Oh, don't even make me think of it!"

"Nell—" He seized my wrists.

I pulled them away. I was tired of being seized for the day, even by one who made my pulses leap with a strange combination of anticipation and dread.

"Look. I've brought you a present."

And from his pocket he produced a bit of folded tissue. His unwrapping fingers revealed a length of carved ivory, quite exquisite.

He held it up, a circle, not a length.

"What on earth?"

"A cure for seasickness from the Indian Ocean. A bracelet."

"A bracelet? For me?"

"Two," Quentin said, grinning like a street conjuror as he produced a twin to the first.

"Quite lovely, but—"

His fingers spread to fan the ivory squares wide. They were threaded on two lines of elastic. "Try them on."

He'd taken my hand despite my objections and was slipping one bracelet over my fingers onto my wrist.

"Goodness! They snap as tight as a sleeve-band."

"Exactly. The gentle pressure cures seasickness on the Indian Ocean. It can do no differently on the Atlantic."

"You're sure of this?" I asked as he installed the second bracelet on my other wrist.

"I've seen it work. You just wear them for the duration of the voyage."

I frowned. "They may attract attention."

"What do you care if you can take the air on deck and eat dinner at the captain's table?"

"Those two activities have never been among my ambitions."

"But I'm rather shallow and will enjoy it. I'd rather you enjoy it with me."

I had only one thought: *What would Nellie Bly do?*

"I'd be delighted," I said.

And was.

The next day, in late afternoon, we all stood on the deck of the *Alsatia* and watched the crowds on the dock dwindle into a waving gray mass. Lady Liberty in the harbor grew smaller and smaller.

Irene and Godfrey leaned against each other at the rail, silent and smiling, happy to be heading home and in each other's company after a long separation.

My gloved hands rested on the rail, the ivory bracelets both pinching and peeking out of my jacket sleeves.

The wind was intense, but one of the dozen new hat pins Irene had bought me anchored my hat, my Nellie Bly–broad-brimmed hat.

Quentin anchored me also. I could feel him behind me, see his hands bracketing mine on the rail.

I felt quite well in one way, but full of fluttering butterflies in another.

A week. Onboard. Alone with Quentin, for obviously Irene and Godfrey intended this voyage as a second honeymoon.

" 'Twas a consummation devoutly to be wished. . . ." And feared. I had been deserted even by my infirmity, seasickness. I was on my own, with Quentin.

What would come of it, I couldn't say, but I was not the woman in the square before Notre Dame Cathedral in Paris who had almost swooned at being familiarly addressed by a strange man in alien garb two years ago. Quentin.

Oddly enough, I recalled Lola Montez at that moment, and with some throb of sympathy I'd never expected to feel for such a notorious woman.

How many times had she stood at the railing of a departing or arriving ship in her life, hopeful or fretful? How often had she fallen in love on shipboard, and lost love on shore?

What had she thought when seeing New York and its hubris of high-rise buildings for the first time? The last? She'd resolved to live out her life here, and only her hated mother came to help her bid adieu to it. Not one man came who had toasted her, feted her, admired her, loved her, lost her . . . in life.

What had she really felt, when all was said and done?

I would never really know. Nor would Irene. But we would always wonder, and in that way alone Lola lived on.

Coda:

Sex, Lies, and Obfuscation

〰️

*We believe that many overtures have been made to draw the celebrated
Countess of Landsfeld from her retirement in Grass Valley, and
exhibit her once more upon the stage in this city, but thus far, they seem
to have failed. . . . We may therefore give up all hopes of seeing the
celebrated 'spider dance' for some time.*

—PATRICK HULL, EX-HUSBAND, IN *DAILY TOWN TALK,* 1855

Pity the scrupulous academic who tries to untangle the history of Eliza
Rosana Maria Dolores Gilbert James Heald Hull, better known for
half of her life as Lola Montez.

Copious printed materials from both the nineteenth and twentieth
centuries about this larger-than-life figure abound. In addition there's
the testimony of her own autobiography, lectures, play, and book on beauty.
Still, the truth about Lola remains as elusive as the phantom arachnids she pursued through her petticoats over thirteen years and three continents in her infamous "spider dance."

She is supposed to have inspired the old saw that became the title of a
Broadway musical song a hundred years after her death: "Whatever Lola wants,
Lola gets."

Her play, *Lola Montez in Bavaria,* was very likely the first "docudrama" and the first play in which the principal actor was also the subject. Years later, Buffalo Bill Cody would start his performing career by enacting his own very different adventures in the same way.

As for information about Lola found with the Huxleigh diaries, along with fragments from other sources of the time, including Nellie Bly and, most interestingly Sherlock Holmes, the truth of many of these facts, including her late-life religious conversion, has been recorded by history.

(Lola Montez did indeed visit the Magdalen Asylum, a refuge for "fallen women" that was more enlightened than many. Bishop Henry Codman Potter was a social and political reformer dedicated to improving the lot of the poor. On the Lower East Side he instituted missions, workingmen's clubs, day nurseries, kindergartens, and even sought to "uplift" the saloon environment.)

The only new documentation are the musings from the "Dangerous Woman" herself. These present a provocative revision of Lola's interaction with Cornelius Vanderbilt. Whether fortunes in gold had been transported from California to the Vanderbilt burial vault or kept there, no source can verify this. What has been historically documented is that Pinkerton guards kept twenty-four-hour watch on the Vanderbilt mausoleum for fifty years. In light of the events related in this book, one has to wonder why, if not for some secret and literally subterranean reason.

Just four years after the time of these events, the U. S. government faced economic collapse. It was only saved by the enormous gold reserves of certain prominent financiers, such as J. P. Morgan. And the Vanderbilts? Perhaps.

Within five years, Alva would divorce William Kissam Vanderbilt, charging adultery. Shortly after marrying Consuelo to the English duke mama selected for her, Alva remarried. Her second husband was Oliver Hazard Perry Belmont, son of August Belmont and a divorced man himself. Rumors even before the events shown in this book linked Alva and the younger Belmont. Willie Vanderbilt had been in the papers even earlier for maintaining a mistress abroad. The mayor of New York had to unite Alva and Oliver, as no clergyman then would marry a pair of divorced persons.

Not even scandal could sink the S. S. *Alva,* although the enormous yacht her first husband had named in her honor did indeed sink after being hit by a passing freighter shortly before their marriage finally foundered. After her divorce, Alva reported that "society was by turns stunned, horrified, and then savage." The friends who cut her dead came around in the end. "I always do everything first," Alva said. "I was the first girl of my 'set' to marry a Vanderbilt.

I was the first society woman to ask for a divorce. . . . Within a year ever so many others had followed my example. They had not dared to do it until I showed them the way."

She also showed them the way to snaring blue bloods abroad. She was implacably determined to marry her daughter Consuelo to Charles Spencer-Churchill, the young duke of Marlborough, to further her own social ambitions. In that way she matched Eliza Gilbert's mother and her actions of roughly sixty years before. Consuelo Vanderbilt's eighteen-year-old heart belonged to a New York society man, but Alva kept her daughter prisoner at home, denied mail as well as visitors. Alva even shammed a heart attack and blamed Consuelo, also threatening to shoot the American suitor dead if Consuelo attempted to contact him.

The arranged marriage was bitterly unhappy from the first; the duke also had given up a "true love" for the injection of American money that would save his immense Blenheim Palace. After two children and ten years the couple separated.

Alva Vanderbilt Belmont later became a leader of the women's suffrage movement. When Consuelo sought an annulment of her loveless marriage to Marlborough twenty-five years later to make a love match with a Catholic man, Alva testified that she'd used threats of suicide and murder to force Consuelo into her first marriage and won her daughter's annulment. Consuelo remarried happily.

History has always dismissed Lola's anger against the Jesuits and her frequent public charges that their vengeance pursued her the rest of her life. When she was a prime influence on King Ludwig in Bavaria, though, she did persuade him to make liberal reforms. Her advice encouraged him to dismiss the Jesuit clerics among his cabinet and advisors, to grant freedom of the press, and to support a more secular form of government that was, in fact, the wave of the future in Europe.

So the foes seen here still pursuing Lola after her death bear out that enmity, and reflect the Bavarian populace's anger at the huge sums of money King Ludwig lavished on his Lolitta's residence, furnishings, and wardrobe. Compared to what his grandson spent obsessively building immense and lavish castles, Ludwig's generosity to Lola was a pittance. Latterday Bavarians longed for the days of Ludwig I, so it's not impossible to think that a by-blow heir less likely to be tainted by madness might appeal to some . . . especially as a shadow ruler for the ousted Ultramontanes.

Both the king and Lola denied that she was ever his mistress. Despite the romantic and sexual nature of their letters, Lola's most recent and thorough biographer, Bruce Seymour, could find evidence that the king and Lola were physically intimate only twice. The king was sixty when they met, and Lola was passing herself off as in her early rather than late twenties. Both seemed to enjoy drama more than anything.

Those who wish to study the facts for themselves can find numerous biographies and reference books about Lola Montez, and even more contradictions.

Fiona Witherspoon, Ph.D., FIA[*]

November 5, 2003

*Friends of Irene Adler

Spider Dance

A Reader's Guide

Perhaps it has taken until the end of this century for an author like Douglas to be able to imagine a female protagonist who could be called 'the' woman by Sherlock Holmes.

—GROUNDS FOR MURDER, 1991

To encourage the reading and discussion of Carole Nelson Douglas's acclaimed novels examining the Victorian world from the viewpoint of one of the most mysterious woman in literature, the following descriptions and discussion topics are offered. The author interview, biography, and bibliography will aid discussion as well.

Set in 1880–1890 London, Paris, Prague, Monaco, and most recently New York City, the Irene Adler novels reinvent the only woman to have outwitted Sherlock Holmes as the complex and compelling protagonist of her own stories. Douglas's portrayal of "this remarkable heroine and her keen perspective on the male society in which she must make her independent way," noted *The New York Times,* recasts her "not as a loose-living adventuress but a woman ahead of her time." In Douglas's hands, the fascinating but sketchy American prima donna from "A Scandal in Bohemia" becomes an aspiring opera singer moonlighting as a private inquiry agent. When events force her from the stage into the art of detection, Adler's exploits rival those of Sherlock Holmes himself as she crosses paths and swords with the day's leading creative and political figures while sleuthing among the Bad and the Beautiful of Belle Epoque Europe.

Critics praise the novels' rich period detail, numerous historical characters, original perspective, wit, and "welcome window on things Victorian."

"The private and public escapades of Irene Adler Norton [are] as erratic and unexpected and brilliant as the character herself," noted Michael Collings in *Mystery Scene* of *Another Scandal in Bohemia* (formerly *Irene's Last Waltz*), "a long and complex *jeu d'esprit,* simultaneously modeling itself on and critiquing Doylesque novels of ratiocination coupled with emotional distancing. Here is Sherlock Holmes in skirts, but as a detective with an artistic temperament and the passion to match, with the intellect to penetrate to the heart of a crime and the heart to show compassion for the intellect behind it."

⊰About This Book⊱

Spider Dance, the eighth Irene Adler novel, opens in New York City in the late summer of 1889. Irene Adler Norton and her biographer-companion, spinster Nell Huxleigh, are still searching for the mysterious "Woman in Black" who may have been Irene's mother. They continue on their own, missing the third leg of their domestic life in Neuilly, near Paris: Irene's barrister husband, Godfrey Norton, who is on business in Bavaria for the Rothschild banking family, which often employs one or more of the threesome as its agents.

This leaves Irene and Nell with a trio of acquaintances in New York City, possible allies, or rivals, in their personal quest. When murder most violent enters the picture, so do Irene and Nell's uneasy associates in investigation—Sherlock Holmes and the enterprising American "stunt girl" newspaper reporter, Nellie Bly. Quentin Stanhope, an old acquaintance, British agent, and likely romantic interest for Nell, is also in New York. He should be Nell's and Irene's staunch ally, but he's been commissioned to keep Nellie Bly quiet about their shocking pursuit of Jack the Ripper (after the Whitechapel "horrors") in Paris the previous spring. This means paying far more court to the vivacious young daredevil reporter than to reserved Nell.

⊰For Discussion⊱
Related to Spider Dance:

1. It's often been noted that protagonists in genre fiction, like mystery, traditionally don't have parents, or very visible parents, or children. This novel continues the search for a mother Irene Adler may not want to know, much less the father she never knew either. Why is she so adamant about being indifferent to her forebears? Why do you think parents and children might encumber such characters? Certainly Holmes and Watson were parentless as far as readers were concerned. Are there other favorite detectives you can think of who are singularly alone in the world? What kind of parents would you imagine Miss Marple to have had? Nero Wolfe? The only facts Doyle gave about Irene were that she had been born in New Jersey, was therefore American, and had sung grand opera. What history would you invent for her, instead of this one? Why did the author choose to give Adler the background and milieu she is developing in the American-set novels, *Femme Fatale* and *Spider Dance*?

2. Three women with varying personalities and goals are involved in tracing Irene's history. Sometimes they cooperate and sometimes they compete, as is also the case with all three in relation to Sherlock Holmes. What characteristics do you admire in each of the three women? What don't you like? Motherhood, real and mentoring, is an element of this novel's plot and theme. Who were the "good" and "bad" mothers in the book? How did the cultural imperatives of the time distort the mother-daughter relationship? The character most capable of evolving during the novels is Nell Huxleigh. Is she changing during this novel and the others in the series, and does your opinion of her change as well? What is your opinion of Nellie Bly and Nell's fear of her? *The Drood Review of Mystery* observed of *Chapel Noir*: "Douglas wants . . . women fully informed about and capable of action on the mean streets of their world." How does *Spider Dance* contribute to this goal?

3. New York City has always been a major setting for American fiction. Did anything about the depiction of it in this book surprise you? How many elements did you glimpse in their infancy then, which have become staples of contemporary American life? For instance, Joseph Pulitzer was just entering the newspaper business then, but the journalism awards given in his name today are the most prestigious in the country. How much can history teach us? Can history change our opinions of our own times?

Do you like to read historical novels for the facts of the time period or the attitudes, and how much do you think you can trust such evocations in fiction? Often, historical novelists say, they're challenged on the accuracy of facts that are absolutely true, but seem too modern. Are you encouraged to do more reading about the historical periods you encounter in novels?

4. Mesmerism, or hypnotism, is a minor factor in these novels: it's even hinted that Irene Adler received her last name from a little-known reference in a novel about a famous fictional mesmerist, Svengali. *Trilby,* the eponymous heroine of the George du Maurier (father of Daphne) novel that features Svengali, was hypnotized by him to sing beautifully although she was tone deaf. Svengali married her and forced her to tour as a singer. *The Phantom of the Opera* by Frenchman Gaston Leroux arrived in 1911, more than a decade after du Maurier's *Trilby,* and was far less popular than it is at the present time. It too featured a "monster" training a helpless young woman to sing.

Why, besides the ever-popular Beauty and the Beast parallels, did this theme of women forced to sing by taskmasters create two immortal characters, both of them men and villains? Another minor historical figure named Adler is mentioned in this book. Can you think of any other historical Adlers who might be suitable candidates for Irene's Father? You could make a game of assigning historical "parents" to fictional characters. The intersection of history and fiction can produce fascinating hybrids.

5. Sherlock Holmes has been resurrected as a character by countless writers since Doyle's death in 1930, but by very few women. Writers claim he is a very hard character to change, that even Doyle did better with stories in which Holmes was not too dominant. How is Holmes's character evolving in this series? Which aspects of Holmes as you first encountered him in fiction or film do you feel are immutable, and which allow for change? Does his associating with these particular characters, the three women, two of them liberated American women, throw a different light on his character?

Three Englishmen are continuing characters the novels: Irene's husband, Godfrey Norton, Holmes, and Quentin Stanhope. How do these men differ from each other? How do they each relate to the three women, and how is that different with each man?

6. Douglas has said she likes to work on the "large canvas" of series fiction. What kind of character development does that approach permit? Do you like it? Has television recommitted viewers/readers to the kind of multi-volume storytelling common in the nineteenth century, or is the attention span of the twenty-first century too short? Is longterm, committed reading becoming a lost art?

For discussion of the Irene Adler series:

1. Douglas mentions other authors, many of them women, who have reinvented major female characters or minor characters from classic literary or genre novels to reevaluate culture then and now. Can you think of such works in the field of fantasy or historical novels? General literature? What about the recent copyright contest over *The Wind Done Gone,* Alice Randall's reimagining of *Gone with the Wind* events and characters from the African-American slaves' viewpoints? Could the novel's important social points have been made as effectively without referencing the classic work generally familiar to most people? What other works have attained the mythic status that might make possible such socially conscious reinventions? What works would you revisit or rewrite?

2. Religion and morality are underlying issues in the novels, including

the time's anti-Semitism. This is an element absent from the Holmes stories. How is this issue brought out and how do Nell's strictly conventional views affect those around her? Why does she take on a moral watchdog role yet remain both disapproving and fascinated by Irene's pragmatic philosophy? Why is Irene (and also most readers) so fond of her despite her opinionated personality?

3. Douglas chose to blend humor with adventurous plots. Do comic characters and situations satirize the times or soften them? Is humor a more effective form of social criticism than rhetoric? What classic writers and novelists use this technique, besides George Bernard Shaw and Mark Twain?

4. The novels also present a continuing tension between New World and Old World, America and England and the Continent, artist-tradesman and aristocrat, as well as woman and man. Which characters reflect which camps? How does the tension show itself?

5. *Chapel Noir* makes several references to *Dracula* through the presence of Bram Stoker some six years before the novel actually was published. Stoker is also an ongoing character in other Adler novels. Various literary figures appear in the Adler novels, including Oscar Wilde, and most of these historical characters knew each other. Why was this period so rich in writers who founded much modern genre fiction, like Doyle and Stoker? The late nineteenth century produced not only *Dracula*, Doyle's Holmes stories, and the surviving dinosaurs of *The Lost World*, but also *Trilby*, *The Phantom of the Opera*, *The Prisoner of Zenda*, *Dr. Jekyll and Mr. Hyde*, among the earliest and most lasting works of science fiction, political intrigue, mystery, and horror. How does Douglas pay homage to this tradition in the plots, characters, and details of the Adler novels?

❧AN INTERVIEW WITH CAROLE NELSON DOUGLAS❧

Q: *You were the first woman to write about the Sherlock Holmes world from the viewpoint of one of Arthur Conan Doyle's women characters, and only the second woman to write a Holmes-related novel at all. Why?*

A: Most of my fiction ideas stem from my role as social observer in my first career, journalism. One day I looked at the mystery field and realized that all post-Doyle Sherlockian novels were written by men. I had loved the stories as a child and thought it was high time for a woman to examine the subject from a female point of view.

Q: *So there was "the" woman, Irene Adler, the only woman to outwit Holmes, waiting for you.*

A: She seems the most obvious candidate, but I bypassed her for that very reason to look at other women in what is called the Holmes Canon. Eventually I came back to "A Scandal in Bohemia." Rereading it, I realized that male writers had all taken Irene Adler at face value as the king of Bohemia's jilted mistress, but the story doesn't support that. As the only woman in the Canon who stirred a hint of romantic interest in the aloof Holmes, Irene Adler had to be more than this beautiful but amoral "Victorian vamp." Once I saw that I could validly interpret her as a gifted and serious performing artist, I had my protagonist.

Q: *It was that simple?*

A: It was that complex. I felt that any deeper psychological exploration of this character still had to adhere to Doyle's story, both literally and in regard to the author's own feeling toward the character. That's how I ended up having to explain that operatic impossibility, a contralto prima donna. I tend to describe Irene as a "dark" soprano to avoid assigning her either the erroneous contralto voice or the not-quite-right mezzo-soprano voice. It's been great fun justifying Doyle's error by finding operatic roles Irene could conceivably sing.

Even more satisfying has been reinventing an Irene Adler who is as intelligent, self-sufficient, and serious about her professional and personal integrity as Sherlock Holmes, and far too independent to be anyone's mistress but her own. She also moonlights as an inquiry agent while building her performing career. In many ways they are flip sides of the same coin: her profession, music, is his hobby. His profession, detection, is her secondary career. Her adventures intertwine with Holmes's, but she is definitely her own woman in these novels.

Q: *How did Doyle feel toward the character of Irene Adler?*

A: I believe that Holmes and Watson expressed two sides of Dr. Doyle: Watson, the medical and scientific man, also the staunch upholder of British convention; Holmes, the creative and bohemian writer, fascinated by the criminal and the bizarre. Doyle wrote classic stories of horror and science fiction as well as hefty historical novels set in the age of chivalry. His mixed feelings of attraction to and fear of a liberated, artistic woman like Irene

Adler led him to "kill" her as soon as he created her. Watson states she is dead at the beginning of the story that introduces her. Irene was literally too hot for Doyle as well as Holmes to handle. She also debuted (and exited) in the first Holmes-Watson story Doyle ever wrote. Perhaps Doyle wanted to establish an unattainable woman to excuse Holmes remaining a bachelor and aloof from matters of the heart. What he did was to create a fascinatingly unrealized character for generations of readers.

Q: *Do your protagonists represent a split personality as well?*

A: Yes, one even more sociologically interesting than the Holmes-Watson split because it embodies the evolving roles of women in the late nineteenth century. As a larger-than-life heroine, Irene is "up to anything." Her biographer, Penelope "Nell" Huxleigh, however, is the very model of traditional Victorian womanhood. Together they provide a seriocomic point-counterpoint on women's restricted roles then and now. Narrator Nell is the character who "grows" most during the series as the unconventional Irene forces her to see herself and her times in a broader perspective. This is something women writers have been doing in the past two decades: revisiting classic literary terrains and bringing the sketchy women characters into full-bodied prominence.

Q: *What of "the husband," Godfrey Norton?*

A: In my novels, Irene's husband, Godfrey Norton, is more than the "tall, dark, and dashing barrister" Doyle gave her. I made him the son of a woman wronged by England's then female-punitive divorce law, so he is a "supporting" character in every sense of the word. These novels are that rare bird in literature: female "buddy" books. Godfrey fulfills the useful, decorative, and faithful role so often played by women and wives in fiction and real life. Sherlockians anxious to unite Adler and Holmes have tried to oust Godfrey. William S. Baring-Gould even depicted him as a wife-beater in order to promote a later assignation with Holmes that produced Nero Wolfe! That is such an unbelievable violation of a strong female character's psychology. That scenario would make Irene Adler a two-time loser in her choice of men and a masochist to boot. My protagonist is a world away from that notion and a wonderful vehicle for subtle but sharp feminist comment.

Q: *Did you give her any attributes not found in the Doyle story?*

A: I gave her one of Holmes's bad habits. She smokes "little cigars." Smoking was an act of rebellion for women then. And because Doyle shows her sometimes donning male dress to go unhampered into public places, I gave her "a wicked little revolver" to carry. When Doyle put her in male disguise at the end of his story, I doubt he was thinking of the modern psychosexual ramifications of cross-dressing.

Q: *Essentially, you have changed Irene Adler from an ornamental woman to a working woman.*

A: My Irene is more a rival than a romantic interest for Holmes, yes. She is not a logical detective in the same mold as he, but is as gifted in her intuitive way. Nor is her opera singing a convenient profession for a beauty of the day but a passionate vocation that was taken from her by the king of Bohemia's autocratic attitude toward women, forcing her to occupy herself with detection. Although Doyle's Irene is beautiful, well dressed, and clever, my Irene demands that she be taken seriously despite these feminine attributes. Now we call it "Grrrrl power."

I like to write "against" conventions that are no longer true, or were never true. This is the thread that runs through all my fiction: my dissatisfaction with the portrayal of women in literary and popular fiction then and even now. This begins with *Amberleigh*—my postfeminist mainstream version of the Gothic-revival popular novels of the 1960s and 1970s–and continues with Irene Adler today. I'm interested in women as survivors. Men also interest me of necessity, men strong enough to escape cultural blinders to become equal partners to strong women.

Q: *How do you research these books?*

A: From a lifetime of reading English literature and a theatrical background that educated me on the clothing, culture, customs, and speech of various historical periods. I was reading Oscar Wilde plays when I was eight years old. My mother's book club meant that I cut my teeth on Austen, Eliot, Balzac, Kipling, Poe, poetry, Greek mythology, Hawthorne, the Brontës, Dumas, and Dickens.

In doing research, I have a fortunate facility of using every nugget I find, or of finding that every little fascinating nugget works itself into the story. Perhaps that's because good journalists must be ingenious in using every fact available to make a story as complete and accurate as possible under deadline conditions. Often the smallest mustard seed of research swells into an entire tree of plot. The corpse on the dining-room table of Bram Stoker, author of *Dracula,* was too macabre to resist and spurred the entire plot of the second Adler novel, *The Adventuress* (formerly *Good*

Morning, Irene). Stoker rescued a drowning man from the Thames and carried him home for revival efforts, but it was too late.

Besides using my own extensive library on this period, I've borrowed from my local library all sorts of arcane books they don't even know they have because no one ever checks them out. The Internet aids greatly with the specific fact. I've also visited London and Paris to research the books, a great hardship, but worth it. I also must visit Las Vegas periodically for my contemporarily-set Midnight Louie mystery series. No sacrifice is too great.

Q: *Why have the reissued paperback editions of three of the first four Adlers been given new titles?*

A: After *Good Night, Mr. Holmes* and its sequel, *Good Morning, Irene* were published in the early 1990s, another mystery novel titled *Good Night, Irene* came out. The very similar title formats caused great confusion in the publishing industry over several books. When I resumed the Adler series after a seven-year hiatus and the first paperbacks were almost out of print, it was an opportunity to end the confusion for good, as well as update the covers. *Good Night, Mr. Holmes,* the first Adler novel, retains its title and will be reissued in January of 2005. *Good Morning, Irene* is now in print as *The Adventuress*, and *Irene's Last Waltz* is now in print as *Another Scandal in Bohemia.* The reissued, retitled editions also have the original title on the cover, for readers' information, and the new titles all relate to Conan Doyle's foundation story, "A Scandal in Bohemia." I made some small revisions in the reissues, including correcting a time-line glitch resulting from the seven-year hiatus.

Q: *You've written fantasy and science-fiction novels, why did you turn to mystery?*

A: All novels are fantasy and all novels are mystery in the largest sense. Although mystery was often an element in my early novels, when I evolved the Irene Adler idea, I considered it simply a novel. *Good Night, Mr. Holmes* was almost on the shelves before I realized it would be "categorized" as a mystery. So Irene is utterly a product of my mind and times, not of the marketplace, though I always believed that the concept was timely and necessary.

Selected Bibliography

Browder, Clifford. *The Wickedest Woman in New York*. Hamden, CT: Archon Books, 1988.

Bunson, Matthew E. *Encyclopedia Sherlockiana*. New York: Macmillan, 1994.

Burrows, Edwin G., and Mike Wallace. *Gotham: A History of New York City to 1898*. New York: Oxford University Press, 1999.

Coleman, Elizabeth Ann. *The Opulent Era*. New York: Brooklyn Museum, 1989.

Crow, Duncan. *The Victorian Woman*. London: Cox & Wyman, 1971.

Doyle, Arthur Conan. *The Complete Works of Sherlock Holmes*. Various editions.

Du Maurier, George. *Trilby*. New York: Oxford University Press, 1999.

Forman, John, and Robbe Pierce Stimson. *The Vanderbilts and the Gilded Age: Architectural Aspirations, 1879–1901*. New York: St. Martin's Press, 1991.

Holdredge, Helen. *The Woman in Black: The Life of the Fabulous Lola Montez*. New York: G. P. Putnam's Sons, 1955.

Homberger, Eric, with Alice Hudson. *The Historical Atlas of New York City: A Visual Celebration of Nearly 400 Years of New York City's History*. New York: Henry Holt, 1994.

Jackson, Kenneth T., editor. *The Encyclopedia of New York City*. New Haven and London: Yale University Press, 1995.

Jay, Ricky. *Learned Pigs & Fireproof Women: A History of Unique, Eccentric & Amazing Entertainers*. London: Robert Hale, 1987.

Keller, Allan. *Scandalous Lady: The Life and Times of Madame Restell, New York's Most Notorious Abortionist*. New York: Atheneum, 1981.

Kroeger, Brooke. *Nellie Bly: Daredevil, Reporter, Feminist*. New York: Times Books, 1994.

Mackay, James. *Allan Pinkerton: The Eye Who Never Slept*. Edinburgh, Scotland: Mainstream Publishing Company, 1996.

Montez, Madame Lola. *The Arts of Beauty; or, Secrets of a Lady's Toilet. With Hints to Gentlemen on the Art of Fascinating*. New York: Chelsea House, 1969 reprinting.

Montez, Lola (Countess of Landsfeld). *The Lectures of Lola Montez*. New York: Rudd & Carleton, 1858.

Patterson, Jerry E. *Fifth Avenue: The Best Address*. New York: Rizzoli, 1998.

Seymour, Bruce. *Lola Montez: A Life*. Binghamton, NY: Vail-Ballou Press, 1996.

Varley, James E. *Lola Montez: The California Adventures of Europe's Notorious Courtesan*. Spokane, WA: Arthur H. Clark Company, 1996.

White, Stuart Edward. *Gold*. New York: Grosset & Dunlap, 1913.

For Fun:

Tierney, Tom. *Ballet Stars of the Romantic Era: Paper Dolls in Full Color*. New York: Dover Publications, 1991. (La Lola as a paper doll with four costume changes.)

About the Author

❦

"Highly eclectic writer and literary adventuress Douglas is as concerned about genre equality as she is about gender equity," writes Jo Ellyn Clarey in *The Drood Review of Mystery.*

Carole Nelson Douglas is a journalist turned novelist whose writing in both fields has been a finalist for, or received, fifty awards. A literary chameleon, she has always explored the roles of women in society, first in daily newspaper reporting, then in numerous novels ranging from fantasy and science fiction to mainstream fiction.

She currently writes two mystery series. The Victorian Irene Adler series examines the role of women in the late nineteenth century through the adventures of the only woman to outwit Sherlock Holmes, an American diva/detective. The contemporary yet Runyonesque Midnight Louie series contrasts the realistic crime-solving activities and personal issues of four main human characters with the interjected first-person feline viewpoint of a black alley cat PI, who satirizes the role of the rogue male in crime and popular fiction. ("Although Douglas has a wicked sense of humor," Clarey writes, "her energetic sense of justice is well-balanced and her fictional mockery is never nasty.")

Douglas, born in Everett, Washington, grew up in St. Paul, Minnesota, and moved with her husband to Fort Worth, Texas, trading Snowbelt for Sunbelt and journalism for fiction. At the College of St. Catherine in St. Paul she earned degrees in English literature and speech and theater, with a minor in philosophy, and was a finalist in *Vogue* magazine's Prix de Paris writing competition (won earlier by Jacqueline Bouvier Kennedy Onassis).

Chapel Noir resumed the enormously well-received Irene Adler series after a seven-year hiatus and with its sequel, *Castle Rouge,* comprises the Jack the Ripper duology within the overall series. Two more Adler novels, the New York City–set *Femme Fatale* and *Spider Dance,* have followed. The first Adler novel, *Good Night, Mr. Holmes,* won American Mystery and *Romantic Times* magazine awards and was a *New York Times* Notable Book of the Year. The reissued edition of *Good Night, Mr. Holmes* will appear in January 2005.

e-mail: cdouglas@catwriter.com
Web sites: *www.carolenelsondouglas.com*
www.catwriter.com